Ellyn —
Enjoy Maggie's story

COMPLICITY

JANE FLAGELLO

ZIG ZAG PRESS LLC

ISBN-13: 978-0-9961237-4-7

Editing by Demon for Details
Cover design by WickedSmartDesigns.com
Interior formatting by Author E.M.S.

Zig Zag Press LLC
Williamsburg, VA
2017

Published in the United States of America

OTHER BOOKS BY JANE FLAGELLO

Fiction

Gotcha!

Bamboozled

Non-Fiction

The Change Intelligence Factor: Mastering the Promise of Extra-Ordinary

CHAPTER 1

Williamsburg, Virginia

"Here. Let me help you with that." Nadine Steiner-Greene, one of the *Williamsburg Beacon's* top reporters, and Morgan Kasen's BFF, held out her hands. "And how did the romantic dinner go?"

Morgan held up two Tupperware containers, cocked her head and shot Nadine a classic arched-eyebrow look.

"That good, huh? Dish, girl. Tell me all about it."

"Turns out he can't go with me to the Outer Banks for a getaway weekend…because he's engaged."

"Ouch! Not good. What's all this?"

"This is what remains of my ill-conceived romantic dinner. Leftover chicken parmesan and salad. You're gonna love it."

"Glad I forgot to bring lunch." Nadine took the containers out of her hands, and Morgan reached back into her car to grab a third Tupperware container of risotto, and a cardboard tray holding two grande coffee cups from Starbucks.

"We do have coffee here, you know."

"I know. It's hot chocolate for Eli, but he wasn't in his

usual spot. Hasn't been for a few days. Have you seen him?"

"No. I figure he left on his own, or was told to move. When I was at the Food King a few days ago, I overheard some of the employees complaining about his little tent city in front of the store. Said he drove away business."

"Maybe." Morgan didn't sound convinced as her eyes scanned the surrounding parking lots. "Think I'll go look for him after our morning staff meeting. Don't want to miss it in case Bob assigns me a juicy story."

Nadine looked at Morgan, saw in her a woman much like herself when she was just starting out, a fledgling reporter hungry for the big story. Once upon a time, many years ago, she was Morgan's journalism teacher at NYU. Now she was her friend. Funny how the passage of time makes age irrelevant.

After retiring from the *Washington World Herald*, Nadine joined the *Beacon* staff. When Morgan moved back to Williamsburg and went to work for the *Beacon* too, they got reacquainted and clicked as friends. Nadine took Morgan under her wing, mentoring her, pushing her to find her own big story to write.

"It will come. You're a good writer. Hang in there. It takes time."

Morgan heaved a big sigh. "I didn't get a master's in journalism so I could spend the rest of my life writing the crap I'm doing now. I keep pitching Bob a story idea about the homeless problem in Williamsburg, but he hasn't given me the go-ahead yet."

"Why wait for his permission? Write it. Make it great. If he doesn't want it, I'll pitch it to some of my contacts."

"That would be awesome."

Nadine swiped her security ID and held the door open. The two of them headed for the staff kitchen to put the leftovers in the fridge.

"You know what I always say...if something's not working, you're the only one who can fix it. Look at me. Retirement wasn't working for me, so I got back in the game."

"Big comedown. The *Washington World Herald* to the *Williamsburg Beacon*. Not sure that's exactly what I'd call back in the game."

"Smaller game, but I still get to write stories that shake up the powers that be, even if their power is confined to this small college, tourist-centric burg."

Two hours later, the staff meeting over and calls returned, Morgan headed out on foot to search for Eli. She guessed he wouldn't have gone far, since he'd been a fixture in front of the Food King for the past few months. Management would shoo him away every few days. He'd come back a few days later, and there'd be a truce until they shooed him away again.

She took a deep breath. It was a crisp, sunny fall day, not a cloud in the sky, no humidity...the kind of day that made her glad to be alive. In spite of her previous night's disaster, she found herself enjoying her walk along the worn, debris-strewn path behind the Food King, adjacent to the railroad tracks.

She had stopped to talk to Eli on a whim one blustery January morning when she could see he was shivering. He was skinny, scruffy, and wearing dark-rimmed glasses with duct tape securing one arm to the frame. In Morgan's opinion, formed the first day they met, he didn't have enough meat on his bones. Nothing a few good meals couldn't fix.

That first day she retrieved a blanket from her car trunk and gave it to him. He was so grateful, couldn't thank her enough, and they talked for over an hour. Since then, stopping for a brief chat became part of her morning routine, as did providing him with leftovers from meals she made sure she over-prepared.

Morgan quickly learned two things: he loved hot chocolate, and he was a veteran of the Iraq War. What was more remarkable was how interesting he was to talk to. He knew a lot about a wide range of subjects, history being his favorite. Some mornings, when she brought him hot chocolate, they'd talk politics, and he'd opine about the problems with the VA and an underfunded military.

He told her he'd been diagnosed with PTSD, which caused him problems on his last job as an IT systems analyst. One day, after what he admittedly described as an uncontrollable episode, the company let him go. He didn't blame them, but refused to elaborate on the details. It happened a few years earlier, though he couldn't remember how many. After living on the streets for so long, he'd lost track of time.

Morgan checked her watch. She'd been walking in ever-expanding circles for almost an hour. Time to get back to the office.

Nadine had her shoulder hunched and her right ear glued to the phone when Morgan walked by her office and signaled her to come to her cubicle. Nadine nodded and held up three fingers.

"Any luck?" asked Nadine when she arrived.

"No. I went as far as the creek down behind the Food King, and then circled back behind the store by the tracks. No sign of him or his stuff. I'm worried about him."

"I'm sure he'll turn up."

"I hope you're right. I don't want him to miss the open house at the new free clinic next week. Maybe some of the tests and counseling they're offering can help him get the medications he needs to hold a job."

"You're definitely earning your angel wings, caring so much about Eli." Nadine studied her friend's face. "Don't get me wrong. The extent of your caring is very commendable, but why do you care so much about people like Eli? You don't know them."

Exasperated, Morgan threw up her hands as Nadine plopped into the chair beside her desk. "I know you're goading me, but the better question, Nadine, is why don't more people care? Here's a man who served our country and is now down on his luck, that's all. We're all just a snap of our fingers away from having a devastating tragedy screw up our lives."

"Speak for yourself."

"I am. From experience. When Alan left, I could barely make the rent. Ate a lot of mac and cheese and Noodle-Roni so my baby didn't want for anything. It wasn't Howie's fault his father was a shit. Waltzed in and out of his life just enough to make it hurt all the more each time he took off again. I tried hard to make up for him not having a dad around." Morgan pulled a tissue from the box and blew her nose.

"Just don't go trying to get Eli a job here, okay? I know he said he has IT experience, but let's not go out on a limb and hire him."

"Bob would never go for that." Morgan glanced toward Bob's corner office. She could see him on the phone gesturing wildly to whoever he was talking to.

Nadine picked up on Morgan's expression. "What?"

"Eli's already done a few odd cleanup jobs for me around here, and he's been great."

"Not sure that's the wisest thing to do. What do you think Bob would say if he found out?"

"Don't know. Don't care. But a few weeks ago, Bob couldn't get over how great the break room looked with a

5

fresh coat of paint. The asshole never asked who did it. Probably thought it was the invisible paint fairy."

"That was Eli?"

"Yep. He wanted to pay me back for all the hot chocolates, and when he saw the grimy walls in the break room, he wouldn't take no for an answer."

"How often has he been in here?"

"I let him in every few nights after everyone leaves so he can take a shower in the locker room and clean himself up. Then I zap some of my leftovers so he has a good, hot meal."

"I know you mean well, but—are you *crazy*? He could have gone off on you, and no one would have been here to help you."

"I know, but trust me, I wasn't in any danger. He wanted to repay me—us. He did a great job. You said so yourself." Morgan shook her head. "Something's wrong. He's been gone longer than usual." Her eyes locked onto Nadine's. "I've got to find him."

CHAPTER 2

Gregory Welton graciously accepted a glass of champagne from the flight attendant.

"We'll be landing in Williamsburg shortly, sir."

"Thank you."

Nestled in the handcrafted ivory leather club chair of the G550 cabin, cruising 35,000 feet above America, Greg closed his eyes, enjoying the last few minutes of an incredibly smooth ride. It doesn't get much better than this, he thought. Over the past five years, his company, Elan Health Systems, had doubled in size and delivered rock-solid performance results. No one was complaining.

He felt a light pressure on his shoulder. Opening his eyes, he found himself staring into the face of the devil incarnate, Colton Pollard. Wavy, reddish-brown hair neatly framed a square-jawed face. Piercingly cold blue eyes looked at Greg from behind frameless titanium glasses. A slight hitch at the left side of Colton's thin lips gave him a crooked smile. It was the pastiness of his skin that always unnerved Greg. Colton Pollard might not look like a devil, but he schemed like one.

"Excuse me," said Colton, his fingers pressing more firmly on Greg's shoulder. "Might we speak a moment before we land?"

"Of course," said Greg, straightening up in his chair. "Please sit down."

"I want to make sure we're clear on the details. Your fumble last week during negotiations with that regional group of clinics outside of Minneapolis almost cost us the entire deal. Loose lips sink ships. You do understand this, right?"

"Yes, Colton. I understand." The skin beneath his collar prickled. Trust Colton to bring up his barely-noticeable slip from the previous week's meeting. The client never even heard it. The deal closed. Elan expanded its holdings, getting a much-desired foothold in the Midwest. Colton made millions.

"Good. Let me do most of the talking. I have a way with words, you know."

"Only too well. You can make a shit sandwich sound appealing." Greg laughed, but he knew in his heart he wasn't joking. The man truly did have an uncanny gift when it came to words.

"Somewhat crass, but I'll take it as a compliment. Thank you." Colton leaned forward in a conspiratorial pose, resting his elbows on his knees. "Just to be clear. These people need us to save their asses. Reminds me of your situation several years ago."

Colton's eyes sparkled and his smirk deepened. He could picture his words twisting an imaginary knife deep into Greg's soul. Even though outward appearances had not changed, and Greg was still CEO, he was a figurehead. Having to sell his small clinic to Colton had been a tremendous blow, and the man somehow knew Greg still resented it.

"Delays, bad decisions, and governmental regulations have led to a bloated, underperforming staff at this clinic," Colton continued, "and they've fallen into accepting each other's excuses as normal operations. Health care is booming, but they've missed revenue projections for the past three quarters, haven't met a deadline in years, and are hemorrhaging money."

"It's amazing they're still in business."

"They're not really. We're the white knight. The offer on the table is one point three million dollars. They'll play hardball, hem and haw a bit, claim to have other bidders."

"Do they?"

"Not really. Marva Health was rumored to be interested." Colton chuckled and shook his head, enjoying a private joke.

"What am I missing?"

"That was our rumor." He cleared his throat. "My rumor." He straightened up in his seat. "There will be no other bid. And at some point, I will make that crystal clear."

"Clever."

"Thank you. I want to close the deal at one million, no more. Less if I can get it. I'm figuring it will take the full hour to get to that price. We may have to pretend to leave at some point to choke off their petulance. When I say, 'Gentlemen, we've been talking for a long time,' that will be your signal to close your folder and push back your chair ever so slightly."

"Then what?"

"Follow my lead. I'll stand. We will say our good-byes, do the handshake thing, and head for the door. We may actually have to get close to leaving before they come to their senses."

"What if they don't?"

"Trust me. Martin Salazar is the ultimate pragmatist. He knows the score and will not let this deal go bust."

"Are you sure about that?"

"One hundred thousand dollars in a Nevis bank account sure," smiled Colton.

The two men tightened their seat belts as the Gulfstream made its final approach to the private Williamsburg airport.

A waiting limo whisked them across town to their meeting in a conference room at the Kingsmill Resort.

Tucked away in a beautiful, wooded office park not too far from Busch Gardens and Kingsmill, the medical clinic was the brainchild of a group of doctors who wanted to practice more altruistic medicine. Unfortunately, none of the doctors involved were business-savvy, and like many small, privately owned clinics, this one sank beneath the weight of incompetence and debt more than a month earlier.

Enter Elan Health Systems, the latest entry in the growing field of concierge medical services. Elan owned a growing network of small, private clinics. The invisible force behind Elan's operation was Colton Pollard, who visualized his growing business expanding across the country within the next five years. However, he preferred to remain out of the spotlight, and installed Greg Welton as CEO after he completed the purchase of Greg's clinic several years ago.

Elan's doctors were board-certified in internal medicine, and a physician's assistant and two nurses rounded out the staffing at each facility. Other specialists were hooked into the network and a phone call away. Elan's operational model supported two care options: a pay-as-you-go, no-insurance system, or an extremely exclusive primary patient, retainer-based system, known as EEP. Each practice was limited to a small primary patient roster, because those people paid premium prices for the luxury of having immediate access to a doctor.

Then there was the free clinic. The hefty fees the wealthy retainer patients paid to have a doctor at their beck and call offset the costs of providing a monthly free clinic to the local community. Named the Asclepius Clinic after the Greek god of medicine, the goal of the clinics was to offset rising health care costs, and help people who had been negatively impacted by Obamacare's price increases. So many people weren't poor enough to benefit from medical subsidies, nor rich enough for medical costs not to matter. Up-front deductibles crippled their ability to afford to see a doctor.

Asclepius was like a traveling circus. For three days each month, an elite group of well-paid, specialized medical personnel manned the clinic, seeing anyone who walked through the door. Like the bloodmobile, mobile medical trailers were driven in and set up in a matter of hours. Everything was done in-house for these events: doctor visits, minor outpatient surgeries, a host of different digital imaging technologies and in-house lab work. Asclepius purchased the most common generic drugs in bulk, and prescriptions were filled onsite. Then the units closed up shop and headed to the next Asclepius Clinic site, usually within a fifty-mile radius. These economies of scale allowed Elan Health Systems, the parent company, to control costs. And the man behind the curtain at Elan was Colton Pollard.

Three hours later, Greg and Colton walked out of the meeting strutting like peacocks.

"That went well," Greg said as they walked back to the parking lot.

"Better than well. We'll absorb this clinic into our growing system here in Hampton Roads and expand Asclepius services to add Williamsburg to its itinerary. And we bought ourselves a renowned orthopedic surgeon to boot. Make sure he is well compensated so he's happy. Considering the local population, his skills will be in high demand. Knee and hip replacements are the gravy train from an aging population."

"Do you plan to keep the physical therapy part of the business?"

"Yes. It's already fully integrated. Our wealthy EEP

clients will enjoy having access to their own private physical therapist for their every little ache and pain. Just another service package we can sell them."

Seeing two limousines parked side by side surprised Greg. "We're not traveling together?"

"No. I have other business to attend to." Colton's phone buzzed. He told the unknown caller to wait a moment. "I want you to stay here and oversee this transition. The trailers are already at the clinic."

"You were that confident?"

"Oh, Greg. When will you ever learn not to doubt me?" He touched Greg's face ever so slightly. "We've had a full crew at the clinic for a few days now. Hurley and Vivian are there too, and Tiffany arrives tomorrow to help you. There's a room reserved for you at the Williamsburg Inn."

"But we won't have paying EEP clients yet for the concierge services to offset the costs of running a free clinic."

Colton put his hand on Greg's shoulder. "Greg, I'm counting on you to make it all happen without problems. You *can* handle this, right?"

"Of-of course."

"Good. I've got to take this call. I'll be back next week to watch the official ribbon-cutting ceremony."

At the subtle push from Colton's hand, Greg knew he had been dismissed. He walked away, got into the waiting limo and left. Colton watched Greg's limo pull out of the parking lot. His attention turned to his call.

"Pollard."

"Brother dear."

"What do you want, Winn?"

"That's it? What do you want? No hello, brother. No how are you?"

"I haven't cared how you are for years, and you've never cared how I am, so cut the crap. What do you want?"

"Well, since you put it like that. It's mother. She's dying."

"Again?" He didn't take the bait. "And this concerns me, why?"

"Because she is your mother, our mother."

"She's always dying. And she was never my mother."

"Poor Colton," Winn said, making sniffling sounds into the receiver. Then his voice turned more taciturn. "Small detail. Inconsequential at this point. The assisted living facility called me. I can't get there for a few days. I want you to go."

"That isn't going to happen."

"You can't still be angry after all these years. Your father did what he thought was best."

"My father married your mother for one reason and one reason only. Her money. Which, if I remember correctly, she's left to you in its entirety. Cut me out of the will completely, and gloated when she told me. And no, Winn, I'm not angry. I'm done. I told you that the last time you called, and the time before that."

"But you went the last time I called."

"Foolishly. She was faking it. She wanted to see how fast I'd get there, and somehow she knew I was coming not you. How did she know that, Winn?"

Silence provided his answer.

"No matter. I'm not falling for her wolf cries again."

"You have to go. I'm halfway around the world in Australia."

"Too bad. I'm busy. Send her a stuffed Koala bear with your regrets."

Colton hit the End button with so much force the phone almost slipped from his hand. *Son of a bitch. And that's just what I am...the son—no stepson—of a bitch. A real bitch, and I'll be damned if she's going to reel me in again.*

He got into the limo and poured himself two fingers of cognac. It was gone in one gulp. Refilling his glass, he eased back into the luxurious seat for the return ride to the airport.

Not even fifteen minutes later, Colton's phone buzzed again. This time he looked at the caller ID before answering. One unexpected and unwanted call a day was enough. Besides, the bottle of cognac had worked its magic, significantly dulling his brother's attempt to lay a guilt trip on him, and he was unwilling to play any more games today. Especially since the cognac was nearly gone.

"Pollard."

"We may have a slight problem," said a baritone voice.

"Do I really want to hear this? You are supposed to be the problem-solver."

"I know, and I am, but you do want to hear this. Things got out of hand last night at the new facility. Hurley, the physician's assistant, had a gastro flare-up. Thought he could handle it. Didn't alert Vivian in time so she could cover for him."

"The dumb shit."

"Shit's the operative word," the voice laughed. When Colton didn't laugh, the man cleared his throat and continued. "When I left, everything was locked up tight. Our client was sleeping like a baby, and our donor was too. Or so we thought. Guess he woke up, got scared, pulled the monitors and tubes out and left."

"He left?" *Unbelievable.* "What do you mean he left?"

"Just what I said. His clothes were gone, and so was he. Alarm bells went off because a door opened. Hurley couldn't get off the toilet. By the time Vivian reached the room, the guy was gone. I got there in ten minutes. We searched the entire facility and the surrounding area for hours. Couldn't find him anywhere. And we couldn't exactly call the police."

"What the fuck do I pay you for?"

"To prevent things like this from happening. And this is the first time it's happened. Hurley's been with us a long time, knows protocols, but figured he'd be able to shit and get off the pot because everyone was sleeping."

"Has Hurley had this happen before?"

The hesitation before answering told Colton all he needed to know.

"When were you planning to tell me?"

"When it became a problem. Hurley's a good physician's assistant. One of the best we have. He told me he was on meds after the first and *only* time it happened, and that was last year. I assumed he got his colitis under control."

"And now? What do you assume now?"

"That I have cleanup to do. Which I will do. I just wanted you to know."

"Get back to me when you've handled it."

"Yes, sir."

"Oh, and please handle Hurley too. Permanently."

"Done."

CHAPTER 3

The day dragged on.

Morgan struggled to concentrate on the latest brain-numbing assignment Bob had given her—writing a compelling story to boost ticket sales for the latest Ladies Auxiliary fall festival garden tour. At the morning meeting, he also told her to cover the opening of the new health clinic the following week, and she'd already set up an interview with the PR person for tomorrow.

But she couldn't stop worrying about Eli. Just before five, she poked her head into Nadine's office.

"You busy tonight?"

"No hot plans. It's Sid's poker night."

"Good. Could you meet me back here in an hour? I'm going home to change into my old jeans and hiking boots. I want to go back behind the railroad tracks, deeper into the woods. I know there's an old shack back there. Maybe he's there."

"Dare I ask how you know there's a shack back there?"

"Wild high school days. We used to drink back there and do other fun things that would have made our parents cringe."

"I always forget you're one of the few people I've met

16

who is actually from this town. Then you moved away. And came back, though heaven knows why."

"I'm just a small-town girl who was momentarily lured by the big city lights and the promise of love everlasting, but who loves her small town. Will you come with me? It was really muddy this morning from all the rain, so I want to change my clothes before I go tramping around in the woods. Help me look for Eli. Please."

"No tempting bribes to make it worth my while, like one of your calorie-rich home cooked meals? The chicken parmesan was delicious, by the way."

"Okay. Sure. A meal of your choice, home cooked, or my treat out. With Sid. Or without. We can make it a girl's night."

"Home cooked all the way. Without Sid. He can stay home, fend for himself. Grill sausage or a turkey burger. He'll love it. And with your cooking, I will too. You should have been a chef."

"Thought about it, but then cooking would feel like W-O-R-K work."

"Good point. We can discuss the menu while we search."

"Thanks, Nadine. See you in a bit."

"Nice boots," said Morgan when Nadine got out of her car. "Love the fringe."

Nadine looked like she could have posed for an L.L. Bean catalog when she rendezvoused with Morgan in the parking lot.

"I always try to dress for the job." Nadine swiveled and swayed like a runway model. "Where do you suggest starting?"

"Down by the tracks. I want to check the shack."

Two hours later, dusk settled over Williamsburg. So far, their search had been a bust. Mud and wet leaves clung to their clothes from ducking under low branches and climbing over fallen trees.

"It's getting too dark to see where we're going," said Nadine, after tripping over a fallen branch. "We should probably call it a night."

"I suppose so. I thought for sure he'd be at the shack. Let's at least go down into this gully and check behind that huge tree. I think I see something red."

"You're seeing things, girl, maybe hoping whatever red you think you see is the red hoodie you gave Eli last winter."

"Humor me."

"Isn't that what I'm doing?" She held both arms out from her sides like a tightrope walker as she navigated the steep slope of the hillside.

"Be careful," said Morgan, leading the way. "It's slippery and wet here."

"Shit!" Nadine's feet shot out from under her, and she slid the rest of the way down the hillside, her butt sinking into the mud. "Stop laughing. This could be you."

"Yes. It could be me, but it isn't. Sorry, I know how much you hate getting dirty."

"Help me up."

Morgan extended her hand and helped Nadine regain her footing.

"You're going to pay my cleaning bill." She saw a strange look cross Morgan's face. "What?"

"That's a leg." Morgan took off running, slipping and sliding through the muck. "Shit. Shit. Shit."

Nadine's only option was to follow. When she reached Morgan, her friend was kneeling behind a huge fallen oak tree trunk, cradling a man's head in her lap.

"Call 911."

"That's not Eli," said Nadine, punching in the lifesaving numbers.

"I know." She felt for a pulse as she gently spoke to the unconscious man. "He's still alive. Mister, can you hear me?"

Within minutes, red and blue strobe lights and blaring sirens marked the arrival of police and an ambulance. Paramedics rushed toward them, equipment cases in hand. They worked quickly to stabilize the nearly-dead man while Morgan and Nadine huddled together, watching the professionals in action.

"You found him just in time," said one of the paramedics to Morgan.

"Will he be okay?" she asked, her teeth chattering in the chilly night air.

"Too soon to tell. He's lost a lot of blood. The ER docs at Sentara work miracles, so maybe they'll pull one out for this poor soul. You should go home and change out of those wet clothes before you wind up a patient yourself."

"We plan to," said Nadine. "And get some brandy into our cold bones. Thanks."

"Hey, Rick, what have we got?" asked Detective Knight as he ducked under the yellow tape cordoning off the area, and approached the paramedics attending to the victim.

"Male. Estimating late thirties. Maybe forties. No ID, so a John Doe. Based on his condition, I'd say a street person."

"Overdose? Drunk?"

"Neither. There's caked blood. Looks like he had some sort of procedure very recently. Too recently for him to be out here walking around in the cold woods at night." He swirled his finger in the air. "Severe post-op trauma. This guy should never have been discharged from the hospital. We can roll him so I can show you."

"No need to move him more than you have to at this point. Anything else?"

"Bandages covering a huge cut back to front along his right side. I'll wager an X-ray will find he's missing a kidney."

The detective stared at him. "You're kidding, right?"

"Nope. That's what the cut's placement looks like to me. But I could be wrong. Haven't seen many cuts like the one he's sporting."

"Need to talk to him as soon as he's conscious. I'll make Sentara my next stop after I finish up here."

The detective turned his attention to Morgan and Nadine. Damn. Reporters. He'd never officially met either woman, but one, Nadine Steiner-Greene, had the reputation of a tenacious bulldog.

"Be right with you ladies," he called out.

Knight surveyed the scene and made a few notes while he prayed the paramedic was right, and the man still had a fighting chance to pull through. The question of what type of problem he had on his hands nagged at him. Whether the man was an alive or dead victim changed things. No way to tell at this point what might be significant evidence.

Sadly, it was too dark to see much of anything. Knight took out his phone and snapped several shots of the victim before the paramedics moved him to the gurney. Then he squatted and shone the beam of his flashlight on the ground. Muddy wet leaves and underbrush formed a depression where the man's body had been curled in the fetal position.

The crime scene technicians were already setting up huge floodlights. They would do a complete workup, take more photos, take John Doe's fingerprints and run them through AFIS, make castings of possible footprints, collect anything and everything that could potentially be evidence, and get their findings to him as quickly as they could. Right now it was all supposition based on years of experience.

He took a deep breath, steeling himself for questioning

20

the reporters who found the victim. Slowly he walked up the slippery incline to the two ladies.

"I'm Detective Adam Knight. I understand you two found the man. Okay if I ask you a few questions?" Not waiting for a reply, he continued. "You're kind of off the beaten path here. Not exactly the place for an after-dinner stroll. What were you doing out here?"

"We were searching for Eli," said Morgan. "He's the homeless man who usually hangs out by the Food King on Richmond Road."

"I know who you're talking about."

"I haven't seen him for a few days, and I've been worried, so I asked Nadine to help me look for him."

"Why back here?"

"I talked to him some mornings when I brought him food, and he told me about walking the railroad tracks. I knew there was a shack back here, and I thought maybe he went there, since it's been so rainy these last few days. It would give him some shelter. It was the last place I could think of to look."

Knight switched his attention to Nadine. "Do you know him?" The detective nodded in the direction of the victim being wheeled to the waiting ambulance, keeping his voice steady, no fluctuation, no telltale expression.

"Not really," said Nadine. "I think I may have seen him around Colonial Williamsburg, but never talked to him." She started hammering Knight with questions, the kind that roll off the tongue of an investigative reporter, ending with the most obvious. "Anyone report a missing person that matches his description?"

"Asked like the reporter you are, Nadine."

"Ah, I was wondering if you recognized me."

"Yes, I know who you are. And my answer, like the law enforcement official I am, is no comment." He smiled at his cleverness. "I know you both work at the *Beacon*, but make sure the officer over there has your complete contact information. I'll be in touch if I have more questions."

Morgan grabbed Nadine's arm when Knight headed back to his colleagues.

"Did you hear what the paramedic told him?" she whispered. "That he might be missing a kidney?"

"Yeah. I heard that." Nadine rustled in her tote bag and pulled out a small spiral reporter's notepad and pen. "You think it's true?"

"Who knows? But if he just had major surgery, what was he doing wandering out here alone? Love the notepad, by the way. Do you ever plan to enter the technology age?"

"Funny. Out here electronics would slow me down." She made some notes using her own unique shorthand. Then she looked at Morgan. "What if it wasn't a legitimate surgery? I've heard about it happening."

"What are you thinking?"

"What if he sold his kidney? Or, worse yet, what if someone kidnapped him and stole it? You know, cut it right out without his permission."

"Seriously?" She frowned while her eyes shifted from Nadine to the scene and back to Nadine.

"Yes. A man found in the woods close to death, no ID, signs of very recent surgery, caked blood on bandages."

"Not exactly your everyday sort of discovery while out walking in the woods." Morgan shuddered and rubbed her hands up and down her arms.

"I've heard of selling your blood for money, but that's not legal anymore. Men can sell their sperm, and women can sell their eggs."

"Donate their eggs," said Morgan.

"Semantics. If you get money for it, you're selling it."

"Ah, Nadine, forever the cynic."

"I'm just saying. The internet is loaded with ways to make money selling body parts. All legal. I even saw a story once about making money selling your very healthy poop."

"Yech!"

"When people need money, they're willing to do things they otherwise might not do. So, maybe he did it to himself."

"What do you mean? He certainly didn't cut out his own kidney."

"If he's homeless, maybe he sold his kidney. Money for drugs? Booze? Who knows what? People in third world countries do it all the time."

"It's illegal here."

"Legal-schmegal. Doesn't mean it doesn't happen."

"Cutting out someone's kidney requires a top-notch medical team, and there's no hospital for miles. How did he get here?"

"Good question, which we need to find an answer for."

Morgan shivered. "We've got to go."

"I agree. I can't feel my toes."

Something didn't fit. Detective Knight felt it in his bones last night, while he tossed and turned, trying to get some sleep. He called the hospital before going out to the crime scene this morning, and learned John Doe was barely hanging on. The prognosis wasn't good.

The nurse on duty said he still wasn't conscious. Said she'd call Knight when he woke up. If he woke up. Rather than hang around the station waiting for her call, Knight decided to visit the scene, see what he could see in the morning's light. At least the guy was still alive, he thought, downing his third cup of coffee.

He parked his car in the Holiday Inn parking lot and

walked down the hill to where the two women reporters found John Doe. CSI techs were still hard at work scouring the area for evidence, anything that could tell them what a man, who clearly had very recent surgery, was doing out in the woods by himself.

Knight assumed he was one of the homeless people from in and around Williamsburg, since no missing persons report had been filed. The population wasn't as huge as in some major cities, but Williamsburg had a fair share of homeless, due to the mild winters and kindness of citizens who provided meals and sponsored the local shelter.

"Hey, Detective," said one of the CSIs. "Watch your step. It's really slippery."

"Find anything useful?"

"Not much. We picked up all the leaves and muck where the body was found. Looks like he came over the rise on the other side of the gully." The tech pointed up the hill opposite where they stood. "Found depressions that look like they were made by someone rolling down the hill."

"Interesting." Knight walked the perimeter outside the tape and trudged up hill on the other side. It opened up onto a parking lot at the back end of a brick building surrounded by four large semi-trailers clustered together. He heard generators powering the trailers, and saw enclosed walkways connecting them to one another and the main building.

The place looked deserted, but people must be working, because he saw several cars in the lot. Thinking someone inside might have seen something, he headed for the main building, touching the hood of one car as he walked by it, noting it was warm.

Walking around the building to the front door, he found it locked. The sign over the front door said Elan Health Systems. He remembered getting a notice about an open house for a new clinic scheduled for next week. *This must be the place*.

He knocked once and waited. No one came so he knocked harder. Still no one responded. Cars told him people were there, and a car with a warm hood told him someone arrived recently. He pounded on the door, thinking he was making enough noise to raise the dead.

"Hi there," said the portly, gray-haired woman in purple scrubs who finally opened the door. "We aren't open yet."

"I'm Detective Adam Knight with the Williamsburg police," said Knight as he flashed his credentials. "We had a little incident down the hill at the back of your parking lot last night, and I was wondering if I could come in and ask you a few questions."

"Of course. Please come in. Things are kind of a mess. Boxes all over the place." She moved aside so he could pass into the reception area. "I'm Vivian."

"Nice to meet you." He shook her hand while he studied the room.

"You said something happened out back." She absently touched her fingertips to her lips as she peered out one of the windows facing the side parking lot. "I'm not sure how much help I can be. What happened?"

"Were you here yesterday?" Knight looked directly into her eyes, sidestepping her question.

"Yes. I've been here every day for over a week. The new owners wanted to get a jump on the renovations once they were sure the sale would close."

"That's out of the ordinary, isn't it?"

"Probably. I don't know much about real estate. The old owners closed down last month. Had to. Ran out of money."

"I didn't know that." Knight jotted down a note to check out the previous ownership and the new owners.

"I pretty much do what I'm told. They said show up and

get things started, so I did. And it's a good thing. Place is a mess. All dusty. Feels like I live here. There's so much to do before our grand opening next week. And we aren't fully staffed yet."

"You're here alone?"

"Yes. Everyone's gone out for breakfast. I know they say breakfast is the most important meal of the day, but the last thing I need is to start my day with a big meal. It slows me down, so I volunteered to stay behind."

Knight thought about that and the four cars he saw in the parking lot.

"What time did you leave last night?"

"I didn't. I've been sleeping in one of the patient care rooms. After the second night it got silly driving back and forth to the motel, since everything I need is here. So I brought my things over a few days ago. I can shower, bring in food, and sleep here. Just as comfortable as the motel. And I've been getting way more work done."

Knight noticed her glance out the window again. He saw a shadow of concern cross her face.

She looked back at him, her face now a little paler. "You never told me what happened."

"A man was found in the woods back there." He pointed toward the site. "Looks like he fell down and rolled into the gully."

"Oh. That's awful. Who found him? Was he badly hurt?"

"He's in the hospital now. Still unconscious." He let that sink in a minute. "Did you happen to see anyone lurking around the parking lot last night?"

"No. No I didn't. And the security lighting is still not fully functioning. It gets very dark back there at night. When I do leave, I rush to my car." She paused a moment, her eyes lingering in the direction Knight had pointed. "My stars, why would someone be wandering around in the dark?"

"That, Vivian, is the sixty-four-thousand-dollar question." Knight thought he heard a noise and wandered toward a set of double doors which were propped open. "What type of medical facility is this?" He stuck his head into the hallway. "Looks nice."

"We're a private health clinic. Concierge service. Perhaps you've heard of it?"

"No." He stepped into the hall and looked both ways. The sound did not repeat itself.

"It's the latest twist on medical care, and it's taking off like a rocket. We'll also offer a free clinic to those less fortunate souls among us who can't afford to pay." Vivian came to his side and seemed to be herding him in the direction of the front door. "We have clinics in other locations, too. The closest one is in Newport News. We felt Williamsburg would be a good addition to our company."

"You said you aren't open for business yet? There are no patients here?"

"No. My heavens. There's no one here but little old me. And this really isn't an overnight-type facility. We're not a hospital."

She pulled a brochure off the counter and held it out to him. "Please come to the open house next week. We'll be giving tours of the facility. I know you'll be impressed with what we have to offer."

"Maybe I'll do that."

"You'll have to excuse me, but I really have to get back to work."

"Sorry. I didn't mean to keep you. I'm sure you have lots to do before your opening. Thank you for your time."

He heard the lock click when she closed the door behind him. He made his way back around the building, took out his cell phone and photographed all the cars in the lot. At least he'd be able to run their plates and ascertain ownership. He headed back to the gully, and was doing a slow pirouette from the middle of the lot to look back at the clinic property when he heard the squeal of truck brakes.

A semi-trailer with a rusty orange twenty-foot container on a flatbed pulled up and parked next to the loading dock. He watched the driver get out. It looked like he rang a bell by the loading dock door, and then went around and unlocked the back of the container. Then he disappeared inside the container. Knight copied the six-digit identifier stenciled on the side of the container into his notepad and took a photo with his cell phone. Suddenly a man came out of the building and joined the driver inside the container.

"She lied to me. Sweet, kind Vivian lied to me. She wasn't alone."

A few minutes later, Knight watched and photographed the two men wheeling air tanks into the building. Each man's dolly carried six tanks of assorted colors: green, blue, gray and yellow were most prevalent. They came back out and reloaded, this time with boxes. He couldn't read the printing on the boxes, but he snapped photos of the men and their cache of supplies. The lab would be able to blow up the photos so he could read the markings. And he'd Google air tank standards to learn what the different color tanks meant.

Interesting, he thought. Very interesting.

CHAPTER 4

"Knock, knock," said Nadine when she stuck her head above Morgan's cubicle the next morning.

"Yeeeeess," said Morgan, drawing out her one word response, not taking her eyes off the Wayfair.com website she was browsing. "Have you seen these fabulous lamps?"

"Forget about the lamps. I was talking to Sid last night, after I got out of a very long, hot shower, and we agree. This is your chance. Your breakout story. The one you've been waiting for—to show Bob what you can do. It just fell in your lap."

Morgan stared at Nadine.

"You think Bob will let me write it?"

"Who cares if Bob lets you write it? Just write it." Nadine's hands went to her hips, her frown incredulous. "Aren't your reporter bones aching to dig in to all of this? Are you telling me you didn't go right to the internet when you got home last night?"

"No. I'm not saying that. And yes. I spent the better part of the night online. Even started outlining a story thread or two. Then I came in this morning, and the first person I saw was Bob, who wanted to know when I'd be finished with the story about the Women's Club Golf Outing."

"So, what?"

"The man knows how to take the wind out of my sails, that's all. I don't mean to sound so wimpy."

"You *are* wimpy, girl. You need a new sailboat. The whole homeless thing is ripe for the writing. And a stolen kidney adds the dramatic twist. Bob ain't the be-all-and-end-all of editors." Nadine rolled her eyes. "So, show me, what did you find?"

Morgan plopped the keyboard in her lap. Her fingers flew across the keys, entering search parameters, pulling up results, rapidly opening window after window for different searches.

"Wow. You did do your homework last night. I'm proud of you." Nadine looked admiringly at Morgan. "You can't let Bob dictate your writing life anymore."

"I know. You always tell me if I don't like where I am or what I'm doing, I'm the only one who can fix it. I get that. But at this point, I need this job. No husband helps pay my bills."

"I started my freelance career without Sid. It's hard, but you've been through worse and come out smelling like a rose. There are plenty of other ways to get published and paid for your work. A well-written exposé about the problem of homelessness can blow the lid off this tragic problem, which is being willfully ignored by so many towns and cities across America."

Morgan took another sip of her coffee and looked back at her laptop screen.

"But some of these stories... Homeless people swept up in the night? Mysterious white vans? FEMA camps warehousing vagrants? Jeez, Nadine. Some of this makes me wonder if the conspiracy crazies have been let out of the loony bin."

"How deliciously politically incorrect you are. And it's not even ten o'clock yet."

"Besides, nothing on Google can be trusted."

"That's why they call it research. And where the fun is. Finding out what is, or is not, true."

"What about the kidney angle?"

"That adds another layer of drama to the story. And the one I think offers you the best shot at having your story picked up by one of the national wire services."

Morgan gazed out into space. "I have an old friend, Greg Welton. Haven't seen him in years. Used to work for HHS. Not sure what he's doing now, although I heard he went into private practice. He may be able to help me with the kidney angle."

"Isn't he the guy who introduced you to your first husband?"

"Both husbands. They were his friends in college. He might be a good resource. He knows a lot of people who know people."

"Sounds like a line straight out of *The Godfather*." Nadine laughed at her own joke. "Sorry, couldn't resist. Contacting him can't hurt. He might know someone who can help you. Maybe he has another friend who is ripe to become husband number three."

"Not funny, Nadine." Morgan gave her a twisted eyeball glare. "What angle do you think would work best?"

"Not sure. You're already looking into the homeless problem, and the guy last night looked like he didn't have a pot to piss in, so I'd say start there. Though, if the guy is missing a kidney like the paramedics thought, you have to wonder what the heck he was doing in the woods. Which brings up all sorts of interesting what-if type questions."

"Don't know how well this will play with Bob. He told me to write a story about the new health clinic that's opening next week. I'm interviewing one of their PR people at the Williamsburg Inn this afternoon."

"Just what we need. Another medical clinic. We've got one of those on every corner."

"This one's supposed to be different. Something about concierge-style service, whatever that means."

"How different can it be? First the nurse says get on the scale, which is in the main hallway, so you have to keep all your clothes on, which adds at least four pounds to your weight. Then she says take everything off and put on this gown, opening in the back. The doctor finally shows up, says open wide and say ahhhhhh. He types on his computer for most of the appointment. Asks if you've had your flu shot, shingles shot, pneumonia shot. Then he writes a prescription and says, 'See you next year. If anything hurts before then, call me.'"

"I can see the medical profession isn't exactly high on your love 'em list."

"Sure it is. The less I see 'em, the more I love 'em."

Morgan arrived early for her three o'clock appointment with Tiffany Stamos, the person in charge of spreading the word about the grand opening of Elan Health Systems and its Asclepius Clinic affiliate. She wanted to learn as much as she could about the new clinic for her story, and whether it might be a way to help her friend Eli.

The Williamsburg Inn was quiet when she walked through the doors. Most of the tourists were either out learning about America's colonial capital, on the golf course, or screaming their brains out on the roller coasters at Busch Gardens, or the giant water slide at Water Country USA.

"You're Morgan, from the *Beacon,* right?" said a bubbly Ms. Stamos, her hand already outstretched from the other side of the lobby. "So pleased to meet you. This is so exciting."

"Yes, I'm Morgan Kasen. A pleasure to meet you too, Ms. Stamos."

"Please call me Tiffany. Everyone does."

Morgan registered her initial impression more as snarky jealousy than a pleasure. Tiffany's bouncy, shoulder-length blond hair was tucked behind her ears, which sported large diamond studs, and her sparkling white teeth and effervescence caught Morgan off guard. Tiffany Stamos was sleek, slender, and seemed to automatically assume a picture-perfect pose, not a hair out of place. Her emerald green dress made her green eyes pop, and there wasn't an eye in the lobby, male and female alike, that wasn't focused on her right at this moment.

"I thought we'd enjoy afternoon tea in the Terrace restaurant. The blueberry scones just melt in your mouth, don't you agree?"

"I've never had the pleasure."

"Well, then this will be one of many new experiences for you, compliments of Elan. I can't wait to tell you all about what we have planned for the medical center and clinic here."

Morgan kept pace with Tiffany, but didn't even try to match the bounce in her step. Her gleaming smile at the host in the Terrace Room got them a prime table in front of the oversized picture window overlooking the golf course.

"I just love coming to a new town, and Williamsburg has so much history and charm. We were very excited when the deal to purchase the doctors' failing practice was signed, sealed, and delivered, as they say." Her mouth curved up into a broad smile. "The stars aligned. It was meant to be."

Morgan tried not to stare at over-the-top, giddy Tiffany

Stamos. *How do some women get away with it? Bet men flip over her every word.*

The server approached, and Tiffany ordered almost everything on the small tea menu, only stopping to ask Morgan what she wanted to drink.

Not sure how much of Tiffany's enthusiasm she could take, Morgan got right to the interview. She pulled out her recorder, and got an affirmative nod that it would be okay to tape the conversation.

"I don't want to rain on your parade, Tiffany, but we already have a large cross section of medical professionals serving the community. How does Elan plan to compete?"

"We're totally different. As you know, we're a concierge medical center. We serve a unique clientele. Our patients forgo using insurance for their care. Our EEP's—that means extra-exclusive patients—pay a premium fee for premium service, and save the money they would have paid for insurance. In our model, people only need to purchase a catastrophic care policy, which we also offer. At Elan, we like to say it's like having your own private physician at your beck and call."

"Sounds expensive."

"It is, but so worth it." Tiffany oozed positivity and charm.

Morgan marveled at her zeal. She wondered how many doctors had a hand in crafting Tiffany's flawless complexion, straight nose, and gleaming white teeth. She feigned a cough to stop the runaway catty train rumbling down the tracks of her brain.

"And we have board-certified specialists serving the Hampton Roads area, so whether it's dermatology, gastroenterology, orthopedics, or surgery, we provide better than blue-ribbon care. Our labs, diagnostic imaging, and outpatient surgical facilities are state-of-the-art, and are immediately upgraded as new technologies are approved by the FDA and the AMA. People are willing to pay for that level of care."

"What about those who can't afford the services you've described? Aren't you dividing medical care by socio-economic class?"

"Let's not be naïve, here." Tiffany's hand slid across the table, the sparkle of a huge diamond engagement ring catching the light. She patted Morgan's hand and then retreated. "That's already being done. Most executives have much better health plans than the average company employee. Even Congress managed to write themselves and their staffs out of standard Obamacare to ensure they would continue to have top-of-the-line coverage."

"That's true." Morgan slathered butter on top of the warm blueberry scone the server had quietly placed on the table, and sank her teeth into its sweet goodness. "Oh, this is yummy."

"Told you." Tiffany helped herself to one of the smoked salmon and caviar tea sandwiches. "As far as the inequities in health care go, Elan has taken care of that, too. We have an alternative tier of service, kind of like a gym membership. It's pay as you go. And the best part, the part that gets me most excited," she said, stopping to chew the sandwich she popped into her mouth, "is the free Asclepius Clinic that we offer every month."

"I did read something about that. Tell me more."

"You are coming to the open house next week, aren't you?"

"Yes."

"Then you'll get to see it for yourself. And seeing what we are offering is so much better than anything I could possibly tell you. I'll give you the grand tour myself." With that, Tiffany picked up the recorder and clicked the stop

35

button, clearly signaling the interview was over. "Now let's finish off these goodies and enjoy some girl talk. You can tell me all about yourself and Williamsburg."

New York City

Jesse hailed a cab on Madison Ave, gave the driver the restaurant's address in Little Italy, and buckled in. A small Hawaiian bobblehead doll wearing a purple lei and a traditional grass skirt rocked on the dashboard.

Cab drivers in New York were an eclectic bunch, he thought, every ride a potentially life-altering adventure. Horns blared all around him as the driver weaved in and out between delivery trucks, bicycle messengers, and pedestrians, for whom crossing the street was a contact sport.

Greg's call had surprised him. They'd gone their separate ways after college, although their paths crossed in New York or DC every few years. Greg said he was on his way to New York, hinted he might have a story right up Jesse's alley, and asked if he had time to meet. Even threw in a steak dinner. Jesse wondered what Greg might have for him. The guy was a doctor. What could he possibly have that would interest an investigative reporter?

Suddenly the cab jerked to a stop. The driver put down the fare flag. Jesse swiped his credit card and got out of the cab. At least he'd get a good meal.

"Greg? Is that you?" asked Jesse as he approached the booth at the back of the restaurant. "What are you doing way back here? The ladies are up front, man."

"Hey, Jesse." Greg slid out of the booth and gave his

fraternity brother a warm man hug. "How the hell are you? What's it been? Two years?"

"More like five. Since the last reunion in Atlantic City."

"Oh, don't remind me. My head still hurts when I think of how drunk we all got."

"Yeah. That was some party. We're getting too old for that shit."

They ordered a round of drinks, medium rare steaks with all the fixings, and spent the next hour reminiscing about the good old days at Princeton.

Finally, Jesse pushed his empty plate away. "Okay, we've been here almost two hours. You ready to tell me what's up?"

"I've gotten myself into something." His low voice and stolen glances around the room heightened the seriousness of his words. "No one knows I'm here. I'm supposed to be in Virginia."

"You look really tense. You're making me nervous."

"I'm thinking maybe you could do what you do best, and find out whether my fears are real or I'm imagining things."

"What's happening?"

"You know a few of us doctors got together and started our own clinic a few years ago."

"Right. You were tired of the hospital/insurance scene and wanted to be your own boss. I remember that."

"Well, things didn't go exactly as we planned—"

"Do they ever?"

"Sometimes. Anyway, not this time. My partners wanted to bail, but I wanted to keep going, so I bought them out. Then the shit hit the fan and I was in way over my head. Got a little strung out financially, then pharmaceutically, if you know what I mean."

"I hear ya."

"Then this guy comes along. Seems to know all about my

business. About me. About my problems. He gets me out of bankruptcy—"

"I had heard through the grapevine you were in trouble. Then I didn't hear anything else, so I figured you'd handled it like you always did. Your frat nickname wasn't Fixer for nothing."

"I did, but..." Greg finished his vodka martini and motioned to the server to bring them another round. "I need your help. This guy...the one who got my company out of trouble... He's... He's... Shit, man, I don't even know how to describe what he is. Some of the stuff going down behind the scenes...stuff I'm not supposed to know about...deals he's made doing God only knows what. Let's just say my white knight has gone very black."

Greg downed the martini the waiter just put in front of him and jumped to his feet. "I've gotta go. Been here too long. Gotta get back to Williamsburg before I'm missed." He threw two hundred dollar bills on the table. "I'll call you next week."

Jesse grabbed his wrist. "Can you give me a name? Something to go on."

"You want a name? Try Colton Pollard."

CHAPTER 5

Private island, Florida Keys

All during spring and into the summer, James Hayden religiously scanned the local Palm Beach and Miami newspapers, looking for news about a boating accident that had lit up the night sky. The explosion made the front page of the Palm Beach Post the very next day, with a scant, one-column story below the fold.

Fact—a boat had exploded in the waters off the Palm Beach coast at ten p.m. the previous night.

Fact—one body was recovered, a woman, burned beyond recognition.

Fact—the boat had been rented out by a tour company called Beyond Land Charters.

Authorities were investigating. No further information was available. A plea for the public's help concluded the article. If anyone had any relevant information, they needed to call the police.

Twenty-four hours later, an even smaller follow-up story appeared. The authorities had declared the boat's explosion to be the result of faulty gas line maintenance. The only woman reported missing was Desiree De Maurier, a Sand Isle resident. And Beyond Land Charters, the company who rented out the boat, had never bothered to check the validity of the information on the reservation, since it was paid in advance, and in cash. The police would continue to pursue the investigation if and when more information became available.

It was fall. Months had passed with no additional mention of the incident. Case closed.

"May I refill your coffee, sir?"

"Yes. Thank you, Moss."

Hayden put down the Financial Times, sipped his coffee, and gazed out across the calm, turquoise blue waters. He was home, on his own private island, one of close to seventeen hundred on the archipelago called the Florida Keys. Sitting on his terrace in a silk Gucci smoking jacket, enjoying a late breakfast of croissants, jams, assorted hams and cheeses, grapes and sipping espresso, he laughed at all those from his past who told him he'd never amount to anything. Let 'em rot in hell, he thought. I'm in heaven. No apologies required.

The feelings of peace the view brought him soothed the monster living deep within him—temporarily. He stopped lying to himself about who he was years ago. He was Gemini—twins—polarities—two beings—one good—one evil.

He had made a Faustian bargain to ensure both beings survived—the ultimate deal with the devil. He became an active accomplice to the storm battling within him, and created an alter ego, a persona who gave breath to his other being. It was all about choices, how unrequited desires for wealth and power fueled his choices. He lived vicariously, finding pleasure from seducing others to the dark side of their very human frailties, watching them give in, watching them fall victim, and making oodles of money off their vulnerabilities.

But now this. Payment had been called, and the devil was viciously demanding his due. Unlike many of Hayden's victims, who met their maker quickly, albeit with some pain, the devil had decided to take his time with him. Rich, indulgent living caused, and then exacerbated, his Type Two diabetes. Not obeying his doctor's orders was about to cost him his life. Unless…unless he found a way to turn things around.

"Will you be going out today?" asked Moss as he cleared away dirty dishes.

"No. I'm going to catch up on some reading and relax. I'll be having dinner in. See about getting some lobster. I've got a taste for tetrazzini."

"With respect, sir. Is that wise?"

"The hell with wise." Plates rattled when he slammed his fist on the table. "It's what I want."

Moss flinched slightly. "Very good, sir. I'll be back shortly."

Hayden reached for an Arturo Fuentes Opus X cigar and waited for Moss, his caporegime, ever-faithful companion, bodyguard, assistant, chief-cook-and-bottle-washer, to leave the terrace. One quick clip, and his fourteen-carat gold, double-bladed guillotine cutter opened just the right amount of the cigar's surface to create the perfect smoke. Lighting up and taking a puff, he blew the first smoke ring into the air, its gossamer tendrils blending into the wispy clouds.

Loyalty, he thought. The only quality that truly mattered. He'd saved Moss's life years ago in a street fight with a guy hopped up on PCP. Moss had been too drunk to defend himself, and had a lot to lose if the police arrested him. He'd stepped in and ended the fight with the kind of finality that assured Moss the druggie would never come after him again. They both walked away unscathed, innocent victims.

And now Moss was trying to return the life-saving favor. He was right, of course, lobster tetrazzini was a poor meal choice. Too rich, too buttery, too much for his kidneys to process. He would need extra time on dialysis to cleanse the waste his failing system couldn't. But dinner would be oh so good going down.

Hayden left the table, took off his robe, and sank into the hot tub. The warm water soothed his tired bones. When Moss got back from town, he'd have him arrange an afternoon massage. He settled deeper into the water and leaned his head against the tub's side, positioning the jets to pummel his lower back.

Soon it would be over, one way or another. He puffed his cigar and blew delicate smoke rings into the air. The past few months had not been without their challenges, but overcoming impossible odds was his forte.

Transplant or dead. Those were the options the doctors placed before him. Having someone else's kidney put in his body was his solution of choice, but kidneys were in high demand. The transplant list was long—close to one hundred thousand, and growing longer every day. It could take five to ten years to receive a kidney from a dead donor, a living donor even longer. When you factored in the additional requirement of tissue-matching, the numbers didn't work in his favor.

And since waiting was not his strong suit, he'd taken matters into his own hands to find a suitable donor. Arrangements were underway.

The kidney thing was just the latest in a series of challenges. The fickle finger of fate was scratching his ass in others ways as well. The FBI had raided and closed down the Sand Isle Inn, a lucrative brothel he owned along the Southeastern coast of Florida. He loved that his primary business interests played off the fantasies of men. Sex, drugs, power, control. Most men didn't have them in their real lives. He provided all of them in the world of make-believe—online or onsite—and made a fortune daily. But to everything there is a time, and knowing when to make a graceful exit was crucial in his line of work. After the FBI raid, he gave the order to close down several inns and halt recruitment, the term he used to describe the process of procuring ladies for the brothels.

Moss tied the boat up to the pier, then got back on board and pulled a beer out of the always-stocked cooler. He sat down on the bench seat in the back of the boat and took a swig. Cold beer felt good in the late morning's heat.

He needed some time to himself. His mind was cluttered with thoughts from the past, because events in the present were spiraling out of control. He'd been living with a psychopath for the better part of two decades, but Hayden's cruelty had remained apart, separate, removed from Moss's daily interactions with him.

Last spring it hit home. He couldn't get the image of that dark night out of his mind. Hayden, standing at the floor to ceiling window of his Palm Beach penthouse, pressing the button on a cell phone, and the instantaneous explosion on the ocean's horizon.

Moss swallowed a sob and blinked back tears. Dawn's life was ended so swiftly. So easily.

A flock of seagulls soared overhead, which got him thinking about the fleeting passage of life. He'd been at Hayden's side since well before he adopted the James Hayden moniker, when he was good old JJ.

He'd sworn allegiance to his old friend the night before he left to join the Marines. They'd been drinking and doing some weed. A fight broke out, someone pulled a knife, and the rest—while not exactly history—left Moss questioning his memory about how it all started, and what really happened. All he remembered was sitting on the curb with an ice pack on the cut above his eye, listening to his best friend JJ lie to the police so convincingly that he found himself questioning the details of the fight.

The next morning, so cold by Memphis standards Moss could see his breath, he waved good-bye to JJ and Dawn, his two best friends, and climbed on the bus for Parris Island.

A lot changed during the ten years he was gone. Once he and his friends had been cut from the same cloth—purgatory-poor, raised by God-fearing parents who worshiped the whip as a teaching tool. Moss took the military route to manhood; JJ and Dawn stayed on the streets.

While he finished his beer, his thoughts drifted back to his homecoming party at Hammond's bar so many years ago. Like countless turning points in his life, the party remained fresh in his mind, like it happened yesterday. His conversation with JJ that night was vividly etched in his memory, word for word, because it had set in motion a chain of events no one could have predicted.

They had been the three Musketeers. But that night there were only two. The JJ who walked into Hammond's bar was so fashionably dressed Moss had trouble believing it was really his old friend. Where was the grungy kid he left at the bus stop? This JJ was a different breed.

A round of drinks and a few minutes of talk confirmed the feeling, he no longer knew his childhood best friend. The years had been good to JJ, but Moss couldn't stop wondering about the source of his good fortune.

"It's the ultimate freedom, man," said JJ late into the night of drinking. "The bitch. Claimed I got her pregnant. No way. I shoot blanks. Can anyone say vasectomy?"

"Are you sure you were shooting blanks?" asked Moss. "I heard it took a few months for all your little soldiers to die."

"Don't know. Didn't care."

Moss saw JJ look away. Something's off, he thought.

"She's gone. I'm free."

"How long ago was this life-altering decision?"

"A few months, man. It's the bomb. My gear works just fine. Can screw whatever walks. No damn rug rats coming out of me." JJ signaled for another round. "Got me thinking. How many men want to do the same thing? Have their fun and walk away? I figured lots. There was money to be made. So, I opened for business. And let me tell you, man, business has been booming."

"I can see that. You don't look anything like the old JJ."

"I'm not. That guy, he's gone. I'm James Hayden now." JJ picked up his beer and took a big swig. "We can do this, man. You and me. Like old times. The three musketeers."

"But there are only two of us here. Where's Dawn? It's not like her to miss my homecoming party."

"She's gone, man. Forget about her." JJ had grabbed Moss's shoulder and squeezed hard. "You're back now. Just you and me. Do you know how much money I've made in the last three months alone?"

"No."

"A shitload. And that's just around Memphis. I'm expanding. Heading for the coasts. Less puritanical in their views. I could use a man with your skills by my side. We'd be unstoppable."

"Let me think about it. It's late. I gotta go."

"Don't go. You're not in the military anymore. Loosen up. Have some fun."

Moss threw some money on the table and headed out into the night. Something was definitely off. Where was Dawn? JJ claimed not to know where she was. Said they lost touch a few months ago. His lack of eye contact told Moss there was more to his story.

He found Dawn two days later, about forty-five miles away, in a one-horse town with more bars and gas stations than schools. She was waitressing in a shithole diner. And she was pregnant—very pregnant.

Tears filled her eyes when Moss came through the door, and she raced into his arms. Were her tears because she was happy to see him, or because she was ashamed of her pregnancy? He never knew. She took her morning break, got them both coffee, and led him to a booth in the back.

When she joked that the baby was the result of a one-in-a-billion shot, he knew JJ was the father. She begged him to never breathe a word. This had to be their secret. He swore on his Marine Corps oath he'd take it to his grave. He remained at her side through the delivery of a beautiful baby girl, and they never spoke about it again.

So long ago, thought Moss, as he opened his eyes and checked the time. *Gotta get moving.* Being gone too long made Hayden nervous. He got off the boat, gave the line one final tug to make sure the boat was secured to the cleat, and headed to the mini-mart to get dinner supplies. His arms full, he crossed the parking lot to the dock where the fishermen brought in their catch and selected a three-pound lobster. Before he walked away, he pulled out the prepaid phone he'd bought at the mini-mart and made a call. It was answered in two rings.

"Yeah?"

"Something's up. Not sure what. More testy than usual. Everything okay on your end?"

"Nothing out of the ordinary here. She's working her ass off as usual."

"Okay. Stay sharp. Call me if anything happens. Anything. You got that?"

"Got it."

Disconnecting the call, he chucked the phone into a fly-infested trash bin, where it sank beneath fish heads, skins and guts, the remnants of the fishing fleet's now-clean daily catch. He got back on his boat and headed out.

CHAPTER 6

Williamsburg, Virginia

Detective Knight marched down the hospital's second floor ICU corridor, determined to talk to John Doe regardless of what the doctors said. A former Army Ranger, he stood an imposing six four, with sandy hair cut close, and muscles on top of muscles filling out a navy blue golf shirt tucked into black Dockers. He could have stayed in the military, but decided to go the civilian law enforcement route, securing a master's in criminal justice, and settling in Williamsburg to be close to his aging parents.

He needed answers, and John Doe had them. Or at least, he hoped he did. Uncovering the who, what, when, where, how and why of what happened to the man would be daunting unless John himself could fill in the myriad of blanks.

"Detective Knight," said Dr. McKenna. "How good to see you."

"You too, Doc." His pulse kicked up as his gaze slid the length of her, all five feet two. And though scrubs weren't figure-flattering, his vivid imagination made up for it. His muscles tightened in the wrong place. He'd coolly faced enemy fire, but struggled mustering up the courage to ask Debra McKenna out. He clamped down, pulled his mind away from the path of arousal, back to the here and now.

"I hear our patient is awake. Can he talk?"

"Yes, but I don't know how coherent he'll be. He's been rambling all morning about Aruba and his ticket to paradise. Hasn't said much more than that. He understands he's in the hospital."

"What's the prognosis?"

"Not good. He's got a very bad sepsis infection. We're giving him some strong antibiotics. Hope they work. If they do, he'll have a long, slow recovery."

"What happened to him?" He enjoyed talking to Debra McKenna. She was a pert little redhead who came up to his shoulder. She'd joined the Sentara team about a year ago, a competent doctor. John Doe was getting the best care possible.

"Simple nephrectomy. Someone took out one of his kidneys. They did it the old-fashioned way, full cut rather than laparoscopically. I don't believe they let him leave the hospital. Medical protocol calls for a two- to seven-day hospital stay, depending on the condition of the patient."

"Shit." Knight blushed at his use of the invective. "Sorry. Who would do something like that?"

"Not any reputable doctor I've ever met." McKenna pulled out her scrunchie, scratched the back of her head and redid her pony tail. "You know, I've read about cases like this, but we're talking third-world countries. Not here."

"What do you mean, cases like this?"

"Men who mysteriously lose a kidney. This man—" she said, nodding toward the room where John Doe lay. "Let's just say he did not get the best medical care, which tells

49

me it might not have been his choice to give up a kidney."

"Considering how and where we found him, that is a classic understatement."

They both heard the ping. She pulled her phone from her pocket and looked at the text. "Gotta get back to the ER. Nice seeing you."

"You too. Thanks, Doc."

Detective Knight nodded to the officer standing watch outside John Doe's door and approached the patient, who was now clean and safe in a guarded hospital room. Someone had given him a good sponge bath, and cleaned his thinning hair of mud and caked leaves. His clothes were nowhere in sight. Knight made a note to bring him some fresh clothes for when he left the hospital. Monitors beeped and hummed, recording his vitals, and ensuring the slightest variation would attract someone's attention.

His eyes were slits, but Knight felt them on him. *What must he be thinking?* He threw back his shoulders, straightened his posture, and held up his credentials in John Doe's line of sight. Hundreds of questions swirled through his mind. He wanted to complete his interview before anything else happened to the man.

"I'm Detective Adam Knight." He stopped, waiting for John Doe to acknowledge his presence. He thought he saw a nod of recognition so he continued. "I need to ask you a few questions about what happened to you." Too official-sounding, he realized, and with his height, he was towering over the man in the bed.

Honey, not vinegar.

He softened his voice and pulled up a chair close to the bedside.

"Can you tell me your name? Anything about what happened to you?"

"I don't know," said John Doe, running his tongue across his chapped lips. "I don't remember much."

There was something broken, lost, in this man's dull gray eyes. Whoever did this to him, their callous disregard for him as a fellow human being couldn't go unpunished. The man deserved justice for what he'd survived.

Knight held the straw of his water jug to the guy's mouth while he took a sip. "What's the last thing you do remember?"

"Thanks." The man dried his mouth with the sheet, his eyes cast out the window.

Knight's stomach knotted as he assessed the rail-thin man lying in the bed, cheekbones protruding, eyeballs sunken into the sockets. Detached eyes, making eye contact with you, but not really seeing you. He guessed his own thumb and index finger could easily encircle John Doe's wrist.

He watched him fidget in the bed, rubbing his eyes, picking at a loose thread on the top sheet, looking out the window, and then quickly looking away, struggling not to make eye contact with the one man trying to help him.

Knight's phone buzzed. He didn't want to look away, but knew it might be important to the case.

"Excuse me a moment." He gently touched the man's shoulder, turned, and walked to the doorway. "Knight here." Listening more than speaking. "Thanks. I'll be in shortly."

Walking back to his seat by the man's bed, he said, "Mr. Hobbes. That's your name, yes? Jason Hobbes?"

A flash of recognition crossed the man's face. "Jason Hobbes," he repeated softly, "that was me, a long, long time ago. Now..." His voice trailed off. "Not so much."

"Mr. Hobbes, I want to find out what happened to you. What can you tell me to help me? Who did this to you?"

"No one," his voice was raspy, each word a struggle. "I

51

did it to myself. Years ago. No one to blame but me."

"What you might have done to yourself does not explain the fact that, according to the doctors, you've recently had an operation where someone removed one of your kidneys. Do you remember that?"

Silence. Hobbes turned his head away.

"Mr. Hobbes," said Knight softly, "you couldn't cut out your own kidney, so someone else did this to you. What can you tell me about that?"

"Paradise. My ticket to paradise. Aruba, Bahamas, Monte Carlo. Montego. Wherever I want to go. All paid for. Warm. Worth it." With that Jason Hobbes, the former John Doe, drifted off.

What the hell does that mean?

The Beach Boys tune "Kokomo," popped into Knight's head. Remembering the ratty clothes Hobbes was wearing when he was found, and connecting it to his missing kidney, and ramblings about a trip to paradise, had alarm bells sounding in Knight's brain.

He watched Hobbes's even breaths, and couldn't help but wonder what a more youthful, robust version of the emaciated man lost in the bed next to him might have been like. And how he got from there to here. A star athlete in high school? The quarterback who got the girls? Took the lead in all the plays? All conjecture. So much promise trampled by the ups and downs of a reality he was unprepared to live.

There, but for the grace of God, go I.

Suddenly all hell broke loose. The monitors went crazy, blaring sirens calling others to arms. Doctors rushed in, and Knight walked out, bumping into Nadine Steiner-Greene.

"What's happening?" she asked, knowing the answer even as the question left her lips.

"He's crashing. Was talking to me one minute. Rolled his

head to look out the window. I thought he fell asleep. Then the shit hit the fan."

The interview with Tiffany Stamos was a total waste of time. Morgan learned nothing she didn't already know from reading the advance PR tip sheets and articles written about Elan Health Systems. At least the next item on her "to-do" list would be more satisfying.

She walked into Sentara hospital holding a small green plant with bright cobalt blue foil paper wrapped around the pot. A huge yellow bow secured the foil paper to the pot and gave the plant a cheery look.

Nadine was meeting her at John Doe's room, and had just texted her the room number. She took the elevator to the second floor, where disinfectant slapped her nostrils as soon as the elevator doors opened.

Hospitals all smell alike, like death.

The chaotic scene that greeted her confirmed her feelings, which were further validated by the announcement currently being broadcast.

"Code Blue, Room 202."

She saw nurses and doctors race into a room down the hall, eager to do what they could to save a life. Morgan spotted Nadine and Detective Knight leaning against the wall outside the same room.

"What's happening?" she asked while squeezing the life out of the plant's plastic pot.

"He's coding," said Nadine. "Spiked a fever. Major infection. Guess spending time outside in the cold after someone cuts out your kidney is not good for your health."

Looking at Knight, Morgan asked, "Were you able to find out his name or anything about him?"

"Jason Hobbes. His name's Jason Hobbes. A vet. Earned a purple heart in Iraq."

"Wow. This is so sad," said Nadine. "Another story that needs telling. Too many of our bravest living on the streets and winding up like this."

"Based on your reputation, Nadine," said Knight, "I'd say this type of story is right up your alley."

Just then sad-faced doctors and nurses walked out of the room, their battle against death lost.

"We're so sorry. There was nothing we could do," said one of the doctors, flipping his stethoscope over his head.

"No. He can't be dead." Morgan was surprised at the surge of grief. "You're supposed to save him, give him blood transfusions, meds, something."

"We like to think we can save them all," said the young doctor, "but in his case, the infection was too advanced. I am sorry for your loss." They moved as one down the hall to the nurses' station.

One last nurse came out of the room. Her gray hair and the lines on her face spoke volumes about her years of dedicated service and experience. She could see Morgan's distress and went to her side.

"I'm so sorry for your loss. We weren't expecting him to have visitors, not from what Detective Knight said last night. Are you family?"

"No. Just someone who cared."

"You're the person who found him, aren't you?" The nurse's hand gently rested on Morgan's arm.

"Yes. We were looking for someone else and stumbled onto him last night."

"At least he didn't die out there in the woods all alone. You can go in if you want to." She stepped to the side and her hand swept in the direction of the doorway.

Morgan took a step toward the door and stopped.

"No. That's all right. I-I think I need some air." She hurried away alone, absently placed the potted plant down on the counter in front of the nurses' station, rushed past the elevators, and slammed the stairway door open.

"I better go with her," said Nadine. "Mind if Morgan or I call you later, Detective Knight? Maybe you can give us some insights about how you see the homeless issue around here, and how this man's death might connect. Who knows? Working together might give us a better chance of finding some good solutions to a complex problem."

"You okay?" asked Nadine when she caught up to Morgan in the parking lot. "You're taking the death of a guy you didn't know awfully hard."

"No, I'm not okay." Morgan wiped away a tear. "I know I'm supposed to say yes, I'm okay, but the truth is I'm not okay in any way, shape or form." She was huffing and puffing, terribly out of breath. Her chest heaved, and she found herself gasping for air.

"Want to talk about it?" Nadine leaned against Morgan's car.

"Transference."

"Come again?"

"I'm worried about Eli, and I'm transferring that worry and sadness onto the guy we found, John Doe. No one's life should end like this."

"I agree. Alone is no way to leave this world. But many people do. And I'm not just talking about the elderly who find they've outlived their friends, and don't have family close by who care enough to be there at the end."

"Or care enough to be there at all."

"Families are funny things."

"Tell me about it." Morgan blinked back tears and hung her head for a moment. "Mine is so messed up. Look at me. Divorced twice with a confused son who only calls me when he needs money, and is somewhere in Europe trying to find himself."

Her air quotes tied to the words "find himself" spoke volumes to Nadine. She slowly put her arm around her friend.

"I haven't heard from Howie in weeks." Morgan's voice wobbled. "So much for social media. I text. Get nothing. I have this recurring dream that I'm going to die just like John Doe. Alone."

"No you're not. And that's a long way off, so don't even think about it. What's up with you, anyway?"

"Things are out of control, that's what. Don't you feel it?"

"Mercury's retrograde. Of course things are screwy. What do you expect?"

Morgan sniffled and hiccuped. "You're kidding, right?"

"Yes. Sorry. Couldn't resist. Thought it would lighten the moment," Nadine said while she stroked Morgan's back.

"Everything is so messed up. All the things I used to take for granted... Then whoosh," she said, snapping her fingers, "they're gone. Nothing lasts."

"We've lasted. Next to Sid, you're the closest thing I have to family."

"But what if it's not enough? What if *I'm* not enough?"

"Okay, this conversation is too morbid to have without strong adult beverages. Go on. Get in. Follow me home. I'll call Bob and make up some excuse why neither of us is at work. Then I'll send Sid out for steaks. We'll drown our sorrows in a hearty Cabernet while he slaves over a hot grill and waits on us hand and foot. You'll stay the night. And tomorrow morning Sid will take us out for waffles."

"I love waffles."

"I know you do, honey. I know you do." Nadine hugged her friend, holding her tight. She could feel the raw tension in her friend's body melt away as her soft sobs rinsed away her grief and fears.

CHAPTER 7

Sand Isle, Florida

Out of the corner of her eye, Carolyn saw an unmarked brown van pull into the driveway of the small beach cottage she and Kyle shared on the grounds of Le Maschere, the compound Marco owned. Kyle had been instrumental in helping her find her daughter last spring, and he was slowly becoming a very important person in her life.

Last month she agreed to move into his place to test whether their relationship could withstand the pressures of twenty-four/seven cohabitation. He argued the money she was spending in rent could be better spent, since his place was rent-free, and they were together every night. A convenient, rational argument, she thought. So like a guy not yet ready to commit.

Even though the van couldn't have gotten onto the property without clearing front gate security, she was still cautious. Vigilance had become her permanent friend after the untimely death of Desiree De Maurier five months ago. The boat she was on for a sunset cruise exploded. She and Kyle had been on his sailboat, the Victoria B, miles from the explosion, but they saw the glow of the fire light up the horizon. It remained an unsolved case, raising more questions than answers about how it had occurred, and whether it was an accident—or not.

"Yes?"

"Mrs. Carolyn Conrad from Bangor, Maine?"

"Yes?" Carolyn peered through the plantation shutters at the man on her doorstep. He was tall, about six foot two, she estimated, and had long, thinning brown hair pulled back into a ponytail. He wore plain clothes, a sage green golf shirt and jeans. Not exactly a uniform, no insignia. She thought it curious that he included her hometown when verifying her identity.

"I have a special delivery package. I just need your signature." The man waved a manila envelope in the air. When she opened the door, she saw a large box at his feet. She quickly signed for the items and thanked him. Securing the envelope under her arm, she reached down for the package.

"It's heavy, ma'am. Want me to carry it inside for you?"

"No, I can manage. Could you just put it into my arms?"

"Sure thing, ma'am."

"Oh, it is heavy." Carefully readjusting the box, Carolyn closed the door with the back of her foot and the weight of her body.

Walking into the kitchen, she slid the package onto the counter, and examined the envelope, noting the return address was an Orlando law firm, Kohlmeier, Kraft and Boules. Pulling a kitchen knife from the block on the counter, she deftly slit the envelope open and pulled out a neatly typed letter on crisp, white stationary. There was a second envelope with her name handwritten on it, the writing shaky.

Carolyn opened the more official-looking letter first. It

was short and to the point. Four lines of type on gold-embossed letterhead, not including the dear ma'am or the sincerely yours.

The law firm was following the directions of its client, Desiree De Maurier. It had recently learned about her death. At her request, the enclosed letter and package were herewith delivered to Carolyn Conrad of Bangor, Maine. It ended with an apology for the delay because it took them some time to locate her.

Strange, thought Carolyn. It wasn't like she and Desiree were close friends. In fact, they weren't friends at all, at least not in Carolyn's mind. Their meeting at mah jongg tournaments, their so-called friendship, was a ruse perpetrated by Carolyn, who believed Desiree could lead her to her missing daughter, Amelia. And she was right. Amelia was now safe, out of the clutches of the sex trafficking ring that held her prisoner for years.

Then Carolyn opened the second letter. Like her name on the envelope, it was written with a shaky hand.

Dearest Carolyn,

There aren't words to express my heartfelt sorrow. I know our friendship was not what it appeared to be. Yes, Carolyn, I know. And by the time you read this letter, I'll be gone, and unable to express my regret for the harm I have caused your daughter, and the pain I have caused you. Know that if I could have safely ended that pain, I would have done so.

I have only one small request, one I am confident that, with your skills, you and only you will be able to fulfill. And I am praying that you will put aside any feelings of anger you may have and help me.

All my worldly possessions, except what you received with this letter, are left to my daughter. Yes, I have a daughter, too, one I love and have not seen since the day she was born. Find her. Protect her as I know only you can.

Please accept these two gifts as a token of my repentance. Everything you need to carry out my last request, to protect my daughter, is in the package you now have. The dragon is the key.

Thank you. Forgive me.

D

Tears welled in Carolyn's eyes.

She knew! Knew I wasn't some lonely housewife going to tournaments to get away for awhile. That's impossible. How could she have known?

Carolyn's curiosity turned to the package. The kitchen knife shook in her hand, but she finally managed to use the tip to cut into the tape securing the carton on all sides. After ripping open the flaps and pulling out the bubble wrap, Carolyn beheld the top of a beautifully carved antique chest. Slowly, she lifted it out of the box.

It was a mah jongg set. She'd seen photos of chests like this one when she did her research and learned how to play the game.

"Desiree gave me her mah jongg set," she breathed.

She ran her fingers over the top of the chest, the wood soft to her touch, the carvings deep. The image of a different fire-breathing dragon was expertly carved into each side, with the symbols for the four winds tiles—north, south, east and west—placed in each of the four corners. On the top there was an intricately carved garden scene depicting a dragon walking across a bridge, about to enter a cave. The brass handle was positioned so it fit into the scene as part of the glistening bridge over the river. The chest was stunning.

What craftsmanship!

Carolyn couldn't wait to open it, sure the tiles would be equally exquisite. She saw sets of small hinges indicating where the chest opened in several different places, but she couldn't find a visible latch or slot to insert a key. Then again, she didn't have a key. Lifting the chest and shaking it gently, she heard rattling sounds like tiles clicking against each other. But, try as she might, she couldn't find a way to open it.

She picked up Desiree's letter and reread it. It mentioned two gifts. There had to be more.

Removing the remaining bubble wrap from the box, she found a small, green velvet drawstring bag. She could feel something inside.

"Must be the key."

She separated the bag's ties and turned the bag over, expecting a shiny brass key, matching the brass on the handle, to fall into the palm of her hand. To her surprise, brilliant, emerald green eyes stared up at her. Desiree's white jade dragon pendant looked up from her palm.

She stared at it, shocked. Questions bombarded her thoughts.

Wouldn't she have worn the pendant for an evening's boat ride with a dear friend? She wore it every day, everywhere. Why didn't she wear it that night? A premonition of trouble?

Holding Desiree's prized possession in her hand, Carolyn was now convinced the reason for the explosion that killed her five months ago was far more sinister than a faulty gas line.

One badly burned body was found after the boat Desiree was on exploded, and preliminary identification was made using the charter company's records. The boat was rented, with her listed as its only passenger that evening. Carolyn told police she remembered Desiree saying she was going boating with an artist friend of hers named Andre, but without a last name, finding him proved futile.

Carolyn always wondered what happened to Andre, the boat's captain, and its crew. Desiree wouldn't have been steering it herself, and she wasn't serving herself food or beverages, that's for sure. But no one reported anyone else missing.

"Hey, what's up?" asked Kyle as he walked in the back door, his arms full of groceries. Putting the bags down on the counter, he ambled over to Carolyn and wrapped his arms around her waist from behind. She leaned back into him.

"One of the benefits of being so close to the office," he whispered in her ear as he planted soft kisses on her neck, roving down to the edge of her petal pink tank top.

She turned around and slid her arms around his neck. His mouth found hers, and his kiss was long and deep.

"A girl could get used to this."

"And I want you to." He kissed her again, hungrily, his tongue and hers twisting, exploring, his fingertips brushing her nipples, which rose to attention at his touch.

"I love you, Carolyn Conrad. I've never said that to any woman, and I can't stop saying it to you. With all my heart, I love you."

"I love you too," she said, tilting her head and looking into his hazel green eyes. "You are the surprise of my life. What started as a nightmare is ending like fairy tales do, happily ever after."

"God, you're beautiful." He tucked a wisp of blond hair behind her ear, his boyish grin belying the power of his masculinity. A former SEAL, Kyle was instrumental last spring in rescuing her daughter and smashing the sex trafficking operation holding her and nine other women prisoner.

"Delivery guy just dropped off an interesting package," she said, resting her hand on top of the box.

"How interesting?"

"Very. Check this out." She handed Kyle Desiree's handwritten letter and watched him read it. "Interesting, yes?"

He blinked and stared at her. "She has a daughter? Wonder if Marco knows."

"Probably not. Then again," she continued thoughtfully, "what Marco knows and doesn't know always surprises me. Regardless, he'll know it soon enough. I'm going to ask him if Brett and I can take some time away from our current research into who's running the sex trafficking ring, and take a stab at figuring out who Desiree's daughter is, and where she is."

"You think there may be a connection to her death?" asked Kyle.

"It's possible. The police haven't closed the case yet. They may tell the public the boat had a faulty fuel line, but privately, I hear they are leaning toward murder, premeditated murder. Someone wanted her dead."

Kyle finished the train of thought. "And when they failed to get the job done by poisoning her at the Mah Jongg tournament, they implemented Plan B. Are you and Brett any closer to figuring out who *they* are?"

"Not really. We're still slogging through all the shell companies embedded in Shale Enterprises, the only actual name we have for any company associated with Metamorphosis, the Sand Isle Inn, and Desiree. It's been slow going."

"I'm sure Daniel and the FBI will appreciate anything you turn up. Look what you guys uncovered about the Inn. If it wasn't for you and Brett, let's just say things might have turned out very differently."

"There are hackers and there are *hackers*. And then there's Brett, the cyber wizard."

"True. Your methods and law enforcement's methods might eventually complement each other." He started to unpack the groceries. "What's in the box?"

"Her antique mah jongg set. She showed me a picture of it once, and it's gorgeous. And look what else she sent me." Carolyn picked up the small, emerald green velvet pouch and dumped the white jade dragon into her palm.

"Wow. How the… She sent you that?"

"Yes. Her most prized possession." Carolyn thought about the letter. "Then again, considering her letter asks me to find her daughter, maybe this pendant isn't her most prized possession. Maybe her daughter is. I suspect the knowledge that she even has a daughter has been a well-kept secret, one very few people, if anyone, knows."

"It says find and protect her daughter. Protect her from what?"

"Or from who?" Carolyn scrunched up her face. "Or is that whom?"

"Who knows? Who cares?"

Carolyn and Kyle gazed into each other's eyes for a long minute. "Maybe she thought someone was going to harm her? And her cryptic the-key-to-everything-is-the-dragon comment raises a host of questions in my mind."

"Mine too," said Kyle. He put the milk and eggs into the fridge and started to take vegetables out of the little plastic bags when he realized Carolyn was staring out the window, seemingly lost in a trance.

"What's up? You seem tense, far away."

"I'm thinking about Desiree. Giving up her daughter. Never having known her. And now asking me to find her and protect her. After what she did to me, to Amelia, what made her think I'd help her?"

"She knew you. Knew the type of person you are. Bet on your kind soul, your loving heart."

"We weren't together that often. A few days two or three times a year over the course of two years. It's not like we shared a room and got into intimate, girlfriend conversations. We mostly played mah jongg and went to dinner."

"You can learn a lot about a person over dinner and at a gaming table. Ask any croupier in Vegas. The one thing they excel at is reading the players at their tables. Desiree lived and thrived in that world. And she wouldn't have been a successful madam without a keen sense about people."

Carolyn took a breath and heaved a sorrowful sigh. "I can't imagine giving up Amelia when she was born."

"You didn't have to. Maybe Desiree felt she had no choice."

"Doesn't that seem strange to you?"

"Yes, but I'm not her, and I wasn't living in her skin. Can't judge her decisions. She probably was young, scared, pregnant and alone. Who knows what I might have done under those circumstances?"

"You couldn't be under those circumstances. You know, the pregnant part."

"Minor technicality. You know what I mean. No one knows what they would do until confronted by the situation. And we're all different. Her experiences led to her decisions. You might have made a different decision. Anyway, I learned a long time ago not to judge others."

Carolyn snuggled into his side and felt him nuzzle her hair. She felt safe and at home in his arms. She traced her finger from Kyle's lips down across his smooth chest, encircling one nipple and then the other. His muscles pulsed at her gentle touch. Her hand slid lower and then she pushed herself away.

"Wait a second. If you're here, who's in the office? TJ and some of the guys are still at a security conference. Brett's not back from vacation until tomorrow, and I'm here."

"Tina and I are holding down the fort. Told her I needed to run a few errands after work. We made a deal. I'd go run my errands now while she watches the place, and I'll do the last hour alone so she can leave early. I think she has a hot date."

"You think you can handle it alone?"

"Hey. Not nice. I can answer phones. With Marco, Marissa and Sophia away, too, it's been dead quiet all morning. Our deal benefits both of us. She said she'd text if something comes up."

"Just like a guy. Always leaving a woman to do the important work." Carolyn put her arms around his neck and wiggled her hips against his. She felt his appreciation harden.

"Cute. A little bit of professionalism please, ma'am. This is sexual harassment. And if you keep this up, Tina is going to be holding down the fort alone longer than planned."

Kyle's mouth covered hers, her lips parted while they enjoyed a little bit more afternoon delight.

"Hmmmm." She purred as he planted a kiss on top of her head. "Professionally speaking, would you use these strong muscles and put this box on the dining room table?"

"I'd rather use my strong muscles to hold onto you a little longer."

"Rein it in, mister," she laughed pulling away. "There's work to be done. Time for play later."

"Promises, promises."

"And have I ever not delivered on a promise?" She loved that her quirky smile aroused him.

"Not that I recall."

"Then the sooner I get started on unraveling this puzzle, the sooner we can move on to more fun types of things."

"Your wish is my command," said Kyle as he hefted the box and followed her into the next room.

CHAPTER 8

Williamsburg, Virginia

Morgan and Greg Welton had known each other forever, had spent every childhood summer together at Blue Mountain camp. They always called those times the good old days, before they had to go out and earn a living. When she called him saying she needed his help for a story she was writing, and learned he was in Williamsburg, they made plans to meet for dinner at Opus 9.

"Are you trying to sneak up on me?" giggled Morgan who seemed to be able to sense his presence behind her before she actually saw him.

"Doubt I could ever sneak up on you."

Morgan slid off the barstool and into his arms. "It's so good to see you." A long, warm hug ensued. "I can't believe you're actually here in Williamsburg."

"I'm as surprised as you are. Delighted, really."

The host appeared at Greg's side.

"I think our table is ready. Here, let me take your drink."

After following the host through the crowded restaurant, they settled into a quiet booth.

The server approached the table. "May I get you something to drink, sir?"

"I'll have a scotch on the rocks, please."

"It's been too long. How have you been?" Morgan couldn't help but notice how tired Greg looked. "You look like you've been burning the candle at both ends."

"Work's been overwhelming. A lot of travel. I just flew in from New York, and we just closed a big deal here."

"In Williamsburg?"

"Yes. I thought it was going to be a quick trip, which is why I didn't call you. But it looks like I'll be here for a while. And your call asking for my help made my day."

"What are you doing here?"

"Opening a clinic."

"Impressive."

"I'll be spending more time here, too, so we may be able to see each other more often. Do something more than these quick, catch up with an old friend, dinners. It's been too long." He slid his hand across the table and placed it gently on top of hers.

Smiling at him, Morgan pulled her hand back, fumbled for her reading glasses and picked up her menu. "That's great. We'll be able to hang out a bit. Like old times."

"What looks good?" asked Greg, opening his menu as the server approached to take their dinner order and replenish their drinks.

"Everything is good here."

"Tonight is my treat, so order to your heart's content."

"Thank you." To the server, she said, "I'll have the filet, medium rare, and the baked potato with sour cream and creamed spinach."

Greg said, "This is going to be easy. Double that and bring a bottle of Domaine du Vieux Chateau Neuf du Pape."

"Very good, sir." Menus were taken away. A young lady approached with a camera.

"May I take your photo? Compliments of the house."

"That's nice," said Greg.

"It's a new service, sir. A way to give guests a nice memento of your evening here at Opus 9. Now get cozy." She waited while Morgan and Greg moved closer and leaned their heads together. "Smile."

Two snaps later, the young lady smiled sweetly. "Thank you. We'll have it for you on your way out."

Greg watched her walk away, noting that she didn't stop at any other tables.

"So, you're here on business?" asked Morgan.

"Yes. I'll admit to a hefty meeting schedule over the next few days with colleagues, but tonight I'm all yours." His smile went from ear to ear, his eyes twinkling. "You know, I've always considered you the one who got away. I should never have introduced you to Alan. Who knew you'd marry him!"

"Didn't last long. We were too idealistic back then. He wanted to shake up the world, or at least his little corner of it. One of us needed to have his feet—her feet—firmly on the ground. Get a real job. Make some money to pay the bills."

"Where's Alan now?"

"Off in Africa somewhere. Doctors without Borders. Hope he keeps his head down. Even Howie hasn't heard from him in a while."

"And how is your wandering son?"

"Still wandering. Thanks for asking. Not sure where I went wrong with him. He flunked out of college, but finally finished his degree through one of those online degree programs. He can't keep a job, alienates everyone with his my-shit-don't-stink-I'm-the-smartest-person-in-the-room routine. He's off backpacking through France."

Morgan averted her eyes and blew out a breath, wanting very much to change the focus of their conversation. Talking about her son always twisted her heart. "Oh, look, here's dinner. I'm starved."

Several servers descended on their table. Plates with a savory array of food were placed before each of them while Morgan hoped Greg couldn't hear her stomach growl…until she heard his doing the same.

"Excuse me," he smiled. "I haven't eaten all day." He refilled their wine glasses. "This looks great. A toast. To old friends." His eyes sparkled. Glasses clinked.

"So, you mentioned on the phone you want to pick my brain for a story you're writing. Won't take long. Not much there these days. What do you want to know?"

"I want to know about kidneys. Kidney transplants to be exact."

Greg started to cough and reached for his water glass.

"Are you okay?"

"Yes," Greg croaked. "Went down the wrong pipe."

"You're a doctor. You should know better than to talk with your mouth full."

"What's got you interested in kidney transplants?"

"My friend Nadine and I found a man in the woods the other night. He was almost dead, and did die the next day. I overheard one of the paramedics tell the detective that he thought someone had removed one of the man's kidneys. I looked online and saw how much kidneys go for, and I thought there might be a really good story here."

"You're going to write a story about organ donation? That's great. There are never enough organs to match the need."

"Not really the donation side. I'm thinking more along the lines of the black market in organs. Way more exciting. Nadine threatened to write it if I don't."

Greg felt himself shudder.

"Sounds interesting. It's a dangerous business, black market organs. You sure you want to investigate something so dangerous?"

Her eyes sparkled at him. "Yes. It's my big break, a chance to show my editor that I can write about more than garden clubs, grand openings and obituaries."

"I don't want you getting hurt."

"Thank you. I don't plan to get hurt. Who would want to hurt me?"

"People invested in making sure the whole black market organ business stays below the radar of any number of federal health agencies, and the FBI, who would all shut it down in a heartbeat. It's illegal in this country. Lots of powerful people would go to jail."

He took a hefty sip of wine, straining to keep control of his voice.

Morgan skewered a piece of steak with her fork and waved it in the air as she spoke. "With technology advancing as fast as it does, I'm sure someday soon they'll be able to make replacement organs on 3-D printers, but for now they have to rely on donations. And too many people are waiting on donor lists—dying while waiting on donor lists. I've been doing a lot of reading about organ donation."

"I can see that." He could feel her watching him. "It's not really an area I know much about. And I've been out of the actual practice of medicine for a while. Doing mostly administrative type things. So I don't think I can be much help."

"Bummer. I was hoping you would know tons about it. Do you know anyone I can talk to?" She noticed his hand shaking a bit as he held his fork. "Are you okay?"

"Yes, I'm fine." He refilled both their wine glasses, forcing himself to concentrate on holding his hand steady. "I can't think of anyone off the top of my head, but let me ask around for you. You seem really excited about this."

"I am. I especially like the ethics angle. If it's ethical to sell something you own, like a car or a home, why isn't it ethical to sell a part of your body? You own your body, don't you?"

"You do and you don't."

"Spoken like a politician, not a doctor." She took a sip of wine. "And for some body parts—like sperm or eggs or plasma—selling those is totally legal." She pulled out her iPad and started swiping through screens.

"You carry your iPad with you?"

"Everywhere I go. You never know when you're going to have to write something down. Anyway, get this." She gently touched the back of his hand. "The 9th U.S. Circuit Court of Appeals, that's the very liberal court out west, declared it was okay to compensate bone marrow donors. Donors in places like Arizona, California, Hawaii, Guam, Idaho, Alaska, Montana, Nevada, Oregon, and Washington can get up to three thousand dollars per donation. The article said it takes eight weeks to recover. Do the math, Greg. Someone can donate bone marrow six times a year and make an easy eighteen thousand dollars. Just for bone marrow. And science has perfected the process so stem cells can now be harvested directly from blood. Not as painful a process as it used to be."

Big blue eyes stared at him, looking for some sign, some interest. She pressed on. "Who gets to decide which parts are okay to donate and which aren't?"

"Congress passed a law against selling body parts years ago."

"Yes, I know. NOTA, the National Organ Transplant Act. I read that some entrepreneurial man was setting up a way for people to sell organs, and he'd take a commission on the sale. Congress put a stop to it and passed a law."

"And established a task force to decide who gets an organ when one becomes available."

"This task force, what gives them the power to decide whether someone lives or dies?"

"Congress did. And their educated opinions."

"Opinions are like assholes. Everybody's got one."

"Whoa. Nice mouth over dinner." Greg took a deep breath and looked around the room. "Any chance we can talk about something else?" He saw a great change of subject at the next table. The waiter was serving a soufflé. "How about we focus on dessert?"

Greg followed Morgan home and pulled into her driveway behind her. She walked back to his car just as he got out.

"How about a nightcap?" he asked. "Some cappuccino or espresso?"

Greg stroked her cheek gently with the backs of his fingers. He studied her face, noticing the upturned perkiness of her nose, the rosy moistness of her lips, the cool blueness of her eyes, framed by the longest lashes he had ever seen. Every time they met, she would give him a warm hug and friendly kiss, and her lashes would brush against his cheek, sending a tingle down his spine. He wanted more.

"Another dessert, perhaps? The non-fattening kind?"

Morgan's eyes met his.

Not again. Tell me he isn't going to put the moves on me again.

She felt the beginning of a giggle take hold of her insides. She pressed her lips tightly together, working to control the burst of laughter bubbling up inside her, to keep it from exploding out loud. Maybe she needed to apply herself more, get herself into the right mood somehow.

Gingerly, she placed her right hand on his chest. "We've tried this before. Remember?"

He covered her hand with one of his own. "I remember. The first time you were between husbands. And Ruthie and I had just filed for divorce. Then you married Marv. Another one of my friends, I might add. How about you stop linking up with my friends and go for the real deal? Things are different now."

"How so?"

"Neither of us is in a committed relationship. We're free agents."

His cocky smirk annoyed her. "And you know this about me, how? Have you been spying on me?"

"Of course not."

Morgan noted the upward twitch of his eyebrows. He blinked and averted his eyes.

Did he just lie to me?

"I'm just reading the tea leaves," he said softly.

"We didn't have tea."

"You know what I mean. We went through our entire dinner, and you never once mentioned another man."

Greg leaned in, trapping Morgan between him and his rental car. "If this were a taxi, I could say something cute like the meter is still running. Shall I pay him and tell him to go?"

"The only meter that's running here is yours," she laughed, hoping to ease a very awkward moment. "Let's take this slow. I had a really nice time at dinner. And you said you'll be in Williamsburg for a few weeks opening your new clinic, which is really exciting, so we can plan a few more lunches and dinners. Let's see where it takes us. How does that sound?"

He heaved an exasperated sigh. "If I must. But, I'm telling you now, I'm quite the catch. Successful doctor—CEO of a major health care provider—what more could you want?"

"I don't know right now. It's too soon for me. And just so you know, I did just end a relationship with someone, and I'm not sure I'm ready to jump into another one. Think I need some breathing room."

"I understand." He remained silent for a moment, scanning her face. "Maybe we can have breakfast."

"I've got a morning meeting that I don't dare miss. And since you didn't know much about the black market for kidneys, I've got a full day of research ahead of me."

"Okay. I give up." He raised his hands in surrender. "Promise me you'll think about...about us...the possibility of an us."

"I promise."

Morgan tilted her head up, positioning herself for his good-night kiss, glad their evening was ending as a draw— no winner—no loser. He leaned in, kissing her gently.

"Good night. Sleep well. I'll call you in a few days."

"Sounds good." She gave him another peck on his cheek.

He got into his car, backed out of her driveway, and headed back toward town.

She waved as he drove away, and then walked into her garage and hit the button to lower the door.

Nope. Nothing. Like kissing my brother. If I had a brother.

CHAPTER 9

Williamsburg, Virginia
One week later

Elan Health Systems couldn't have asked for better weather for the clinic's opening day—a brilliant blue, cloudless sky and crisp fall air. The red, white, and blue balloon arch over the main clinic entrance fluttered in a slight breeze. The band from Jamestown High School played the national anthem during the opening ceremonies, and other crowd-pleasers. Many in the crowd clapped and sang along.

Dr. Greg Welton lined up next to the mayor and several local dignitaries, and handed the mayor an oversized pair of shears. Everyone smiled for the photographer, and then the mayor cut the huge red ribbon precisely at ten o'clock.

Colton Pollard watched from the sidelines. He shunned any active part in the festivities, preferring to move around with the crowd of visitors, listening to their unedited comments. At one point, he sidled up to Tiffany Stamos and complimented her on a job well done. Holding her elbow, he guided her away from the crowd and into one of the unoccupied treatment rooms.

"Thank you for all of your hard work on this project. You've done a spectacular job."

"Thank you, Mr. Pollard. It's been my pleasure to work for Elan and bring medical services to such a needy population," she gushed and beamed.

"Hold out your arm, please." He slipped a hand into his pocket and pulled out a glistening string of gorgeousness. "A small token of our appreciation." He wrapped the gleaming diamond bracelet around her delicate wrist and hooked the clasp.

"Oh," she gasped, blushing. "This is too much. I can't accept this."

"Of course you can. And you will, Tiffany. You've earned it. We are very impressed with your work. Now, go and enjoy your party." He remained locked on to the swivel of her hips as she walked away, grateful that such a pretty face and fantastic body had brains to match.

Colton preened in front of the mirror before heading back to the festivities. His father had once told him his own delusions of grandeur and egomaniacal narcissism would be his undoing, and believed his genius level IQ was the root of his problem. No one was smart enough to compete, and Colton shunned those with lesser abilities like he would a leper. His poor father suffered a fatal heart attack less than a week after he made those comments.

Tiffany felt heat rise from within her, like she'd swallowed a hot coal, as she returned to the lobby. She felt the weight of her new bauble around her wrist. Pulling together the grand opening in under a week had been a royal pain in her ass, but knowing the stringent demands of her employer, she'd left nothing to chance.

Clowns, jugglers and face painters moved through the crowd entertaining the children. Platters of donuts and pastries, carved watermelon baskets of fruit chunks, mini cheese and spinach quiche, and carafes of coffee, tea and hot chocolate filled several tables for the opening ceremonies. Lunch-type foods would replace the breakfast fare at eleven o'clock.

Colorful brochures detailing the clinic's different levels of service were picked up by guests as quickly as a staffer could replenish the piles. The well-trained staff gave tours of the facility, where several modular medical trailers augmented the totally renovated brick and mortar clinic. Guests toured the lab trailers, the treatment rooms, the outpatient surgicenter trailer, and the diagnostic imaging trailer. The state-of-the-art equipment blew everyone away, as well as Elan's promise that the equipment would be continually updated when new technologies were approved by the FDA.

The biggest buzz of the day was the free monthly Asclepius Clinic. Guests were amazed that so much could be offered to an underserved population. They were clearly impressed with Elan's Robin Hood approach.

Morgan and Nadine were enjoying the festivities. Morgan arrived earlier in the day to cover the ribbon cutting, and returned with Nadine after five, when more substantial hors d'oeuvres and adult beverages were served. They were scarfing down the chicken crostini, caviar canapés, and shrimp skewers, offered by uniformed servers weaving their way through the crowds.

"I love how all the mobile units connect," said Nadine. "Reminds me of the Habitrail my hamster lived in when I was a kid."

"You had a hamster?"

Nadine enjoyed Morgan's look of surprise. "Yep. Her name was Sam."

"Knowing you, it's hard to picture you with a pet rat."

"Not rat. Hamster."

"Same thing." Morgan followed Nadine out of the interconnected trailer complex and back to the clinic's main lobby. "This is very impressive. They must have some mega-rich financial backers to pay for all of this. When Greg and I had dinner the other night, he was very proud of what he had created."

"And he should be. You'll have to introduce me to him when he shows up."

"Definitely. I'm surprised I don't see him. This is his big event. I saw him get in his car right after the opening ceremonies, but I haven't seen him since then." She took a sip of wine. "You've got a funny look on your face, Nadine. What are you thinking?"

"That humans are interesting creatures. We resent it when the government redistributes our wealth, but are very willing to do it ourselves. Look at that long line of people, eager to sign contracts and make initial payments on the spot. This place is expensive, but they've bought into the concierge concept, knowing that part of their costs go to support the free clinic."

"When we do it, it's our choice. Not a choice being forced down our throats by others. We give from the heart because it means something to us. Because we care and want to show that caring. When the government does it, we have no choice about where our hard-earned dollars go. And the government wastes tons of money."

"Amen to that."

A server passed and Morgan reached for a triangle of spanakopita.

"Love these. I could probably eat the entire tray."

Nadine stopped the server with bacon-wrapped shrimp. She put one in her mouth and put two more on a small plate, before looking around, studying the people in the room.

"I wonder who that man over there is," said Nadine. "I've been watching him. He seems very interested in what's going on, but he's not really engaging anyone in conversation. More of a wallflower, hanging back, observing. Acts like a manager I once worked for at a small diner. Even when we were crazy busy, he'd stand back and watch everyone work. Never so much as filled a customer's coffee cup."

"He was here this morning, too. No clue who he is. Good dresser. Love his tie. I can ask Greg when I see him. Or I can go talk to him. Remember, I'm here in an official capacity. For the *Beacon,* doing a story."

Morgan put down her plate, pulled out her iPad and started to walk toward the man. Nadine quickly pulled her back.

"Would you mind if I go first? There's something about him. I'm getting a creepy vibe. Give me five minutes, then come over."

Morgan acquiesced. Not her first choice, but the right one to make on behalf of her former teacher, her mentor, her friend. Nadine was in the sunset years of a once-thriving career, whereas Morgan's career had plenty of time to sprout its flowers. She could give her BFF this moment.

Nadine took a circuitous route to her target, who was leaning against the wall next to one of the decorative, fern-filled planters brought in to add warmth to the lobby.

"Great event, wouldn't you agree?" she said, walking up on his right side. He barely budged when she spoke, so her efforts to surprise him seemed to have failed.

"Yes, it is comforting to see so many people from the community show up to support the clinic."

"Nadine Steiner-Greene," she said, extending her hand.

"Colton Pollard." He offered his right hand, then placed his left on top of hers, making a hand sandwich.

Nadine felt trapped by this gentle gesture, and pulled her hand away.

"You work for the *Beacon*, don't you?"

"Yes. How did you know?" Taking a sip of her wine, she asked, "Have we met before?"

"No, we haven't. I have this thing about reading local papers when I visit a new town. I saw your photo and byline on the story you did about the local kerfuffle over Dominion power lines going across the James River. Don't you just love that word, kerfuffle?" He made a slight curling flourish with his hand. "It has such a ring to it. Takes the sting out of even the most intense argument. Good article."

"Thank you." Her internal radar zinged her. *Who is this man and why is he here?*

"And you are not exactly unknown. Your previous work, as a syndicated reporter for the *Washington World Herald,* is infamous for the corruption you exposed. You're the female Woodward and Bernstein, a very talented investigative reporter, an articulate writer, who is able to promote her point of view effectively."

"Thank you again. Are you with the Elan organization?"

"An innocent observer. I was in town, heard about the Elan Clinic opening, and its subsidiary free clinic services, and thought I'd check it out. Health care is a growing industry."

"Are you involved in health care?"

"Tangentially. Consider me an entrepreneurial investor. Always looking for the next big thing."

"Not sure I'm familiar with that line of work. What exactly does an entrepreneurial investor do?" Before he could answer, Morgan came up to her side.

"Colton, this is my colleague, Morgan Kasen. She's a human-interest reporter at the *Beacon*."

"The *Beacon* certainly has good taste when it comes to hiring reporters. With all due respect, two lovely ladies." Any further conversation was interrupted when his cell phone chirped.

"Excuse me." Without looking at the caller ID, he walked outside, out of reach, without answering her question.

Nadine tracked his exit. She exhaled.

"Saved by a phone call."

Colton looked at the caller ID as he walked away. He hit the talk button. "Your report, please."

"Everything has been taken care of." The baritone voice did not elaborate, respecting Colton's preference for brevity.

Colton smiled. "Very good. Thank you."

He ended the phone call, feeling even more pleased with himself. Success might be its own reward, but Colton wanted more, craved more. Uber-success. Uber-rich. Through the doors, he could see Nadine Steiner-Greene standing where he left her—watching him.

She's curious about me. Not good.

While he stalled a moment to consider his options, a bing alerted him to an incoming text. His eyebrows knit as he read it. Trouble in paradise. His associate just lied to him over the phone, and his lie could not stand. Yes, the main problem had been taken care of, and the missing man conveniently died, but, according to this text message, what was done created a new problem. He died in public. At a local hospital. The police were now involved. Okay, he thought, police can be handled.

The text told of a bigger problem. Greg Welton had gone rogue. He'd been photographed recently meeting with two different reporters, Jesse Sinclair and Morgan Kasen, on two different nights.

How interesting, thought Colton, considering he just met Morgan Kasen. Inconsequential. A nothing. A fly. But her more inquisitive friend—Nadine Steiner-Greene. Now there was a problem in the making, a loose end, better tied up sooner rather than later. The other name was unknown to him. He texted back for the operative to track down Jesse Sinclair and send details.

"Ah, Greg. What are you up to?" he mused, knowing at this point it really no longer mattered.

He placed a call, got the response he wanted. Through the doors he could see Nadine and Morgan were still watching him. He smiled at both ladies, lifted his hand and gave a two-finger salute good-bye. Turning, he walked briskly to the limo. The driver snapped to attention, holding the door open.

"Back to the airport, please. And notify your counterpart in DC to be at Dulles when my flight lands."

Washington, DC

Three hours later, Colton walked into the lounge at the Hay-Adams Hotel. He noticed a few couples sitting at tables around the room. The bar was empty except for one lone man nursing a beer. Not wanting to stand out, he took the stool to the man's right and ordered a Grey Goose martini.

"How's it going," asked the man casually, as the bartender placed Colton's drink in front of him.

"Good. It's been a good day." He took a sip. "And you?"

"Can't complain." The man took another sip of his beer and turned to Colton.

"Parker Kent, Greenleaf Investments," he said, offering his hand and a business card. "We deal in antiquities." Colton felt the raw strength behind the man's handshake, and knew antiques were the last things on his mind. His refined attire, an Armani charcoal gray suit, white, collared shirt and red print tie belied his true profession. Parker Kent was a handyman, a finisher, a problem-solver, a man who got the job done.

"Colton Pollard. Nice to meet you." Colton handed him one of his business cards. "May I buy you a drink?"

"No. Thank you. I've got to be going," said Parker, looking at his watch. He finished his beer, slipped Colton's business card into the inside pocket of his jacket, and slid off the barstool. "Nice to meet you."

He left a twenty on the bar and walked away. Stopping at the bell captain's desk, he retrieved his suitcase. The doorman had a limo waiting.

"Where to?" asked the driver.

"Williamsburg, please. I'll tell you which hotel when we get closer."

Parker settled in for the ride.

As the limo headed out of Washington, DC traffic and picked up Route 95 for the trip south, he pulled Colton's card out of his pocket. Two names were written on the back, followed by a web address. He plugged it into his phone and two photos popped onto his screen.

The methods were his to choose. Colton didn't care how he got the job done, only that it be accomplished ASAP, quietly, without fuss, without fanfare. He poured Chivas into a crystal glass from the limo's bar, leaned back in the seat, and stared out the window.

❖

Williamsburg, Virginia

Nadine's internal curiosity meter was screaming during her drive home from the open house. She raced past Sid, her hello kiss barely brushing his cheek, and headed straight to her office. Her butt slid into her chair as her fingers hit the MAC keyboard and opened Safari. Her search target, Colton Pollard.

"Hello to you too," said Sid, following her into her office. "What's up?"

"Just need a few minutes, hon. Got to look someone up while it's fresh in my mind."

Sid stared at his wife. When she was like this, in full-throttle reporter mode, nothing stopped her. The place could burn down around her.

"Dinner's good to go whenever you want it."

"Great." Not the least bit hungry after all the food she just consumed, she smiled up at her husband. "I'll be right there."

Her few minutes turned into two hours. She was so totally engrossed in the information showing up on her computer screen, she had no sense of time passing. After an hour, Sid brought her a sandwich and a glass of wine, and retreated to his La-Z-Boy to watch TV.

Nadine didn't have much to go on—just a name, Colton Pollard. Her Nexus-Lexus search pulled up several men with that name. Instinct told her it was the guy with the least amount of information. That trail led to an innocuous company, Global Initiatives, and a grainy photo of a much younger man. But the features matched the man she had just met.

"Gotcha." She grinned at her good fortune. "You can't hide from me." She took a bite of the turkey sandwich Sid had quietly put on her desk. "Let's see what some of your global initiatives actually are."

She typed Global Initiatives and hit enter. The little icon spun round and round. Nadine took another bite of her sandwich and wiped mayo from the corner of her mouth with her index finger. She sipped her wine watching the icon spin and spin.

Then it stopped.

"Bingo."

Several articles appeared linking Global Initiatives to medical services in several third world countries. There were stories of small traveling clinics providing much-needed medical services to tribes in countries on the African continent, people in remote villages in India, and natives on islands in Southeast Asia she couldn't pronounce. Basic antibiotics and vaccines, items Americans took for granted, were a large part of their services. They supported outfits like Doctors without Borders.

"I wonder if Morgan's ex-husband Alan might be able to shed some light on these guys." She made a note to ask Morgan to see if she could get in contact with Alan.

Soft footsteps approached from behind.

"It's late, love. Time to stop and come to bed."

"I'm sorry. I got so involved. I forgot about you. About us."

"Not the first time," he said, kissing the top of her head. "Won't be the last. What's got you hooked?"

"A man I met at the clinic opening," she said, standing and shaking out her arms and legs to loosen up her joints after sitting at her computer for hours. "There's something about him that doesn't fit. He seemed out of place, and I can't put my finger on why I think so."

"And that's what I love most about you." Sid wrapped his arms around her and kissed her cheek. "You care. You get so involved in your stories because you care about the people whose stories you are telling."

"Thanks for understanding." She hit save on the page of

notes she had typed and closed the cover of her MAC. "Enough. I'm tired. Let's go to bed."

"Better words were never spoken. Want to fool around?" He tickled her waist, then took her hand and led her away from her office, hoping he could get her mind off her work as easily.

CHAPTER 10

New York City

It had been more than a week since dinner with his old friend Greg, and Jesse still couldn't manage a decent night's sleep. This time he gave up at five, headed to the kitchen, and flipped the switch to start the coffee brewing.

In his world, coincidences mattered. His dinner conversation with his old college friend had aligned with a TV documentary that captured his interest a few months ago. He put it on the back burner while he took a much-needed vacation, but now he was back, well-rested, and the story was front and center in his mind, especially after the few tidbits of information Greg shared. Jesse poured a cup of coffee and headed into the living room to cue up and watch the documentary again, glad he had DVR'd it.

Thirty minutes later he was fired up. He'd watched the story twice, taking notes the second time around. The yellow legal pad sitting next to his laptop was full of chicken-scratch, circled words, and lines connecting those circles. Reaching for his phone, he surfed his previous calls list, found Greg's number, and hit dial.

A groggy voice picked up on the third ring.

"Hello."

"Greg, it's Jesse."

"Jesse? Shit, man, do you know what time it is?"

"Yeah. Sorry for the early hour."

"Right."

Jesse could hear sheets rustling and Greg's early morning coughing, throat-clearing routine that he remembered from their college days. Then he heard the familiar liquid hitting liquid sound and the toilet flush.

"Greg, you listening yet?" Not waiting for an answer, he plowed into his pitch. "That problem we talked about at dinner. Your white knight going dark. Remember?"

"Yeah. You said you'd look into it. From the tone of your voice, it sounds like you found something."

"Don't know yet, but I'm on my way down there to do my thing. Where are you staying?"

"Williamsburg Inn."

"Whoa. Too pricy for my bank account. I'll call you when I get there. Can we meet tonight so you can give me more solid details?

"Sounds good. Let me give you a different cell number to call."

Jesse wrote down the number. He had planned to suggest Greg buy a prepaid cell phone. The fact that he already had one both surprised and worried him. Smart, he thought, to use a separate phone in case his suspicions turned into facts that might prove uncomfortable for a few people.

"One more thing," said Greg. "You still do that ninja, Kung-fu shit?"

"Yeah. I keep up. Can't let my Recon buddies down when we go play Army in the mud."

"There's a complication."

"How so?"

"Went to dinner with an old friend who lives down here and works for the local paper. She told me she was looking into a story with similar details. She may be in over her head, and I don't want her to get hurt."

"Ah, a friend of the female persuasion?"

"Does it make a difference?"

"Not unless she's cute, unmarried and likes to fool around."

"Don't read too much into my concern, but watch out. She has a history of liking my friends more than me. Actually married two of them way back when."

"Two?"

"Yeah. Neither worked out for different reasons. Husband number one was too idealistic, and number two was too egotistical. In my opinion, both were too stupid to know a good woman when they had one." He paused for a moment to think about what just came out of his mouth. "I'd be lying if I said I wouldn't enjoy something more intimate with her. But she's not the wham-bam-thank-you-ma'am type."

"Point taken. What's her name?"

"Morgan Kasen."

"Like it. Has a nice ring to it."

"Cool your jets. See you when you get here."

Jesse clicked off the call, got his third cup of coffee, and slid onto one of his kitchen stools. He reread his notes and diagrams, trying to isolate the angle that would make the story pop, be a Pulitzer-worthy investigation. Then he initiated a Google search to see what more he could learn.

The search results astonished him. Too many to read through now. He had to get on the road if he wanted to make Williamsburg at a decent hour. Throwing some clothes in his bag, he headed for the shower, his mind buzzing as he considered different angles for his investigation.

Of course, Greg sharing the bit about a female friend looking into the same story added an interesting twist. He could ply his charms and see what she'd uncovered, maybe promise to partner with her. Or he could be a jerk, take what she had, and run with it on his own.

He turned the hot water on full blast and lathered up. Steam filled the glass enclosure, warming his bones. The story line was good, and the female complication made it fun. Checking her out would be his first order of business.

Sand Isle, Florida

"I'm so glad you all could come." Carolyn greeted her friends at the door.

"Wouldn't miss it for the world," said Marissa. "Any excuse to play mah jongg for a few hours works for me."

"And with Desiree's set," laughed Sophia. "That's too good to pass up. Glad you waited for us to get home from our New York shopping trip."

"Wine and munchies are in the kitchen. Help yourselves. It's a beautiful afternoon, so I thought we'd play on the lanai."

Marissa poured the wine while the others filled their plates.

"I like what you've done to the place, Carolyn." Marissa adjusted one of the plantation shutters. "Kind of has a woman's touch now. You and Kyle getting along?"

"It's been interesting. He's getting used to my less-than-military spit-and-polish ways. Can't bounce a quarter off my bed anymore. When I got out, that was the first thing I stopped doing. And when I did it absentmindedly, I'd go back and mess up the stupid bed. There is nothing about me I'd classify as shipshape, but I'm really trying since this is his house." She bit her lip. "How long does it take to stop feeling like a guest?"

"Don't know," said Marissa. "What I do know is you two have a lot going for you. I'm sure you'll figure it out. Kyle's a great guy."

"I'll vouch for that," said Rosa. "He's like my second husband. He and TJ are so tight. He's been part of our marriage since the beginning, and I love him. I want him to be happy, and I've got to tell you, there's a spring in his step, and he's smiling more than I ever remember since he met you."

The ladies moved out to the lanai and gathered around the table where Carolyn had placed Desiree's mah jongg set.

"Look at these carvings." Marissa glided her fingers across the garden scene carved into the top of the chest. "A very gifted artisan did this work."

"How do you open it?" asked Rosa. "I don't see a latch."

"That's why I invited you over. I knew you'd be eager to play, but we can't play until we figure out how to open the chest. There's no key, no keyhole, no latch. I'll admit it. I'm stumped, and so was Kyle when I showed it to him. He was ready to take a sledgehammer to it."

"Men! If only a hammer could solve every problem." Marissa took a sip of her wine. "Did anything else come with it?"

"Yes. Two letters. One from a lawyer and this one." Carolyn took a paper from the side table, put her glasses on and read it out loud. When she was finished, she put the letter on the table and looked at her friends, repeating the last line, "the dragon is the key."

"What does that mean?" asked Sophia.

"That's what I've been trying to figure out since it arrived last week. Had to let it go for a few days because Brett and I got busy, then he left for a few days R&R."

"And we were shopping," added Marissa.

"But now you're here and I don't want to waste any more time."

"Did you get anything else, you know, other than the chest and the letter?" Sophia asked as she sat down at the table and busied herself examining the chest, turning it this way and that, running her fingers over the hinges and around the carvings.

"This," said Carolyn, pulling something out of her pocket and holding it out for everyone to see.

"Oh…my…God," gasped Marissa. "Her pendant. She sent you her dragon pendant?"

"She wore it every day. But if you have it, that means she wasn't wearing it the night she died. Wonder why." Sophia's comments were directed to no one in particular. "I can't believe she wasn't wearing it on her first outing since getting out of the hospital."

"That's what Kyle and I have been trying to figure out. I know she had it on every time I was with her. Unless…" Carolyn eyes moved from one lady to the next. "Unless she knew."

"Knew what?" asked Rosa.

"Knew she was on borrowed time, that the boat trip might prove less relaxing and more dangerous than usual."

"But she went anyway?" Sophia continued to examine the chest while she spoke. "That doesn't make sense. If she had any suspicion her evening on the water might not be the relaxing evening she anticipated, why the hell did she go? Why didn't she beg off?"

"Maybe she thought she had no choice." Marissa sounded ominous. "That it was only a matter of time. Someone got to her at the mah jongg tournament. Maybe she figured she couldn't escape her fate."

"You could be onto something, Marissa. She made arrangements while she was still in the hospital in Orlando for a lawyer to get this to me in the event of her death. And she was wearing the pendant when I visited her right before the fatal boat trip, so I'm guessing she sent these things to the lawyer between when I saw her last and when she was killed."

Marissa was silently rereading the letter.

"She was definitely putting her affairs in order. Listen to this part… 'I have only one small request, one I am confident that, with your skills, you and only you, will be able to fulfill. All my worldly possessions, except what you received with this letter, are left to my daughter. Yes, I have a daughter too, one I love, though I have not seen her since the day she was born. Find her. Protect her as I know only you can.'"

Incredulously, Marissa said, "She has a daughter?"

"Who would have ever imagined that," said Rosa, "considering what she put those women through." And then Rosa looked directly at Carolyn. "What she put your daughter, Amelia, through. The nerve of her asking for your help. I don't know how she could think…" Her voice trailed off and she was silent for a few seconds, fear etched across her face, obviously thinking about what could have happened to her own daughter, Bella, if things had been different. "What are you going to do?"

"What she asked me to do. Find her daughter."

"How?" asked Marissa.

"If, as she says in her letter, she hasn't seen her daughter since the day she was born, I'm guessing she put the baby up for adoption. Based on what I learned when I was searching for Amelia, Desiree was from the Memphis area. When Brett gets back from vacation tomorrow, I'm hoping we can steal some time away from what we're doing for Marco, and try to hack into Memphis adoption records, using the name Dawn DeSoto."

"You are good," said Marissa. "That was one of the names Brett found on some of the documents related to the Sand Isle Inn. So smart."

"What do you think she meant by protect her?" asked Rosa. "Protect her from what?"

"Or from who?" added Sophia.

"Don't know, but like she said, the dragon is the key," said Carolyn, "and this chest has five dragons carved into it. Maybe one of these holds the key, whatever the hell that means."

The ladies turned their full attention to the wooden chest sitting on the table before them.

"And we can't play mah jongg until we figure out how to open this chest," said Marissa. "Such incentive."

"How deliciously mysterious." Sophia reached out her hand and wiggled her slim, impeccably manicured fingers in Carolyn's direction. "Give me the dragon. I've got an idea."

She took the dragon and fiddled with it for a moment, her index finger traced the carving on the pendant.

"I love jade. It's so soft and cool to the touch."

Then she did the same thing on each dragon carving on the chest. Her finger kept going back to the dragon carving on the lid. She turned the pendant over and placed it carved side down on the chest lid, jiggling and wriggling it, until it suddenly snapped into place.

"Voila," she cried, putting a little pressure on the dragon, her eyes wide with anticipation. They all heard the click. Everyone watched the top and sides of the chest pop open, revealing a tray of beautiful, hand-painted mah jongg tiles.

"These are gorgeous," said Marissa lifting one of the tiles

to the sunlight. "It's almost translucent. I can't wait to play with them."

Carolyn reached into the top tray of tiles. Nestled between the tiles was a silver flash drive. She lifted it out.

"Awesome. Great work, Sophia. I think we've found our key."

CHAPTER 11

Williamsburg, Virginia

"I found Eli," said Morgan, when she stuck her head in Nadine's office. "He's back in his spot in front of the Food King. After I saw him, I drove to Starbucks and got him a hot chocolate."

"Fantastic. Where's he been?"

"He said a guy came around and offered him a job. He was cleaning out one of the old motels on the other side of town. He said there were other guys there. They got three meals a day and slept in one of the motel rooms. Got paid a hundred dollars."

"Bet that made him feel good. There's nothing like earning a few bucks to put some spring in your step." Nadine picked up her coffee mug and blew on the toffee-colored liquid. "Go get your coffee and come back. Have I got stuff to tell you about what I found last night after I got home from the open house."

"Oooh. Sounds delicious. Be right back."

Morgan was back in under five minutes with her coffee and donuts. "Sugar to keep us strong."

"Sugar adds pounds." Nadine shrugged her shoulders. "Hell, give me that chocolate-covered one."

"Here." She passed Nadine the donut and took a sugar-glazed one for herself. "What did you find?"

"That man we met, Colton Pollard."

"Gave me the creeps. And what about the way he talks? So highfalutin, putting on airs, like he's trying to impress us."

"Made him sound gay to me. Not that there is anything wrong with being gay."

"Relax. You're talking to me, remember?"

"Anyway, I looked him up. Couldn't find much specifically about him. I did find the name of a company associated with him, Global Initiatives. It's got its fingers into all sorts of pies around the world."

"Such as?"

"Medical clinics in third world countries that still don't know from indoor plumbing. Pharmaceuticals and vaccines in underdeveloped places no sane person has any business visiting, unless they want to catch some rare, fatal disease that makes your organs melt, and blood pour out of every orifice."

"Not on my bucket list."

"Mine either." Nadine took a bite of her donut.

"How does he make his money?"

"His bio, which was long on platitudes but sparse on facts, says he became a millionaire inventing some app that did something no one needed, but everyone got hooked on using. He sold the rights to some big powerhouse for five billion dollars. Still gets royalties."

"Love capitalism."

"Then he bought a small startup medical clinic. Obamacare passed, and the rest is history. He's been opening these private clinics all over the country."

"But they're free clinics. He can't make money from

free clinics, and he didn't strike me as the altruistic type."

"Not all of it is free, remember. There's a free side, a pay-as-you-need it side, and the very expensive concierge medicine side." Nadine finished her donut and thoughtfully licked the remaining chocolate off her fingers.

"What? I can see something else has your journalistic juices glowing hotter than a bonfire at a pep rally."

"Eloquently said." Nadine's admiration for Morgan shone in her eyes. "Two things. First, I don't see how either Elan's patient pay program or the concierge program could fully underwrite the costs of the free clinic."

"Good point. Medical care is expensive, and offering free care, state-of-the-art free care, must be financially draining."

"My thought exactly. Where's the money really coming from? Which leads to the second thing nagging at me. There was one article that came up on my search that talked about a town in India, Gurgaon, where people were selling their kidneys. It was a huge scandal. The doctors involved got stinking rich and then, when they were caught, got long prison sentences."

"At least they caught them. Prison seems too good for them. Maybe they should have had a doctor take out one of their kidneys. You know, the old eye-for-an-eye philosophy."

"Ouch! A little spiteful, don't you think?" Nadine held her coffee cup in the air as she continued reading something on her screen. Finally, she looked up at Morgan. "It was fascinating reading. Sid finally had to come drag me away."

"Do you think there is any connection to the man we found?"

"That's what I'm wondering. John Doe was missing a kidney. This new clinic opens, offering free services that don't seem to be covered by the paying side of the business. A distinguished-looking man, who just happens to be in town at the same time as Elan's grand opening, owns a company, Global Initiatives, that is somehow connected to medical initiatives in third world countries, where poor people regularly sell their kidneys."

Morgan's arched eyebrow emphasized her questioning look. "Coincidence?"

"Maybe. But I did see Global Initiatives mentioned in a different article that also mentioned the same town, Gurgaon."

"You're thinking, what?"

"Did they get them all? Just a gut feel. It was a huge operation, and it's been my experience that the people at the top of big, illegal operations have a way of disappearing before they're caught. The raids usually sweep up the little guys. So, I'm just wondering out loud whether the authorities were able to find everyone involved."

"You can't possibly think the guy we met, Colton Pollard, is somehow involved in an international scheme to procure kidneys. This is Williamsburg, Virginia, not Juarez, Mumbai, or Istanbul. That kind of stuff doesn't happen here."

"Where better than someplace like here? Who would suspect a thing? This is Williamsburg, the colonial capital of America. Wholesome and pure, like freshly fallen snow. Hiding in plain sight."

"A bit farfetched for me. But the kidney angle—trafficking black market organs—does kick my homeless story up a notch. Makes it a really juicy story."

"Pulitzer-worthy story." Nadine telegraphed her belief with a hard stare.

"How do we prove it?"

"Don't know yet. Wasn't your first husband involved with Doctors without Borders?"

"Yes. He's somewhere in Africa, doing good things for poor people."

"Can you get in touch with him? I want to know if he knows anything about Global Initiatives."

"I can try. I'll do the triple whammy—text, email and voice. Maybe one of them will get through to him."

"Good. Go do it. Then come back. Let's put our heads together and plot out the angle this story needs to take."

Two days of gray clouds and misty drizzle had finally given way to a hazy sunshine. Morgan walked into Barnes & Noble, and headed straight down the main aisle of the store—a woman on a mission. The bathroom called. She and Nadine were meeting at The DoG Street Pub for lunch, then shopping and a little girl time. Reemerging from the ladies' room, she wandered over to the sale table.

She noticed him immediately. He was hard to miss, standing just inches away on the other side of the table. Tall, she guessed around six foot, with athletic good looks, a full head of curly dark hair with the slightest threads of silver weaving in and out, salt and pepper stubble, and warm, caramel brown eyes. He looked like trouble, the kind she might fantasize about. Goose bumps cascaded down her neck and arms.

"What looks interesting?" he asked.

"Nothing really. Just browsing."

"How about this one?" He held the book up so she could see the cover. "The Impressionist Works of Claude Monet."

"Tempting. I do love Monet."

"Me too." The corners of his mouth curved up. "Look at that. We've not yet met and already we have something in common."

"Excuse me?"

"Too forward?" he chuckled, revealing a wicked-nice smile.

"Presumptuous is more like it. My mother always told me not to talk to strangers."

"And yet, here you are, talking to a perfect stranger. Did you always do what your mother told you?"

Morgan couldn't help laughing. "Rarely ever."

"Good. Could I interest you in continuing to disobey your mother upstairs over a cup of coffee?"

Wolfish grin and man dimples. "Can't. I'm meeting a friend for lunch across the street."

"Rain check?"

"You are persistent, aren't you?"

"Yes, I am. One of my more endearing qualities." His eyes twinkled at her.

"Look," said Morgan adopting a teacherish tone, "I'm sure you're a very nice man, and there are hundreds of women, maybe thousands—"

"Thousands?" he interrupted.

"Funny. Anyway, I'm really not interested."

"How can you know you're not interested until you get to know me?"

"My how you do go on."

"Come on. A cup of coffee. What could it hurt? We're in a public place."

"Thanks, but no thanks. I've got to go."

"Tomorrow, then. I'll be here tomorrow—upstairs in the cafe—at two o'clock. I'll wait for you, and when you get here, I'll buy you a cup of coffee. Even throw in a pastry. You look like a chocolate kind of lady."

"Big spender."

"Generosity is another one of my better qualities. I'll see you tomorrow." He winked and walked away, heading for the front door.

She followed behind him, not wanting to catch up, but wanting to see which way he went.

Hmmm, nice butt. Can't be much space between where his jeans start and his boxers, or briefs, or speedos end.

Leaning against the store's front doorjamb, careful to stay in the shadows, she watched him cross Duke of Gloucester Street.

Will he turn around? Will he look back?

And then she saw it, just as he reached the Colonial Williamsburg ticket booth. A quick half head turn over his left shoulder. Not too much, but she saw it clear as day. *He's checking to see if I'm watching him.* She quickly ducked back inside the store as a group of ladies, all wearing red hats and purple boas, pushed through the doorway and blocked her view.

Good. If I can't see him, he can't see me. Her teeth pulled at her lower lip. Then he disappeared into the parking lot behind the ticket window.

Do butts make the jeans, or do jeans make the butt?

The man does look good, good enough to—

Stop it. Don't go there.

Her pulse skipped a beat. Warmth radiated through her. Hot flash.

Shit!

Morgan let out a long breath, an almost-disappointing sigh mingled with it.

Should I meet him?

She had a whole day to consider whether to show up or ignore this handsome hunk of a man.

What is it about older men? They look more distinguished, more handsome as they age. He seemed so eager to get to know me.

Too eager perhaps?

It's only for coffee. Oh, and a pastry. He ain't cheap.

She felt a smile brighten her face. It had been a long time between chance encounters.

CHAPTER 12

Sand Isle, Florida

"I heard you got an interesting package," said Brett, when Carolyn joined him in the security office at Marco's compound.

"News travels fast."

"Yes, it does." He and Carolyn were working on a special project for Marco, digging into the life of Desiree De Maurier, formerly known as Dawn DeSoto, trying to find concrete links to whoever was behind the Sand Isle sex trafficking and prostitution ring they busted last spring.

"I'm so glad you're back from your vacation. The only thing that stopped me from plugging this flash drive into my laptop was my fear of getting a virus or uploading something that would crash my system." Carolyn handed Brett the slim silver drive and pulled up a chair.

"Smart decision." Bret swiveled his chair.

Four screens, several keyboards, two laptops, a desktop, and a high-speed printer fought for space in his corner office domain. His two hundred-plus collection of bobblehead dolls ringed the room. Two personal photos completed the scene—one of his parents, the other a rag-tag group of bearded men looking like refugees from a war-torn Middle Eastern country. They were in fact his buds, his team, his brothers in arms.

"My security software is top notch, so I'm glad you waited." Brett plugged the drive into one of his laptops, interlocked and inverted his fingers, and cracked his knuckles. He ended his personal start-up ritual by rubbing his palms together.

"You're acting like a kid in a candy store."

"Seriously?" He looked her square in the face. "A flash drive hidden in an antique mah jongg game chest, delivered to you by a lawyer, at the request of a woman who was in the hospital after being poisoned at a mah jongg tournament, and who ran a brothel, where your daughter and nine other girls were being held against their will, and who died as a result of a mysterious explosion on a rented boat where she is shown as the only person on board, owned by a company that appears to have gone out of business a year ago?"

Brett took a long breath. "Are you kidding?" He chuckled. "It doesn't get any better than this."

"Hopefully there will be something on this flash drive that will give me the information I need to do what she's asked me to do—find her daughter and protect her from whatever or whoever wants to harm her."

"Curious that she automatically assumed you'd do for her what she was unwilling to do for you."

"Or unable." Carolyn felt a twinge of sadness. "I know. Weird. But she paid the ultimate price. That explosion was not an accident. Maybe she had no choice."

"And you have a choice."

"Yes. And I'm choosing to help. Desiree left this drive to me for a reason. She needed my help, asked me for my help, and I'm going to give it to her."

The screen came to life. Two folder icons appeared.

"Not much there," said Carolyn.

"Keep the faith. Good things come in small packages."

"As my four foot eleven inch granny used to say, so does dynamite."

"Funny."

Brett clicked into the first folder. It contained a lone JPEG image. He clicked it open. They found themselves staring at a scanned birth certificate for a baby girl, dated August 20, 1983. The mother's name was Dawn DeSoto, and the father's name, JJ Henry. The space where the baby's name would go simply said Baby Girl.

"It's a start," said Carolyn. "Confirms what she said in her letter. She had a daughter. How sad that she never gave her a name. Guess she wanted to let the adopting family name her."

"Wonder why she gave her baby up for adoption? How old was Desiree? In her fifties? Girls being forced to give up babies was over and done with way before Desiree found herself in trouble. Lots of unmarried girls had babies and kept them twenty, even thirty years ago."

"Good question." Her eyes stung, and she had to swallow back a sob. She'd spent five hellish years searching for Amelia. Giving up her own daughter would have been a bridge too far. She stood, took a deep breath, and blinked tears away. "I'm getting coffee. Want some?"

"Mountain Dew."

"How about the other file?" asked Carolyn, walking back in and placing the soda can on his desk. "Let's see what's in that one."

"On it." Brett clicked into the folder. "More folders, labeled by year. These are all Excel files." He opened the first one. "It's a ledger. Kyle was right. Desiree was a bookkeeper. These are records of transactions. There are years and years of them. Looks like the first one is labeled Memphis, 1984."

"Memphis? That's where I found that first photo of Desiree, dancing with a man on a riverboat. Only her name was Diana Delacroix then."

"Call Marco. He needs to get over here and see this. I think we've found the missing piece of the puzzle."

Williamsburg, Virginia

Morgan pulled open the back door to Barnes & Noble at one fifty. She had talked herself into meeting her handsome stranger. The familiar *"It's a public place,"* coupled with *"what have I got to lose?"* won the argument going on inside her head.

She scanned the store. Not very crowded, but it was Tuesday afternoon. She took a deep breath, walked the length of the store to the front, and waited while an elderly couple helped each other onto the escalator. She chose the stairs. At least she'd have an excuse if her breath seemed hurried when she met him.

Here goes nothing.

An old familiar feeling, like the edgy nervousness before a first date, accosted her as she started up the stairs. She recognized the feeling instantly.

"Chill, girl," she chided herself. "He's just a guy, and this isn't a date. It's just coffee. You ain't marrying him. He probably won't even be here."

As she reached the top of the stairs she felt every muscle in her body tense. She blew out a breath and plastered a smile on her face as she turned toward the cafe.

There he was, sitting alone at a table by the window, watching the escalator and the stairs. He stood when he saw her. A broad grin spread across his face as his eyes met hers.

"Not the smartest thing I've ever done," she mumbled to herself. "Then again, I've done dumber. Here goes nothing."

She headed for his table, feeling like a giddy schoolgirl on the way to her first dance, and not the mature, accomplished woman she actually was.

"Thank you for coming. I wasn't sure you'd show." He held up his wrist and pointed to his watch. "And five minutes early, no less."

"Don't get carried away. Around here you can never tell about traffic or finding a parking space. Colonial Williamsburg is notorious for lots of the first and very few of the second."

"Since my inducement was coffee, what can I get you?"

"An iced latte sounds good."

He started to go—

"And don't forget the pastry you promised me," she said. "I'll have a brownie."

"I knew you were a chocolate lover. Iced latte and a brownie coming right up."

Again she found her attention riveted on his butt as he walked away. She was a butt girl, pure and simple. Had been all her life. There was something about the way butts moved...one cheek up, the other cheek down...mesmerizing...enticing. Clothed or naked, it didn't matter. Unconsciously, she moistened her lips, her tongue ran sensuously across her upper lip and back along the bottom.

"Here you go, my lady."

"From brash yesterday to formal today. How quaint."

"How long have you lived in Williamsburg?" he asked as he sat down.

"What makes you think I live here?"

"Just a hunch," he said.

"On and off for most of my life. Did some time in New York."

"You make it sound like a prison sentence."

"No. Just New York. I'm more of a country girl, like a quieter lifestyle. I moved back here last year. Inherited my parents' home when they died, and I'm slowly doing a complete renovation. It's not that old, but the layout needed to be opened up."

"Intriguing."

"Intriguing?" she repeated. "You see me across the sale table at the bookstore, we meet for coffee, and I tell you I'm doing a home renovation, and you find that intriguing? You've led a sheltered life."

"I pictured you a freewheeling, well-traveled reporter type. Kind of like your pixie hairdo. Low maintenance, easy, breezy." His eyes scanned her face.

"Thank you, I think."

"You're welcome. It looks cute on you." He sipped his coffee and took a bite of his donut. "Houses take work."

"Tell me about it."

"Next to boats and wives, they're the ultimate money pits. Something always needs repairing or replacing."

"I take it you're not a house type of guy. You clearly don't own a razor. Don't they pay you enough wherever you work to buy a razor?"

He stroked his stubble.

"Sure they do," he said, "I'm trying the look on for size. I take it you don't like it."

"Has to grow in some more, get fuller."

He stroked his chin again, flashing another flirty smile. "And I travel too much to own a house. An apartment suits me fine."

"And where, pray tell, is said apartment? I'm guessing you're not from around here."

"Don't I look like a Williamsburgite?"

"No. And you don't look like your average tourist either. That's the curious part. What is a guy who looks like you doing wandering around Colonial Williamsburg alone, picking up women?"

"I wasn't picking up women. I simply asked you to have coffee with me."

"Right." Morgan broke off a piece of her brownie and waved it in the air. "But why?"

"Does there have to be a why?"

"There's always a why, a reason, a motive. So, who are you? What's your motive? And don't think I didn't catch that wives are a money pit comment." The brownie piece finally made it into her mouth.

"My name's Jesse Sinclair. I'm a journalist. Work freelance."

Wariness had the hairs on Morgan's neck standing at full attention. *Odd that we're both reporters.*

"Jesse Sinclair. Sounds elegant. Makes a good byline. Is it your real name?"

Jesse smirked as he extended his hand to shake hers. "Jesse Schwartz. Nice to meet you, Morgan."

"How very ethnic."

"Not white bread enough for the masses. After a pile of rejections, I decided to play their game by their rules. They wouldn't hire Jesse Schwartz, but they eagerly accepted every article I submitted as Jesse Sinclair. I learned fast."

"Shades of anti-Semitism rearing its ugly head?"

"Maybe. Who knows? I made a decision. If you can't beat 'em, join 'em. I wanted a career in journalism, and was willing to do what it took to make it happen. I know who I

111

am inside. What's a name? A label, an identifier for others."

"Good for you. So, what are you doing here in Williamsburg?"

"Doing a follow-up on a story I did a few years ago after the BASF plant closed. The whole environmental cleanup thing."

"I remember that plant. There was a huge uproar over possible contamination. It kept the locals wagging their tongues in the 'My Two Cents' column for weeks."

"'My Two Cents?'"

"It's a column in our paper, the *Williamsburg Beacon*, where residents can write in and say whatever they want. Some ask for recommendations, you know, like who knows a company that power washes homes. Some people offer comments about local restaurants, or ask for things they need. Some complain. It's fun to read."

"I'll have to make sure I get a copy of the paper and check it out while I'm here."

Morgan sipped her latte. "The BASF land is ripe for redevelopment. Area is called Grove. Part of it runs along the James River. They've been wanting to develop the land for years. Would certainly be an economic boom to the area. Ideas like a resort, marina, amusement park, golf community get pitched, but every proposal gets shot down."

"Why?"

"Traffic and environmental concerns is what they say. Can't have the tourists glow in the dark. Not good for business." She laughed holding up her hands, framing her face. "And some of the land borders Ft. Eustis."

"If the land is that close to a military installation like Ft. Eustis, then I'll bet the Army is against it."

He talked about different angles he was investigating for his follow-up story. She heard his tone change and wondered which side of the issue he was supporting.

"You're dangerous."

"Dangerous could be a good thing. Personally, I prefer unpredictable." His mischievous smirk returned with a vengeance.

Morgan felt herself flush. She coughed to hide any redness he might see. "Do your charms work on everyone?"

"Most times. Are they working on you?"

"Sorry to disappoint, but I'm not falling for your routine. I don't plan to be another notch on your conquest belt."

"What makes you think I have such a thing?"

"I notice you're not denying it."

"Neither confirming nor denying," he said, finishing the last bite of his donut. He watched her shift positions, tickled that something he said caused her to lose her composure. "Just kidding. Can't a man hope?"

He found her disturbing, fascinating, alluring; her low, sexy laugh enticing, her sass stimulating. He wanted her. And he hadn't wanted anyone in a very long time. Women were a complication his life didn't need.

Warmed by his easy smile, she found herself momentarily fantasizing about a romp in the hay with him.

"It's not going to happen. Not sure where I saw it, but one definition of hope is delayed disappointment. If I were you, I'd stick to writing. Though I do find your lopsided grin appealing in an odd sort of way. So what I said stands. Dangerous."

Then again, she thought, there is something happening here. She could feel an undercurrent, a crackling of sexual energy arc between them while they bantered, while they flirted, while they... What were they doing exactly?

And suddenly it didn't matter. Whatever this was, it was fun. His smile was magnetic. He pulled her in. She could feel a smile wanting to burst forth when they sparred like they were doing now. She crossed her arms over her chest, noting the hardness of her nipples when her thumb brushed against one.

Morgan took another sip of her latte and finished her brownie. "So, now, what's your reasoning behind the wives are money pits comment?"

"Ah, we've gotten to that. I see you don't forget what people say to you."

She tapped the side of her heard. "Mind's like a steel trap."

"It's nothing. Let's just say I'm not a proponent of having my heart ripped out through my nose with a blunt instrument without anesthesia."

"Very descriptive. I take it you've ridden the love merry-go-round once or twice."

"No comment." He watched her squirrel up her face and added, "Okay, made it down the aisle once. Painful memories I swore never to repeat. I learn from my mistakes."

A disconcerting silence suddenly hung over the table.

"I've got to go." Morgan finished her coffee and stood. "Can't say this hasn't been interesting. Good luck on your story. Hope you find what you're looking for."

He stood too. "Thanks. I'm going to be in town for a while. Maybe we could grab dinner some night?"

"Maybe. Let me think about it."

"Don't think too hard. You know what they say, thinking rots the brain."

"Haven't heard that one before. You just make it up?"

"Sort of. Nothing to think about. Don't think. Do."

"Cute. So Yoda."

"It's only dinner. If it doesn't work out, you can dump me."

"There is that." She slung her purse on her shoulder. "'Bye. Thanks for the latte and the brownie."

"Any time," he called out behind her as she walked away.

Morgan walked out of B&N into brilliant sunshine, zigging and zagging to avoid the tourists who flooded Duke of Gloucester Street. How weird, she thought. I just spent an hour with a stranger, having coffee, talking about this, that and the other thing, his work mostly. She could see his face in her mind—a kind face, almost Santa-ish, the twinkle in his eyes when he smiled, and appreciated for the umpteenth time his very nice butt tucked into snug jeans.

He'd asked her to dinner, but he hadn't asked for her number. Of course he didn't need it. He knew where she worked.

Throwing a quick glance behind her to see if he followed her out, she suspected there might be more to Jesse Sinclair than met the eye. Was their chance meeting really by chance? A sense of foreboding made her shiver like someone walked over her grave, and a new realization took hold in her consciousness. He was lying. Concealing something. But what? And why?

CHAPTER 13

Washington, DC

The Gulfstream waited patiently at the general aviation area at Dulles for its lone passenger. It was fueled, the flight plan filed, the crew ready to go for the short hop to Williamsburg.

Flying private is the best, thought Colton. *No one knows anything about anything. No TSA bullshit. Only the FAA knows where you're going or where you've been. And you can change directions without much fuss.*

Colton marched across the tarmac like a man on a mission. And he was.

"Morning, sir," said the steward when he entered the main cabin.

"Good morning. Coffee, black, please."

"Yes, sir. We're cleared for takeoff as soon as you're ready. And this envelope came for you a few minutes ago."

Colton handed the steward his suit jacket, took the envelope, and settled himself into one of the swivel chairs. He buckled up, smiled and said, "Let's go."

Wheels were up in under fifteen minutes. Once they were

at cruising altitude, the steward brought him breakfast. Colton took a mouthful of oatmeal, opened the envelope, and pulled out two photos. One photo showed two men enjoying drinks and dinner in a secluded booth at what looked like a New York steak house. There were celebrity photos adorning the walls and signs reminiscent of the roaring twenties. The second photo showed one of the same men with a woman, again enjoying dinner, but this time at what looked to be a fancier restaurant. There was a red X through the face of the man who was in both photos.

"More coffee, sir?"

"Yes, please."

Colton leaned his head against his seat back. By all outward appearances, he was what he claimed to be, an entrepreneurial investor, a successful businessman. His shadow world held his secrets, the strings he pulled, how he really made his money.

Quietly, he said to himself, "Thank you, again, Mr. Kent. Another problem soon to be solved."

The doorbell rang at one p.m. sharp.

"Penny, the brew witch, is here." Hayden got up from the table and headed for the chaise lounge where he would sit for the next few hours while receiving his dialysis.

"Hayden," said Moss. "Penny is here to help you. She's your care partner." He rolled his eyes as he got up to answer the door.

"Care vampire is more like it. If she really cared, she'd give me her kidney."

Moss stopped. "What part of attitude is everything don't you get? Besides, a stranger giving you a kidney is far and away more than you could expect most people to do. But you could be a little nicer to her. Your life has gotten significantly better since she started coming to help you."

Hayden scowled. "You'd give me your kidney if we were a match."

"Yes, I would. We've been together a long time." Out of hearing range, he muttered, "but thank God, we're not a match."

Opening the door, he said, "Hey, Penny. How are you today?"

"Good. And how is our patient?"

"Grumpy."

"So, no change?" She laughed, her freckles dancing on her nose. "It's rough on everyone in the beginning. Give him time. He'll get used to it."

"You don't know Hayden. Getting used to things is not his style."

She followed Moss out to the lanai. "Mr. Hayden. So nice to see you. How are you feeling today? Have we been getting our exercise and sticking to our proper diet?"

"Stop the pleasantries. Just hook me up, go sit down somewhere until I'm clean, and shut up."

Penny shot Moss a look and got to work. Once the dialysis was underway, she sat down on the opposite side of the lanai, out of Hayden's sight, and pulled out her knitting.

"Is there anything I can get for you?" Moss stood at Hayden's side while the machine started churning.

"A kidney match."

"Wish I could."

"Don't sweat it. I'm working some magic of my own, and may have a line on one that has a good chance of being a perfect match."

"Really?" Moss felt his jaw tighten. "What's up?"

"Don't want to talk about it now. I've got a few more calls to make to verify. Let's just wait and see what happens.

Then I'll be all too happy to send the brew witch packing and tell you all about it."

Williamsburg, Virginia

Jesse's research was pulling him in too many directions. He'd driven up to DC yesterday to see a friend and got stuck in traffic. As the hours ticked by with him inching along, he called Greg and changed their tentatively planned dinner from last night to tonight. He was bone tired when he hit the bed at the Residence Inn, his home away from home.

And now he was getting a later start than he planned. Although the hotel offered breakfast, the room was crowded with families and screaming kids. It was nine-thirty when he pulled into the parking lot at Panera on Monticello, in desperate need of strong coffee and something sweet.

The restaurant was full of gray-haired senior citizens table-hopping to chat with friends.

Is this what I have to look forward to? Retirement's gotta suck if it is.

He ordered coffee and a chocolate croissant, and snagged a table outside figuring, since there was a slight breeze, the seniors would stay indoors.

Freelancing unleashed him from other people's demands and schedules. Freelancing also fed his lazy side. This morning, when his phone alarm sounded at seven a.m. to wake him, he shut it off and rolled over.

Since his dinner with Greg in New York a few weeks ago, he'd done quite a bit of online research on Colton Pollard, hitting all the major search engines. Nothing he found pointed to anything that would hint of scandal. In fact, he found very little on the man, which ignited his suspicions and investigator instincts all the more.

Jesse made a few phone calls to friends at both the IRS and the FBI, pumping them for information about Pollard. Both friends wimped out, too fearful of being caught, losing their pensions, and winding up indicted. In their minds, the big guys got away with their crimes, and the grunts went to jail.

Failing this line of inquiry, he sent a text to a black hat friend-of-a-friend. Jesse loved hackers, worshiped their skills and the information they uncovered. He never questioned how they did what they did, or its legality. For this guy, money talked. They agreed on five hundred dollars.

While waiting for his second cup of coffee to cool, he picked up the local paper. A byline name leapt out from a story on the front page. Bells and whistles clanked in his brain.

"Nadine Steiner-Greene. She's here? In Williamsburg? What the f—."

Before he could finish his outburst, his phone buzzed. Caller ID told him it was his hacker.

"Pay dirt! I earned my money and then some, man. Where do you want it sent?"

Jesse gave him an email address. The hacker would send the information as soon as he received notification from PayPal that the money was in the account of All-Seeing Eye, LLC. Thirty minutes later all transactions were completed, and Jesse was scrolling through information that was definitely worth way more than five hundred dollars. The hacker had found offshore accounts and deposits he couldn't link to a particular person or company, but where Pollard's name showed up in some capacity. He promised Jesse he'd keep digging.

Pollard was dirty, no question about it. The only question

was how dirty. And, based on the amount of information downloading onto his MAC—very dirty. Up to his eyeballs dirty. Jesse planned to spend the rest of the day at the local library sifting through what the hacker sent to isolate what he wanted to share with Greg tonight at dinner. Couldn't give him too much at once. Didn't want him choking on his crab cakes.

After cleaning up his trash, he headed back to his car, contemplating his next move with Morgan. The chance meet at B&N went as planned. She saw his smile, his man dimples a match for her own, and was hooked. Happened all the time. How could she resist? Here he was—a tempting, dark-haired, distinguished-looking, smooth-talking hunk of a man, if he did say so himself—in the prime of life, inviting her to rendezvous for coffee. Adding the he'd-wait-for-her line gave the invitation just enough mystery. He knew she'd show up.

How fortuitous that she worked at the same paper as Nadine Steiner-Greene. Talk about a surprise. The bigger surprise came from her innocent passing comment about the story she was working on about the homeless, something similar to the story he was really in Williamsburg investigating. He hated lying to her, dangling the BASF follow-up piece, but a well placed, little white lie served everyone.

Nadine Steiner-Greene was a different matter. He remembered the glowing tributes to Nadine when she left the *New York World* to move to DC, and then a few years ago, after she retired from the *Washington World Herald*.

How did she wind up here?

"What if I make one of those you-don't-know-me-but-have-I-got-a-story-for-you phone calls that investigative journalists would kill for, and see if I can hook her into partnering with me. I wonder if she'd bite." With her help, he thought, he was guaranteed to win a Pulitzer, could already imagine it sitting on his mantel.

He let the image take root in his mind while he walked inside to refill his coffee and buy another chocolate croissant. By the time he returned to his table, he knew his answer.

"No. Can't do it. I work alone." He chuckled because he could hear Arnold Schwarzenegger's voice from the movie *Eraser* warning the Vanessa Williams character, "I work alone."

Alone worked for him. More freedom to follow leads and hunches without a lot of explanation. He hated having to explain his every move. A former boss warned him against the loner role, admonishing him for his preference, saying he'd never make it big in the newspaper business following that path. But listening to, let alone taking, unsolicited advice was not one of his better qualities. He didn't want to play the game.

CHAPTER 14

Morgan had been at her desk all day, skipping lunch. She inhaled every Google entry she could find about disappearing homeless people, and was finding the stories had common threads. First, upset constituencies storm city hall meetings, complaining about people sleeping in the parks, urinating in public, wandering the streets, eating out of garbage bins. Then the city council votes to fund more shelters, but the homeless don't show up, preferring the anonymity of the streets. Then, one by one, the homeless people begin to disappear.

A chilling YouTube video told the story, with ample B footage of run-down neighborhoods, and men warming themselves around large garbage can fires, spliced in. A local TV station reporter somewhere in the Midwest told about a resident walking his dog late at night who reported seeing a white panel van roaming the downtown section of the city where the homeless congregated. He said he saw the same van over the course of several nights. Then it was gone, and so were some of the homeless.

The ominous voiceover asked the question: *Have the homeless simply moved on or is it foul play?*

The reporter had no answer. What he did know was that the city's problem had been solved.

Doesn't anyone care?

Morgan rubbed her eyes and stared out the window while the voice in her head answered her own question.

Yes, I care. The Elis of the world deserve better. We're each a snap of our fingers away from being homeless, living paycheck to paycheck. It only takes one incident, and we could be in dire straits too.

Slam! A hand and some loose pages landed on her desk, causing her to jump.

"Didn't mean to startle you," said Bob, his hands perched on his hips, fingers splayed. "But now that I've got your attention, mind telling me what this drivel is?"

Her eyes caught the top line in bold caps, FLOWERING FUN.

"It's the piece I did for the garden tour." She tried to sound strong and positive about the piece, knowing her boss could be a real ass.

"I can see that, thank you very much."

He moved closer to her, the stench of cigarette smoke invading her senses. He put one hand on the back of her chair and thumped the fingers of his other hand on her desk. He stopped thumping, elevated his right index finger to thumper-in-chief, hitting the pages again and again and again.

"What I don't see is any connection to what we do here. You know, journalism? Pardon my French, but this sucks."

"It's a garden tour, Bob, not the next coming of the messiah. What's there to say? Time, date, locations, silent auction for charity at the luncheon. Same as last year and the year before that. Will be the same next year." She stopped for a moment. "Maybe we could plan a hit. You know, dead body found between the roses at the old Victorian house on

Scotland Street. That would breathe some excitement into it."

"Snide remarks won't get you off the lifestyle desk. Fix it. Beef it up and have it back to me within the hour."

Ignorant schmuck.

Then remembering the slippery slope to homelessness and her own tenuous, paycheck-to-paycheck life, she swallowed her pride. "I'm sorry I let you down, Bob. It won't happen again. I'll do a complete rewrite and get it back to you."

"See that you do."

Morgan watched him strut away. He'd never been more than a second-rate reporter. But he didn't have to be good. His family owned the *Beacon*. Nepotism at its best. Nadine was right. It was time for a change. And with the right story, that change could happen sooner rather than later.

Colton exited the elevator on the fourth floor of the Williamsburg Inn.

"Sir, is your room on this floor?" asked the uniformed officer who stood sentry.

"Yes. What's happened?" He feigned surprise at the flurry of activity.

"There's been an incident. No need to worry."

Flashes popped. Men and women in blue jumpsuits and white paper booties busied themselves behind yellow crime scene tape cordoning off a hotel room at one end of the corridor. At the far end of the hall, he could see a Hispanic-looking woman, dressed like a maid, wringing her hands and sobbing.

"Did someone die?"

"Yes, sir. Housekeeping found a body this morning. I'm afraid that's all I can say at this time."

"May I go to my room? It's down there," he said, pointing in the opposite direction.

The officer let him pass. Colton smiled as he walked the length of the hall. He stopped at the last door, turned, noted that no one was watching him, and slipped into the stairwell, walking down one flight of stairs before exiting. Then he strode down the hall to the bank of elevators, pressed the down button, and scratched another item off his mental to-do list.

Greg Welton's flapping tongue didn't know when to quit. Two dinners in three days with unknowns didn't feel right. Something had to be done.

Colton had called Hendrix. "I'm sending photos. Find out who they are and what they do. Quickly, please."

Hendrix successfully ferreted out their identities in record time. Within two hours he had delivered two complete dossiers to Colton. The first dinner was with an old friend; the man, an investigative reporter. The woman was also an old friend, also a reporter, on the lifestyle desk at the *Williamsburg Beacon*. Colton realized he'd made her acquaintance at the Elan open house. Reporters. Next to lawyers, reporters were the scum of the human food chain.

Oh, Greg. Did you keep your mouth shut? Dinner with a good-looking woman I can understand. What might you have shared during pillow talk? And the guy? Fraternity brother or not, loose lips sink ships and yours has hit rock bottom.

A phone call to Mr. Kent of Greenleaf Investments followed his reading of Hendrix's report. Another contract. Another untimely end to a promising, if misguided, career.

Seeing the crime scene tape blocking off the hall at the Williamsburg Inn made him chuckle. It would take days for the ME to ascertain cause of death. And knowing the operative he'd hired to do the job, there would be nothing for the crime scene investigators or the ME to find. It would be chalked up to a simple myocardial infarction, experienced by a well-fed, out of shape CEO. Case closed.

Moss's nerves were frayed. While his calm outward demeanor never faltered, his insides were screaming. In his mind, Hayden's veiled comment about ending dialysis soon could only mean one thing. He found a viable donor. The question that ping-ponged in Moss's brain was whether that viable donor was Darby, the daughter Dawn and Hayden conceived so very long ago, when he thought he was shooting blanks. As his daughter, she had the best chance of being a solid match.

For years, Moss had watched from a distance, a sentinel on duty, holding true to his promise to Dawn that he would watch over her daughter. And he'd hired others to watch with him and for him, since he couldn't be there all the time.

The baby Dawn gave up for adoption so many years ago had been lucky. She was adopted by a wonderful couple who loved her dearly and supported her goal to become a veterinarian. She worked hard to achieve her dream, and had grown into a beautiful woman, who now had a daughter of her own.

Dawn would have been so proud if she only knew, if she could have forgiven herself for her very human transgression. But she wouldn't allow herself that comfort, that privilege. Every time he tried to tell her about her daughter, and her granddaughter, the work Darby did caring for abandoned animals, she shut him down faster than ice melting on a scorching Miami sidewalk in August. Her self-flagellation was relentless. It was her punishment for what she had done, for what she did, for the choices she made, for the life she led.

He desperately wanted to see Darby, but he was in the Florida Keys and she was on the Eastern Shore of Virginia. A check-in call to his man at the scene would have to do. Telling Hayden he had errands to run, he took the launch to the mainland. Then he drove twenty miles down Route One to a bustling tourist town he never frequented, bought a prepaid cell phone at the mini-mart, and walked out onto the local fishing pier.

Moss walked the full length of the pier, constantly monitoring the activity around the waterfront. Families were fishing off the pier, some picnicking on the beach, a few children even playing in the ocean. Everyone was minding his or her own business.

"Checking in." Moss's man had secured a job working for Darby at her fledgling animal sanctuary. "Picked up an odd vibe. You need to be on your toes."

"What's happened?"

"He dropped a comment about a kidney match. It's probably just some ordinary person, but I'd rather be safe than sorry. Has anything happened on your end? Any strangers in town? Anyone that seems out of place?"

"Not that I've seen. Some drifter came by a few weeks ago asking about work, but when she said there was nothing, he moved on."

"Did he move on?"

"Good question. Thought I saw him a few days ago. Tried to get closer, but I lost him."

"Where is she now?"

"In the barn. One of the horses is giving birth."

Moss scratched his head contemplating his options. "Wish she was closer so I could see her. It's been a long time."

"She's awesome. Been in the barn all night. Won't leave

her horse. Wrangler's her favorite. She raised her from a colt."

"Doesn't surprise me. Okay. Stay alert. Stay close. Closer than usual. I don't know what he's up to, but something has got him excited."

"I'm on it. I'll put a tracker on her Jeep."

"Good. Call me with anything."

Moss left the pier and drove back to the dock where the launch was tied up. Before boarding, he stopped at the mini-mart and bought some groceries so his doing errands lie would pass the sniff test.

"Where have you been?" The tenor of Hayden's voice demanded an answer.

"I had some business to attend to," said Moss. "And I stopped for groceries."

"Business? Really? You expect me to believe that?"

"JJ—"

"Don't call me that."

"Sorry." Moss bit his tongue. Every once in a while he'd slip and call his oldest friend JJ. If looks could kill, he'd be dead a thousand times over. Considering the current stakes, he could kick himself for his slip of the tongue. In his most conciliatory tone he replied, "Hayden, what you choose to believe is out of my control. But yes, I expect you to believe that I had something important to do."

Hayden eyed him suspiciously. "You've been gone a lot more lately."

"No more than usual. You're just more aware of things, because now that you're on dialysis, you've lost some of your own independence."

"Damn right I have." His face reddened. "Do you think it's fun being hooked up to that damn machine, watching your blood flow in and out?"

Moss remained silent. Hayden's baited question wasn't worth the argument any answer would cause.

"I've been doing a lot of thinking," said Hayden.

"I'm sure you have. A life-threatening illness does that to people."

"Things are going to change around here. I'm closing Shale Enterprises. Whoever raided Sand Isle was very good. It touched too close to home."

"I'm not so sure Sand Isle wasn't just a rare opportunity when fate brought discrete pieces together to make a whole. A crazed mother searching for her missing daughter got lucky and stumbled onto Sand Isle, and got some much-needed help from equally crazed parents who were pissed their own daughters had behaved stupidly."

"Interesting description." Hayden watched Moss move through their shared space.

"You want to tell me what you're working on? What business you keep slipping away to handle?"

Moss smiled. What he was planning would certainly surprise Hayden.

"Not telling. Just some small investments to put to work all the money you pay me."

"How deliciously mysterious."

"I think I'll keep my efforts under your radar a bit longer, if you don't mind. I think you'll be impressed."

"Have it your way. Only, I'd appreciate a heads-up the next time you plan to disappear."

"Will do."

CHAPTER 15

Sand Isle, Florida

Carolyn and Brett joined Marco for lunch on the patio by the infinity pool. The cascading waterfall's soothing, trickling sounds contrasted sharply with the roar of the ocean not two hundred yards away.

"Desiree must have been one worried lady," said Carolyn. "These entries go back decades. She kept meticulous records, but wasn't as good with codes. Brett broke her encryption easily."

"It wasn't very sophisticated. Basic number-letter swap."

"Maybe not, but you two did a good job," said Marco.

"Thanks," said Brett. "We only printed out the final few months from the Sand Isle location. There are years and years of entries on this flash drive."

"And these lists go way beyond Sand Isle," said Carolyn. "New York, DC, Los Angeles. There are inns in most major cities across the US. There's also an international file."

Brett took another bite of his panini. "She definitely knew the importance of information."

"But why?" asked Carolyn. "Why keep all this?"

"Blackmail?" offered Brett. "Insurance?"

"Insurance? From what?" asked Carolyn.

"From whom may be a better question." Marco shuffled the pages in his hands. "She wanted protection, and keeping records with names, dates and amounts was the only way she felt she could get it."

Marco paused to study one page. "Some prominent names here, people who would want this information to remain secret. I know some of them, and they would have a lot to lose if their private playtime activities at the Sand Isle Inn were to get out. The humiliation would be overwhelming, career-ending, not to mention the cost of the divorces and custody battles."

"Didn't work," said Carolyn. "Someone got to her."

"Whoever is at the top, orchestrating all of this, is disciplined, intelligent and resourceful—very resourceful—to pull off the boat explosion and leave no trace."

"He certainly avoids the limelight," said Carolyn.

"I sense a fatal flaw. Some might call it a virtue. Kind of reminds me of me," said Marco. His eyes got a faraway look. Although retired now, he'd once been a world-class con man, feasting on the frailties of other people.

"What might that be?" asked Carolyn.

"He believes circumstances dictate behavior. And if he controls the circumstances, then he controls behavior."

"So?"

"So, he endeavors to control circumstances. Take the brothel business. He played on a very human male weakness, and set up the means, through an intermediary, of course, to provide a quick fix."

"Of course. Desiree, right?"

"I suspect she was one of many intermediaries. There are more layers and levels to the Sand Isle Inn and Metamorphosis operations than there are particles of sand on the beach out there." Marco took a long swig of his beer. "Whoever is at the top covered his tracks brilliantly."

"Put the nightclub operation in place and hire young, hotshot wannabes to dangle the carrots and hook the rabbits." Carolyn looked from Marco to Brett. "Then sit back and enjoy the goodies and the promise of anonymity."

Marco took another bite of his panini and continued to peruse the printout.

"Whoever is behind this is making an effing fortune," said Brett.

"And that is what we need to find out. Who is behind this, at the top. Then we feed Daniel the information, because it's right in line with the FBI task force he, Jim Greene and Mac run. Working with Interpol and their counterparts across the globe who aren't on the take, they might just have enough with this cache to close the entire operation down for good." Marco sipped his beer. "And there are others out there who could lend a discreet hand."

"Others?" asked Carolyn.

Marco reached over and squeezed her hand. "You don't want to know."

"Great," said Carolyn. "Anything we can do to bring down this operation and put this son of a bitch away for a long time. I don't want any other parent to go through the hell I did for the past five years if I can help it."

"It won't be easy. He has another trait. Patience." Marco's thumb followed a bead of water sweating down the side of his beer bottle. "We are dealing with a very patient man, one who takes pleasure when the ultimate revenge is enacted."

"You think he killed Desiree, don't you?" asked Carolyn.

"Yes. Maybe not directly. He probably has people do the dirty work."

"Doesn't make sense. She was loyal to him."

"Until she wasn't. What happened to call her loyalty into question remains unanswered. But something happened to turn her."

"And caused her death. Sad, really," said Carolyn.

"Speaking of Desiree." Marco finished his beer. "How is the daughter search going?"

"Slow," said Brett. "I'm searching through births from the date shown on the certificate. Might be easier if she had given the baby a name."

"Probably wanted to leave that to the new parents," said Carolyn.

"Anything on the father?" asked Marco.

"Nothing yet," said Brett. "Henry seems to have been a popular surname in and around Memphis about the same time."

"What if…" began Carolyn. "What if Desiree and this JJ Henry, assuming they were a couple, got their start there…in Memphis? She was Dawn DeSoto then. What if JJ Henry also changed his name? What if they ran the first brothel together? That was where I found the first photo of her—dancing on a riverboat. The baby was an inconvenient accident, and instead of aborting it, she put it up for adoption."

"Interesting theory," said Marco.

"To piggyback on Carolyn's what-ifs," said Brett, "I've been thinking about the name thing. Desiree changed her name, but kept her initials. What if the father, JJ Henry, did the same thing? I can write an algorithm to search all variations of men with J H initials who were living in the Memphis area at the time. Like driver's licenses, high school graduation records, library cards."

Carolyn laughed. "Someone involved in a prostitution racket doesn't strike me as the library card type. But if we search police records and find anything on prostitution arrests connected with Dawn, maybe we'll get lucky and find someone else who was involved who has the initials J H." Carolyn opened her laptop. "He could have been her pimp."

"What we don't know is whether the guy was a local, or someone passing through town that Dawn had a one-nighter with."

Carolyn tapped a finger on her mouth and thought about it for a moment. "He wasn't a drifter. He meant something to her. I'd bet money on it."

"You sound very confident," said Marco. "What makes you so sure?"

"Women's intuition. She would have left the father space blank if he was just some guy passing through town who knocked her up." Carolyn looked up, watched a noisy seagull fly across the sky until it was out of sight. "How she did what she did to young women when she had a daughter of her own is beyond my understanding."

"Keep at it. You two are a solid team. If anyone can find Desiree's daughter, you can." Marco picked up a cookie and took a bite. "I've got an appointment. Stay as long as you want. Take a swim. Enjoy the view."

Williamsburg, Virginia

The wait time increased exponentially as each hour ticked by during the first day the Asclepius Clinic was open to patients. People started lining up outside the doors before seven o'clock in the morning. And the clinic didn't open until nine.

"Eli, go get in line, and I'll join you after I park my car."

"Thank you, Miss Morgan. You're very kind to bring me

here, but I don't want you getting your hopes up. I'm not sure there's much they can do for me."

"Let's not jump to conclusions until the doctors have had a chance to examine you."

"Yes, ma'am."

Eli got out of her car and shuffled to the end of the line. He'd taken a shower early this morning in the *Beacon's* locker room, before any of the staff showed up for work. Morgan gave him new clothes. He brushed his hand against his new T-shirt, flicking a hair off his shoulder. He tugged at the waistband of his new jeans.

"She got me all dressed up," he said to no one in particular, wondering if a straitjacket was as stiff as his new jeans.

The woman in front of him in line turned to look at him. Seeing he was talking to no one, she moved closer to the people in front of her, widening the space between herself and Eli.

Eli drummed the fingers of his left hand against his leg. He looked back to the parking lot. "Miss Morgan is really good to me," he said to the woman in front of him. "She got me these clothes and…and…and…"

If looks could kill, he'd be lying flat on the pavement after the woman's eyes cut right through him before she inched farther away.

Morgan found Eli halfway up the line. Their conversation was cut short when the clinic doors opened. At the front door, Morgan recognized a smiling Tiffany Stamos, dressed in navy blue slacks with a cream blouse and oversized blue beads around her neck. She wore a white lab coat with her name embroidered above the name of the clinic on the left side.

"Welcome, everyone. We're so glad you're here." While her words might have fallen short, her smile reached the back of the line. The crowd pulsed forward.

"No need to push. Everyone will have an opportunity to meet with our doctors. As you step inside, please take one of the clipboards our staff members are handing out and fill out the information as best you can. The information you give us will help our doctors better care for you. Thank you. Come on in."

The room was a sea of perky staff members in white lab coats. They moved from person to person, guiding them to seats and helping them complete the paperwork. When Eli walked through the door, he was given a plastic card with the number fifteen on it, and one of the clipboards. He and Morgan found seats against the far wall. He stared at the clipboard on his lap and the pen shook in his hand. Lost eyes turned to Morgan, pleading for help.

"I'm not sure I can do this, Miss Morgan."

"Don't worry, Eli." She took the clipboard from him and began to fill in the spaces, asking him questions. "When you go in to see the doctor, just tell him what you remember about what the VA doctors told you. Let them examine you. And I'll be right out here when you're done."

"Won't you come with me?"

"I can't, Eli. It wouldn't be right. I'm not family. If you run into trouble, you can send the nurse out to get me."

When his number was called, he followed the nurse toward the double doors into the examination area. He turned to give Morgan a mournful look. She gave him a wink, a smile, and a hearty thumbs-up. The nurse escorting him could see his trepidation and placed her arm around his shoulder as she swiped her ID. The double doors opened with a swoosh, and she guided him through.

Two hours later, Eli walked back into the waiting room smiling from ear to ear.

"It was great. They were great. You should have been there." His face flushed as he gushed about the care he received. "The rooms are all damn-spanking new. Everything is so clean. I've never seen equipment like what they have. Not anything like it at the VA."

"This is really good to hear, Eli. I'm so glad it went well for you."

He rubbed his upper arm. "Kind of stings. Got a few shots."

"Really? Just like that? What shots, if you don't mind me asking?"

"Not at all. Let's see." He held up his hand and counted on his fingers. "They gave me a flu shot and a pneumonia shot. Then they asked if I'd had chicken pox when I was a kid. I said yes. Figured I did. All kids get chicken pox. But I don't really remember. I remember having the measles. My brother and I had them at the same time. So did my cousin, so we all were sick together. It was a hoot." He laughed and Morgan could see how badly he needed a dentist. "My mom, she was ready to pull her hair out. And they gave me a shot for something called shingles."

He thought a moment. "Guess that's it. There was another one but I don't remember what it was for. Hurt like the devil." He scratched his head for a moment. "Oh, and they took some blood. Said they were going to do a complete work-up. Mentioned all sorts of letters that I guess named the tests, but I don't remember any of them. Maybe they figure they'll be seeing me on a regular basis."

"Would you like that, Eli? Most people do see a doctor at least once a year. Kind of like a tune-up for a car."

"If I'm here, sure. Why not? It's free. And they were nicer to me than at the VA. Gave me these pills and told me to take one each day."

Morgan took the pill bottle to read the label. Valium, ten

milligrams to be taken daily. She wondered what Eli had told the doctors that resulted in the valium.

"The doctor said if anything showed up on the tests, they'd call me. Well, they'll call you, because that's the number they have."

"And I'll come get you, and we'll come back here together."

"And they want me to come back next month for a follow-up visit. Want to see how I'm doing on them pills. I said okay, but I'm not sure I can do that."

"Why not?"

"Not sure I'll remember." He looked away from her, down at his feet.

"We'll remember together." She placed her hand over his and gave it a warm squeeze. "I'll put it on my calendar, and I'll make sure you make your appointment. I see you every day when I bring you hot chocolate. We can count down the days together."

He looked at her, staring into her eyes. "Why are you so nice to me? I don't understand."

"Because you are a nice person. Because you served our country, gave up part of yourself so I can enjoy the freedoms people like you fight to protect for me. Because inside you there is so much good that is struggling to see the light of day. And if I can help you—"

"Whoa. No one ever talked to me like that before. I just did what my father did before me, and his father did before him. Got out of school and enlisted."

"And that's why I'm honored to help you. Because you did that. Generations before you did that. Helping you is the very least I can do."

"How are you doing?" asked Nadine. Sitting on her back

deck, she watched Morgan contemplate the question, noticed her long pause before answering, saw her lips twitch and turn down.

"I'm fine, really. You don't have to worry about me."

"Why don't I believe you?"

"What's not to believe? Everything is great. Eli got to see the doctors at the clinic this morning, and it looks like they are going to help him. Because of your prodding, and with your help, I'm pulling together what could be the story of my life, and I had coffee with an interesting stranger at B&N the other day. It's a beautiful afternoon. We're enjoying eating, drinking, and playing Siamese mah jongg. Sid, your one-of-a-kind husband, has volunteered to make us dinner again. The sunset is going to be spectacular. This crab garlic dip you made is delicious. All's right with the world."

Morgan dredged a Triscuit through the dip, snagging a huge dollop of the rich cream cheese and crab concoction. After chewing it slowly, she washed it down with wine, draining her glass.

"Wait. Back up. What guy?"

"There was this guy. The other day, when we were meeting for lunch, I was early so I went to B&N to kill some time. This guy struck up a conversation. He invited me for coffee. I said no because I was meeting you, but then he said he'd be there the next day at two and would wait for me to show up."

"That's crazy."

"I know," she giggled.

"And?"

"I showed up. He's a reporter, a very handsome reporter. Jesse Sinclair." She filled another cracker with dip. "Funny, though."

"What?"

"He knew my name. I've been wracking my brain,

replaying what I remember of our conversation, and I don't remember telling him my name. I must have, though, because he used it. And now that I'm saying that, I remember he also knew I was a reporter. He said something like my haircut matched me being a fun-loving, freewheeling reporter. Anyway, we had coffee, talked about the stories we were working on, and that was it. So, see. I'm fine." Morgan raised her glass in a mock salute.

Nadine's radar shifted to high alert.

"Pardon me, but you don't sound fine. You're going to need more wine."

"Ya think?"

She reached out and refilled Morgan's wine glass, finishing the bottle. Then she fetched another bottle of Chardonnay from the fridge on the deck.

"Not sure I can do all this. Pull it all together. Make it all work." Her heavy sigh confirmed Nadine's fears. "My atelophobia is kicking up big time."

"Love that you found a name for it. Makes it sound so serious, like a real disease."

"It is serious. Atelophobia, the fear of not being good enough, not meeting others' expectations. I've battled it all my life. Do you know how many people go through life secretly harboring this fear? That they'll be found out—found wanting—not good enough, not smart enough, not perfect enough. The old fake it till you make it."

"You can count me among the group," Nadine said. "But I thought you were getting over your confidence issues. Look at everything you've accomplished. And going after this story will focus your energies as nothing else can."

"In my never-to-be-humble opinion, you never get over it. You just learn to hide it. Until something happens that rattles your protective walls to their foundations."

"You'll be fine. Trust me." Nadine finished her wine and

refilled her glass. "Tell me about the clinic visit. Was that Ramos woman there?"

"Stamos. Tiffany Stamos. Decked out in all her bubbly glory." Morgan ran her finger around the rim of her glass. "Sorry, that wasn't nice." Morgan took a large gulp of wine, ashamed she'd again fallen into jealousy mode.

"Don't be sorry. Jealousy is one of my favorite deadly sins. What do you envy most? Her size? Her clothes? Her jewelry?"

"God, you make me sound so petty." She thought for a moment. "How she seems to have her act so together. I know she could be dying inside, but on the outside, she is one together woman."

"I know. I loved watching her in action at the clinic opening. You'll have to introduce us."

"You asked about Eli's clinic visit. There were so many people there, but he seemed to do well. He was nervous at first, but when he came back into the waiting room, he was all smiles. He said they took good care of him, took blood, gave him a full round of preventive shots and a thirty-day supply of ten milligram valium pills."

"Oh, I could use those."

"Couldn't we all? Just to take the edge off our workaholic, aggressive, charged, doggedly determined, type A personalities." She lifted her glass toward Nadine's and they clinked.

"Here's to all of us overachieving, type A women," said Nadine. "And the men who love us and put up with us," she added, smiling at Sid, who had come out to the deck looking rather serious.

"What's up, hon? You don't look so good."

"I had the local news on while I was making dinner. They found a man's body at the Williamsburg Inn."

"You're kidding," said Nadine.

"I'm afraid not. I think you know him, Morgan. Greg Welton."

"No...no...no. That's impossible. I was just with him a few days ago."

"That's the name the reporter said. The CEO of Elan Health Systems." Sid sat down across from Morgan.

"We just had dinner. I was asking him if he knew anything about black market organs or anyone who could help me. He said he didn't. But it was strange…"

"What?" asked Nadine.

"I don't know. He seemed worried when I told him what I was working on. He even told me to be careful."

The three of them sat in silence for a moment.

"He can't be dead. How? What happened?"

"There weren't many details."

"I'm so sorry." Nadine came over to her side as she made eye contact with Sid.

"Thanks." Morgan's eyes filled with tears. "We were old friends."

"Friends?" asked Sid.

"Yes. I've known him for years. Did I tell you he tried to put the moves on me after dinner the other night?"

"Again? Didn't you two try that before?"

"Yeah. A long time ago." Morgan shuddered. "Like kissing my brother. And now he's dead."

CHAPTER 16

Private Island, Florida Keys

The information had been painstakingly slow in coming, but heaven-sent once received. Hayden lifted his cell phone and retrieved the text. It had come in a few weeks ago, and he saved it. It was the first thing he looked at when he awoke each day, and the last thing he read before he closed his eyes to sleep. The news was life-changing—priceless.

Dawn had a kid. My kid. A baby girl. My last fertile shot. My soldiers went swimming, and they produced a daughter.

The bitch never told him. She'd given the baby up for adoption the day she was born, and the records were sealed. Didn't even name her, though she named him, JJ Henry, as the kid's father. Hallelujah!

How lucky for him that he'd found the birthday card stuffed with five one hundred dollar bills on Desiree's desk the day he made a surprise visit to the Sand Isle Inn. The envelope was addressed to Dr. Darby Dratton in Wachapreague, Virginia, wherever the hell that was. When he asked Desiree about it, she'd gotten flustered. Most unlike Desiree. Nothing rattled her. But something in her eyes told him she was lying. Why lie about a birthday card unless she was hiding something?

Thinking back, he remembered Dawn disappearing for some months when they were just starting out. He was furious with her at first, but she'd come crawling back to him full of apologies. They'd been a great team ever since, made each other rich beyond either of their wildest dreams.

His curiosity aroused, he put his best man on it. Not Moss. He always had a soft spot where Dawn was concerned. Even accused Hayden of killing her a few weeks back. His guy paid off a clerk in the Memphis records department. Big money. The clerk would never have to work a day in her life again. Records were unsealed. Basic detective work followed, and he tracked her down. His man texted that he had her in his sights.

Hayden had a choice. He could have played it straight, gone to see her, introduced himself, apologized for abandoning her, and asked flat out for her help. But what if she turned him down? What if she told someone about this worthless piece is shit of a so-called father she'd never met, who came calling out of nowhere because now he needed her kidney? His survival instincts offered a better plan. Why ask for what you can simply take?

It would be over soon. She'd be tested for blood and tissue matching. If there was a five- or six-point match, like he prayed there would be, she'd disappear for a few days and return home a little sore, and with a new scar. If they weren't a good match, she'd wake up at home that much sooner.

"Is it exclusive?" asked Hayden.

"As exclusive as it gets. Private cottage overlooking the ocean. Other guests can't see you, and you can't see them.

Small lap pool and hot tub. There is a private room for your caregiver while you recuperate, and he or she, whichever you prefer, is with you 24/7. All meals are provided when you want them, and consist of what you want."

"Sounds perfect."

"You'll fly into Williamsburg the morning of your surgery, and fly out the next day in a private, medically equipped jet. Plus, you'll have a doctor and a nurse practitioner at your side the entire time."

"I have a friend who may join me. Is there space for someone else to be with me? Another bedroom?"

"If you think it's necessary, it can be arranged. We'll reserve one of the cottages with three bedrooms."

"Do that. Availability?"

"Whenever you're ready, the facility will accommodate you."

"Excellent. Set it up. The sooner the better" He ended the call. One detail down, one major detail to go. Was there a tissue and blood type match?

"You seem pleased," said Moss when he brought Hayden an afternoon snack. "Who were you talking to?"

"A travel agent."

"Where are we going?"

Hayden cast a shadowed glance in his direction. "I'm not sure *we* are going anywhere. I may be taking a short vacation without you. Does that upset you?"

"No. Surprises me. Especially now that you're on dialysis."

"That may end soon." Behind the facade of pleasure, one point crystalized for Hayden. Every day was precious now, every moment of delay costly.

"Who is better equipped to care for you than I am? No one knows who you really are." Moss stood across the room from Hayden. "Except me, that is."

146

Hayden fixed his gaze out to sea. Soon the sun would set, igniting the sky in hues of pink, red and purple. He looked back at Moss, whose cold stare had not wavered.

"No one cares who I am. People only care about themselves, getting their needs met."

"Is this what you tell yourself to make it all okay? The whores? The drugs?"

"Find a need and fill it." Hayden grinned. "Prostitution. The oldest business in the world fills a need. The drugs? Well, why not take advantage of the basest of all human weaknesses? The need to feel good, if only for the moment."

"I'm not so sure that's true."

"Bullshit. You know it's true. I'm simply capitalizing on an opportunity. Man's gotta eat, right? And he likes them young and pretty and docile. If I wasn't doing it, someone else would."

Moss seethed. Hayden was right about a huge segment of the male population.

"You were just like me once upon a time. Then you went and joined the fucking Marines. I don't know what they did, but you came back a different person. Shit, you grew a conscience."

"I came back a man with honor, not a street thug."

"I liked you better when you were a thug. This holier-than-thou bullshit could get you killed—get me killed."

"Like it got Dawn killed?"

"Don't fuck with me, boy. Friendship only goes so far. I gave you a job, a life, travel, the best of everything my money could buy. And all I asked for was a little loyalty."

Moss held his stare, eyes locked, a veritable non-fluid pissing contest.

"You think you're so smart. You know so much. You have no idea what I'm really capable of."

"Keep thinking that, Hayden. Your arrogance will be

your undoing." A wave of anger rolled through him, and he swallowed hard to regain at least a semblance of control.

"Loyalty is your Achilles' heel. You demand it from me, demanded it from Dawn. But your fatal flaw? You offer little in return. Certainly not loyalty. Sure, the money, the lifestyle, the best of everything. But your price is too high. And when we balk, you push us away, most times permanently. You never answered my question. Did you kill Dawn?"

"What difference does it make? She was becoming a problem, getting soft, growing a conscience. Kind of like you. She was a liability."

"She was your friend, my friend."

"She was—" Hayden hesitated, seeing fire in Moss's eyes. "She was a problem. And the problem's been solved. Gone away. Good riddance."

"You bastard."

"Excuse me, Mr. High and Mighty. Might I remind you that you live rather well on my generosity? She did too."

"And I've served you faithfully, paid for it with my life."

"Poor you. If you'd stayed in that shithole town, you'd be working in a fucking cat food factory or dead by now. You were a drugged-out mess when you came back and begged me for a job."

"It's how you make your money that concerns me."

"Funny, it never bothered you before. One's morals often depend on the size of the deposits in one's bank account. I don't remember yours being that big before you came to work for me. What bug is up your ass?"

"No bug. I know the truth, and I want you to admit it. You killed Dawn. Pressed the button. I saw you. We were the three musketeers. One for all and all for one."

"Go fuck yourself." Hayden stormed out of the room. It wasn't the first time he and Moss had gone around about

Dawn, and it wouldn't be the last. Why did Moss care about her so much? She was old history. Made no sense.

Williamsburg, Virginia

"Nadine, there's a man in the lobby asking to speak with you." The receptionist handed Nadine a business card. Surprise registered on her face. She got up and walked into the lobby.

"This is a surprise," she said, approaching Colton Pollard with her hand outstretched.

"I hope not an unwelcome one. I thought we might have coffee so I can tell you all about what an entrepreneurial investor does."

"Sounds interesting. Let me get Morgan. She's doing a story on Elan and Asclepius and I know she'd be interested to learn what an entrepreneurial investor does too, and how it all fits at Elan."

Nadine left him standing alone. He didn't mind because his plan was working. He'd hoped she would invite Morgan to join them. For some reason women liked to travel in pairs. They went to the bathroom together, shopped together, and now were going to join him for coffee, together.

"You remember Morgan?" she asked as they approached him.

"Yes. So glad you could join us."

"We'll go to Aroma's. It's just down the block in Colonial Williamsburg, and it won't be crowded this time of day. You can tell us all about your business ventures."

Two hours flew by. Colton pretended to relish being in

the spotlight, delighting the ladies with tales of his entrepreneurial conquests. He gave them both pens with his company's name, Global Initiatives, on them. Alarm bells went off in his head when their questions about his business interest in the clinic began to feel more like an interrogation. Abruptly, he stood up and pulled his phone from his pocket.

"Anything wrong?" asked Nadine.

"I'm not actually sure. My phone has been vibrating in my pocket. It must be important. Would you excuse me for a few minutes?" He stepped away from the table and took the call. Nadine kept her eyes glued to him.

"Something's up," she said to Morgan. "Bet he comes back and says he has to go."

"You think?"

"I know. Our questions were making him squirm for some reason. Wish I knew why. Here he comes."

"I'm sorry, ladies, but something has come up, and I've got to leave. Please stay and finish your coffees. I'll take care of the check on my way out. It's been a pleasure." He handed them both business cards. "Let me know if there is anything else I can help you with. And don't be shy about staying in touch."

"We won't," said Nadine.

"The only thing missing from his stories," said Morgan while she and Nadine walked back to their office, "were names, dates, and details."

"You noticed that too? Every question we asked was answered—"

"In a very longwinded fashion," interrupted Morgan.

"But with few concrete details. Incredibly frustrating."

"He didn't seem to like any of my questions about the free clinic part of the business."

"There ain't no such thing as free." Nadine tossed her

empty coffee cup in a trash bin. "I know Elan charges a lot of money for its concierge level of care, but it can't be enough to cover the costs of all the advanced technology we saw on the tour."

"Did you catch his discomfort when I started to talk about the story I'm working on about missing homeless people?"

"Yes. I wondered about that. Didn't help matters when I threw out my story twist about a link between missing homeless people and illegal trafficking in organs. He got so red, I thought his head was going to explode."

"He covered it by answering his phone…which, by the way, I didn't hear ring or chirp or buzz. I think he faked the call. We hit a nerve. There's something there. I can sense it."

"Sounds like your reporter nose is sniffing full blast." Nadine touched the side of her own nose. "Good for you. I'm so pleased you're getting into this story. And once it's finished, I plan to pitch it to a friend at the *Washington World Herald* who owes me a favor."

"You'd do that for me?"

"Yes. It's your break. I got mine years ago when someone did something nice for me, and now it's my turn."

From a safe distance, Colton discreetly watched the ladies walk back to the newspaper office. It had been a pleasant conversation until Morgan started talking about missing homeless people. And when Nadine added her theory about nameless people stealing their organs and killing them, he practically jumped out of his seat. Revisiting his retort, that investigating missing homeless people and linking them to black market organs is the type of sensational journalism that sells newspapers, regardless of whether it was true or not, seemed to squash the idea, but should they dig too deep, it could present him with a host of problems. Dare he enlist Mr. Kent's services again?

With a wave of his hand, his limo appeared at the curb.

"Back to the Inn, please."

"Certainly, sir."

Settling into the back seat, he poured himself a drink and considered his options. He needed to give these two ladies a new focus, re-direct their attention, give them something else to investigate. He considered who was the more dangerous of the two women. Morgan Kasen seemed too much of a novice. Her bubbly gushing told him she was working on her first big story. She'd require watching.

Nadine Steiner-Greene was an entirely different matter. She was the pro, and clearly she was providing direction to Morgan. *Yes, Nadine is the ringleader, the more dangerous of the two at this point. Perhaps it's time to alter the direction of her life.*

CHAPTER 17

Morgan rubbed her eyes, laced her fingers, and raised her arms above her head in a big stretch. She'd been online for hours, and her head was ready to explode from everything she was learning about cadavers donated to science, organ trafficking, and transplants. "Parts are parts" was her favorite saying when it came to ordering fried chicken, but when it came to human beings, she found the practice of selling body parts of the dearly departed gross.

"Incentives are everywhere." Her self-talk got louder. "Selling human body parts is big business. People are worth more dead than alive. Call it a donation, and hint that I can win a gift card or a trip, or be entered into a sweepstakes, or make this month's rent, then it's okay. What bullshit."

The more she read about the worth of a cornea or a lung or a section of liver, the uglier the situation became. "Jack off and get a hundred and twenty-five dollars for your sperm. Be willing to go blind in one eye, and here's a gift card for your cornea."

Then there were the body brokers, legitimate companies that brought in corpses for medical seminars held in posh hotels. She knew she'd never look at a hotel ballroom the same way again. She could see the hotel's daily schedule marquee in her mind's eye. Tonight in the Winchester Room is the Taylor wedding, and tomorrow ABC Medical Technologies is training doctors on laparoscopic surgery, using a new device sure to improve their technique.

"Ugh! Of course, once science is done with you," she muttered, "they'll cremate your remains for free and return them to your loving family. Guess the only question is, did you get all of Aunt Sally's remains?"

It was almost five o'clock when Morgan drove up the ramp in the parking garage, going around and around until she finally found an empty parking space on the top level. Lots of empty cars, but no people. While fumbling to put her phone in her purse, she dropped her keys, the clanking sound echoed in the cavernous space when they hit the cement floor.

And then another sound. *What was that?* A shiver ran down her spine. *Was someone there?*

"Stop it!" she admonished herself, turning around twice to see if she could see anyone. "Of course there's someone here, on at least one of the floors. This is a public garage." She bent down, retrieved her keys, and seeing her reflection in the car window, ran her fingers through her hair, straightening out the spiky ends.

"My imagination is getting the best of me. This is Williamsburg, Colonial Williamsburg. Nothing bad happens here." *Yeah, right. Bad stuff happens here like it does everywhere.*

Emerging at street level, she headed for the new restaurant she and Nadine decided to try for dinner, since Sid was at his weekly poker game. It was in one of the old houses on Scotland Street. Nadine had described it as an exotic little French bistro with an excellent wine list, gooey French onion soup, interesting salads, crusty bread, and to-die-for chocolate mousse.

As Morgan approached the restaurant's door, she saw Nadine standing with a crowd of tourists waiting to cross Henry Street. She waved wildly, and succeeded in getting Nadine's attention. The light changed, and Nadine, totally focused on her phone, allowed the throng of tourists to shepherd her across the street. Morgan could see her shrug as she waited for the next light to turn and the Don't Walk signal to change to Walk.

Why couldn't the damn traffic system stop all the cars and allow pedestrians to cross diagonally?

The light changed, and the waiting crowd surged forward, but Nadine stopped because her attention was distracted by something on her phone. A puzzled look crossed her face as she looked at the screen. She put the phone to her ear as she started to cross. Suddenly a black SUV shot out from nowhere, appeared to careen out of control, and slammed into her.

Her body grew wings. It flew into the air. Whomp! It smashed onto the hood of the SUV, rolled off, and landed with a dull thud back on the sidewalk in the midst of horrified screams.

Morgan froze in place momentarily.

And then the noise of chaos returned in a rush.

"Nadine!" A blood-curdling scream ripped out of her throat, and for a moment the world tilted, and her vision narrowed to almost a pinpoint.

People were screaming, "Someone call 911." Cell phone cameras recorded the chaos.

Morgan pushed through the growing crowd. Rubbery legs carried her to the side of her best friend, who was a crumpled mass of human flesh lying twisted and bloody on the sidewalk. She knelt down beside Nadine, sobbing, afraid to touch even her hand. Clumps of what had to be brain matter, and a puddle of brownish-red blood, haloed and pooled around her head. Nadine's eyes stared off into nothingness, her neck wrenched unnaturally to one side, and Morgan could see a bone sticking out of her mangled right leg. One look. Morgan knew. There was no hope. Nadine was dead.

When she heard the sirens wail in the distance, she glanced up automatically.

The SUV hadn't moved.

The driver's side window slid down. Steely blue eyes stared at Morgan through slits in a black stocking cap for what felt like an eternity, but was barely a moment. Goose bumps rushed up and down her skin.

Then rage replaced them, and she started to get to her feet, but before she could take a step, the SUV's window went back up, it backed up, made a U-turn, and sped away.

The ambulance and police took its place.

"Oh, God. Please, God. Fix this. Make this better."

Morgan knelt again beside Nadine's body, eyes burning with tears, cold and shaking from anguish and rage…and terror…because the SUV driver's blue eyes had remained riveted on her like a tiger crouched to spring. A crowd surrounded them, close enough to see what was happening, but far enough away to disconnect mentally from the gruesome scene.

Morgan felt strong arms pull her to her feet while the paramedics went to work.

"I'm Officer Spencer. Here. Let's go over to my car where we can talk."

In a fog, she complied. Soon she was sitting in the passenger seat of a black Chevy, clutching a wad of damp tissues in her shaking hands, tissues stained with her mascara and her lipstick.

"Here. Have some water." The officer twisted off the white cap and handed her a bottle of Aquafina. "I'm Officer

Spencer," he said, reintroducing himself. "You know the victim?"

"Yes." Morgan's voice barely a whisper. "Nadine...Nadine Steiner-Greene."

"What can you tell me about what happened?"

The water bottle dangled loosely in her hands.

"It was so fast. She was standing on the corner...waiting to cross. I-I think her phone must have rung, because she looked at me and wiggled it in her hand. Then she put it to her ear. Then—" Her throat locked.

She took a sip of water, put the bottle in the cup holder, pulled clean tissues from her purse, and wiped away fresh tears. "Then...I-I don't know. There was this SUV...black." Her throat squeezed almost shut. "It was just there and Nadine...Nadine...she's...she's...oh my God."

She concentrated on Officer Spencer's kind eyes, slowing her breath, and with a newfound certainty, strengthening her voice.

"Oh my God. He hit her. He aimed right for her. The light was red, and he shouldn't have been moving. But he was. He hit her. She flew—like a rag doll. And then she hit the hood of the car—that sound—that awful sound—and then she was on the ground."

She buried her face in her hands and began to sob again. Officer Spencer squatted down to comfort her. He'd been doing his job long enough to know any comfort he might offer would pale against her grief.

When her sobs subsided a bit, he asked, "Is there anything you remember about the car?"

"It was black. I don't know the make or model. Some type of SUV, like you always see in presidential motorcades." She took a long gulp of water and reached out her hand, grabbing his sleeve. "He looked at me."

"Who looked at you?"

"The driver. His window went down and he stared at me."

"Can you describe him? Would you recognize him if you saw him again?"

"It all happened so fast, but it felt like slow motion. His face was covered. He was white. Had cold eyes—blue. Icy. Cold. Empty."

"Okay." He jotted down some notes. "Then what happened?"

"I heard the sirens. He must have heard them too, because he looked in his rearview mirror. Then he backed up and sped away."

"Thank you, Ms. Kasen. You've been very helpful. I am so sorry for your loss. I've got your contact information, and someone from the Williamsburg PD will be in touch if we need to talk to you again."

"Slow down, Morgan. I can barely understand you," said her Uncle Daniel.

They had reconnected after he retired from the NYPD and moved to Williamsburg to start the next chapter of his life with his new wife, Rachel. He told her to call if she ever needed anything.

"I'm putting my phone on speaker so I can take notes while we talk."

"It happened so fast. One minute she was there, crossing the street and then—wham." Her words tangled with her sobs.

"Oh, Morgan. I'm so sorry."

"And I saw him."

"What do you mean, you saw him? You can identify the guy?" Daniel's detective radar shifted into high gear.

"No. His face was covered by one of those stocking masks. But his eyes. I saw his eyes. Piercing. Blue. Lifeless.

Cold as ice. I'll never forget them. And I started screaming."

"What did the police say?"

"What could they say? It happened so fast. It was a big black SUV with tinted windows, the kind you see all over DC or New York, driving around VIPs."

"Did anyone get a license plate?" he asked.

"There were no plates. The police looked at the photos from everyone's cell phones. The SUV didn't have plates." Morgan stopped talking.

"Morgan, you still there?"

"Yes," she said softly. "Uncle Daniel, this was not an accident. They were waiting for her. I'm sure of it." Strength had returned to Morgan's voice. "She was distracted. Got a phone call. Didn't cross with everyone else. She was all by herself. That's why no one else got hurt."

There was a moment of silence.

"Morgan?"

"I'm here. I was just thinking, Sid must be devastated. I've got to call him."

"Don't do it alone. Please. Wait until Rachel and I get to you. Where are you now?"

"I'm home."

"We're on our way."

Time seemed to stand still, one minute bleeding into the next while hurried arrangements for Nadine's funeral were made. It had been a horrible two days, and probably far worse for poor Sid.

Friends and family filled the small synagogue this morning, and many were here now, in Nadine and Sid's home, making the traditional shiva call. Morgan always felt that one good thing about being Jewish, among many others, was that burial was handled swiftly, traditionally within twenty-four hours. And then the family was left to mourn and remember. So many friends wanted to speak at the service. Their obvious affection and respect, conveyed in their stories, brought tears to everyone's eyes. Nadine was beloved.

Morgan walked up the sidewalk alone.

A pretty little girl wearing a pink sundress and hot pink Crocs, with pink ribbons holding her strawberry blond ringlet pigtails in place, opened the door. Sid was close on her heels.

"Hi," the girl said in a sweet, childish voice. "I'm Madelyn."

"It's nice to meet you Miss Madelyn," said Morgan.

Sid held the door open, welcoming Morgan inside.

"I'm so sorry I didn't get much of a chance to talk to you at the service this morning," he said. "You and Nadine were such good friends, and I hope you know how much she loved working with you." Sid ran his fingers through his still-full head of snowy white hair, looking around for…something…someone. Morgan suspected he was automatically looking for Nadine to share the moment, and her heart broke for him.

His eyes landed on Madelyn, who slipped her hand into his and beamed up at him. "Needless to say, it's been kind of crazy around here."

"Please, don't apologize," said Morgan. "I can't imagine how hard this has been for you and your family."

He picked up the little girl and bounced her in his arms. Her giggles filled the room. "My son and daughter-in-law are here somewhere, and I'd love for you to meet them. As for this little munchkin, for now, she's mine, all mine." He snuggled his face into his granddaughter's cheeks and gave her a big kiss, which had her erupting in even more giggles.

"You and Nadine had a very special relationship, Sid. She talked about you all the time. Loved you so much. I always envied her."

"Thank you. And thank you for coming. Please, get something to eat. There's so much food. A shiva visit isn't complete without lots of food."

The afternoon wore on. She found Sid holding little Madelyn in the kitchen when she was ready to say her good-byes. Clearly, his granddaughter brought him comfort, and Morgan was so glad she was here for him.

"Sid, I'm leaving now. If it's okay with you, I'd like to continue working on the homeless story Nadine was helping me write."

"Of course it's okay with me. There's no reason or need to ask. From what I understood, it was your story. She was helping you. That's what had her so excited. It would be a shame to lose all your hard work by stopping now."

"She was researching a different angle. I'm wondering if she left any notes around that could help me pull it all together. See where she left off, and figure out what needs to be investigated further. She was a note-taking queen."

"Anal when it came to writing things down," said Sid. "Never wanted to trust her memory. I'm sure there are notes here somewhere. I-I haven't thought to look for them. I'm sorry."

"No. Please. There's nothing to be sorry for. I wouldn't expect you to look for notes right now. What I'd like to do is come by in a few days, when it's convenient for you, and look through any notes she might have left here. She always warned me to keep the really important stuff I was working on at home, on my own computer, not leave it at the office."

"She got scooped once very early in her career, and she learned that lesson well." He lowered his granddaughter to the floor, taking care to make sure she was stable on her feet. "She's getting heavy," he laughed. "They grow up so fast."

He filled Madelyn's sippy cup with apple juice and handed it to her. "Come by any time. We weren't religious, so I'm pretty sure friends making shiva calls will dwindle to none in a day or so. Looking for her notes will give me something to do, something to occupy my mind."

CHAPTER 18

A white panel van pulled down the dark alley behind the movie theater, its headlights providing the only illumination.

"There," said the driver, pointing to a red dot blinking on his navigation screen.

At the end of the alley, the van made a sharp right turn, and stopped at the edge of the blacktop adjacent to the woods. After a few minutes, the side door slid open. A thin man in a white lab coat got out of the passenger side, and, keeping his head down and his back to the building, approached the small group of men huddled in the darkness under blankets, talking.

"Hey. How are y'all?"

No response. Three pairs of eyes stared at him.

"I'm Dr. Edwards from the free clinic on the other side of town. I think I met some of you when we opened."

The men exchanged glances with each other. One seemed particularly leery of the stranger, getting up and moving slightly away from the others. It looked like he was preparing to bolt into the woods.

"Anyway, I'm looking for Caleb Stone."

"What for?" asked one of the two men still seated.

"Caleb, that you?" asked the doctor leaning closer,

pushing his black framed glasses up on his nose.

"Might be. What do you want to know for?"

"Do you remember me?" Without waiting for a response he crouched down on his haunches to be more at eye level with Caleb. "I'm Dr. Edwards. We met the other day at the clinic."

"Yes, sir. I do remember you." Caleb stood up and brushed his right hand on his pants before extending it to his visitor. Dr. Edwards was clean-shaven, square-jawed, and Caleb remembered thinking he smelled like the ocean. He wore a white shirt with a red and blue striped tie that reminded Caleb of an old barber pole.

"You were mighty nice to me. Asked me all sorts of questions. Gave me those shots and the pills."

"Have you been taking the pills?" asked Edwards as he stood up.

"Yes, sir. I surely have been doing what you told me to. I wouldn't want you to think I didn't appreciate your kindness."

"Good." Dr. Edwards glanced around. "We got some results back from the tests we ran the other day, and there are a few things we'd like to check out."

"It's mighty nice of you to come all the way out here to tell me. Should I be worried?"

"No, Caleb." Dr. Edwards beamed a warm smile. "Don't worry at all. It's all good. Do you think you might be able to come with me?"

"Like now?"

"Yes. If you could come now, it would be great."

"Be happy to oblige, Doc." Caleb started to collect his things.

"Here, let me help you." Dr. Edwards bent down and started to help Caleb gather his things.

"Thanks." Caleb wiped his sleeve across his nose. "Can't

be too careful. Never know what's gonna happen to your stuff if you just leave it out here. Here's my cart," he said, grabbing the bent handle of a metal push cart. "My home away from home."

"We can put your things into the van. They'll be safe in there. And when we're done, we'll bring you back here, or take you wherever you want to go."

"Thanks, Doc. How'd you ever find me back here?"

Dr. Edwards coughed, thinking about the locator implant placed under Caleb's skin as part of the testing procedures the day he visited the clinic. "Why, you told me where you hang out. You said, sure as I'm standing here, that behind the movie theater was your favorite place. Don't you remember?"

"I surely don't, but that don't mean it didn't happen." He took off his red Washington Nationals baseball cap and scratched his matted-down, dirty hair. "Can't say I remember too much of anything these days."

The van's driver joined them. He and Dr. Edwards put everything Caleb owned in the world into the van.

"Let me help you get in," said Dr. Edwards.

Caleb turned around and looked at his friends. "See you guys in a couple of hours. If anyone comes looking for me, tell 'em I went fishing." The guys all laughed and grumbled some words of encouragement. Caleb ducked his head and got into the back seat of the van.

"Now buckle your seat belt," said Dr. Edwards as he hopped into the passenger seat next to the driver. "We wouldn't want anything to happen to you on our way to the clinic."

Ambition knows no age boundaries. While several of his freelancing buddies wrote puff pieces, counting the days to retirement, Jesse still had Pulitzer on the brain. He desperately wanted one. He just needed the right story.

The call from Greg Welton had him salivating and got his heart pumping. He knew he'd found his holy grail. Greg's tale of shady dealings, strange comings and goings of people the staff said were guests, not patients, odd orders and missing supplies at several clinics, had the right three elements: secrecy, greed and power. The only name Greg shared was Colton Pollard. And everything tied neatly to the PBS documentary he had watched so many times, he nearly had it memorized.

His instincts sparked. He knew he was onto the story of his career. Sex was all it lacked, and he bet if he dug deep enough, he'd uncover some lascivious lusting or gratuitous sex. He'd called Greg to say he was on his way to Williamsburg, jumped in his car, and hit the road, ready to make his Pulitzer dreams come true.

He'd been in Williamsburg over a week, nosing around the new clinic, making friends, digging into both Greg's and Nadine Steiner-Greene's untimely deaths. He also learned about the homeless man Morgan and Nadine found in the woods who was missing a kidney. It was all too much, too fast, too coincidental. There had to be a connection.

Morgan. Morgan Kasen. His surprise. Thinking about Morgan was really what disturbed his sleep. She was…well, she was more than he bargained for at this point in his life. After his one and only disastrous marriage, he'd been a confirmed bachelor.

But her smile, and the way her blue eyes flashed when her temper got riled up, ignited a spark he hadn't felt in years…hell, decades. He wasn't a saint, had women in his life, but there was something about Morgan Kasen that was different.

At three a.m., he gave up. Pulling on his jeans and a T-shirt, he headed for IHOP, the closest thing to a twenty-four-hour diner in Williamsburg. Pancakes, eggs, and bacon would soothe his savage soul.

His was one of three cars in the parking lot. He took a booth by the window, ordered the Bacon Temptation Omelette, and pulled out his laptop. Praying the cholesterol-laden meal wouldn't kill him, he reviewed his notes while waiting for his food.

He had a slew of questions he never got to ask Greg, and the best way to honor his old friend would be to follow the trail of bread crumbs he laid out when they had dinner. His own research into Colton Pollard revealed a spider web of companies and subsidiaries. How they all fit together, and Pollard's role, were the keys. He had to make sense of what he and his black-hat hacker uncovered.

Breakfast arrived, and he pushed aside his laptop. *Bacon has got to be a natural aphrodisiac.* He took a bite of the omelette. *Oh, my God, this is good.* He refilled his coffee cup and drenched his pancakes in syrup, glancing at his laptop screen again.

His chewing slowed as his mind revved up.

Morgan walked through IHOP's door and headed right for him, her approach strong and steady. She stopped at the table's edge.

"You lied to me." Her voice was shrill.

"What? No hello?"

He gestured for her to sit down. She remained standing, her blue eyes trained on him like twin laser beams.

"Don't get cute with me. You know what I mean. You lied." She straightened her shoulders. "I checked. There's no story about any remediation from the old BASF plant with your name on it."

"Are you following me?"

"Yes. How's that for honest?"

"A bit too honest, maybe. How'd you know where to find me?"

"Trackers are cheap. Radio Shack on Monticello had the perfect model. Something about our meeting didn't seem kosher, so I followed you back to your motel and slipped it under your back bumper the other day."

"Clever girl."

"Don't change the subject. You lied."

"I didn't lie. I just wasn't completely forthcoming."

"Half-truths are lies in my world. You lied. Period."

"Can we talk about this?"

"What's there to talk about? You just admitted to lying—"

"No. I admitted to not being completely forthcoming. I may have misrepresented a bit, colored a few facts, added some flourishes here and there. There's a difference."

"Bullshit." Her expression unforgiving, she continued. "In my world lying is the eighth deadly sin. Should be the first. Probably causes most of the others. You lied to me." Her eyes pinned him in a furious glare that showed no signs of letting up.

He opened his mouth to speak.

Her left hand shot up nose high, palm out, fingers taut. "Stop before you even start," she snarled through clenched teeth.

The audacity of her approach surprised him. "If I stop, you won't get the answers you want. What do you want to know? And please, sit down."

She slid into the booth opposite him.

"I did do a story on the land owned by BASF and the environmental remediation currently underway."

"Then why couldn't I find it?"

"Because it never actually got published. It was shelved, never to see the light of day." He rubbed his hand across his stubble, feeling annoyed about it all over again. "Something, or rather someone, more exciting grabbed the headlines. Osama Bin Laden. My story was supposed to appear the day news of Bin Laden's killing broke. I'll be happy to show it to you. It's on my computer as a constant reminder of how fast things can change."

Morgan reached over to the next table, grabbed a clean mug and poured herself a cup of coffee. "I need an answer to a question that's been bothering me."

"We don't want anything bothering you, so ask away." Jesse pushed his plate into the center of the table and offered her his fork. She picked up a slice of bacon with her fingers.

"I know you're looking into Nadine's and Greg Welton's deaths. And a friend at the hospital said you were there asking questions about the homeless man who died. My question is why. Why are you digging into these deaths? They have nothing to do with the BASF plant or any chemicals leaching into the James River." Morgan's expression demanded an answer.

"Have to."

"Not true. No one has to do anything."

"You don't believe in have-tos?"

"No, I don't. We do things, even things we think we have to do, because we want to. Deep down inside, we know that whatever it is we label as a have-to teaches us who we are. And all of us want an answer to that eternal question. Who am I? What am I made of? What am I all about? Why am I here?"

"Now that's profound." He cut and forked a small stack of pancakes and dragged them through the syrup on his plate, stuffing them in his mouth and chewing slowly. He took a few sips of coffee, then gave her one of his signature disarming grins. "Pop psychology 101. Did you get that from a fortune cookie?"

"No." She finished the slice of bacon and took another

one. "Think about it. Whatever you're doing, there is always something in it for you. You get something out of it, even if it's feeling shitty. Who knows, maybe you like feeling shitty. So, what's in this for you?"

Jesse didn't answer. Five seconds…ten seconds…thirty seconds…a minute. His silence unnerved her.

"Jesse?"

He turned away from her, staring out the restaurant's window, at the lonely road, increasing the mental distance between them. He expelled a heavy sigh, and a lightness washed over him, almost as if her questions had lifted the weight of the world and freed him.

"For the sake of full disclosure, I need to tell you something. Your friend, Greg Welton? Small world. We were fraternity brothers at Princeton. Hadn't seen him but two or three times at reunions, but then I got a call from him, and we had dinner in New York a few weeks ago. He told me about some scary shenanigans at Elan. Said he felt like he got sucked into quicksand. And this guy who really owns it all behind the scenes. Made the guy sound really scary. Said he tried to quit, but the guy threatened him."

Jesse scooped up a forkful of his omelette, put it in his mouth, and chewed slowly.

"I'm fulfilling a promise. Not a promise I made out loud. One I made to myself the other night, when I learned Greg was dead. I knew then," he stopped talking and looked into Morgan's eyes, "like I know now, he was murdered. Nadine, too. Murdered. Probably by the same person. And since you're expanding your homelessness story to include the possibility of a connection with organ trafficking, someone may come after you. What if you're next?"

"Next? Next to what? To die?"

"That, my dear Morgan, is the million-dollar question."

"A bit melodramatic, don't you think?"

"I don't know what to think. But it's time we found out what's going on, and who's at the bottom of this, don't you agree?"

Morgan slumped back into the corner of the booth. Now it was her turn to stare out the window. Her hands white-knuckled her coffee mug.

"Earth to Morgan. Can I refill your coffee for you?"

"Huh? Oh, yeah. Sure." She held out the mug, straightened up, and rested her forearms on the table. "The day Nadine died. The SUV. The driver. He looked at me."

"What do you mean?"

"The driver rolled down the window and stared at me. I'll never forget those stalking-tiger blue eyes. They seemed to look right through me while I knelt by Nadine's lifeless body. I see them every night when I close my eyes."

"I rest my case."

Morgan shook her head. "After you met with Greg in New York, that's when you started investigating the connection between his clinics, missing homeless people, and organ trafficking?"

"Yes and no. It's all about timing. Greg caught me when I had finished up a grueling story. I was beat and needed a vacation. I'd seen a documentary a few months earlier, but when he and I met, I was too strung out to pay attention to what he was saying. Went on vacation down to the islands. Nothing but sun and sand."

"And women and booze, if I can edit your story."

"Cute. But what I really got was a look at poverty. And it started me thinking. If I was dirt poor, would I sell my kidney to take care of my family?"

"Good question."

"When I got back, I watched the DVD again and started digging. And the deeper I went, the more intriguing it was.

171

The documentary was riveting. People in third world countries routinely sell their kidneys to feed their families. They only get a small fraction of the actual price the recipients pay to the brokers. Kidneys are big business."

"Nadine was pitching this very idea to me a few weeks ago, as a way to give my story on the homeless teeth. There are laws against it."

"Here, maybe, but not in India, or China, or lots of other places. You know how Google searches tend to link to other related topics?"

"Yes. Costs me hours of time when one of those tangents hooks me. What did we do before Google?"

"I think they call them libraries. Anyway, I got hooked. I found another story about missing homeless people. Somewhere in the Midwest. White vans driving around in the middle of the night and—voilá—by morning a city's homeless population has diminished considerably. Where did they all go?"

"I saw that story too. But there wasn't anything in it about organ trafficking."

"Do some creative math. Put two and two together. The guy you and Nadine found in the woods was missing a kidney, right?"

She nodded, refilled both their coffee cups and took another piece of bacon off his plate.

"What if someone was willing to pay a lot of money to get a kidney, or piece of liver, or God knows which organ they needed to save their life? The waiting list for organ donation is years long. Many people die before their name ever gets to the top."

"Jeez, Jesse. If what you're saying is even remotely true… Shit!"

"What?"

"We met a guy at the new clinic here in town. Had coffee

with him a few days ago. He got really nervous when Nadine mentioned the very same idea to him. Left in a hurry."

"Interesting. Remember his name?"

"Yes." She thought for a moment as she sipped her coffee. "Colton…"

"Pollard." Their voices chimed in unison.

"I've been digging into him, too," said Jesse, finishing his omelette. "It was the only name Greg gave me."

"He told us he invested in viable business ventures. I'm guessing he invested in Elan Health Systems, which owns Asclepius Clinics, the free clinic that serves the homeless."

"From what I could find, he is the only investor in Elan. He owns it lock, stock and barrel."

"His company's name is Global Initiatives."

"I know." Jesse sipped his coffee. "Can I make a suggestion?" His wolfish grin returned with a vengeance.

"What?"

"Let's pool our resources. Work together. I'll be honest with you—"

"Trying something new?" She shot him a look that could thaw a glacier. "Why didn't you tell me what you were working on when we first met? Which I'm guessing was no accident."

"I didn't want to spook you, and you're right, our meeting was not an accident. I don't want to say I was following you or stalking you, but, okay, I admit it, I was following you. Greg gave me your name."

"That's how you knew my name. Wonderful," she snickered, not bothering to hide her sarcasm.

He loved how hard she was working to remain cool and collected. He could see the skin just above her cleavage blush, and her nipples poked through the soft blue sweater that clung a bit too tightly to tempting breasts. He was having trouble with his own thoughts wandering into uncharted territory, and the hard-on pressing against the zipper of his jeans wasn't helping.

Jesse groaned, got up, came around the table, and pushed into her side of the booth seat. "I want a Pulitzer out of this. We can do it together." He reached up and pushed a hair away from her eyes.

"Stop. Just stop." There was that intriguing blush above her cleavage again.

"What?"

"Flirting with me." She put her hand against his chest, pushing him back. "Planning to open a can of worms, are you?"

"Too late. Already opened...for me anyway." He nudged her chin and lifted her face toward him, his thumb rubbing across her lips. "You have very kissable lips. I'd really like to kiss you right now."

"Excuse me?"

"You heard me. And I'm thinking you're thinking the exact same thing."

"Like what?"

"You're wondering how it would be, if we kissed."

"There's presumptuous you again."

"Tell me I'm wrong. I dare you."

"In your dreams."

She retreated, wedging herself into the corner of the booth, folding her arms across her chest protectively, hands hugging her elbows tightly. Over the years, scars from the relationship mistakes she'd made had carved deep ruts into her psyche, grooves with sides higher than the Rocky Mountains. Scaling them to trust this man would be a monumental undertaking, one she was unsure she was ready to attempt.

"Yes. Ever since we met for coffee, I wake up smiling."

"And a pastry. Don't forget about the pastry. The brownie was delicious."

"Look, Morgan—"

"You…you. Be quiet and let me think."

"Think away."

"Stop grinning. I can't think straight with you grinning like that."

"Like what?" Jesse moved his body square with hers in the tight booth. Her hand found its way to his chest. For one long moment, she left her hand there, felt his heart beating. Then she pushed him away.

"It's inevitable, you know. The two of us," he said. "We're going to wind up making love. It can be now, or it can be later. But trust me, we are going to hook up."

"What makes you so sure?" She arched her eyebrow at him.

He took her hand and pulled her to him. His lips found hers, and a long, intimate kiss followed. His tongue pushed its way into her mouth, meeting barely any resistance. Then he let her go.

"The hard part's over. We've kissed. You let me know when you're ready to move to second base."

"That's not the first base I remember."

"I know. Thought I'd go for a home run right off the bat. You know, we're not spring chickens, not getting any younger. Why waste time?" His fingers brushed her cheek.

"Stop that. We have work to do."

"All work and no play…"

"Work now, play later."

"Promise?" Jesse gently lifted her hand to his lips. His eyes never left hers.

"If you're good." She tingled when his warm lips touched her skin.

"Oh, don't you worry your pretty little head. I am very, very good."

"Stop it."

Surprising feelings were emerging inside her, ones she knew better than to entertain with this rascal. She might have been a journalism major, but she recognized chemistry when she felt it. There was something birthing between them. Unexpected, unwanted, and deliciously inviting.

Jesse held up both hands, palms out, in surrender. "I'm not doing anything, but since I'm clearly upsetting you, I'll take myself back over there. I didn't realize I was so irresistible."

"You're not. I just can't think straight when you're this close." Morgan felt her insides trembling. She had to force herself to concentrate on what she was doing. Her body had other plans, as long-dormant sensations tingled inside her.

"It's a gift. My curse. My cross to bear." He slid out of the bench seat and moved back to the other side of the table.

"I'm game. We can try it."

"Making love?"

"No. Working together." Oh, God, she thought, this could get very complicated. "But only if we share the byline equally and alphabetically."

"Alphabetically means your name goes first." He thought for a moment and then smiled at her. "I can live with that."

"A Pulitzer with my name on it sounds mighty fine. Nadine would be very proud of me." She extended her right hand across the table.

CHAPTER 19

Sand Isle, Florida

"Okay, here's what I've got." Carolyn and Marco were staring at Brett's computer screen. "It looks like Desiree's daughter was adopted by someone in the military. The name is Rayburn, Major Thomas Rayburn. He was stationed at Arnold Air Force base in the 80s. Did some time at MacDill, then Aviano in Italy. Ended his career at Langley AFB in Virginia."

"I wouldn't mind being stationed at Aviano. Give me Italy," said Carolyn.

"Down, girl. You just want to go shopping. No need to travel all that way. You can shop the world online."

"Thanks, Brett. Shopping's not my thing. It's the food that interests me."

"Back on track, please," said Marco. "What else did you find, Brett?"

"Major Rayburn had a daughter named Darby. Married name Dratton. She's a veterinarian. Went to Virginia Tech. Lives on the Eastern Shore in a town I have no clue how to pronounce. Spelled W-a-c-h-a-p-r-e-a-g-u-e."

"Any family?"

"Husband. Died. Afghanistan. Was a pilot. Has a daughter. Brianna. And listen to this. In addition to her vet practice, she runs an animal sanctuary."

"That's cool," said Carolyn. "Don't know her, but I like her already."

"The odd thing is, I'm not the only one searching her records. Don't ask me how I know this, and I could be wrong—"

"You? Wrong? Surely you jest." Carolyn gave Brett's shoulder a little push.

"Sarcasm does not become you. As I was saying. I could be wrong, but I think someone else has been looking for Darby. I found a digital footprint showing her records were recently accessed electronically. Whoever it is, isn't using Tor, so I'm thinking he is not a skilled hacker like moi."

"There you go again," teased Carolyn, resting her hands on his shoulders while she read the information scrolling up on his computer screen.

"Do I want to know what Tor is?" Marco's dour expression broadcast his lack of interest in the intricacies of technology. He was truly a bottom-line man.

"Probably not," said Brett. "Encryption software. It encrypts at each level, and the data relay only goes to the next level in the chain. The user sees one level of information. Great tool for anonymous communication."

Brett could actually see Marco's eyes glaze over.

"Think of the layers of an onion. The receiver only gets one layer. The rest remains hidden."

"Harder to track?"

"Exactly," said Brett. "Much harder."

"Why didn't you just say that?" Marco shook his head and finished his coffee.

"Wonder who else is looking for her?" asked Carolyn.

"Finding out might tell us who Desiree wanted me to protect her daughter from."

"I think you're right," said Marco. "When we find out who's looking for Darby, we'll know what we have to do to protect her."

"Let me see if I can link to an IP address with a name and location attached. Whoever this is, he is using a proxy server, and bouncing off other servers. Could take a while."

"Do your thing." Marco headed for the door. "Keep me informed."

Eastern Shore, Virginia

The only direction he'd been given was to make no waves. Get the girl. Make her disappear—without fanfare, without hoopla, without a sound. How he did it was his choice.

This was his kind of job, and he was already salivating over his promised payoff. A cool half million. Someone wants her bad, he thought, licking his lips as he watched Darby go about her daily routine. He'd been watching her for the better part of a week, and her routine didn't vary.

Up at dawn, shower and dress, wake her daughter, get her dressed, fed, and onto the rainbow-colored bus to Little Horizons Day Care by seven thirty. A quick meeting with Ken Bennett, the man who runs her small animal sanctuary, and then she leaves for the veterinary clinic. Works until five, then heads home.

Her live-in nanny takes care of the household chores, cleans, cares for Brianna after school, and prepares dinner. Everyone eats together around six, and then they go their separate ways for the rest of the evening. On nice nights, she and Brianna take a short walk. Other nights, it's puzzles or games or TV. Get ready for bed, sleep, and repeat the next day.

The perfect storybook life, he thought while watching her through high-powered binoculars, as she sat on the front porch swing, licking an ice cream cone and laughing with Brianna.

"Wouldn't mind having her lick something for me," he said out loud to no one. He checked his watch. Tomorrow night was go night. Everything was timed down to the minute. He'd deliver the package, earn his money, and disappear.

Williamsburg, Virginia

Detective Adam Knight was out of his element.

Nothing—not the Army, not facing down bad guys, not working his way up the law enforcement ranks to detective—prepared him for dating. He felt a bead of perspiration trickle down his back when Dr. Debra McKenna walked into the restaurant. He almost didn't recognize her out of her scrubs, without her stethoscope around her neck. Dressed in a cream sweater that hugged her curves, tight jeans, and boots, she was even prettier. He felt his pulse quicken.

"Thanks for meeting me for dinner." Adam stood and pulled out a chair for her.

"Thanks for inviting me. I don't get much time off, and it's nice to be sitting across the table from a smiling, healthy face, not staring into the eyes of someone bracing for the bad news I usually have to deliver."

"I hope you like Italian. Giuseppe's is my local favorite."

"Works for me." Debra settled herself into her seat and smiled across the table at him. She opened the menu. "What's good?"

He felt a twinge in his chest and knew he was smiling back. "Just about everything. I usually go with the fish special. Love how the chef mixes all the flavors."

"Sounds good."

Knight watched her across the table. Her auburn hair shone like crisp autumn leaves kissed by sunlight, and fell below her shoulders, framing her face and making her blue eyes pop. Like so many redheads, she had a mass of light freckles that seemed to dance when she spoke, set off by a golden tan.

"Looks like you've spent some time in the sun this summer, and haven't been totally cooped up in the hospital."

Debra's arms were crossed in front of her chest. "Guess my freckles are out of control." Her fingertips went to her nose, and her face blossomed into a big smile. "I live across the street from the reservoir in Toano, and I love to kayak. I'm out there as often as I can be. Doesn't take much to haul a kayak into the water."

"You look great. What was the word you just used? Healthy. I suspect after a day in the ER getting out on the water must feel wonderful."

"It's calming, peaceful." She took a sip of water. "Do you kayak?"

"Done it a few times."

"Good. Maybe you can join me sometime. I've got two kayaks."

"Sounds like fun."

Dinner was a nice, easy affair, and time seemed to float by. Knight was struck by how easy Debra McKenna was to talk to, to be with. She laughed at his jokes, shared some of the crazy happenings in the ER, in exchange for him telling her about some of his most harrowing experiences.

"Uh, oh," said a tall man approaching their table, buffeting Knight on the shoulder. "Here's trouble. I didn't think they let people like you in here."

Knight stood and shook hands with the new arrival, then did the introductions. "Reggie, this is Debra McKenna. She's one of the ER doctors at Sentara. Reggie manages the not-so-busy Williamsburg Airport down by the winery."

"Busier lately than I've been in a long time." Reggie turned his attention to Debra. "Nice to meet you."

"So, they're keeping you busy and out of trouble?"

"Too busy to get into any trouble. Since old man Tremble forked over the money to lengthen the main runway, we've been getting all sorts of rich people landing their private jets. Tremble's the stingiest man you'll ever meet. Bet he still has his recess money."

"What made him do it?" Knight sensed Debra's discomfort right when the question left his mouth, and he regretted extending Reggie's time at the table.

"Business. He wants more business. And it's paying off for the cheapskate. Been seeing some beautiful flying machines. Wouldn't mind taking a spin in any one of them."

"I didn't know you had your pilot's license, Reggie."

"I don't," he laughed. "But I can appreciate beauty when I see it." He winked at Debra. "That's why Tremble spent the money to lengthen the runway. He wants to expand the airport's capabilities. Private aviation removes the hassles of flying commercial. We've even had a few medical transports popping in and out recently."

"Really?" Knight looked at Debra. "Doesn't seem like the normal, everyday type of aircraft to come here."

"Who knows? Gotta go. My friends are waiting for me. Nice meeting you." Reggie excused himself and moved off to join his group of eight at a long table in the back of the dining room.

"What's up?" said Debra. "I can almost see the wheels turning in your head."

"Sorry." He thought about it for a moment. "Medical transports are usually for emergencies, right?"

"Yes, or used by people with serious conditions who require specialized care their local hospitals and doctors can't provide."

"Just wondering." He refilled both of their wine glasses and ordered two cappuccinos when the server passed their table. "Do you think you could check and see if Sentara has ordered any flights?"

"I can ask around. As long as you don't need names. Names would be a breach of patient-doctor confidentiality."

"No. No names. I can get them if I need to through proper channels."

"What are you thinking?"

"Nothing specific. If someone was going to need a medical transport, I'd think the hospital would be the starting location."

"Makes sense, but remember, we aren't the only hospital in town. And doctors could schedule something out of their own offices, plus, the patient or the patient's family could do it."

"Interesting." He smiled at her across the table. "What can I say? Curiosity goes with the job. Hard to turn it off when I hear something that doesn't fit the usual pattern of activity, even when I'm off duty." Knight finished his wine and made a mental note, just as their dessert arrived, to check out who might be using a medical transport.

Rachel opened the door to find Jesse holding wine and flowers.

"Thanks so much for coming tonight. A good dinner and

some relaxing conversation is just what you need right now."

"I appreciate the invitation. I've heard so much about you. These are for you," he said, handing her a bouquet of Shasta daisies. "Sounds like your neighbors are having one hell of a party."

"Yes, it does," said Rachel, glancing down the street. "Come on in. These are so pretty. Thank you so much. Daisies are my favorite. How did you know?"

"I didn't, but based on everything Morgan has told me about you, I suspected you might enjoy them. Also brought some wine. Didn't know what we were having, so I brought both red and white."

"Thank you. Morgan and Daniel are in the kitchen. She's telling him about the story you're working on."

He heard them before he saw them. Voices raised in heated conversation.

"You little rebel, you. Watch what you're doing with that knife before you cut yourself, and we have to go to the twenty-four-hour clinic." Daniel kept half an eye on her while turning the steaks over and over in the marinade, making sure each one was fully coated in the garlic, olive oil and wine mix.

"Think about it," said Morgan, waving a paring knife in the air. "What if it is true? No one misses the homeless."

"You're serious." Rachel's expression and her frown broadcast her disbelief. Grabbing the scissors, she busied herself cutting the ends off the daisy stems and arranging Jesse's gift of flowers in a vase.

"You bet I am. They're invisible. Someone could easily snatch them off the streets and do whatever to them. So many are on drugs, or are alcoholics, or mentally unstable. They can't protect themselves."

They stopped arguing long enough for Morgan to introduce Jesse to Daniel. As they shook hands, Jesse could tell Daniel was sizing him up. The twinge in his gut told him he cared what Daniel thought of him more than he expected to, and wondered whether it was Daniel's cop side or his uncle side that was taking his measure.

Jesse took a deep breath and chimed in to get the conversation back to where it was before he entered the room. "We really don't know what we've got yet. There are a lot of loose ends in our story."

"The bottom line," said Morgan, "is that we have a huge homeless problem in this country. And, other than giving lip service to it, not too many people, with enough power to make change happen, are engaged enough to find a solution."

"We are a rich country. How do we allow this tragedy to continue?" asked Rachel.

"We elect self-serving politicians whose only concern, or rather their primary concern, is to get reelected. Homelessness is a great election-year issue, but it touches so many people in so many different ways, it's difficult to get your brain around and solve." Jesse felt himself flush, heard the anger fueling his words. "Not meaning to be too cynical here, but it's a rigged system. Our precious senators and representatives don't have time to implement solutions, because they're flying off on their latest junkets to study the mating habits of the dodo bird on an exotic island in the South Pacific, or some such nonsense."

"At taxpayer expense, of course," added Morgan.

"Of course," laughed Jesse, opening the red wine. "Who wants red?" Three hands went up, including Jesse's. Rachel asked for white. He filled four wine glasses and handed them out. "Why pay your own way when you can have hardworking taxpayers fund your vacations?"

"This can't be happening," said Rachel. "I mean, how is it possible?"

"It is happening," said Jesse, adamantly, "and it's possible because most average Americans are too busy working their asses off, taking care of their families, and trying to put food on the table. They're trusting that the politicians they send to Washington have their best interests at heart."

"That'll be the day," said Daniel. "You just said it. The only thing most politicians care about is winning the next election. Don't care what party they're from. They go in average citizens, altruistically wanting to serve, and come out millionaires and billionaires, clinging like vipers to their so-called seats. Remember when Scott Brown won Teddy Kennedy's seat? The Kennedy seat. Like the Kennedy family owned it."

"We're clearly onto something important. Throw in the long-shot chance that there may be a connection to black market organ trafficking and, wow, it's the story of the century." Jesse finished off his wine and headed for the sideboard to refill his glass and top off everyone else's.

"And we can only hope our efforts to expose what's really going on will produce results," said Morgan.

"Are you sure you want to do this?" asked Daniel. His expression telegraphed his displeasure at his niece's decision. "Nadine, and your friend Greg, were probably killed because of their involvement with this story. If you two keep digging—"

"I need to do this for Nadine's sake," she said, looking affectionately at her uncle. "I know you care about me and are worried. But she saw this story as my big break. More important than that, we have an opportunity to make a huge difference, blow the lid off of a cruel and inhumane practice, and help a lot of people."

Jesse raised his glass, and the others followed suit. "May our efforts to expose these bastards never waver."

"Enough! I'm hungry. Honey, get the steaks on the grill so we can eat," said Rachel.

CHAPTER 20

Morgan picked up Eli bright and early on another beautiful fall day. She turned off the engine on her Camry and looked over at her passenger.

"Thank you so much, Miss Morgan, for driving me over here, and for letting me give the clinic your phone number so they could contact me."

"It's my pleasure, Eli. Do you want me to go in with you to keep you company?"

"No, ma'am. I'll be fine."

"What exactly are the doctors planning to do?"

"Well," said Eli, dragging out the word while he searched for an answer. "They said they wanted to run some tests."

"Did they tell you what kind of tests?"

Eli averted his eyes and looked out the window.

"It's okay if you don't remember. And I don't mean to pry. It's really none of my business, but I want you to know that I'm here for you, that I care about you."

"I know that, Miss Morgan. I really do. You've been so nice to me all these months, bringing me food, letting me shower at your office." He picked at his cuticles. "To be honest, I don't remember what they said. I do remember they said they'll use what they learn from these tests to help me get better."

"That's all we want. For you to feel better."

"Then maybe I can get a job and begin to repay you for all your kindness."

"You just get well, Eli. I don't want anything more."

She leaned over and gave him a light peck on the cheek. "You have my cell number. When you're done, call me, and I'll come pick you up."

He got out of the car and slowly walked into the clinic, stopping briefly at the door to wave good-bye.

When he walked into the lobby a blast of cold air sent a chill down his spine. The temperature difference between the humidity outside and the lobby surprised him.

"You'll get used to it in a minute, honey," said a kind-looking gray-haired older woman behind the reception desk. She wore a flowered jacket over hot pink scrubs. There was no one else in the waiting area. "How can I help you?"

"I'm Eli. I'm here to see Dr. Edwards. He left a message with my friend Miss Morgan, because I don't have a phone. And when I called him back, he said he wanted to run some more tests."

She smiled warmly at him. "Let me check my roster of incoming patients. It's going to be a busy day, and I want to make sure I get y'all checked in and settled in your room before the rush."

"Thank you kindly, ma'am."

"Here you are. Eli Jackson. I see you're here for some tests. And that you'll be staying with us for a few days."

"A few days? Dr. Edwards didn't say anything about that."

"Yes, dear. That's what my records say. And my records are always right." She stood up and came around the counter, gently slipping her arm through his.

"Yes, ma'am."

"Have you eaten today? Some of the tests require a blood sample, and you need to have fasted for ten hours."

"Yes, ma'am. Miss Morgan bought me breakfast before she dropped me off."

"Miss Morgan? Is she related to you?"

"No, ma'am. I don't have me any family. It's just me. Miss Morgan is a friend."

"Okay. Let's get you settled. Dr. Edwards will be here soon. You may have to stay another day, because some of the tests can't be done for ten hours after you eat."

"I'm so sorry, ma'am. I didn't know."

"Not a problem." She patted his arm. "Everything will be just fine. You'll see."

Eli walked next to her to the double doors where a sign read Authorized Personnel Only. She swiped her ID badge in front of a silver plate and the doors swooshed open. He heard a loud click after the doors swooshed shut behind him. Slowly, they made their way down one corridor and then another.

"Wow. All these halls look alike. I'm sure I'd get lost here if you weren't with me."

"We won't let you get lost, honey. Don't you worry. We're here to help you."

One more ID swipe through another locked door brought them into a room with six beds. She stopped at the one with a number two hanging down from the ceiling.

"Here we are, Eli. Your home away from home for the next few days."

She slid a plaid curtain out from the back wall on one side of his bed and then another on the other side of the bed, creating a small, somewhat private alcove.

"What we need you to do now is get comfy. Here's a gown to put on with the opening in the back. You can put your clothes in this cubbyhole. If you need to use the restroom, it's just past the number six, over there, hanging from the ceiling. Do you see it?"

"Yes, ma'am. I surely do."

"Splendid. You go ahead and get comfy, and I'll be back in a few minutes."

Morgan watched Eli go through the door into the clinic. She felt a sharp pain shoot through her jaw. She opened and closed her mouth a few times to relieve her knotted jaw muscles.

Something didn't seem right to her. When she first brought Eli to the clinic, they had decided to use her cell number as his contact information. When she received a call for him yesterday, she let him use her cell phone so he could return the call and find out what they learned from the original set of tests. Eli told her they wanted to run more tests. He was so excited. She didn't have the heart to push her questions and doubts on him. But they were there.

She looked around the deserted parking lot. It was nine a.m., and there were only three other cars in the clinic's lot. A beat-up white Chevy that had to be a dozen years old, with part of its bumper held on with duct tape, a silver mini-van with decals of a man, woman, three kids, a dog and a cat on the back window, and a pea-green Kia. No Mercedes. No Lexus. No BMW.

Was there a doctor in the house?

Something didn't feel right. She pulled out her cell phone, drove past each car and snapped a photo of each license plate.

She wished Eli could remember what type of tests the doctor said he was going to run. Beyond that, Eli's problems were mental, not physical. He'd call when he was done. She needed something to do in the meantime to hold back the worry.

"Got a sec, Uncle Daniel?" Morgan stood on the deck watching Daniel weed a small flower bed. "Rachel said I'd find you back here."

"For you, always. And what I'm doing isn't half as important as talking to you. Weeds grow. We pull them. More grow. Vicious cycle."

"Kind of how I feel about dusting. A thankless job." She waited while he brushed off his pants and joined her on the deck.

"I need an objective second opinion about the information I've been finding on Elan."

"Let's go into my office. Looks like we're going to need space to spread out."

Morgan followed him into the house, her arms loaded down with papers and a large document tube. He took the tray of lemonade Rachel had waiting for them on the kitchen counter and headed down the hall.

"The look on your face tells me you found something interesting." He poured lemonade for both of them. "Show me what you've got."

He smiled at his niece, who really was more like a second cousin once removed, from a side of the family his mother didn't exactly enjoy. Ah, families. You can pick your friends, but you're stuck with your family. Their reunion had been one more pleasant surprise since he moved to Williamsburg. She chose to use the uncle label, and if it made her feel comfortable, then who was he to object?

"Coincidences. I'm not screaming conspiracy here, but you know what they say—what *you* always say—about coincidences." She put down the papers and pulled a large sheet of white craft paper from the tube.

"Let's hang it on the white board with these magnets."

The two worked together to get the unwieldy visual unrolled and hung up. They stepped back, shoulder to shoulder, Daniel rubbing his chin as he looked at a map of the United States with red, blue and yellow dots in different places.

"Colorful." He handed her a glass of lemonade. "Explain please."

"For my article on homelessness, I started mapping cities that had large homeless populations, mostly in warmer climates. Those are the red dots. When I got sidetracked by news clippings of cities where homeless had gone missing, I decided to map those with yellow dots. Remember Jesse and I mentioned this at dinner."

"Yeah. I've been wondering about that. Even made a few calls after you brought it up, to see what the Bureau might have on the subject."

"Thanks, Uncle Daniel." She put her glass of lemonade down and went to her chart. "Bob, my editor, told me to cover the Elan Clinic grand opening and write a puff piece about it. I was reading through their brochures." She paused and looked at her uncle to see if he was showing signs on interest.

"Okay." Daniel strung out the word in a sing-songy manner. "And? Don't keep me in suspense."

"It was all pretty random at first. Different states. Different cities. Different causes of death. Nothing to really connect them. Until I added the blue dots for the Elan Clinic locations. The yellow and blue dots... They overlap."

Daniel took a step closer to the map. And Morgan watched his face for any sign that she might be onto something.

Not wanting to leave anything to chance, she added, "The cities where homeless have been reported missing, and where some have later shown up dead, are the same cities where Elan has clinics, give or take fifty miles." She remained silent for a few minutes to give him time to process what she was saying, what he was seeing. "What do you think? Am I on to something?"

"You may be, but it's too soon to draw any conclusions from what you've found so far."

"Okay, but you think I may be onto something, right?"

His silent nod gave her hope, hope that she was onto the story of a lifetime. Her next step would tell.

"Thank you for meeting me, Mr. Pollard." Morgan stood and shook his hand as he joined her at the table. It was after one, and the lunch crowd at Opus 9 had thinned considerably.

"Actually, I was surprised to get your call. Pleasantly surprised, I might add. And please, call me Colton."

"Of course, Colton. Why were you surprised?"

"You've been under a lot of stress lately. The tragic loss of two of your friends coming so close together as they did. I thought you'd be taking some time off to regroup."

"How did you know that Greg and I were friends?"

"I'm not sure. He might have mentioned you in passing." He kept his eyes pinned to hers as he answered her question. "And Mrs. Steiner-Greene's death was in the newspaper."

"I miss her terribly. Diving into my work helps ease my grief."

"Concentrating on work does push the sadness to the back of your mind for a few hours." Colton accepted a menu from the server who had come to the table.

"Thank you." Morgan smiled at the server when he handed her a menu. "I know Nadine wouldn't have wanted me to do anything less. And Greg's death was so sudden. We were old friends, but it wasn't like we saw each other very often."

They both ordered glasses of Chardonnay and selected the crab cake special for lunch. Morgan put her reading glasses back in her purse.

"It's been a difficult time for both of us." She dropped her napkin into her lap.

"What do you mean?"

"Well, Greg was the CEO of Elan Health Systems."

"Greg was a loyal member of the Elan family, and I'm sure he will be sorely missed."

"And you're more than a... What did you call it? An entrepreneurial investor. Elan is one of your companies, isn't it? That's why you were at the open house last week. You *are* Elan."

Colton took a sip of wine and smiled. "I see you've been checking up on me."

"Not on purpose, I can assure you. I'm working on a story, and your name came up in my research. I'm sure Greg's death has put a damper on the opening of the new Elan clinic here."

"A little, but Tiffany Stamos came to the rescue. She's a trooper. I don't know what they would have done without her."

"I was very impressed with her when I interviewed her for the story the *Beacon* asked me to write about the grand opening."

"So was I when I met her. That's why I suggested the Elan team hire her. Stole her away from the cruise line she was working for."

The waiter brought their lunches, refreshed their wine, and wished them a pleasant meal.

Colton reached for the salt and said, "I'm curious, Morgan. You said my name came up in your research. What kind of story are you working on?"

"Like I mentioned when we had coffee, I've been researching homelessness. A homeless man died here a few weeks ago." She looked at Colton to see if he had any reaction.

"How awful."

"Yes. We, Nadine and I, found him in the woods. By the time they got him to the hospital, there was nothing they could do to save him."

"How very upsetting that must have been for you. Yet another death touching you so closely."

"I didn't know him. But I have made friends with a homeless man, Eli, who has taken up squatting residence outside the Food King, across from my office at the *Beacon*. He suffers from PTSD, and I've been trying to help him."

"That's very kind of you. Most people pass by the homeless without a glance. They're invisible."

"Not to me, especially since I've gotten to know Eli." Morgan dabbed her mouth with her napkin. "In fact, he's been taking advantage of the free services of the Asclepius Clinic part of Elan. I dropped him off there this morning."

Disappointed at the lack of visible reaction to her comment, she continued. "The doctors want to run more tests. I can't help but wonder what that's about."

"They're trying to help him. You said it yourself."

"Yes. And that's why I wanted to have lunch with you. You know how one thing leads to another when you're doing research. I have so many questions about the free clinic and the services you're offering. Since you're the top guy, and you're in town, and we met at the open house, I didn't think you'd mind."

"Of course not. Ask away. What would you like to know?"

"Well—." She hesitated and looked down at her plate, dragging her fork through her garlic mashed potatoes. "I'm thinking there's a connection between the untimely deaths of homeless people in different parts of the country and organ trafficking."

She stopped talking and waited for him to fill the silence. Nothing. She took a sip of her wine and plowed on.

"According to the news articles I've read, when many of these people were autopsied, they were missing a kidney. A few were missing a section of their liver." As she spoke the last few words, she raised her eyes and locked onto his.

Nothing. Not a blink. Not a flinch. Not a movement.

"How awful. And if there is merit to your story, I'm sure the authorities will be very interested." Colton finished his last French fry, dredging it slowly through the ketchup on his plate. "But I don't see how I can help you."

"I'm thinking you might be able to give me some insight into how such a thing could happen. Your business sense could help me put a more objective spin on what I'm learning. Street people dying missing a kidney. It's all so upsetting." She broke off a piece of bread from the basket and took her time buttering it.

"I was wondering if—and I know it's a lot to ask—but I was wondering if maybe you could play the what-if game with me. It's what Nadine and I used to do to flesh out stories. And now I'm working on this story, and she's gone, and I've got no one to play with. You're involved with these clinics, so you must know something about clinic operations."

"Unfortunately, my role is more of a silent investor. I don't get involved in the day-to-day operations of any of my businesses."

"Oh." She tried not to overdo her faux disappointment. "I was so hoping you could help me. There is all this research swirling around in my head." She made a swirling motion with her finger to emphasize the point. "Research on the homeless. Research on the black market sale of organs. Did you know kidneys were the most popular organ sold on the black market?"

"No, I didn't know that." Colton reached for his water and eyed her over the top edge of the glass.

"I guess it goes on all the time in countries like India and China. And lately the authorities have been uncovering more organ trafficking operations here in the US. My Uncle Daniel, who's retired NYPD, and is on a special task force with the FBI, is looking into these sorts of things."

"Well, then, he's your expert. You should ask him your questions."

"I have, and I do. But his head is all detective. He knows nothing about business. I thought, with your connection to Elan, and your business savvy, you might be able to help too." Morgan sipped her wine. Colton remained silent.

"One interesting thing I did was track where the dead street people have been found. You know, on a map with different color dots.

"How enterprising. Did you notice a pattern?"

"Yes, as a matter of fact I did. But only because I was also putting the finishing touches on the story about the Elan and Asclepius Clinic operations for the paper. My editor, Bob, doesn't think my writing skills are good for anything but fluff pieces. This story is going to be my big break."

"I see."

"Which is why it's so important to me. And why I need all the help I can get." Morgan put her fork down on her plate and pushed it away. "Anyway, there I was, listing where your clinics are located for one story when I suddenly realized that many of your clinics were close to where the homeless bodies had appeared. So I got more dots, and used yellow for the dead homeless people and blue for your clinic locations."

Again, Morgan stopped talking, waiting for, hoping for, some reaction.

Nothing.

She continued. "It was amazing. The proximity of your clinics to these deaths was almost a perfect match."

"That's incredible. Are you saying you think there is a connection between the deaths of homeless people and the Asclepius Clinics?"

"I guess I am."

"Seriously?" He sounded slightly agitated now. "That is one incredible leap. You can't believe the Asclepius Clinic has anything to do with those deaths. Or the black market sale of organs."

He reached for his wine glass, touching it to his lips.

"This is very concerning." He finished his wine, but kept the empty glass in his hand. "If Elan has people operating in the shadows, doing anything like what you are implying…" He shook his head and put his wine glass down. Leaning in and looking her straight in the eye, he asked, "Do you have any concrete evidence to back up what you're saying?"

"Nothing specific at this point."

"That's good to know." He cleared his throat and leaned back in his chair. "The Elan operation is a thriving business enterprise, on the cutting edge of health care reforms. Doing something so illegal…so awful…so immoral, doesn't fit the good work they do. What would be their motivation for doing such horrendous things?"

"I don't know. My uncle says when he was a New York detective trying to solve a murder case, he always looked to the seven deadly sins for motivations. I think the one that fits best here is greed."

"That would fit. There is a lot of money flowing in and out of health care these days." He wiped his mouth with his napkin and laid it on his empty plate. "I must say, Morgan, all of this is very disconcerting. If any of what you're saying turns out to be true...well... I must call my legal team immediately to extricate myself from any and all dealings with Elan and Asclepius."

"Then you really know nothing about the internal operations of the new clinic that opened here?" She couldn't believe he was still denying his complicity. His calm outward demeanor clashed with what she saw happening in his eyes. His pupils were dilating, becoming huge black pools across the table.

He's working hard to stay calm.

"No. I'm sorry I can't be of more help."

She ran her index finger around the rim of her wine glass. "Do you know someone I can talk to at the clinic who might be able to shed some light on what I've found?"

"You know, I really don't." He made a show of looking at his watch. "And I am afraid I must be going. I've got another appointment this afternoon with a banker. You know how bankers are. Prompt, very formal people. I don't want to be late. But please stay and finish your wine." He signaled the server for the check.

"Please, my treat," said Morgan, slightly giddy that she had finally gotten a rise out of him. "After all, I invited you to lunch. And if you do think of anything that might help me, please give me a call." She held out her card as she stood to shake his hand.

"Thank you. It isn't often I have a beautiful woman buy me lunch." He pocketed her card without looking at it. "If anything comes to mind, I'll be sure to call."

"Enjoy your meeting." She remained standing while he left the restaurant. Watching through the window, she saw his limo pull up to the curb. He was talking on his cell, but jumped in the back, not waiting for the driver to open the door.

She wondered. Was he a man hurrying to his next meeting, or hurrying to make a fast escape from this one?

CHAPTER 21

It had been a long day. Morgan dreaded telling Jesse about her lunch with Colton Pollard, but since they had agreed to partner on the story, she knew she had to fess up. They declined her aunt's offer to come for dinner again, and stopped for Chinese takeout on the way back to Morgan's place. The skies opened up, and it started to pour just as they pulled into her garage.

"Nice storm," said Morgan as thunder boomed and lightning lit up the darkening sky. She kicked off her shoes. "My life is usually very dull. And I like it that way. I'm not cut out for this cloak and dagger stuff."

"What do you mean? Most of what we've found so far is circumstantial at best." He took two glasses out of the cupboard and poured the wine.

"About that." She took a long drink of wine, stalling while she got out plates and set the table. Jesse busied himself opening the little white food containers.

"About what?"

"You're not going to like this, but after I dropped Eli off at the clinic this morning, something just didn't feel right."

"Such as?"

"The cars in the parking lot, for one thing. There weren't

201

enough of them, and they were all wrong. None were cars a doctor would drive."

She turned too fast, they bumped together in the small space between her kitchen sink and island. Her wine sloshed over the edge of her glass onto the floor. Grabbing paper towels she bent down to wipe it up.

Jesse knelt to help her, just as she straightened and they bumped. He stayed on his knees for a moment, then got awkwardly to his feet and took the dirty towels out of her hands. He turned away, tossed the dirty towels in the garbage, and finished his wine.

"Thirsty?"

"Just on edge," he said. "That's all. The wine will relax me, help me think."

"It makes me sleepy. We'd better eat or I'll fall asleep in my General Tso's chicken."

They sat across from each other at the small kitchen table and dug in.

"Okay, what did you do after you dropped Eli off that I'm not going to like?"

Time's up. Can't delay the inevitable.

"I called Colton Pollard and invited him to lunch."

"You didn't."

"I did. And I told him my theory. What we've been working on. I didn't mention you at all, but I did talk about the colored dots on the map I made, and about the missing homeless, and the bodies showing up with missing parts near Elan clinic sites."

"You're just full of surprises," said Jesse, refilling her wine glass.

She caught the flash of anger in his eyes. "Don't be angry with me. We know there's a connection. You said it yourself. I just took the bull by the horns and went for the gold."

"You're mixing your metaphors." He turned away briefly, and his eyes were blazing when he looked at her again. "Greg was really frightened of him, and look what happened to him. He's dead. And let's not forget about Nadine's death. I'd bet money he had something to do with it. Maybe even ordered the hit. And from all you've described, it was definitely a hit. If Pollard's as involved in these deaths and what's happening with the homeless as we think he is, what's going to keep him from coming after you?"

He shook his head, then added quietly, "I think you just painted a giant bull's-eye on your back."

Morgan sat quietly for a minute. "I'm sorry. One thing led to another. After I dropped Eli off at the clinic, and spoke to my uncle, I don't know what happened to me. I got caught up in everything, and I made the call inviting Pollard to lunch. I didn't expect him to accept, and when he did, I was stuck."

"You could have called me to join you."

"I thought about that, but figured I might have a better chance of getting a rise out of him by myself. Using my feminine charms and all." The corners of her mouth curved up.

"You're safe. That's all that matters." He slid his hand across the table and touched hers. "We know there's a connection. We've just got to find the key to open the floodgates."

"Now who's mixing metaphors? Do you forgive me? I know we're in this together, and I was always planning to tell you. Chalk it up to me idolizing Christiane Amanpour, the fearless female reporter, who goes wherever she needs to go, wearing a shmata on her head, and does whatever she needs to do, to get the story."

"You're kidding, right? She's not half as good as Nadine was."

"I know. But still, I wanted to be her when I first started journalism school. Nadine used to kid me about it all the time."

"Okay, you're forgiven. But let's not have a next time."

"Agreed." She raised her wine glass to his.

"Eat. Your food is getting cold."

The sounds of two hungry people devouring dinner combined with the light dinner music playing on the radio.

"Good station. Or did we hit it at the right time?"

"No. WMBG 740 plays great music all the time. Good mix of oldies and new stuff. Nothing hard, and no rap."

Morgan started to clear the table and saw Jesse get up. *Ah, housebroken. He's going to help me.* He picked up their plates and took them to the sink. Watching him scraping food residue into the garbage, she found herself paying attention to his body. He was taller than she, though not too much taller. His lean, athletic physique told her he cared about his health and appearance. The man had muscles. He worked out. How comfortable he seemed in her home.

The Four Seasons song "December 1963" came on the radio and Jesse pumped up the volume.

"I love this song. Saw Jersey Boys when it toured here a few years ago."

"Can you Lindy?" Jesse asked from behind her before taking her hand and twirling her around. She found herself in his embrace.

"I think so," she said, following his lead.

He was whirling her and twirling her.

"You've got these moves down."

"Always loved to dance, and there's something about doing the Lindy that speaks to me. A throwback, for sure. Four Seasons music gets me moving."

She was in his arms, strong arms, arms that made her feel safe for the first time in weeks. Dancing with him was fun.

And she needed a dose of fun badly. The tension drained from her shoulders and Morgan felt herself relax.

Jesse whirled her around one last time just as the song ended. The dance in his head didn't. It was easy to forget all the craziness going on when he was with her, when he held her. Like he did now. And for the moment, he didn't want to let her go. She smelled of lavender and lace, roses and raspberries.

He folded her into his arms, bent his head slightly and took her lips, covered them with his mouth, ready to retreat if he felt the slightest hesitation on her part. What he felt was a woman melting into his arms.

And it felt right, like he was home.

Soft, gentle, warm, lips like honey sugar spun by the Gods. "Hmm...nice."

She broke their embrace and looked at him, gasping for air.

"I-I" she stared up at him, watery-eyed. "I don't know what to say. With everything that's been going on, I..."

He touched a fingertip to her lips and drew her back to him. "Shhh. Nothing to say. Just enjoy the moment." And he kissed her again. Stronger now, more probing.

When they parted, he sighed. "I don't know, call me crazy, but there is something about you that...that...well."

He slid his lips along her cheek to her mouth. At the slightest nudge of his tongue she opened to receive him. Her arms found their way around his neck, and she gave in willingly to his kiss.

After tracing the line of her neck with kisses, he paused to nibble behind her ear. Morgan tilted her head back, and Jesse's lips found their way to the ultra-sensitive hollow in the middle of her collarbone. A moan escaped her.

When they parted, Morgan gazed at him, her eyebrows

knitted, her face flushed. The pulse in her neck was skittering like a pebble thrown across a pond.

Jesse savored her, inhaling deeply, taking in every ounce of her.

"Maybe you should go," she said, a lump rising in her throat "before—"

"Before what?"

"Before—" Her voice trailed off.

A sudden crack of thunder, a scream pierced the air, and Morgan leapt into his arms.

"Who screamed?"

"You did," said Jesse pulling her close. "Don't worry. You're safe."

Morgan pushed herself out of his embrace, walked over to the plantation shutters, looked out into the rainy street, and then angled them downward.

"You like fixing things, don't you? Making wrongs right. Making everything all better."

"Yeah, that's me. Mr. Fix It. I hate when scum get away with stuff common folks, like you and me, would get twenty years' hard time for."

"I could see that in your articles. You're David to the world's Goliaths. But I'm not sure you can fix whatever is going on here."

"Never know until you try." He was in front of her, cupped her face in his hands, and gazed into her eyes with a heartfelt sigh. He knew it wasn't the right moment to take whatever was sparking between them any further.

Timing is everything.

"Right now, let me try to calm your nerves. Got any green tea?"

"More wine sounds better."

"Green tea to soothe. You're stimulated enough. If you don't have any, I've got some in my backpack."

206

"You carry around green tea?"

"Yes. Never know when I'm going to need to calm down. Tea works for me. Besides we just had Chinese. It's an unwritten rule. We've got to have tea."

He filled the teapot and set the water to boil. How much space do I give her, he wondered, watching her flinch at every boom of thunder.

"Some storm." Flashes of lightning revealed frayed nerves and the tension on her face.

"You've been keeping me rather busy lately," said the voice on the other end of the line. "Do you know what time it is?"

"Losing a bit of sleep at the rates you charge is the least of your concerns. I'm sure you're enjoying spending the fruits of your labors."

"Definitely. However, too many occurrences can get us—me—noticed."

"One last assignment, and I'll be on my way. You'll never hear from me again."

"Sad. You've been a very good client."

"Mr. Kent, I'm confident Greenleaf Investments will find another client with equally interesting and challenging needs, and equally deep pockets."

Colton gave Kent the target and ended the call. His head dropped against the headrest of his rental car which was parked in the lot adjacent to the *Beacon's* offices. Through the trees, he could see Morgan's car.

He'd been watching her all night, saw her come home with a man, stood in the rain and watched through the kitchen window while they ate their cute little Chinese takeout and danced in the living room. He hadn't expected to see her friend leave, figured he was there for the night, but many of his recent expectations had not materialized as planned.

He followed her to work. He knew he shouldn't have, but she was getting too close for comfort with her digging. She had become a problem, one that needed to be handled. And until his handler arrived, he needed to keep tabs on her comings and goings.

CHAPTER 22

Eastern Shore, Virginia

"Dr. Dratton," a sleepy voice said into the receiver. She rubbed her tired eyes so she could see the red digital readout on the clock. Three o'clock.

"Dr. Darby. Are you there? You gotta come quick. It's caught in the rocks. I'm sure it's got a broken leg. It's neighing in pain."

"Slow down. Who is this?"

"Dr. Darby. I didn't know who else to call. You gotta come. I'm at the beach just off Main Street by the marina. Please, Dr. Darby. I know it's early, but she's in pain. I can tell."

With that, the line went dead. To Dr. Darby Dratton, one of three local vets who rotated being on call for after-hours emergencies, neighing translated to a horse.

"What's a wild horse doing down by the beach? They usually don't roam this far south."

Rolling her legs off the bed, Darby reached for her jeans. A huge yawn caught her, and she stopped to stretch her arms behind her back. Her dedication to furry critters was so strong, she didn't think twice about going out in the middle of the night to help. She put on socks and UGGS, and buttoned a flannel shirt over her T-shirt, secured her long, honey blond hair in a ponytail, and took a quick glance in the mirror.

"Not classy, but at three in the morning, who cares?" she said to her reflection. "Damn it, why does this shit always happen when it's my night to be on call? Never happens to Tony or Dennis when it's their turn." Casting her eyes upward, "Next time, God, could you pick someone else's on-call night to have an animal be in trouble?"

Darby peeked into Brianna's room. Her sweet bundle of love was curled up, sound asleep, with Snoodles, her raggedy stuffed dog, firmly tucked under her arm. Pink shadows danced across the ceiling from her Princess Ariel nightlight. Darby tiptoed to her bedside, adjusted the covers, and lightly kissed her daughter's forehead.

When she got down to the kitchen, she scribbled a note for Ashley, her college student slash nanny slash housekeeper, saying she'd gotten a call that an animal was in trouble at the beach, and she'd be back in a few hours. No point waking her at this ungodly hour. She made two Keurig pods of coffee and poured them into her Virginia Tech Tervis mug. Two packets of Splenda and a shot of half and half, had her morning hit of caffeine tasting just the way she liked it. After taping the note to the refrigerator, Darby grabbed her phone and her medical bag and ran out the door.

The cold breath of morning seeped into her bones. She pulled her jacket closed, zipped it to her chin, and wrapped her scarf around her neck. When she turned the key, the engine of her Jeep Grand Cherokee roared to life, and she drove down her long driveway and out onto Route 13. Quickly, but carefully, she drove through deserted streets of Wachapreague and headed north out to the small community beach. A mist dampened her windshield when she neared the water and she flipped on her wipers to clear the glass, noting the arc of dirt bordering the now-cleared windshield.

Darby was a no-nonsense, stubborn-as-a mule, tough-as-nails Air Force brat, raised by military parents serving their country across three continents. Putting down roots had no meaning for her. Neither did long-term relationships. With two major exceptions. A minor miscalculation before her hubby left for Iraq five years ago produced the best thing that ever happened to her, a daughter, Brianna. Her daughter and the animals in her care meant the world to her. They were her life, her very breath. And the only things that could get her out of a warm bed on a cold morning.

She pulled into an empty lot by the marina in record time and cut the engine. No other cars in sight.

Curious.

The caller said she'd been walking along the beach when she stumbled over the poor creature. Why anyone would be walking along the beach in the dark never crossed Darby's mind until now. Questions popped into her head, disconcerting questions that caused goose bumps. Where was the caller's car? There aren't any homes for miles. Darby pushed the questions away, focused instead on the job ahead of her, saving a helpless animal or, if need be, putting it out of its misery.

The moon, veiled by a thin wisp of clouds, cast a silvery path out across the ocean. She could hear surf lapping against the floating docks. Carefully stepping between the rocks, she walked down to the shoreline. The beach was as deserted as the parking lot and the roads had been. *Someone's messing with me.* Nothing visible as far as she could see in both directions. But the female caller had sounded frantic. It was one of the wild horses, and the caller said she could see movement, so it wasn't dead. Dr. Darby, she said, you have to come quick.

Thinking about it now, Darby knew that most, if not all, of the wild horses were farther north, on Chincoteague Island. She hadn't really stopped to consider that when she got the call. After chalking it up to a cruel hoax, Darby's skin prickled as her safety concerns resurfaced. She quickened her pace back to her Jeep.

When she got back to her Jeep, she let out a breath she didn't realize she was holding and took one last look around. Just as she touched the door handle, a searing pain charged through her body, like someone holding a hot iron to the small of her back. Her blood-curdling scream awoke the heavens. Her body went rigid. Then her knees buckled, and she went down.

A black panel truck appeared out of nowhere. A man dressed in all black hopped out and joined his buddy, who had been lying prone on the ground about twenty feet from Darby's Jeep. One hoisted her over his shoulder in a classic fireman's carry, while the other opened the back cargo doors. It was over almost before it began. Darby Dratton was gone.

Somewhere

She opened her eyes. Blurry images surrounded her. An intermittent bleep broke the room's silence.

Where am I? What's happening?

A foggy haze shrouded her thoughts.

She remembered answering a call to help a wounded animal: her job, her avocation, her life. And in return, she found herself plunged into a surreal hell.

Darby pushed herself to move. Her body refused to respond. Her arms wouldn't move, nor her legs, when she tried to get up. She looked down at her wrists and feet to find straps held them fast.

She moved her eyes from side to side, trying to make sense of her surroundings. A soft green light just above her head cast shadows around her. Its source? A hospital-type heart monitor recording the bleeping image of a heartbeat. Slowly she realized she was watching her own heartbeat. Her shirt and jeans were gone, replaced with a hospital gown.

Was I in an accident?

Her tongue ran across dry lips. Gasping for breaths, she strained against her bonds. Pungent antiseptic smells hit as she sucked in air. Bleach. Disinfectant. She swallowed hard, and did a body scan like her yoga instructor taught her. Starting at her feet, she mentally moved up her body—toes...ankles...knees...stomach...chest...neck...head.

Nothing hurts except my throbbing head.

More images in the room came into focus. Yes, this was a hospital room, and she was lying on an examination table. There was an IV attached to the back of her hand. She could see the slow drip of fluid entering her through the tubing.

Adrenalin fed her rising fear, her heart racing as she fought to breathe through her increasing panic. Blood pumped through her veins, her pulse increasing. She watched the numbers climb on the monitor. One twenty. One thirty. One forty.

Calm down, Darby. Calm down.

She slammed her eyes closed and started to count, taking a slow inhale with each odd number and a full exhale with each even number.

Five...six...seven...eight...nine...ten...

When she opened them again, a muffled scream escaped her. Nothing had changed. Her eyes darted around the room.

The voice inside her head cooed gently.

Calm down so you can think.

Turning her head to the left, she realized she was not alone. A stout woman was wiping down the counter, oblivious to her distress.

"Excuse me. Ma'am. Can you help me?"

No response.

She raised her voice and she repeated her request for help. Then she saw the ear buds, thin white wires running into the woman's smock pocket. Music was shutting out everything else.

"Ma'am," she screamed, using all the air her constricted lungs could hold.

Darby saw her turn.

"You're awake."

She was older, gray-haired, portly, breasts like one huge pillow, giving Darby the impression of an elderly aunt.

"That's good. We weren't sure how long you'd be out." The woman moved to her bedside and busied herself checking the IV connections, taking Darby's vitals, and making notes into an iPad. "I'm Nurse Vivian. You're important to us, and we've been monitoring your progress carefully."

"Where am I? What happened?"

"Oh, honey, I'm sure you have lots of questions. And the doctor will answer all of them in due time. For right now, you just try to relax. Okay, sweetie?"

Darby could hear Vivian humming.

"Why am I tied down?"

"We've restrained you so you can't hurt yourself if you try to get up."

Prisoners get restrained. People held against their will get restrained.

"What time is it?"

"It's just about noon, hon," she said looking at her watch. "You've been asleep for a few hours. Do you need to use the bathroom?"

"Yes." If she could just get untied, get to her feet, maybe she could run.

"Well, you can't use the actual bathroom." Smiling, she picked up a white plastic bedpan and came to the side of the bed. "I'll help you lift up your bottom so I can slide the bedpan underneath you."

Darby struggled to gain control of her muscles.

"You're going to have to do a little better than this, dear. Come on. Lift up. There you go."

Vivian slipped her hand in the space between Darby and the bed, pushed up and slid the bedpan into place.

Darby fixed her eyes on the woman. *How can I get this kind-looking person to help me? What will it take? What do I need to say to turn her from foe to friend?* As much as she tried to resist it, tears rolled down her cheeks.

"Please help me. I don't know what I'm doing here. Where I am? Help me."

Her pleas fell on deaf ears.

"It's okay, honey. There, there. You'll be fine. The doctors are going to take good care of you."

"What doctors? Where am I hurt? I don't feel any pain."

"All done?" asked Vivian, ignoring her questions. She slid the pan out from under her. "Not much there, but I'm sure you're more comfortable now. You just rest. I'll be back in a bit."

"No. Please! Don't leave me."

Too late. Vivian was gone. And Darby was alone—alone

with her thoughts, alone with her fears, alone with her prayers.

Private Island, Florida Keys

"Talk to me. What have you got?" Moss answered his cell, and his breath caught in his throat.

"She's gone."

"What do you mean she's gone?" Time slowed. *This can't be happening. All my precautions gone to shit.*

"Not sure how or where. Wasn't here this morning when I went to check in for morning rounds. Ashley, she's the nanny, found a note taped to the refrigerator. Said she got a call about a hurt horse and would be back soon."

"Did you check the video?"

"Next on my list. Wanted you to know first."

"Do it. Then call me back. I'm on my way."

Moss went berserk. Beyond crazy. Rage pumped through his veins and fueled his anger. He threw his coffee cup against the far wall with a resounding crash, splashing its dark brown contents in a Rorschach pattern on the cream-colored paint.

I promised Dawn I'd protect her. I promised. Shit. How did this happen?

Walking in circles around his bedroom he dragged his hands across his bald head and down his face. He knew. As sure as he had breath in his body, he knew Hayden was behind Darby's disappearance.

How did he find her?

Moss headed into the bathroom and splashed cold water on his face. Lifting his head, he looked at his reflection in the mirror. Quick as a snake, he hammered his fist into the mirror, smashing it into a thousand pieces, glass shards sticking out of his knuckles, droplets of blood trickling down his fingers.

He showered and packed some clothes. Then stopped dead in his tracks.

What should I tell Hayden?

He couldn't very well leave without telling him something. He needed a plausible lie.

Blood from his knuckles seeped through the bandage he'd wrapped around his hand. Decision made. He opened the window that overlooked the driveway and tossed his bag into the bushes. Then he headed into the living room to find Hayden.

"What's up?"

"Had a bit of an accident." He held up his hand, bright red blood soaking through the bandage. "I'm taking the launch and going to the 24-hour place in town. Be back in a few hours."

Not waiting for a response, he hurried out the front door, retrieved his bag, and headed for the boat. He hopped into the launch, started the motor, stowed his bag, threw off the lines, and slowly pulled away from the dock.

"God, help me," he cried, gripping the wheel tighter and tighter with each passing mile, his knuckles gone white, his agitation intensified. "I've got to find her. Her life can't end this way."

He had a long drive ahead of him. Even driving all night, it would take him more than a day to reach the eastern shore of Virginia, time he'd spend brooding and worrying and berating himself for not doing more to protect Darby.

"Damn it. What more could I have done?"

The question hung in the air as the launch reached the mainland. He tied up the boat and headed for the parking lot

217

where he kept his car. Opening the windows and turning the air conditioning on full blast, he considered the path not taken, security options not engaged.

It wasn't the most elaborate security system available, and the salesman had a hard enough time convincing Darby to install the few cameras, motion sensors, and alarm system she did agree to. Her excuse was hard to argue with. She lived in the country, far from the city crazies. Out here, people trusted each other. The salesman countered with her isolation and the overarching importance to be warned about a possible intruder, especially since she had a five-year-old daughter. Saying that won the day, and a basic system was installed around her home.

But the note she left for the nanny made it clear she'd left on her own. He pulled up the apps he installed on his phone to monitor her comings and goings.

Where was her car signal? Did the tracker's battery conk out? Why wasn't her phone pinging?

He knew she'd never turn off her phone, in case there was an emergency about Brianna.

People don't disappear.

And if, as he suspected, Hayden was involved, he was going to need some muscle.

CHAPTER 23

Sand Isle, Florida

The phone chirp stopped TJ in his sandy tracks. He and his daughter, Bella, were out for their morning run. Their occasional father-daughter thing had become ritual after Bella's kidnapping.

Her brush with death had changed her, and he and Rosa were doing everything they could to help her recover from the experience. Bella, the joy of his life, was now somewhat sullen, more careful, more withdrawn.

The caller ID showed a blast from his past, a familiar name that could only mean one thing. A fun party was in the offing.

"What's happening, bro?"

"Sorry to bother you, man, but I need a favor."

"What kind of trouble are you in this time?" All thoughts of partying disappeared. He knew this voice. Moss's somber tones had TJ on full alert. Serious. Deadly serious.

"Not me. Someone I care about. Think I may need some backup."

"You got it. What's up?" asked TJ.

"Got a small problem up in Virginia. Eastern Shore. I'm on my way now. Been driving for hours. A dear friend's daughter has gone missing. Someone I swore to protect. Could use a few good men."

Memories crashed into TJ's brain. He looked at Bella splashing her feet in the ocean and felt his throat close up. He almost lost her less than six months ago. A wave of emotions swamped him.

"Tell me."

"Don't know much. She left a note saying she was going out on a call, and no one has heard from her since. Tracker in her car isn't working, and her phone isn't pinging."

"Think I can spring a few of the guys. When do you need us?"

"Yesterday."

"Let me clear it with Marco. I'll text you an address in Virginia where we can meet. You got a plan yet or are we winging it?"

"All wings at this point. May know more by the time you get your ass up here."

Somewhere

Her mind willed her arms to move, straining against the restraints, but nothing happened. A swirling haze fogged her sight. Still groggy, she thought she heard voices.

Were they real or imagined?

Shadows passed before her eyes.

"Stop. Please stop," she wailed softly, but no one was listening to her.

She watched a tall, thin man, fully gowned in surgical

attire, his protective mask in place over his nose and mouth, put a tray of stainless steel instruments—scalpels, forceps, hemostat clamps, retractors—on the counter above her head.

Surgical instruments. Someone is going to do surgery? On me? Why?

"No. *Please.* Don't do this." But she still didn't know what "this" was—what they were preparing to do to her. She could feel her heart pounding, thumping like it would burst out at any moment. Her throat tightened with terror, dry as the Mohave Desert.

Finding it increasingly difficult to tamp down her growing dread, Darby squeezed her eyes shut, willing her nightmare to end, praying for someone, anyone, to appear, to help her, to rescue her from whatever was about to happen.

She felt a light touch on her arm and opened her eyes. She was back. The frumpy, curly-haired, big-bosomed nurse was back.

"You came back. I-I don't remember your name."

"I told you I would," she said, patting Darby's arm. "Vivian, dear. My name is Vivian. Don't you fret over a small detail like my name. You relax, now. I'm going to take a little blood."

She stiffened and jerked her arm when the woman touched her again.

"No, no, no," said Vivian calmly. "That won't do. Just relax, sweetie. We're not here to hurt you."

Affixing a tourniquet above Darby's elbow, she said, "Make a fist." She tapped lightly at the vein. "You're going to feel a little pinch. There. Hold still. Just a moment more." She reached up and released the tourniquet.

Darby scanned her face. *How can such a kind-looking woman be so heartless? Doesn't she understand I'm being held against my will. Why won't she help me?*

"All done. Now tell me true. That wasn't too bad, was it?"

Terrified, Darby could hardly speak. "Sorry, I'm...I...please let me go. I won't tell anyone, I swear. Please help me. Tell me what's going on. Why am I here?"

"Why you're here to do one of the most unselfish, noble things anyone can do for another human being."

Unselfish?

Noble?

"What are you talking about? Are you out of your mind?"

Her body heaved. Tears ran from the corners of her eyes, tickling her cheeks as they fell into her hair. The nurse plucked a tissue from a box on the counter and gently wiped them away.

"Shhh. Calm down. You're here to give the gift of life, to save a man's life, your father's life."

Darby's mouth fell open. "Can't be. There must be some mistake. My father's been dead ten years. Cancer took him. It took my mother last year."

"Of course he's alive, dear," she said, gently patting Darby's shoulder. "You rest now. It's going be a while before we get started. One of the doctors got held up. I'm going to give you a mild sedative to help you rest. Sorry I can't get you something to eat." A needle pierced the IV tubing. She pointed to one of two IV bags hanging above Darby's head and smiled. "This one's got the real kickapoo joy juice. You'll get it when we're ready to get started."

A deep sob caught in Darby's throat as her new reality sank in. She was lost. Her fate, whatever it might be, was out of her control. She understood the magnitude of her problem. No one knew where she was. No Lone Ranger was coming to save her.

Brianna's sweet face appeared before her. Tears welled up in her eyes and rolled down her cheeks.

Will I ever see Brianna again? She'll be so alone, feel so abandoned, when Mommy doesn't come home.

That's what had happened with her daddy. He left one day, dressed for war, and didn't come home. Brianna didn't remember him, but she slept with Snoodles, the stuffed dog he gave her, every night, clutched tightly to her side.

What Darby needed was a solution. Her dad had taught her to remain calm, assess her situation and make a plan, but a dull haze was clouding her thinking, making it impossible for her to clearly process her predicament in a useful way.

Williamsburg, Virginia

"Berger." Daniel put down his slice of pizza and picked up his phone without checking caller ID. Even off duty, he answered his cell with an air of authority.

"Hey, Daniel. It's Marco. How are you two newlyweds doing?"

"Enjoying the life. Can't believe I waited so long. But my little bride was definitely worth waiting for."

"Bet you're grinning ear to ear right now."

"Busted! You don't miss a trick, do you?"

"Nope."

"Funny you should call. Were your ears ringing?"

"Should they be? You been talking about me?"

"Not you so much as Brett and Carolyn. Been working on something here that could use their unique research talents."

"Small world. Want to put up with a few houseguests for a day or two or three? TJ's heading up your way to help out a friend."

"Anything I can do?"

"Not sure. Might be. He's coming with Kyle, Tina and

Brody. Can easily add Carolyn and Brett to the party since you're wanting their skills."

"Sounds like the whole gang." Daniel found himself wondering what could be happening to send Marco's best security people in his direction. "Rachel will be excited to see Carolyn. Got any details you can share?"

"Not much. Possible missing person case. Don't think it's anything like the last time. Friend of TJ's. Not sure of all the details."

"Our house is their house. You coming?"

"Not sure yet. My arm could be twisted to come see that pretty wife of yours."

"What part of she's married don't you understand?"

"Think I'm beginning to understand it more and more."

"You and Marissa getting serious, Mr. Confirmed Bachelor? You know, it's never too late."

"Who knows what tomorrow will bring? Anyway, what's up on your end that you need Brett and Carolyn? Isn't the FBI network good enough for you?"

"My niece has gotten herself into something. She's been investigating missing homeless people since she literally tripped over an almost-dead man in the woods, who happened to be missing one of his kidneys."

"Ooh, not good."

"There's more. Then her best friend gets herself killed— hit and run—right in front of her. A former boyfriend, though she never thought of him in that way, suddenly dies of a heart attack. And a homeless man she's befriended is missing."

"A lot of dead people up your way. Maybe I don't want my people going up there."

"Too many dead people, if you ask me. Something's going on. I'm just not sure what. But I think the homeless guy who was missing his kidney is the key. And I could sure use Brett's special extracurricular talents, if you catch my drift."

"He's yours for as long as you need him. Make sure you have a lot of Mountain Dew on hand. The guy inhales the stuff."

Tiffany Stamos relaxed in her hotel room in the main building of Wellington Manor, her feet propped against the wall behind the antique four-poster bed, while she played with her new diamond bracelet, twisting it to catch the sun's light. The colors of the rainbow bounced around the walls as the sun reflected off the stones. She loved diamonds, and would do almost anything to acquire them.

Almost anything.

Had she overstepped all semblance of conscience this time? Was this job worth what she was paying morally? Ethically? How low was she willing to go? The questions plagued her more and more lately.

Maybe she was raised by wolves. Her last foster mother had screamed these words at her after she had kicked and bitten her, then bolted out the door for freedom, never to return. She was put into the system at five. It had raised her. Seven foster families in all. She learned fast. And the lesson? Eat or be eaten.

Eavesdropping was bad, but what she recently learned about the after-hours activities of Elan and the Asclepius clinics was reprehensible. And she was in too deep now to be able to claim plausible deniability. She not only knew what was going on after hours, she was orchestrating it.

How complicit am I? Can diamonds really buy my silence?

Maybe she had a moral compass after all.

Mr. Pollard was certainly a generous boss. They met six months ago on a chartered yacht. She was the social director, seeing to his every need during his private cruise of the Mediterranean. When the cruise ended, he asked what motivated her. "Diamonds," she replied flippantly.

The picture he painted, to be the public relations front person for one of his companies, Elan Health Systems, was hard to resist. Come work for me, he said, and more diamonds than she could imagine would be hers for the taking. All she had to do was be ambitious, exceed his expectations, and earn them. She accepted on the spot and never looked back. And diamonds she got. Every time her work exceeded his expectations, he gave her some new bauble. First earrings. Then larger earrings. Now this bracelet.

The knock on her door had her reliving her gymnastics days, rolling her legs over her head and coming to a standing position next to the bed. She even popped her arms into the air like the gymnasts do in the Olympics when they complete a routine. She'd once held that dream, now long dead due to a bad fall that ruptured her Achilles tendon. On to new dreams, she thought, as she went to the door and saw her visitor through the peephole.

"Mr. Pollard," she said as she opened the door. "How nice to see you." Stepping back so he could enter, she asked, "How may I help you?" Every time she asked this question, her fear was that he would ask for more than she was willing to provide. Her saving grace was his effeminate mannerisms, which led her to believe she was not his type.

"I'm checking on our most recent arrivals. I want to make sure everything goes smoothly."

"Everything is taken care of. Our first guest, Mr. Green, arrived two days ago, and is secluded in Patriot's Villa, down the hill from where we are now. His benefactor has been at the clinic for a few days. All tests are proceeding perfectly. Looks like a match made in heaven. The procedure is set for tonight."

"Good. That's what I like to hear."

He was standing right next to her, in her space, and it was all she could do not to step away. He repulsed her.

"Our other guest, Mr. Gold, arrives shortly. He is booked into the Patrick Henry Villa, which is at the center of the winery. His procedure is scheduled for the day after tomorrow. His benefactor arrived last night, and is being kept sedated and comfortable."

"Was there any problem acquiring this provider?"

"None that have been brought to my attention. Though I do admit, it is easier when we find the providers for our services than when one of our guests arrives with a predetermined benefactor."

He smiled at her and stroked her cheek. "It's the things we don't know, Ms. Stamos, that can be our undoing. And Mr. Gold is a very special guest, paying a great deal of money for our exclusive services. Please ask a few more questions of our team to ensure that nothing you don't know right now can come back to haunt you, or me, later."

"Of course, sir." Tiffany shivered and rubbed her arms.

"Are you chilly?"

"No. I'm fine." She moved to the mini-fridge and took out a bottle of water. "May I offer you something?"

"No. I must be going."

"Mr. Pollard, if I may. I was wondering…" Her voice trailed off as she second-guessed the wisdom of asking the question burning in her mind.

"Yes. What were you wondering?"

"Well, it's a question I always ask potential employers. And I asked you when you hired me, but you didn't answer. You never told me what happened to the person who had this position before me. I'm sure there was someone coordinating your public relations and guest services before you hired me."

"Yes, Ms. Stamos, there was someone before you. And someone before that person too."

"And were those people promoted? Was that why the job was vacant?"

"No, Ms. Stamos. Those people disappointed me. And I had them cut up in little pieces and fed to the alligators in the Everglades."

"Oh!" Her stomach twisted, and for a second she felt like she was falling.

"I'm kidding, Ms. Stamos. Really. Relax. Like most people who leave jobs, they left to pursue other opportunities."

"Th-Thank you for telling me." She took a big gulp of water, gripping the plastic water bottle tightly so he wouldn't see her hand shaking.

"Do you have any other questions?" His smirk broadcast his delight at her shock.

"No. No, sir. And I'll check with our team to make sure there are no surprises awaiting us."

"Good girl. Dinner is at eight at Cafe Le Canard. I hear they make the best she-crab soup and escargot in Williamsburg. Don't be late."

"I won't."

As she closed the door behind him, Tiffany couldn't help but wonder if his joke was more truth than fiction.

CHAPTER 24

The plane landed smoothly at the small private airport in Williamsburg, and the limo was waiting for its lone passenger, James Hayden. A uniformed chauffeur held the door open for him, and then went to retrieve Hayden's five pieces of Louis Vuitton luggage.

Within five minutes, the limo pulled up to wrought iron gates behind which sat Wellington Manor, a European-style hotel nestled at the center of six hundred acres of vineyards. The driver pushed the intercom button, and gave his passenger's name as Mr. Gold.

"Welcome to Wellington Manor. Please bear to the left at the fork in the road, and then make a right turn when the road ends. The driveway to your villa will appear on the right, about a quarter mile down the road. Our welcome team is waiting for you there."

Slowly the gates opened. The driver pulled ahead, following the directions to navigate a winding road through the vineyard. Wellington Manor's exclusive villa suites afforded special guests an exceptional level of privacy. Through the window, Hayden saw vines bursting with grapes ready to be harvested. Within minutes the driver pulled up to the front door of a French-style villa.

The hotel manager was waiting for him. When Hayden got out of the limo, the man snapped to attention.

"Welcome, Mr. Gold. I'm Mr. Pfeiffer, the hotel manager." He was impeccably dressed in a light gray pinstripe suit, white shirt, and midnight blue tie. His silver-gray hair gave him the distinguished air of an older gentlemen, the gentlemanly air further enhanced by a slight British accent. "Here is your room key, sir."

"Thank you." Hayden strode into the suite with Pfeiffer a respectful distance behind him.

"We've fully stocked the bar area, as you requested, sir. Menus are on the table for any meals you desire. You are welcome to dine here on your private patio, or join our other guests in the restaurant. The manor's limo is at your disposal for your entire stay."

His bags were brought into his suite by a young bellman in a hunter green and brown uniform, complete with pillbox-style hat. The guy looked like he was barely old enough to shave. "Shall I unpack for you, sir?"

"No. That won't be necessary." He handed the kid a twenty-dollar bill and watched his eyes brighten.

"Thank you, sir. Will there be anything else?"

"No. All I require is privacy. I don't want to be disturbed."

Mr. Pfeiffer gave the bellman a dismissive nod, and he vanished. "This is our most secluded villa," he said. "Your patio looks out over the vineyards. Please let us know what you might require, and we will be honored to provide it for you."

"Thank you."

"I realize you just arrived, and, with all due respect, I notice your stay is open-ended. Do you have any idea yet how long you'll be our guest?"

"Not at this time. I have some plans that are just now

taking shape. I should know within the next day or two when I'll be leaving."

"Very good, sir." Mr. Pfeiffer gave Hayden the slightest bow and retreated from the villa. He let out a huge breath as he got into the waiting golf cart and sped off toward the main hotel and his office.

Introductions were made, hugs and kisses exchanged, and plates piled high with breakfast treats.

"We weren't expecting to see you, Marco," said Rachel, giving him a warm embrace.

"I'm not staying. Just thought I would hitch a ride, drop in, say my hellos and drop off the fruit. One of the advantages of owning the plane."

"Well, I'm glad you came." Rachel held up a grapefruit to her nose and inhaled. "Yum. I love fresh oranges and grapefruit."

"And I love that we got past the little hiccup in our history." The twinkle in his golden-brown eyes caught her eye. "There was a time, young lady, when—"

"Are you flirting with me, Marco?" asked Rachel. "I'm a married woman," wiggling her ring finger and winking at Daniel, "and my honey carries a gun."

"If I remember correctly, your nuptials took place at my home, Le Maschere."

"Yes. And it was beautiful. Your home, the ocean, the sunset. The entire day was something I'll always treasure." She hugged him tightly.

"As for the gun, well, hell, carrying is the new black." He lifted his pant leg to reveal his own piece snugly hugging his ankle.

"You should have brought Marissa."

"She and Sophia are packing for their shopping trip to Paris and Milan. There's still time for you to join them."

"Paris? Milan? Not for me," she laughed. "Williamsburg is a very laid-back community. I don't have any place to wear the latest Paris fashions."

"So, how's your job with the Feds working out for you?" Marco asked Daniel while he poured himself a cup of coffee.

"It's okay. The contract is only for a year. My choice whether to re-up or not."

"Red tape and formal protocols driving you crazy yet?"

"Nope. That's what Jim Greene's for. He's FBI all the way. Mac and I are both former NYPD, so we don't know from red tape. We just do our Brooklyn cop thing. Jim clears the field and covers our asses. It's working well so far."

As everyone settled into places around the dining room table, Jesse questioned the extra chair. "Adam…Detective Knight…said he'd stop by this morning," said Daniel.

"He's investigating the homeless man I found in the woods, who unfortunately died later," added Morgan.

Marco turned to Daniel. "Sounds like you've been busy," he said. "Why don't you go first? Tell us what's going on. Then TJ can bring you all up to speed on his friend's problem."

"Sounds good." Daniel took the lead, giving a thumbnail sketch of events—knowns and unknowns. "Can't say it hasn't been interesting around here lately."

"Looks like we got here just in time," said Brett. "You've got a lot of unknowns."

"We know. If we had all the answers, we wouldn't need you." Daniel smiled, giving both Carolyn and Brett appreciative nods.

"Aw, shucks," said Brett. "It's nice to be needed. Am I blushing?"

"The FBI sex-trafficking task force I've been working on

with Jim and Mac has a division that delves into black market organ trafficking. Based on what we've been able to piece together, it looks like small town Williamsburg may be one of several nondescript cities housing a shadow medical clinic operation doing illicit surgeries."

"And we think two people, Nadine Steiner-Greene and Greg Welton, are dead because they got too close," said Jesse.

"I thought Greg had a heart attack," said Rachel. "That's what the ME said, according to the newspaper."

"There is no way I believe his death was an accident," said Daniel. "But it will be weeks before the full toxicology comes back, and I don't feel like waiting and letting the trail go cold. My gut's telling me it's all connected."

"But why?" asked Rachel.

"Usual motives for murder are power, greed, jealousy, and revenge," said Daniel. "Greg had power. He was CEO of Elan. Morgan, you've said he wasn't the greedy or the jealous type, so that leaves revenge."

"Revenge?" repeated Morgan. "For what? What could Greg have done that would have someone want to take revenge on him? There wasn't a mean bone in his body."

"It wasn't revenge at all," said Jesse. "He was a threat. When I had dinner with him, he told me he'd learned something about Elan that worried him. He was scared. Visibly scared."

"That's not good," said Daniel. "Wonder what he learned that necessitated eliminating him?"

"We were supposed to meet for dinner the night he died," said Jesse. "He was going to lay it all out for me, what he found, what he thought might be going on. When he didn't show and didn't answer his cell, I made a wrong assumption. That he got cold feet. I should have checked on him."

"Don't beat yourself up, Jesse," said Morgan. "Whatever he was going to share got him killed, and Nadine, too. Her husband, Sid, gave me her notes. She was deep into the organ trafficking side of the story, and researching Colton Pollard."

"Who's he?" asked Carolyn.

"A man whose name keeps popping up," said Morgan. "It looks like he's behind a grotesque twist in my human-interest story about homelessness."

"The thought of someone randomly cutting out another person's kidney makes my skin crawl," said Rachel.

"And doing it without their permission is unconscionable," said Tina. "I know it goes on all the time in third world countries, but here?"

"Yes, here," said a booming voice from the hallway. "I let myself in. I hope that's okay."

"Of course," said Rachel. "Everyone, this is Detective Knight."

"Nice to meet y'all." He helped himself to coffee and headed for the lone empty chair. "What is it they say? Everything's for sale. It's just a question of price. And everything's negotiable."

"But who's getting paid? Not the guy Nadine and I found in the woods. You can't tell me he got paid for his kidney."

"He didn't, but somebody did."

"Who?" pressed Morgan.

"Not sure yet. I sent out feelers to nearby communities, and got some surprising results." Knight took his place at the table. "Other local cities have had homeless people disappearing and then showing up at the local hospital, or dead, a few days later, minus one of their kidneys or a lobe of their liver."

"And you think this clinic is involved?" said Carolyn. "That's a huge leap. There are dozens of medical clinics and mini-surgery centers in communities. What is it about this clinic that's got you focused on it?"

"Interesting question," said Knight. "Wolf among the sheep. Paid the place a visit the day after Morgan found the homeless man. Watched them unload canisters of gases and boxes of supplies. My detective gut is telling me it isn't what it's touted to be. And we all know, once aroused, detective instincts are hard to quell."

A knowing glance shot between Daniel and Knight.

"What's got your instincts in an uproar?" asked Kyle. "Got to be more than a few gas canisters and some supplies."

"How about the fact that the woman I spoke with there lied to me?" he chuckled. "Said she was alone, but I saw a man come out the loading dock door when a truck pulled up." Knight's eyes connected with each person at the table. "How about a free clinic that for three days a month is the Mother Theresa of clinics to the poor, the indigent, anyone and everyone who needs free medical care. And on the other twenty-something days, it's either gone—"

"What do you mean gone?" Kyle had been walking around the table refilling everyone's coffee, but he stopped, his concentration on Knight's explanation of events.

"Think traveling circus. They've got these huge semi-trailers, mobile medical units like they use in Iraq or at disaster scenes. When their time is up at one place, the trailers close up shop and go someplace else."

"You're kidding," said TJ, who had been quietly listening, his attention split between what he was hearing and the needs of his friend Moss, whose plea for help had initiated this trip north.

"Nope. It's all in the brochures." Daniel slid a four-color glossy across the table to TJ.

"Slick," he said, flipping through the pages. "I'd guess the guy at the top, running all of this, is one smart dude, smart enough to have a solid exit strategy, one that includes a disappearing act worthy of Houdini."

"This is the first month of operation here," said Jesse. "They had an open house last week. And the free clinic was over two days ago. But the trailers are still here. Nothing's moved on."

"Yet," Daniel added firmly.

"And a friend of mine," said Knight, "who runs the small private airport in town tells me there is a lot of increased traffic there. And some of it is medical."

Knight looked around the table and saw a lot of muscle ready to go. These were the good guys, he thought, ready to play out their boyhood fantasies, chase the bad guys, and save the world. The only thing that changed was the deadliness of their toys. He suspected they were all licensed to carry, so their guns were real, their martial arts skills real, their ability to kill with their bare hands very, very real.

"Just to let you know," he continued, "I placed the clinic under surveillance a few days ago, and there was one particular coming and going that coincided with a medical flight out of the airport that got my attention. Wealthy hedge fund manager, Demetrius Vargos, arrived fully mobile on his own Gulfstream from New York, but left this morning strapped to a gurney on a medical flight. When I checked, the flight was headed for Costa Rica."

Knight tossed a few glossy photos on the table. Some showed a tall, dark-haired, handsome man, maybe in his mid-forties, bouncing down the steps of a plane and walking across the tarmac. Others showed a man strapped to a gurney.

"How do you know it's the same guy? Hard to see his face. Though the dark, curly hair looks like it could be the same guy," asked Tina.

"You just named the problem." He raked his hands through his hair. "There's no way to be sure it's the same guy."

"What are you doing about it?" asked Kyle.

"I actually have a buddy vacationing in Costa Rica. Did you know it's the new cool spot to vacation? I sure as hell didn't. Anyway, he's doing me a favor. Should hear back from him anytime."

"Oh my God." Morgan's outburst got everyone's attention. "I dropped Eli off there two days ago and haven't heard from him. He's a homeless man I've sort of befriended. He was going to have a nurse call me when they finished with all the tests they wanted to run, but when I didn't hear from him, I got worried. I stopped by yesterday to check on him."

"And?" asked TJ.

"And nothing. They wouldn't let me see him. Said visiting hours were over, that I should come back today. I'm heading over there after we're done here. You don't think they... They couldn't... They wouldn't... Oh, my God."

"Don't most hospitals have unlimited visiting hours these days?" asked Brody. "It's not like years ago, when there were specific hours."

"Most do, but not this place. The woman said it would be different if I was family. But I'm not family."

"Why didn't you lie?" asked Brody.

Morgan blushed. "Didn't think of it in time. Didn't think I needed to. Said I was a friend. A very worried friend."

"We've got to cut Morgan some slack," said Jesse. "She's new at this investigative reporter thing. Now me, I would have lied big time to get in there. In fact, I'm trying to think of a way to get beyond the double doors as we speak."

"What do you think is going on there?" Tina looked directly at Jesse.

"Remember the movie *Invasion of the Body Snatchers*?" Jesse looked around the table for signs of recollection from the group. "I think they're body snatchers. Only they're not aliens taking over someone's body by invading it. They take parts. Remove parts. And dispose of the rest."

"That's a big accusation," said Carolyn. "Got anything to back it up?"

"A Frontline documentary that aligns with everything we've been talking about. Two deaths, three if you count the homeless guy Morgan and Nadine found. And a man whose name keeps showing up."

"And my map," said Morgan, pointing to the map of the US hanging on a white board scattered with colored dots.

"I was wondering what that was all about," said Brett. "Colorful."

"Thanks. Where the blue and yellow dots overlap are places where homeless people have gone missing, and then showed up dead, or missing body parts, and where Elan has clinics."

"Interesting," said Carolyn. "I love that you were able to pull together disparate pieces of information to make your case so effectively. Very damning."

"The official ME report is still pending on Greg Welton," said Knight. "Unless the lab finds something in the toxicology, it will go down as a myocardial infarction. And we found a black SUV abandoned up north in Toano, in the Kiss and Ride lot near Route 64, which we think is the same one that killed Nadine. Found some fibers in the front grill that look like a match to what she was wearing. We're having it towed to the lab in Richmond, but I don't expect to find much."

"I hope you find fingerprints or something that will help you find the guys who killed Nadine," Morgan said. "I can still see the driver studying me like prey right after he hit her."

"I'm not counting on it," said Knight. "This guy was a pro and I'm sure he wiped it down before he dumped it."

"Not good," said Jesse. "Wish you had more to go on. We need to catch these guys fast, because Morgan stepped into the crosshairs and had lunch with the guy we think is behind everything the other day."

Knight looked around the table as he stood. "Looks like there is plenty of protection available to make sure she makes it to her next birthday unscathed."

He put his dirty mug on the sideboard.

"And since I don't want to know what you guys are planning...you know, plausible deniability...I'm outta here. Thanks for the coffee, Rachel." He stopped just short of the door and turned back to the group. "You have my cell. If you need help, call."

"Do you know anything about the people inside?" asked Carolyn. "Who's running the show? Who owns the operation?"

"Not enough," said Daniel. "That's why we need you two."

Carolyn nudged Brett in the side. "Guess that's our signal to get to work."

"Do you have any names I can start with?" asked Brett.

"One," said Jesse. "Colton Pollard. Also try Elan Health Systems, Asclepius Clinics and Global Initiatives."

"And Tiffany Stamos," said Morgan. "She's their PR person."

Brett and Carolyn started punching their keyboards as Daniel turned to TJ.

"It's your turn." Daniel scooped up a knife full of cream cheese and started smearing it on half a bagel. "Now that we've filled you in on what's going on here, what's with your friend?"

"Moss and I were Marines together. He stayed, went Marine Recon when I left for SEAL training. We stayed in touch. He should be here soon. I texted him the address."

"Special forces brotherhood," said Kyle. "He's a good guy."

"What's his problem?" asked Daniel.

"Oh, let me," said Carolyn looking up from her laptop. "It's straight out of Ripley's Believe It or Not. You're gonna love this."

"Be my guest," said TJ. "I know better than to stop a woman eager to spill the beans."

"Here's what Brett and I think, based on what we've been able to piece together." She looked around the table and saw that all eyes were on her. "TJ's friend Moss and Desiree were old childhood friends. Desiree, whose real name we know was Dawn, got pregnant, and gave her baby up for adoption when it was born. We think the baby's father, a guy named on the birth certificate as JJ Henry, was also from the old neighborhood."

"And Moss works for him," added Brett. "Has for years. The guy calls himself James Hayden now."

"So…something happened, and the friendship changed. Moss remained loyal to Dawn all these years, probably promised her he'd watch over her daughter. And it looks like he did, faithfully. Until a few days ago, when she went missing."

"Desiree," said Rachel, when Carolyn stopped talking, "that's a name I haven't heard in a few months. Not since we met her at the Mah Jongg tournament in Orlando, where she was one of the poisoning victims."

"Also, the madam of the Sand Isle brothel," added Kyle. "Which is probably why she gave her baby up for adoption. Somehow she knew the path she was heading down was not the kind of life you live if you want to raise a healthy kid."

"Right," said Carolyn. "Desiree actually sent me her antique mahj set. Got it a few weeks ago. I guess, after she was poisoned, she knew her days were numbered. Seems like she met with a lawyer while she was still in the hospital in Orlando, and wrote up a document requiring them to find me if anything happened to her—"

"Like getting blown up on a boat," said Brody.

"Yeah. Like that. Anyway, there was a note asking me to find her daughter and protect her. Guess she didn't think Moss was still on the job."

"Or had been bought off by this Hayden guy who was his boss," said Kyle.

"Protect her? From what?" asked Daniel.

"Didn't say. But here's where we get the Ripley's connection. Brett and I actually tracked the daughter down. And believe it or not, Desiree's daughter turns out to be the same person TJ's friend Moss called him about."

Rachel, who had gotten up for more coffee, whipped around. "You're kidding."

"Small world," said Tina. "The Kevin Bacon syndrome. Six degrees of separation."

"Let me get this straight. The woman who is missing, the woman who TJ's friend Moss swore to protect, is the same woman Desiree asked you to find and protect. Fathered by some guy Desiree was sure was out to kill her and harm her now-grown daughter?"

"Fun stuff," said Brody. "Can't make this shit up."

"We'll know more when Moss gets here," said TJ.

"He's here," said a deep voice emanating from the front hallway. "Stopped to talk to the guy who just left, Detective Knight. Said to come on in."

TJ stood, and both he and Kyle shared bear hugs with Moss.

"Been a long time, man," said TJ. "Must admit that I prefer it when you call about a party and not trouble."

"Trouble's all I got this time around."

Introductions were made and coffee cups refilled.

"I want to thank you all for your help," said Moss after he downed his second cup.

"Wait," said Daniel. "I know you. Seen you somewhere."

"Hoover's house. FBI. Undercover these last few years, working to bring down a very bad man. My mama used to say, 'Don't borrow trouble, your own will find you soon enough.' And she was right. When this happened, it brought it all too close to home."

"What makes you think this Hayden guy had something to do with Darby's disappearance?" asked Rachel.

"He needs a kidney. She's his blood. He's been acting strange these last few weeks. Nastier than usual. Even said he was planning a vacation without me. He barely wipes his own ass without me, so going on vacation without me strikes me as very odd."

"Fair assessment," said TJ. "But you don't know any more than that she is missing. No calls received? No contact made?"

"My guy on-site tells me nothing, no contact. Her five-year-old daughter is really upset. Fortunately, she has a familiar face in the live-in nanny, who will take care of her until I can bring her mother home to her."

"*We* can bring her mother home. You're not alone in this, Moss." TJ put his hand on Moss's shoulder and gave it a warm squeeze. "And here's an interesting twist. The fact that he needs a kidney aligns with what I've just learned these folks are working on. They think there's a black market organ trafficking ring operating at a local clinic here."

"To bring you up to speed," said Daniel, "Jesse and Morgan are doing a recon of the clinic tonight. We don't know if your girl is there, but if she is, we'll find out tonight."

Moss ran his hands over his cue ball-bald head. No sleep,

a long drive, and overwhelming fear for Darby's safety had him by the short hairs. He found no solace in anyone's words of comfort. The wrenching pain of knowing he screwed up had a tenacious hold on him. Things were moving too slowly. There was no time for recon. He had to act, and act fast. He struggled to bridle emotions racing out of control like a wild bronco.

Everyone was talking over each other. Moss's frustration grew. He pushed away from the table, overturning his chair which crashed to the floor.

"I can't sit here. I gotta go."

Not waiting for any replies, he righted the chair and raced out the front door…where he stopped, his hands choking the iron railing as he fought every impulse to lash out, go it alone, charge ahead and find Darby.

"Want to talk about it?"

He turned. The gentle voice matched the kind face, golden-brown eyes, and soft smile.

"Tina, right?"

"Yes. I don't mean to intrude, but you're not the first man I've seen struggling with PTSD symptoms. The invisible nemesis of war."

"Armchair diagnosis?"

"No. I was a medic. Seen it many times before, expect to again."

Moss averted his eyes.

"Whatever memories are haunting you, talking about them helps. Though, I suppose, like TJ, Kyle, and the rest of them, you prefer the macho, go-it-alone route."

He smiled at her.

"Figured as much." She sidled up to him and rested her hands next to his on the railing. "Talking helps, and I do understand. I've been there. It's harder for people like me."

"People like you?"

"Women. We're used to expressing our emotions, but when we exist in your world, we have to deny them, control them more than we're used to. It's hard."

"None of this is war-related. It's older than that. From the before time. About a promise made, one I am not keeping."

"You don't know how any of this will end. That promise is not broken yet. Trust us. Like you, we're very good at what we do."

CHAPTER 25

The pounding on the door wouldn't stop. Lights went on. The front door's lock clicked.

"What's all the fuss about?" demanded a stocky, gray-haired woman in navy blue scrubs who, when she opened the door, found herself face-to-face with a woman struggling to hold a man around the waist, a man who was hopping on one foot.

The injured man's face contorted in a twisted road map of pain and suffering. The woman struggled to hold him up.

"Don't just stand there," she shrieked. "Let us in, and find someone who can help my friend."

"This is a private clinic. It's after hours. There's no one here."

"Bullshit." The woman pushed past her into the reception area. "You're a medical facility. There must be someone here who knows what they're doing."

"Like I just said, we're a private clinic, not a hospital. And there's just me and another nurse here." Looking at the injured man, she asked, "What happened to you?"

"We were hiking by the creek, taking pictures of deer with my new camera, when I slipped and slid down the hill. I think I broke my ankle. I can't walk." Anguish and pain filled his voice.

"It was all I could do to get him up the hill and across the parking lot. I saw lights at the back of the building, so here we are."

Suddenly, the injured man started to wheeze uncontrollably. "I-I can't breathe." His hands clutched his chest. "I think I'm having a heart attack. Help me." He slumped to the floor, his fight for every breath growing louder and louder.

Both women grabbed him and sat him down in a chair in the reception area.

"Don't just stand there," screeched the woman. "Get him an aspirin. He needs oxygen. *Do* something!"

The nurse ran to the double doors, swiped her ID, and pushed through when she saw the security light turn green.

"Don't overdo your part," Jesse whispered to Morgan once the nurse was out of sight, his eyes moving to a security camera tucked into the corner of the room.

"Too much?"

"Not sure. But she's not an idiot. The three energy drinks I chugged are making my heart go nuts, but if she's any good at all, she'll see right through the heart attack thing once she gets me hooked up to a monitor."

"Let's hope we get that far." Morgan nodded to acknowledge that she saw the security camera.

"Help me over to the doors, so when she comes back we're closer to where we want to be and can barge our way through."

"Remember you're in pain, in case someone is watching the video feed." Morgan pulled Jesse to his lone working foot and helped him hobble to a chair by the doors. The doors opened, and the nurse pushed a wheelchair toward them.

"Here, chew this aspirin." She handed him a small, clear plastic cup with a lone white pill in it. "Let's sit him down in the wheelchair so I can take him to one of the exam rooms and check him out. Then we can call 911 if we need to."

"Thank you. I'm Morgan, and this clumsy fool is Jesse." Morgan strained forward to read the woman's name tag, but there was no name on it. Just the logo for Elan Health Systems. "You're being very kind. I'm sorry I yelled at you a moment ago. I'm feeling kind of stressed. What's your name?"

"You're welcome. No need to apologize. I've heard a lot worse. I'm Vivian Blair, the nurse on duty." She wheeled Jesse into the first examination room in the corridor. It looked like every other exam room. She pulled a portable oxygen tank from under the counter and affixed a nasal cannula, allowing the lifesaving air to flow freely into his nose.

"You said this wasn't a hospital. Just a clinic. Do you have patients here?" Morgan remembered the room from the open house tour. She also knew that three hallways branched off from this main hall at the end of the corridor.

"N-no. Not really," stammered Vivian.

"I'm confused. I thought you said you were the nurse on duty. How are you on duty if there are no patients?" asked Morgan.

Vivian blushed. "Your banging startled me. I-I was finishing up some paperwork when I heard you at the door. I'm so used to introducing myself that way, saying I'm the nurse on duty. It comes out automatically."

She wrapped the blood pressure cuff around Jesse's arm, put her stethoscope in her ears, held the chest piece to the brachial artery and began to pump up the cuff.

"Well, we're glad you're here, and very grateful you opened the doors for us."

JANE FLAGELLO

Vivian watched the mercury column as she released the air from the cuff, listening for the rhythmic sounds as blood began to flow through the artery.

"Definitely elevated. Not too bad, considering. One hundred and sixty over one ten. You're probably just worked up after your fall. Do you know what your numbers usually are?"

"Last time I was at the supermarket, I used the machine, and I think I remember it registering one twenty over eighty. But that was a few weeks ago."

"And those machines aren't the best." She unwrapped the cuff and placed it back in its basket holder. "You seem to be breathing better. I think you had a panic attack. What were you two doing out by the creek at night? Don't you know it isn't smart to go wandering around in the dark, especially when you don't know the terrain?"

"Yeah, Morgan. Don't you know it isn't smart?"

"Don't blame me. You were the one who wanted to use your new Zeiss lens to take pictures of deer at night."

"And I dropped the camera. Have to go back to get it. Hope it isn't broken."

"I'll go back and find it."

"What a friend!" Jesse took a deep breath. "My chest doesn't feel as tight. My ankle is a whole other story. Man, it hurts."

"Probably a bad sprain. Could be a fracture. You need to get it X-rayed."

"Can you do that here?"

"No, I'm sorry to say. Our technicians are all gone for the day. And you aren't a patient here. We're a private facility."

"Can he rest here while I go get the car?" asked Morgan. "It's over in the Holiday Inn parking lot. Shouldn't take me more than ten or fifteen minutes to jog over there and get back."

Vivian bit her lip, taking a few moments to consider her answer. "Well, I don't see why not." She looked down at Jesse. "Not like you can go anywhere."

"Can you get me some ice?" asked Jesse. "Not the first time I've sprained or possibly broken something. I know the RICE routine—rest, ice, compress, elevate. Won't be able to rest until I get this looked at, but I can do all the other steps."

"You have done this before." Vivian smiled at him, resting her hand on his shoulder.

"What can I say? One of five brothers. We played rough."

"I can see you're in good hands, Jesse. Let me go get the car," said Morgan. "When you get the ice do you think you could bring back a compression bandage so his ankle won't sustain any more damage?"

Vivian hesitated. "That probably isn't a good idea. We don't really know what's happened to his ankle. I don't want to get sued or anything. But I will let you out and then get him an ice pack."

"I'll take him to one of the twenty-four hour places for treatment. There's one on Richmond Road. Will be a lot cheaper than an ER visit."

"My medical insurance carrier appreciates your economical choice," laughed Jesse.

The women left and Jesse heard the whoosh sound when the doors closed behind them. He was alone for the time being, but knew Vivian would be coming back this way after she let Morgan out of the building. Then she'd either have to go to a kitchen for real ice, or one of the supply closets for one of those strike-and-shake instant ice packs, giving him two blocks of time when he could look around.

First things first. Jesse shoved the flash drive into the laptop Vivian had booted up in the exam room. Why she'd done it he didn't know, because she never actually input any information. But it was a Godsend because she had accessed the system with her password. The flash drive made the internal connection so Brett could let his devilish fingers poke around in Elan's private files.

Eli wasn't sleeping well. He'd been at the clinic for two full days and nights, felt trapped like the fireflies he and his brother used to catch in glass jars when they were kids. His freedom itch needed scratching. Tonight, he tongued the pill Vivian gave him to help him sleep and spit it out when she left the room.

The banging broke the nighttime silence he had gotten used to, and had him sitting up in bed. He swung his legs around, put his feet on the floor, and stood up. More banging.

He looked over at Caleb who didn't move, hadn't moved for hours.

"Something's happening." Talking out loud had become part of his normal everyday behavior, one that caused people who passed by him to think he was slightly off.

Clutching the IV pole with the bag dripping fluids into his arm, he padded into the dimly lit hall. Looking right, then left, he saw no one. More banging. He turned in the direction of the noise. As he approached the next corridor, the lights went on.

Muted voices.

Male and female.

He went to the end of the hall and peeked around the corner to see who was speaking just as the double doors flew open. He quickly pulled back, so they wouldn't see him.

Vivian had told him not to leave his room, to push the big red button if he needed anything. He was disobeying Vivian. And he'd learned not to do that the very first night he was at the clinic. She went from pussycat to man-eating tiger in a flash when he didn't follow her directions during one of the medical tests. Then she went ballistic when he asked for a phone to call Miss Morgan.

Since then, he'd been very wary of her. If she caught him in the hall, would she punish him? Would she stop giving him the medicines she promised would help make him better?

He saw one of those big corner fish-eye mirrors mounted high above his head pointing down the corridor. He could see Vivian wheeling someone into a room. A woman followed behind the wheelchair.

Was that Miss Morgan?

He remained still for a few minutes, straining to hear what they were saying, knowing he was too far away. Then Vivian and the woman went back through the double doors. He crept down the hall.

Jesse's head popped out of the room.

"Who are you?" asked Jesse when he saw Eli hugging the wall and walking slowly in his direction.

"Eli. I'm Eli."

"You're Morgan's friend?"

"You know Miss Morgan?"

"Yes. She's a good friend of mine."

"She's my friend, too. I've been wanting to call her and tell her I'm okay. Miss Vivian keeps saying she'll give me a phone, but I suspect that's not gonna happen." Eli moved closer. "Could you tell her where I am? That I'm okay, but they won't let me leave yet."

"Sure. I'll tell her." Jesse saw a huge smile cross Eli's face. "Could you tell me why you're here? What are they doing to you?"

"Tests. They keep sticking me, taking my blood, giving me pills that make me sleepy." Eli looked at the floor then back at Jesse. "I just want to go home."

251

"And we're going to help you get home. But this has to be our secret. You can't tell anyone you saw me. Can you do that?"

"Sure can. I ain't no fool. I know how to keep my mouth shut."

"Eli, is there anyone else here? Have you seen any other patients?"

"Not rightly sure. Caleb's here. And there was some commotion last night. I saw a gurney go down the hall with someone on it. Couldn't tell if it was a man or woman. Sorry."

"That's fine, Eli. You better get back to your room. My friend won't be able to keep Vivian occupied much longer."

"Your friend?" He looked past Jesse at the closed double doors. "That was Miss Morgan, wasn't it?"

"Yes. But please, you must not say anything about seeing her, or about us talking."

"You got that right. Miss Vivian has a mighty mean streak. Best not to tangle with her." He turned to go, stopped and looked back at Jesse. "Please tell Miss Morgan not to worry about me. But if there is anything she can do to spring me, I'd much appreciate it."

"You got it, Eli. I promise."

They both saw the lights go out in the reception area.

"Gotta go," said Eli.

Jesse watched Eli turn the corner, and then he scooted back into the exam room.

CHAPTER 26

The shrieking alarm woke Morgan. Panic choked off any scream. Screaming was useless. There was no one here to hear her. Living alone did have its challenges.

Flying out of bed, she reached for the gun her Uncle Daniel made her promise to keep loaded in her night table. He was all about self-protection, constantly reminding her that it could easily take police ten minutes after a dispatch alert to arrive at the scene. Nine minutes and fifty-nine seconds too long.

Her heart was racing, her mouth dry, her palms sweaty. The lump in her throat felt like she'd swallowed a bowling ball. She inched toward the bedroom door, alert for any sound she might be able to hear above the screeching alarm. The gun shook in her hands.

She stopped cold in her tracks. "What am I doing? Am I nuts?"

Retracing her steps, she grabbed her cell and locked herself in the bathroom. Fingers, doing their own version of the shimmy-shake, punched in 911.

"911. What's your emergency?"

"This is Morgan Kasen. My house alarm is going off. Help me."

JANE FLAGELLO

"Where are you now?"

"200 Hickory Court. In Berkeley Trace. Locked in my bathroom. Please send the police."

"The police are on their way. Stay where you are. They will come to you."

Blinking back tears, Morgan slid down the wall, scrunched up her knees, wrapped her arms around them, and huddled into the corner behind the bathroom door. Panic knotted her stomach. Bile soured in her mouth. Her pounding heart felt like it would burst from her chest.

It had been a crazy night. The recon at the clinic was exhilarating, but this screaming alarm reinforced, once again, that she preferred less excitement in her life.

She punched in Uncle Daniel's number, grateful he and Rachel lived nearby.

"Yes?" a groggy Daniel answered.

"It's me, Uncle Daniel. My alarm is going off. I'm scared. I called 911. Can you come over?"

"I'm on my way."

Red and blue strobe lights flashed across the bathroom ceiling. Morgan felt herself exhale. Help was here. Her eyes flicked up toward heaven.

"Thank you, God."

She shoved herself up off the floor, unlocked the bathroom door, and slowly opened it.

The shrill whine of the alarm could wake the dead. Putting on shorts, she took a deep breath, then opened the bedroom door. The nightlight cast a soft blue glow down the hall. No one was there, but someone was pounding on the front door.

Racing down the hall and through the living room, she punched the key code into the control panel to stop the alarm. Blessed silence at last.

More pounding.

"Police, Ms. Kasen. Open the door."

Morgan peered through the shutters. Uniformed officers were visible on the porch. She could still hear the deafening alarm echoing in her head, and she put her hands over her ears to silence the clanging. Her tongue stuck to the roof of her dry mouth. Tears streamed down her cheeks. Fighting to regain control, Morgan inhaled deeply through her nose and blew out the air to the count of ten.

"Thank you, God," she said, again glancing upward. Flinging open the front door, she could see Daniel racing up her walkway, his badge clearly visible hanging from a chain around his neck. Rachel was close on his heels.

"Thank you for coming, Officers. I'm sure it must be a malfunction of the alarm." Her words didn't match the fear churning in her gut.

Then Daniel's arm was around her shoulder leading her into the living room.

"Here. Sip this," said Rachel, handing her a small glass of brandy.

"Take care of her," said Daniel. "I'll check in with the police. We'll do a thorough search of the place."

"Thanks." Turning to Rachel, she said, "I'm so sorry to get you up in the middle of the night. I...I didn't know who else to call."

"Shhh. Don't be silly. Of course you call us. We're family." Rachel drew Morgan into her arms.

Morgan nestled into Rachel's shoulder. "What a nightmare. Nadine's death. Greg's. The homeless man. And now this. It's all too much."

"Don't jump to conclusions. We don't know exactly what this is yet. Could be a short in the system."

"Wrong. I know exactly what this is. Whoever killed Nadine is now after me. I've felt like someone's been watching me for a few days now. Probably the driver of the

SUV with the creepy blue eyes. I'm getting too close to whatever is going on at the clinic and making someone very nervous."

She downed the remaining brandy. The mantel clock chimed three.

"Think I better make some coffee and put some more clothes on. It's going to be a long night."

Two hours and several cups of coffee later, Rachel was again alone with Morgan. The police had left, and Daniel was outside doing another walk around the property.

"We're here for you. Don't you worry. Why don't you grab a few things and come stay with us?"

"I appreciate your offer and your hospitality. I really do, but my stubborn, pissed-off streak is rearing its ugly head. Weak, sniveling and afraid is no way to go through life. I refuse to be scared out of my wits, let alone scared out of my own home. Besides, you're newlyweds. I wouldn't want to put a damper on your…activities, if you catch my drift. How can you make spontaneous, mad, passionate love on the dining room table with me around?"

"You've been reading too many romance novels, young lady. We're too old for that. Give me a nice soft Tempur-Pedic, please."

"Well," said Morgan, uncrossing her legs and standing up. "At least I know the alarm system works, and that I have strong locks."

"Locks don't always keep the bad guys out," said Daniel as he came back into the house. "Just makes them work harder to get in. And if they are the really bad sort of bad guys, they know ways to bypass any lock."

"Thanks for sharing, Uncle Daniel. Can't tell you how much safer knowing that makes me feel."

"Do I detect a note of sarcasm?"

"Sorry." Morgan stared at him, raised and lowered her eyebrow. "I'm going to make waffles. Any takers?"

"How can you eat?" Rachel asked, following Morgan into the kitchen.

"I'm hungry. Besides, it will give me something to do." She pulled pancake mix, eggs, butter and cream out of the fridge. "It's almost six. If I get a jump on breakfast, I'll have the whole rest of the day to worry about who's trying to kill me."

"Not funny, Morgan."

"Don't mean it to be." Morgan felt her aunt's unwavering stare. "What?"

"Nothing. I'm just worried about you."

"That makes two of us."

"Three," said Daniel joining the ladies in the kitchen. "I may have overstepped my bounds just now, but I took the liberty of calling Jesse. He's on his way over, so you better make more batter."

"I don't believe you did that." Morgan shook her head. "What did the police say that you're not sharing that prompted the call to Jesse?"

"Not much more than you already know. They said you should call the alarm company in the morning to get it checked, and they'd arrange to increase patrols on your street for the time being."

"And?"

"And what?"

She arched her eyebrow at him and stood silently staring, knowing there was more that he had yet to share.

"Okay. They found a few footprints in the muddy area outside one of your windows, and what looked to be some jimmy marks. The CSI team will be here later this morning to take a casting and dust for prints."

"Thank you. Maybe I'll get a dog," laughed Morgan,

pouring batter into the waffle iron. "A big, mean, Rottweiler."

The front doorbell rang and Daniel left Rachel and Morgan alone while he answered it.

"I'm repeating my invitation for you to come stay with us. Do you really think you should be alone?" asked Rachel.

"Probably not. Probably why Daniel called Jesse. I'll be okay." She got quiet for a moment as she looked down the hall toward the front door. "I can hear him filling Jesse in on what went on here tonight."

"What's up with you and Jesse?"

"Nothing."

"Don't tell me nothing. He's interested in you."

"Don't be silly, Rachel. We're partnering on the story. That's all."

"I know all when I see it, and partnering on a story isn't all. Not by a long shot. I saw the way he looked at you when you came to dinner the other night."

"Seriously?"

"Very. Girl to girl, that man wants to kiss you up one side and down the other."

"Aunt Rachel!"

Rachel laughed and gave blushing Morgan a loving squeeze.

"I've barely been your aunt for a few months, so don't you Aunt Rachel me. These eyes know what they saw. He's nice-looking, and all I'm saying is you might want to take him out for a spin."

As if on cue, Jesse burst into the room.

"Looks like you can't get enough of me tonight," he said drawing Morgan into his arms. "The minute I turn my back, trouble shows up." He looked around the kitchen. "And waffles."

"Can't pass up a meal, can you?"

"You two enjoy. We're heading home," said Daniel, taking hold of Rachel's hand.

"But I made tons."

"Jesse's hungry and waffles freeze." Rachel gave Morgan a knowing smile. "Have fun."

"You're smiling from your nose down, but your eyes are sending me other signals," said Jesse.

Morgan shrugged, since she couldn't think of anything to say. Strike that. Anything she was willing to say.

"Someone is trying to hurt you, or at least scare the living crap out of you."

"They're succeeding on that last part. I am scared, but I don't see what I can do about it. I can't cower in my home. I can't stop living. I *won't* stop living."

"Go to your uncle's. Stay with them until we catch this whack-job." He walked over to her kitchen counter, picked up her cell phone, held it out, and said, "Call them. Ask them if it's okay for you to spend a few nights under their roof until we figure this out."

"I don't need to ask. I know it's okay. Rachel wanted me to come now. But...but they just got married. The last thing they need is me hanging around."

"Then you're going to have to put up with me."

"Excuse me?"

"No arguments. I'm moving in. Purely platonic. I'm sure you've got a guest room."

"A little presumptuous, aren't you?"

"No. I'm concerned for you. I'm here. Available. I'm housebroken. I clean up after myself. I'll buy my own groceries, do my own laundry, make my bed." He threw his head back and let out a full-bodied laugh.

Full-bodied and sexy, she thought, remembering her aunt's words. "How you do go on."

"Helps me out, too. Gets me away from the worn-out motel on Richmond Road. Freelancing doesn't pay until you sell the story. Plus, it will give us more time to work on our story."

"Jesse, I appreciate your offer, I really do, but—"

"Hit me with them...the excuses. It's not right. What will the neighbors say? We just met. You don't know me." He paused for a breath. "Did I cover them all?"

"Pretty much."

He gripped her upper arms with both hands, hard enough to show he was serious, gentle enough so his caring came through. "We've only known each other a short time. I get that. But I care about you. And something is going on here. It got Nadine killed. She's dead. Gone. Greg too."

He paused to let his words sink in. "And if something like that happened to you, and I could have prevented it, I would never forgive myself." His words hung between them. "So see? You'd be doing me a favor."

"You trying to make me feel guilty?"

"Guilt is a wasted emotion."

"That's what Rachel always says."

"A wise woman." He picked up the dirty plates from the counter and carried them to the sink, then turned and faced her. "Morgan, humor me on this one. It's the right thing to do. The smart thing. You don't want to be alone right now."

Morgan paced the narrow space between her sink and the kitchen island, mumbling to herself. She clenched and unclenched her fingers.

"What did you say?"

"Nothing. Just talking to myself. I'm trying to sort this out in my head."

"Morgan, you're not alone." His voice was soft, reassuring, "I'm here. Talk to me. Maybe I can help."

Little things were nagging at Morgan about this new man

in her life. What was her unconscious trying to tell her? She looked at him, soothed by the warmth of his caramel brown eyes, the upward curve of his mouth, the way his arms stood ready to catch her, comfort her, the certainty in his voice.

"To be honest, I am scared. Don't tell Daniel. He'll freak."

"You really think he doesn't know?"

"Humor me. It's one thing for him to think he knows, a whole other thing to hear me say it out loud."

A new sensation pulsed through Jesse. It had barely been two weeks since he met Morgan and got lost in her cornflower-blue eyes. His reaction to her surprised him. She was...was so...

He didn't know what, but whatever it was, it twisted his insides like someone wringing out a wet mop. And it felt good. Could complicate things, but to his mind, complications made life interesting.

And Morgan Kasen was one beautiful complication. He knew she was the real deal. She didn't put on airs, didn't flaunt, wasn't faking. She was a woman he could confide in, whatever he told her in confidence—the good, the bad, the ugly—would be sealed away in her internal vault. Shared with no one.

Strange, he thought. After all these years of being alone, might this horrible cascade of events spawn at least one happy ending? Could she be the elusive other half he'd been searching for while he was busy telling himself he was a confirmed bachelor?

CHAPTER 27

Their biggest problem was not knowing how many employees were in the clinic.

Last night, Vivian told them it was her and one other person. Was that true?

And if there were others, who was medically trained? And who, if anyone, had military training? Those medically trained would offer little resistance when TJ, Moss and the others stormed in for their after-hours visit. But those trained by the military would—should—stand and fight. That's what they were trained to do. Dead bodies were not the goal. Rescuing Darby and any other unfortunate souls trapped inside was.

"If the place is doing what you think it's doing, there should be some type of security. Are you sure there wasn't any last night?" asked Brody.

"None that we saw," said Jesse. "I didn't get the impression that Vivian, the nurse we met, was lying when she said she and another nurse were the only ones there."

"She wouldn't have said that if there were others there, especially if there were security types, would she?" asked Morgan.

"Who the hell knows?" Kyle stuffed a piece of donut in

his mouth. "Jesse, you said she acted weird. Didn't want to let you in and wanted you out of there as fast as possible."

"Our intrusion clearly upset her. I did see cameras in the lobby, and I suspect there were a few in the corridors. I didn't see any, but a small camera could be hidden in the ceiling."

"Something doesn't feel right." said Tina. "Maybe it is just a private clinic, like she said. Anything else would necessitate some level of security I would think."

"How do we want to enter? Stealth? Official-like? Gangbusters?" asked Daniel. "I could call Jim and Mac, get the Feds in on this, so we could wave some spiffy credentials in the faces of anyone we meet."

"I vote stealth," said Moss. "Use our training. Credentials put people in one frame of mind. Guns, fists and whatnot put them in another."

"Which do you prefer?" Brody asked Moss, trying to get a sense of the man.

"The first is more civilized," Moss said. "The second more fun."

"Spoken like a true Marine." Brody and Moss bumped fists.

"But if a shitstorm erupts," added Moss, "then you can call in the cavalry."

"That'll go over big," said Kyle. "I know how much the Feds love to get called last."

"They'll get over it," said Daniel. "If what we think is going on here, if black market organ sales are really happening, the task force I'm on will wind up with it. It's nice to have some unofficial help on the front end."

"Let's not make a federal case of this unless and until we have to," said TJ. "Not sure we need the heavy artillery until we figure out what we're up against." Looking at Moss he added, "Remember the time—"

"Yeah," Moss answered sharply. "No need to bore your friends telling tales out of school."

"But it's such a good one." TJ chuckled to himself.

Jesse looked around the table while the briefing continued. Battle-ready men, armed and dangerous, surrounded him. These men and Tina—the lone woman and former medic, on the mission to specifically handle any medical complications—were in their element here. All thrusters go, full throttle. Jesse's lone thought—glad he was on their side.

He had the easy job. Get Vivian or whoever answers the door to open it enough so he could push his way in. And distract her enough so everyone could sneak in behind him. He found himself praying he'd see Vivian's homely face greet him at the door. Someone else would present problems.

Morgan had drawn the group a map of the facility, mostly from memory of the tour during the open house. There were three trailers attached to the main brick-and-mortar clinic. And a fourth trailer connected everything at the other end. One of the trailers was divided into two operating theaters. A second housed two private rooms, and a larger curtained area where six beds awaited patients. The third housed a lab with impressive state-of-the-art imaging technology and a phlebotomy lab.

Theirs was a simple plan. Breach the fortress, rescue the damsel in distress, exit stage left with all players unhurt. Of course, the plan had a few unknowns. Unknowns breed complications. Complications screw up the best laid plans.

The biggest complication—assumptions. They were assuming Darby was in the clinic, based on Jesse's encounter with Eli the previous night. They were assuming there would only be two nurses on duty, based on Vivian's comments. They were assuming there wouldn't be any security tonight, because there didn't seem to have been any last night.

And they all knew assumptions could get you killed.

Iron-hard determination rode Moss hard. He was determined to find Darby, and end it once and for all with Hayden. He had collected more than enough information for the FBI to make a strong case that would put Hayden away for the rest of his miserable life.

He didn't say much during most of the briefing, more the strong, silent type, but his mind was busy imagining the worst for Darby. His only saving grace was daylight. His gut told him nothing this ungodly could take place in the light of day. And he'd just spoken with Hayden who, after giving him a tongue-lashing, and drilling him another asshole for being gone so long, let him know that he'd be out of touch for the next twenty-four hours. So, wherever the hell Moss was, he better make arrangements to get his ass to the Rio del Playa Resort in Costa Rica the day after tomorrow.

"Maybe we should do another recon tonight," said Tina. "The lack of security thing's got me spooked."

"We don't have time for more surveillance." Moss slammed his hand down on the table, rattling the china. "Whatever is going down, is going down soon. Real soon. Tonight. I'm sure of it. We gotta move."

All eyes stared at Moss. Seconds lengthened to minutes.

"And you are one hundred percent sure of this, how?" asked Daniel.

"Because Hayden is dying of renal failure. Desperately needs a kidney transplant, and is too arrogant a son of a bitch to even consider waiting his turn on a transplant list."

"Why this woman?" asked Brody.

Moss glared at him. "Like I told you, she is his daughter, his only child. Odds are she's a perfect match. And he told me to meet him at some resort in Costa Rica in two days. Whatever is happening is happening now."

"Does it for me," said TJ.

"Me too," said Kyle. "Anyone want out, now's the time."

Eyes met eyes. No one left.

Moss's tone softened. "Sorry. I know I come on like gangbusters sometimes. I hate that I failed to keep a promise I made a long time ago to a dear friend."

"Your boss, Hayden," said Morgan, "sounds like such a creep. What made you stay with him?"

"Dawn. She was the main reason I put up with his bullshit for so long. Being close meant I could keep an eye on him. I didn't like what they were doing business-wise, but I kept my mouth shut. So wrong. I never thought he'd turn on her like he did. That's when I volunteered to take the whole operation down." He nodded to Daniel. "I had to stay and keep collecting evidence for you guys."

"Did you know Desiree was also keeping records?" asked Carolyn.

"No. But it makes sense. She probably thought she could use it to control Hayden, keep him in line."

"Didn't work," said Morgan.

"No, it didn't, which made my job even more critical. Staying close was the only way I could make sure he never did anything to hurt Darby. I failed, and failure is not in my vocabulary. I should have been more vigilant."

"How could you possibly have known?" asked Carolyn.

"Because I know Hayden. He's a narcissistic psychopath. He hates being on dialysis. And he never forgets anything. Some sleepless night, when he was into the sauce and angrier than a hornet, he must have remembered that he blew Dawn off when she told him she was pregnant." Moss took a breath and his tone softened. "And I knew about Darby, that she is his daughter. And finally, I know he has

266

unlimited resources. Nothing stops him from getting what he wants."

Moss finished his coffee.

"Would have been nothing for him to pay some people off in order to gain access to sealed records. Who the hell knows? It's dangerous to underestimate him, and stupid me did just that. And now it could cost Darby her life."

"Okay, then," said TJ. "We go tonight. Brett and Carolyn will monitor our comm links."

"Me, too. You are not going to leave me out of all the action," said Morgan. "I know I don't have the training Tina has, but I can be with Brett and Carolyn." She glared at everyone around the table, daring someone, anyone, to disagree. "An extra pair of hands may come in handy."

"Fine by me," said Brett. "And we'll be ready to send in the cavalry the moment you give me the signal." He coughed. "Ah, Daniel, you're the cavalry."

"Got it. But I'm going tonight. Wouldn't want to miss all the fun. I'll have my phone on speed dial for Jim and Mac."

"Let's hope that won't be necessary," said TJ. "We'd have a lot of explaining to do if it comes to that."

"Better to explain and ask for forgiveness, than get permission. Right, Daniel?" said Kyle.

"The way I liked to play it at NYPD."

"How are you going to square uncovering a black market organ trafficking operation and not telling your people from the get-go?" asked TJ.

"One problem at a time, please. Right now, all we have is speculation, and a friend of a friend possibly in trouble."

"Remember the old westerns on TV?" asked Moss.

"What's this remember shit? They're on cable about two a.m.," said Brody.

"Sleep much?" Moss looked at Brody, the youngest of

the group, with a kind of big brother admiration. He could tell Brody was a good man.

"Well, like in those settlers versus Indians movies, think of us as the scouting party. If we find something illicit, we'll call in the heavy guns, badges, and warrants. But we get Darby out first."

"Good plan. No need stirring up the Feds prematurely," said Tina.

"Works for me," said Brody.

TJ pushed himself away from the table and stood. He knew the challenge of missions like this one—mastering the delicate balance between civilized person and primitive warrior, switching on the kill-or-be-killed gene, and then being able to switch it off equally fast. He made eye contact with Kyle, with Brody, with Tina, with Daniel, with Moss, with Jesse, with Brett, with Carolyn, with Morgan.

"Get some rest. We go tonight. And remember who we are. The A-team. The team that gets the mission done, the team where every member returns from the mission unharmed. The team that celebrates our success together. Let's get 'er done."

"Hoo-rah."

Tiffany appeared at the doorway of the restaurant promptly at eight. She knew Colton hated waiting. Dinner two nights in a row with him tested every ounce of Southern charm she had.

Seeing him sitting alone at a table, she marveled at how normal he looked. He was charming, gracious, generous to a fault. To the people who pleased him. Displease him and he could turn on a dime. She knew now his demeanor was a masquerade, her innocence blown to shreds a few weeks ago, when she accidentally overheard him on the phone. Even being privy to only one side of the conversation had her stomach twisting in knots.

He was a monster, securing organs from unsuspecting people to sell to the über-rich. And now it was clear, she was his accomplice.

Wish I'd known that six months ago. Hindsight. Always twenty-twenty.

"Good evening, Mr. Pollard," said Tiffany when she reached the table. Noticing three place settings, she asked, "Three? Are we expecting someone else?"

"Yes. Mr. Gold, our newest arrival, invited us to be his guests for dinner." He rose from his seat. "Here he comes now."

Hayden joined Colton and Tiffany in the French restaurant of Wellington Manor. He noted the small, intimate setting, the room decorated with genuine Louis XV furnishings, and thought it more fitting for a romantic evening for a couple deeply in love than the business discussion he had planned.

"It's nice to finally meet you, Ms. Stamos."

"You too, Mr. Gold. I mean, Mr. Hayden. Guess we don't need the subterfuge anymore. And please, call me Tiffany."

"I have to tell you, Colton, you have a gem here in Ms. Stamos. She's taken care of every detail to perfection."

"She is a true gem, isn't she?" Colton touched her hand. "I've always been grateful I stole her away from the cruise line. They didn't appreciate her value."

The server poured their wine and took their dinner orders.

"I suspect this will be the last good dinner I'll have for a few days."

"Just until after the surgery," said Tiffany. "I've lined up a private chef for you. He's world renowned, so I'm confident you'll be well taken care of in terms of your diet during your recovery. He'll be at your villa while you convalesce. The day after your surgery, you'll be flown by a special medical transport to a secluded retreat in Costa Rica. There will be a doctor and nurse with you during the flight and at the villa."

"An American-trained doctor?"

"Of course. Only the best for our clients. For the procedure, you'll be under the care of two teams of surgeons, one to do retrieval, the other to do the implantation. They are the best in their fields."

Hayden turned his attention to Colton. "See what I mean, Colton? Every detail taken care of." Returning his attention to Tiffany, he asked, "And how long is the recovery period?"

"As long as you want," said Colton before Tiffany could speak. "There are no standard time frames with our program. It is strictly up to you. You're in charge."

"Good. I prefer being in charge."

"Everything is customized to meet your special needs, and for your comfort," added Tiffany. "The first few weeks will be the most difficult for you. Your onsite medical team will watch for any signs of rejection, and you'll be on a strict regimen of anti-rejection drugs. The villa is yours until you tell me you are ready to resume your normal activities. Then we'll make arrangements to fly you home and finalize any post-operative care you require."

"Who could ask for anything more?" Hayden raised his wine glass. "A toast to a better future for all of us."

Dinner progressed at an elegant pace, the conversation staying on issues of the day that stirred no emotions, no conflicts. The server brought coffee, after-dinner drinks, and a plate of assorted fruits and petit-fours for dessert.

"Ms. Stamos—"

"Tiffany."

"Tiffany. Why don't you go powder your nose? Mr. Pollard and I have some private details to discuss."

Tiffany looked from Mr. Pollard to Hayden and back. Mr. Pollard's slight nod gave her permission to leave. Both men watched her exit the dining room.

"Ah, the simple gifts life provides."

"Yes, and in such a lovely package." Colton turned his attention to Hayden. "Tiffany has a very tiny nose, so she won't be gone long. When you contacted me, you said there were important details we need to discuss. What is so urgent it couldn't wait?"

"Your little enterprise, of course."

"Come again?"

"You didn't think I'd put my life in your hands—well, not your hands exactly, but your clinic operation—without thoroughly checking you out."

Colton stirred his coffee, his eyes glued to the creamy brown liquid. "And what do you think you learned, Mr. Hayden?"

"You're kind of a legend on the dark web. You carry a mystique. Sort of like me. You move through your world with a certain flamboyance, far removed from the real circles within which you operate. Almost more rumor than man."

"And yet, here I am."

"Yes, here you are. I didn't expect to actually meet you. Everything I heard indicated you prefer to work behind the scenes. Why is that?"

"I hire competent people, and there is rarely a need for me to be directly involved."

"Why this time?"

"We had a minor issue at one of our other local clinics recently that needed my direct supervision. And Williamsburg is pretty in the fall."

"So is Zurich." Hayden selected two chocolate-covered

petit fours and examined the strawberries, biting into a plump, red one. He wiped his mouth with his napkin before he spoke.

"But there is something you need."

"And what might that be?"

"A partner."

"And what makes you think I need—or want—a partner?"

"Insurance."

"Insurance? I can assure you my clinics and facilities are fully insured."

Hayden chuckled. "You misunderstand. Not that kind of insurance. Think personal liability. What I am talking about speaks more to your ability to not only continue to do what you've been successfully doing, procuring organs for people such as myself...though in my case, I've done my own procurement. What I am offering you is life insurance, the kind that ensures you continue to live in the style you've become accustomed to."

Silence. Hayden could tell the rationale behind his offer was resonating.

"We have common interests. I need to partake of your services. And you want to continue to offer those very lucrative services. I can also offer you funding to grow your enterprise. And a nice, ironclad...or should I say, platinum-clad...retirement and disappearance clause, should the need arise. It's a win-win."

"Interesting offer." Colton's voice remained calm, but his mind reeled. *The little prick. How dare this insolent turd try to usurp my business.*

"Bottom line, Mr. Pollard. Who would you rather deal with. Me? Or the Feds? One carefully placed anonymous phone call—after my procedure, of course—ends all this."

He waved his fork in the air making tight circles. "And you and the pretty Ms. Stamos go away for a long, long time. Separate cells, of course."

"Of course."

"Though I suspect she isn't your preferred type."

"And the expiration timing of your most generous offer? I'd like to think about it."

"What's there to think about? Do you want to stay in business and remain a free man, or would you rather spend the rest of your life in an eight by ten cell in a maximum security prison, deep underground, only allowed outside for an hour a day?" Hayden sipped his coffee, letting a few moments pass. "And just to show you how on top of things I am, I hear your Williamsburg clinic had unscheduled visitors last night. And your visitors breached the sacred double doors."

Colton felt the muscles in his jaw twitch. *How the hell does he know that? I just heard about it this morning.*

"Considering I am a soon-to-be guest at the clinic, I've already arranged for additional security, inside and outside. They're there now. And tomorrow, when I arrive for my procedure, security will double."

The men made eye contact.

Hayden reached for another petit-four. He held it up, admiring the fancy icing, before popping it in his mouth. "Hmm, sweet." Again, he let silence rule the table. "I must admit to being surprised you don't already have more security at your facility."

"I run a specialized operation with a unique clientele…guests such as yourself, who come and go under the cover of darkness, and don't want or need the paparazzi visible security might bring haunting their every step. So you see, there's not been a need."

"Not exactly true. According to my sources, something has made your newest operation suddenly very popular with several reporters who are looking to make names for themselves."

"Yes. I've met one or two of them."

"And unless I miss my guess, someone in your operation has gotten overeager, exceeded his, or her, authority, causing one reporter to meet with a fatal accident."

"Do tell."

"It's what I heard."

Hayden loved this part of his show. And this evening's dinner had been totally orchestrated by him. Dribbling out bits of information in this manner was like feeding small pieces of meat to a ravenous dog. The dog's attention was riveted on the person doling out the treats, and since it never knew how long the treat train would keep producing, it paid attention to every gesture. Colton Pollard might not like the treats being offered, but Hayden knew he had his full and undivided attention.

"And your CEO, Greg Welton, has also had an unfortunate end to his life. A heart attack was the ME's preliminary conclusion."

"Heart issues ran in his family, I'm told."

"How convenient. Fortunately for me, no such illnesses are to be found in my family tree."

"I see."

"I hope you do. And I hope we can continue our conversation after my surgery. You will come visit me in Costa Rica, and we can nail down the details of our new partnership. My very trusted lawyer has a full dossier outlining the parameters of our arrangement."

Hayden finished his coffee, wiped his mouth, and folded his napkin, placing it on the table. He sat forward in his chair and looked directly at Colton.

"And just so we understand each other, he also has instructions about what to do with the information, should anything untoward happen to me while I am on what he believes is a two-month vacation."

Colton's eyes shot daggers at Hayden.

"Here comes the lovely Tiffany," said Hayden as he stood. "Come, Colton. Let's adjourn to the terrace for an after-dinner aperitif, so I can smoke one of these fine Cuban cigars. Would you care for one?"

Without waiting, Hayden took Tiffany's arm and escorted her through the French doors to the terrace. Heaters glowed and took the chill off the fall evening.

Hayden took a deep breath and said, "Look at those stars. Only away from a major city can you really appreciate the beauty of the stars in the heavens." He pulled out a chair for Tiffany.

Colton followed, wondering how he lost control of the situation. Hayden had him by the balls. He needed to shift his strategy fast to extricate himself from this unwanted intrusion.

CHAPTER 28

They parked the three rented black SUVs at the far end of the Holiday Inn parking lot. The clinic property was about a quarter mile due south through the woods. Eventually Jesse would drive around to the clinic's parking lot for his grand entrance.

"There are enough cars here that ours won't seem suspicious," said TJ. "We'll split into two teams for the approach, then regroup behind Jesse and Kyle for our entrance."

A whooshing sound got their attention. At the back of one of the SUVs, Jesse and Morgan were blowing up balloons with a portable helium tank.

"How are you coming with the balloons?" asked TJ.

"Almost done," said Morgan.

"I hope whoever answers the door will be surprised enough to be caught off guard by the flowers and balloons," said Tina.

"Come on. Women love flowers," said Jesse. "And the balloons should give me enough cover to push my way in, and hopefully allow all of you time to slip in behind me unseen."

"Good plan, in theory," said Brody. "Now we've got to hope it works in practice."

"If it doesn't work, we'll go to plan B." TJ caught a look from Kyle as the words left his mouth.

"What's plan B?" asked Brody.

"Damned if I know." They all burst into laughter at TJ's comment. "Something will show up. It always does. When have I ever let you down?" He quickly looked at Kyle. "No comments from you."

Kyle threw up his hands. "Ain't sayin' nothin'."

"Good. Keep it that way. To continue. In and out. Get who we've come for and leave. I'd like to add leave no trace, but we all know that's not going to happen."

"It should only be so easy." Tina laughed.

"It never is," said Kyle.

"Maybe this time," said Brody.

"From your lips to God's ears." Tina gave Brody's shoulder a warm squeeze.

"Hey, we're the good guys." Brody looked at his fellow warriors. "That's got to count for some good luck."

"Now that you've gotten that out of your system," said TJ. "To continue. Jesse's SUV will be in front of the clinic, so we'll use it to transport the package out."

"Darby," said Moss. "She's not a package. Her name is Darby."

"Right. Sorry Moss." He gave Moss a long, understanding look. "Brody, she's your responsibility. And before you object, Moss, I need your talents elsewhere to ensure a clean getaway.

"Understood."

Brody looked at Moss. "Don't worry. I'll protect her like I would my own sister."

"You even got a sister?"

"Yes. A twin. We're bonded in ways too numerous to count. It's a twins thing."

"Hopefully the pac—ahem, Darby," said TJ, "will be able to walk. If not, improvise."

"Not a problem. Been working out." Brody flexed his bicep.

Another wave of laughter went through the group. TJ knew it was a good sign. Humor helped ease the tension before a mission.

"We have two pairs of night vision goggles," said TJ as he pulled them out of a bag.

Brody picked up one pair and put them to his eyes, looking into the woods. "Jeez, feels like I'm back in sand land."

"Can't be," said Tina. "Too many trees and no sand."

"Ain't that the truth, but I do love the weird, slime-green glow."

"Probably don't need them, but they might give us a slight advantage." TJ adjusted his pack. "Tactical vests, please. I'm not advocating going in guns blazing, but I am strongly advocating a proactive approach. Better safe than sorry."

"What's the old saying? 'Shoot first and ask questions later,' right?" Brody tugged at the Velcro strap of his vest.

"Remember the plan. Get in, find Darby, get out. Minimal rough stuff, unless you have to. Truss and tie up resistance. No dead bodies unless you see no other way."

"What if we're wrong?" asked Brody. "What if nothing is going on there?"

"Then we go out as quietly as we came in. Fade into the darkness." TJ looked each person in eye. "Let's get the job done and come home safe."

While everyone else walked away for a few private moments to get their heads on straight, TJ tried to gauge Moss's mood. He came up alongside him, out of earshot of the others.

"One leader. Me. Making all calls."

"I get it. I'm too close. I know. But—"

"No but. Decide now. You follow my orders, or you're benched. We go without you. You wait behind."

"Can't do that, man. You know I can't."

"Just so we're clear."

"Crystal. I'll be a good boy."

"That'll be a first."

Huddling in the woods in a parking lot adjacent to the Elan clinic, the men mentally prepared for the coming incursion. Physically, they were ready. Gear-wise, every weapon they carried was top of the line. Black was the color of the night. Black and green camouflage paint streaked their faces. Fierce warriors, brothers and a sister in arms, each one the best of the best: a Recon Marine, two SEALS, and two Army Rangers. A retired NYPD detective and a reporter rounded out the team.

"Let's go."

The terrain was flat, easy to traverse. Fallen branches and leaves covered the ground, making it too wet to make any noise while they made their way through the thick woods. Night creatures sang their songs; frogs croaked, cicadas and crickets chirped, an owl hooted in the distance. They separated, hugging the tree line for concealment once they neared the clinic's lot and headed to their assigned go points.

"Comm check," whispered TJ after ten minutes, enough time for Jesse and Kyle to reach the clinic's parking lot, and for Brett to get into position about a mile down the road.

Everyone verified their equipment was working.

"Hold up," said Kyle to Jesse as they approached the driveway to the Elan Clinic. "Douse the lights."

Jesse did as he was told. Kyle grabbed the pair of NVGs he'd taken, put them to his eyes, and scanned the front of the building.

"Fearless." Kyle whispered TJ's call sign into his comm.

"Go Scratch." Kyle never shook his military call sign. Not the best, but very descriptive of the results of a one-night stand in Tijuana many years ago.

"Got movement. Butt glow. Man to the right of the front door smoking."

"Copy."

Kyle watched the orange glow intensify as the man took a pull from the cigarette.

"Security?" asked Jesse.

"Could be."

"Wasn't here last night." Jesse looked through the NVG Kyle handed him. "Morgan and I got someone's attention."

"So it seems." Kyle took the goggles back, again focusing on the man. "Coming your way, Kid."

"Copy," said Brody, whose Kid call sign referenced his time with the team, not his youth.

"Scratch, do your thing. Jesse, stall your entrance until we clear the field," said Fearless. In his head, TJ cursed the arrival of Murphy, of Murphy's Law fame. *Why did he always show up at the worst time, and in the least opportune ways?*

"Copy that."

Kyle got out of the SUV and closed the door without a sound. With long, smooth strides, not a wasted motion, he quickly covered the distance from the head of the driveway to the huge live oak tree across from the front door. He slammed his back against the tree's trunk and concentrated on slowing his breathing.

"Scratch in position."

"See him." Brody trained his night vision goggles on the man as he cleared the side of the building and continued across the parking lot, heading straight for him.

"He carrying?" asked Fearless.

"Nothing visible."

Brody breathed in through his teeth when the man veered away from the building and headed his way. The guy stopped ten feet shy of his hiding place, held what remained of the cigarette between his teeth, unzipped his fly, and took a piss. He tapped his prick to let the final drops fall, zipped up, and took one last drag of his smoke. Grinding the butt out with the heel of his boot, he retraced his steps back to the trailer closest to Brody, stopped, yawned, and lit another cigarette. He took a long drag and then headed back around the building.

"Coming back at ya, Scratch."

"Copy that."

"Almost got a shower. Guy took a piss. Couldn't hold it until he got back inside."

"When ya gotta go, ya gotta go."

"Copper, see anyone?" TJ waited for Daniel to respond.

"Negative." Daniel loved that they had accepted him and christened him with the name Copper because of his years with the NYPD.

"In my sight," said Kyle. "Orders?"

Kyle made him to be maybe six feet tall, with a slight paunch that meant he was slow to move. No visible weaponry didn't mean he wasn't carrying. But it was a strong signal that he wasn't expecting company.

"Scratch, take him down."

Kyle was juiced. To his core, he loved this type of action—the work he was born to do. His military training had polished his natural skills and talents. Working security with TJ was a walk in the park compared to their previous wartime antics. He missed feeling so alive.

Now his alive feeling was coming from a different source. She was blond, had blue eyes he got lost in, and matched his sense of purpose in everything she did. His little cottage now had flowers in the window boxes and throw pillows on the sofa. Yep, his life had changed considerably in the past six months. He liked coming home to her smile, to the way she smelled, to her laugh. He was in love for the first time in his life.

Would it be enough to keep him content? Would it last?

Kyle shook his head to refocus his thoughts. Right now none of it mattered. All that mattered was the mission.

The guy stopped short of the front door, leaned against the brick wall, picked at his fingernails, and took what was clearly the last drag of his smoke. He flung the butt out to the blacktop, fumbled in his pocket and pulled out some keys. He inserted a key in the lock as Kyle came in from behind and got the guy's head in an armlock. Caught by surprise, the man clamped his hands on the arm from hell tightening around his throat, but he proved no match for his assailant. Kyle squeezed harder, until the air left the guy's lungs and he slumped to the ground.

The guy recovered faster than Kyle expected and staggered to his feet. Kyle saw the guy take a step back and his hand go to his waistband. Kyle's ninja moves were faster. A guttural grunt escaped him when the force of Kyle's thrust kick made contact with his solar plexus. He doubled over in pain, clutching his abdomen. The next blow was a right chop behind the neck.

"Nighty-night," whispered Kyle. "Tango down."

Kyle wasted no time. He did a quick pat-down, removed the Sig 226 tucked into the small of the guy's back. He jerked the guy's arms behind him and flex-cuffed him. Duct tape secured his mouth. The only sounds were muffled grunts while Kyle dragged him deep into the underbrush, well out of sight.

"Hold!" whispered Copper as he saw shadows move. "We've got another visitor."

A man came around from the back of the trailers. Daniel crouched behind the dumpster.

Who's this guy? Where'd he come from?

He looked across the courtyard and could see Tina slammed against the side of the building. Not good. If this guy kept to his current path, she was a sitting duck. So much for easy.

"He's yours, Copper."

Stealthily, Daniel came up behind the guy, swept his left arm around his throat and jerked hard. Air swooshed from the man's lungs, and he went down hard. Daniel frisked him for a weapon while Tina rushed over. Together, they dragged the unconscious man behind the dumpster. Flex cuffs and duct tape secured him, and ensured he would be out of commission until someone found him. Hopefully they would be long gone by then.

"Done. No more night crawlers visible out back," said Copper.

"Ditto out front," said Scratch.

"Clark Kent, you're on." TJ had also anointed Jesse with his call sign, since it fit his investigative reporter persona. "Everyone, rendezvous near the front door. Prepare for entry."

"Not again," said Vivian, looking up from her computer terminal when she heard the distant banging. She pushed away from her desk at the nurses' station and started her trek to the main clinic building. With each turn into a new corridor the banging grew louder.

"This isn't happening again," she ranted. "Last night and now tonight. We're closed. We don't do walk-ins." She swiped her ID to open the double doors, turned on the reception room lights, and stomped across the room to unlock the front door. But her attitude took a sharp turn into delight when she saw the bouquet of red, pink, and white roses and mylar balloons that obscured the face of her visitor.

"Surprise!" Jesse peeked out from behind the balloons. "Remember me?"

"Of course. How are you?"

"I'm good, and these are for you." He held out the flowers and balloon bouquet in a way that forced Vivian to back up, allowing him to enter the reception room. "Are you working late again? You must have some backlog of paperwork to be stuck here after hours two nights in a row."

"Well, I-I—"

"Let's get these down to your desk and put the flowers in a vase with some water so you can enjoy them while you work." Jesse barged on, full speed ahead, practically dragging Vivian with him, chatting incessantly, not letting her get a word in edgewise.

He felt his stomach twitch, like a thousand butterflies fluttering their wings in his insides. *What a friggin' rush. No wonder these guys get high on action. This shit rocks.*

"Here, let me get the door for us." Without waiting, he unclasped her ID from her scrubs jacket and swiped it before she could stop him. The double doors opened, and he hooked her arm with his, hustling her into the clinic and down the main corridor. He stopped when the corridor split.

"Which way to your desk, Vivian?"

"Down here, but…but—"

Jesse kept talking and walking, walking and talking, pulling Vivian along. "What a nice facility. You are one lucky woman to work in such a nice place. And so clean, but I guess that goes with the territory. I mean a medical clinic has to be clean and germ-free, right?"

They turned down another corridor and went through a small doorway. The flooring changed, the hall narrowed, and he could tell they crossed a threshold into one of the trailers.

"You had a long way to go to the front door last night. I'm surprised you heard me banging."

"Sound travels, especially at night."

"Well, I am forever in your debt."

"How's your ankle? Looks like you are walking fine."

"Nothing broken. Just a bad sprain. It's taped."

"That's good."

"They said to ice it and stay off it, but I knew I had to come see you, to thank you for your kindness last night."

Finally, she stopped walking, planted her feet and locked her knees. The skeptical look in her eyes told Jesse he needed to quickly connect to the tender spot deep down in her psyche that drew her to nursing in the first place.

She looked Jesse squarely in the eyes. Her voice was more stern than it had been before, with a slight tremble.

"We have to go back. You can't be back here." Vivian put the flowers down on the desk behind her. When she let go, the balloons flew to the ceiling.

"You have to go. Go. Now."

Her arm flew up in a Hitler-like salute, her index finger extended, pointing back down the hall.

"Vivian, don't worry. I won't cause you any trouble. Cross my heart." He made the imaginary X crossing against his chest. "Who's here that's going to see me?"

"They'll know." Her lips quivered. "My bosses...they *will* know. I don't want to get in trouble. I need this job. It pays better than anything else I've ever done." Her face contorted. She was close to tears. "I really need the money."

Dressed in black, TJ, Kyle, Moss, Tina, Daniel and Brody slipped through the front door before it closed and hugged the walls. Brody dashed to the double doors before they closed completely, propping them open with his foot so the rest of his teammates could pass through.

They could see six exam rooms, three on each side of the hall. TJ signaled and they paired off, Tina with Daniel, Moss with Brody and Kyle with him. Room by room, they worked their way down the main corridor.

"Clear," said Tina as she emerged from the last room on the right and rejoined the others where the main corridor came to a T. Three trailers branched off from there.

"That must be the mirror Eli was using to watch the goings on when Morgan and Jesse barged their way into this place." Tina pointed to the ceiling where a corner mirror hung.

"Which way?" asked Moss.

"Crapshoot," said TJ. "The plans Brett downloaded only showed the main building. He couldn't find anything on these trailers. There were too many different possible configurations to be sure which ones Elan used here."

Kyle took Morgan's drawing from his pocket. "Looks like the one on the left leads to various lab areas. The one on the right shows beds, and the center area she labeled as surgical rooms. Looks like there is a fourth trailer that connects to all three and houses the nurses' station."

"We'll split up," said TJ. "Jesse went this way with the nurse," pointing to the left, "so Kyle and I will head down here to join him. Daniel, you and Tina take the right trailer. Brody, you and Moss take center stage." He looked up and got nods from everyone. "We'll join forces at this fourth trailer at the back."

A crashing sound from somewhere in the far right trailer echoed through the silent hallways and got their attention.

"Let's go. Watch your backs. The outside security was unexpected, so there may be more inside."

Daniel and Tina hustled in the direction of the crash. Stealthily, they moved down a short corridor flanked with carts and movable shelving units holding supplies. Tina pointed to her ears, opening and closing her hand in sync with a beeping sound coming from in front of them. Daniel nodded, confirming he heard it too. The corridor opened to a large ward-like space, housing six beds, two of which were occupied. Two men were sleeping, hooked up to monitors and IV bags.

Daniel could see a bed pan on the floor next to one of the beds. He motioned to Tina, who stopped in her tracks. Without making a sound, Daniel crept to the side of the bed and hovered over the man, listening to his breathing.

"Don't hurt me," said the man, rolling over to face Daniel.

"Shhh." Daniel's finger went to his lips and he gently touched the man's shoulder to comfort him, let him know he was safe. "Who are you?"

"Eli."

The name registered in Daniel's mind.

"Morgan's friend?"

"Yes."

"Who's that?" he asked pointing to the other man.

"Caleb." Eli sat up and called across the room. "Caleb, it's okay. You can open your eyes."

Nothing. Caleb didn't move.

"They did something to him. Some sort of surgery. Hasn't moved much since. Nurse Ratched comes and checks on him every now and then."

Daniel chuckled at the *One Flew Over the Cuckoo's Nest* reference. At least Eli hadn't lost his sense of humor.

Tina went to Caleb's bedside and noted his vitals from the monitors. She could see blood oozing from bandages where a kidney might have been. "We need to get him to a hospital."

"Hear you. Ambulance en route," said Brett through her earpiece. "Will come in sans sirens."

Brody and Moss made their way into the center trailer. One narrow hall along the right wall and two doors on the left wall. They stopped in front of door number one and made eye contact. Moss touched the door handle. Unlocked. He motioned that he would go high and Brody should go in low. Slowly Moss pushed down the handle. Brody went right, he went left. Empty. Huge overhead lights hung like an octopus over a gurney, with air tanks and other assorted equipment necessary to perform surgery neatly arranged around the room.

Moss eyed the connecting door to the next room. He tried the handle, but it was locked. They retreated to the main hall and moved to the next door. His heart pounded as adrenaline rushed through his system. Brody squeezed his shoulder, giving him the go sign. Moss quietly pushed the door handle down and rushed into the room, feinted left, Brody on his heels, fanning out right.

The green of the monitor gave the room a surreal glow. And on the bed, strapped down, lay a sleeping woman. Darby. Moss expelled a sigh of relief seeing her, even though he knew their job was far from over. They came up to the side of the bed and could see her vitals from the monitor display.

"Sleeping?" asked Brody in an undertone.

"With the help of some tasty pharmaceuticals." Moss nodded toward the IV.

"What now?"

"Now," said a voice from what had been a locked door between the surgical rooms a moment ago, "we end our charade."

"Hayden."

"Yes. It's me. In the flesh." He held a chrome-plated Beretta Cheetah pointed in their direction. "Did you really think I didn't know about your guardian angel job?"

Moss said nothing. He was too busy scanning the room, absorbing details that meant nothing moments ago and could prove life-saving now.

"Ah, speechless. Love the strong, silent type. Dawn did too. Please put your guns on the foot of the bed." He patted the space and watched them slowly pull out their guns and place them at Darby's feet. "That's good. Now Moss, if you'd be so kind as to join your friend over there." He waved his Beretta at him. "That way you and your friend will be easier to watch…to wound…to kill…if the need arises."

Hayden watched Moss walk around the head of the bed, only taking his eyes off him long enough to retrieve both guns, putting them out of reach on the counter behind him. Moss's panther-like grace never ceased to amaze him, each step a harmonious interplay of mindful flow.

"Dawn always had crappy taste in men." Moss slid his hand along the counter and palmed a scalpel off the surgical tray. "Look what she let you talk her into doing."

"And she had a great life, living in the lap of luxury all those years."

"Until you killed her."

"You still upset about that?" Hayden took a deep breath. "What can I say? All good things must come to an end. Her time was up."

"You egotistical, self-righteous prick."

"Tsk…tsk…tsk. Such language. And in front of a woman, no less."

"Who's out cold, thanks to you."

"She really is pretty. Dawn and I made a beautiful child all those years ago, don't you think?"

"Who you're about to kill for your own selfish interests."

"Don't be so melodramatic. No one has to die here. I gave her life. I'm just taking a part of her back so my life can continue. Here, I'll wake her up and explain it to her. I'll bet she agrees with me." He reached up and stopped the IV flow.

"You scum-sucking piece of shit. All the lives you've destroyed. You couldn't leave your own flesh and blood alone?"

"A rhetorical question, I assume."

A moan from the bed drew everyone's attention. Darby was waking up. Slowly, she moved her head from side to side and blinked several times. She flinched back when she saw two men dressed all in black with greasepaint-streaked faces next to her bed. Looking the other way, toward the door, she saw a man with a gun.

Her words slurred. "What's happening? Who are you?"

"Friends," said Hayden from his position just inside the door. "And they would have you believe I am your enemy." He took a few steps closer to the foot of her bed, motioning Moss and Brody back to the wall. "But actually, I'm your father. I'm sorry it has taken this long for us to become acquainted, my dear, but better late than never."

"My father's dead."

"Yes, yes, yes. Your adopted father's dead. Such boring details. It's my sperm that created you, my DNA that runs in your veins, my genes that have made you great."

Her voice grew stronger with each breath. "You are not my father. Fatherhood takes more than a sperm shot." Her eyes filled with hate. "My dad was a great man. He taught me everything I know. If you're really my father, then you're a shit for abandoning me."

"She knows you, Hayden," Moss said making eye contact with Hayden, "without ever having met you before now." ⸣

290

She looked at the two men in black. "And who are you two? All dressed up like GI Joe, playing Army."

"I'm a friend of your mother's. She and I—we grew up together."

"We all grew up together," interjected Hayden, "and I gave your mother the ability to have a great life."

"Until you murdered her." Moss again leveled the charge without equivocation.

"You killed my mother?" The drug haze was making it hard for Darby to follow the conversation. "My biological mother?"

"Moss thinks so. But what difference does it make? We're together now, and you're going to be a good daughter and help me out by giving me one of your kidneys. And since secrecy has evaporated from this little adventure, I'll even pay you for the privilege of helping me."

Hayden was standing directly over Darby's bed. He moved to gently stroke her cheek with the back of his hand.

She recoiled. "Don't touch me." Fighting against her restraints, she looked up into cold, calculating eyes. "Why are you doing this to me?"

"Why? Because I'm not ready to die, that's why. I need a fucking kidney. We're a six-antigen match, according to your blood and tissue test results. The best." Spittle flew from his mouth. "And because I *can*."

He stepped back and took a long, calming breath. "It didn't have to be this way. You could have cooperated. Let it happen. People live fruitful lives with one kidney."

"You could have asked."

"What would you have said? Sure, Dad. Never met you, but go on, take a kidney. Really? I don't think so. Desperate times call for desperate measures."

"I'm not going to help you."

"Look around, my dear Darby. You aren't exactly in a

position to make that determination. And if you ever want to see your daughter, Brianna, again, you'll be a little more cooperative right now."

Darby's eyes doubled in size and terror transformed her face. "Don't you dare touch her."

"Or what?" Hayden laughed. "You'll do what? Don't you understand? You are nothing but a pawn in all this. What you want has no bearing whatsoever. Translated, that means I don't give a fuck what you want."

"What gives you the right to just help yourself to my kidney?"

"I gave it to you. I gave you two. I'm taking one back. Call me an Indian giver," laughed Hayden. "It will all be over shortly. The doctor I want to perform my half of the transplant surgery has taken a little convincing, but he'll be here soon. A little slice and dice, and you'll be home in time for supper tomorrow night."

"You are an evil man."

"No. Just a man who doesn't want to be hooked up to a dialysis machine while waiting for his name to reach the top of a bureaucratic list made by some government schmucks." His eyes bored into hers as the fingers of his left hand went loosely around her throat. "I'm a man who has the wealth to take matters into his own hands.

"Even with your kidney there are no guarantees. My body could reject it outright, which would be such a waste for both of us. Not to mention years of anti-rejection drugs, close monitoring, invasion of my privacy. There are all sorts of potential complications. Of course, on the bright side, I'll have a functioning kidney, be off that damn dialysis machine, and won't have to endure more visits from Penny, the brew witch. All for the right to live."

Hayden stepped back from Darby's bedside. His eyes darted between Moss and Brody.

"And, please, spare us any heroics. They're really not necessary. My surgeon is the best in the world, and leads a well-trained team for both harvesting and transplantation. He'll make sure both Darby and I come through with flying colors. He understands the consequences of a less-than-stellar performance on his part—for him, and for his family."

CHAPTER 29

Moss watched Hayden's every move like a hawk. The scalpel he palmed remained hidden. He needed the right moment to use it.

Moss knew Hayden liked to pontificate. He was on a roll.

"Your mother. She was one hell of a madam. Managed girls from San Francisco to Shanghai. You should be proud of her."

Darby stared at him.

"But she made one fatal mistake. I warned her, but she didn't listen. Don't keep records, I said, over and over and over again. You don't want any evidence of anything. Ours is a cash business. Take the money and enjoy. Did she listen to me? No. Of course not. Wanted to protect herself. From what, I can't imagine."

"Maybe from you?" said Darby.

"I'm harmless. I just wanted us to have a good life." He looked to Moss. "Wanted all of us to enjoy the good life. And we did, didn't we Moss? Until you went all moral on me."

Moss said nothing.

"So, there was only one thing left to do. Eliminate the problem. As my idol, Don Vito Corleone, the Godfather said, 'It's not personal. It's just business.'"

"But it was personal, wasn't it, Hayden?" said Moss. "You took it personally. Thought Dawn betrayed you."

Did Hayden just flinch? Had his words struck a nerve in this heartless bastard? Moss couldn't be sure.

"You demand loyalty, but offer none in return."

"What do you know about loyalty?"

"Everything. I stuck by your side for all these years. That's loyalty and should count for something. You hide behind the gilded walls you've built on the human suffering you caused."

"I'm a businessman. Find a need and fill it. Business 101."

"Bullshit." Moss knew his working brain was shutting down, and he didn't give a shit. Volatile animal instincts clouded saner judgment, exploding like fireworks on the fourth of July. "That's why you did the deed yourself. Didn't have one of your flunkies do it. Oh, yeah, they set it up. But you pushed the button."

"It was rather amusing. I must admit that I didn't realize you were in the room. But what difference does it make now?"

"It makes a big difference to me," said Darby. "What's wrong with you?"

"He's in a very dark place mentally, Darby. He thinks taking what he wants, and the hell with anyone else, is how the world works."

"Taking someone's body part, *my* body part, is not okay. Do you hear me, Daddy Dear?"

"Position determines perspective." He waved his gun in the air. "And you are in no position to object. I don't think about it the same way you do. Self-interest trumps everything else."

Hayden gazed into Darby's eyes and his mouth softened into a smile.

"You do look like your mother. You have her eyes, her smile. Don't you worry. It will all be over soon. Now it's time for you to go back to sleep."

Hayden reached up and turned the roller clamp on the IV, causing sleep-inducing fluids to flow into her system. Darby licked her lips. She could feel the sedative take effect. Her body seemed to float free from the bonds that held it firmly to the gurney. Colors twirled in her mind. Discordant voices echoed and then fell silent.

Outside the room, TJ and Kyle hugged either side of the wall while considering their best move. TJ couldn't believe what he just heard. Moss had called the guy Hayden. The guy holding the gun was Moss's boss and supposed longtime friend.

Damn it. You don't go pulling guns on friends.

Now they needed to get Moss's attention, let him know they were there, and to be ready to act. TJ's only dilemma— how to disarm Hayden without getting Moss, Brody or Darby hurt—or worse, killed. There was no good move, only poor options and piss-poor options.

He took the chance and peeked around the doorjamb, then pulled back quickly. A minuscule movement. Did they connect? TJ prayed they had.

Moss saw movement from outside the door. Reinforcements had arrived. He slowly moved to the head of the gurney, trying to give himself room to act. His attention remained riveted on Hayden, and Hayden's on him; a mental readiness call, assessing each other's fitness and determination, commitment to finish what they were about to start. Adrenalin pumped through Moss's veins. He was jacked and ready for action. Three fingers popped out of a balled fist behind Hayden's head. Then two. Then one.

TJ and Kyle rushed into the room.

Like a cheetah springing from a tree, Moss leapt forward and tried to plant the scalpel into Hayden's neck, hoping to twist the blade as the two of them flew through the air. Moss landed on top of Hayden, but the scalpel flew from his hand as a gunshot reverberated through the room.

Kyle smashed his foot on Hayden's hand, forcing him to let go of the gun which was swiftly kicked out of arm's reach.

"I got this," screamed Moss. "He's mine."

Both men backed off with their hands in the air. They smiled at each other, reading each other's thoughts. Revenge can be a beautiful thing.

Moss's face was scarlet now. He cracked his fist into Hayden's mouth and started pummeling him mercilessly. Hayden's hands flailed around his head to deflect the worst of the blows.

"Moss, stop. We need him alive. That's an order, Marine!"

TJ's authoritative voice penetrated Moss's anger. He flipped Hayden over onto his stomach, wrenched his arms back, giving them a little extra tug that had Hayden cry out in pain, and grabbed the flex cuffs Kyle held out to him.

Tina rushed into the room and checked the labels on the two IV bags hanging from the pole.

"Give me a minute to get her unhooked." She stopped the IV flow and carefully removed the tube connection from Darby's hand. Then she removed the restraints. "She's all yours."

Brody looked down at his charge, lying so helplessly on the gurney, her face pale, her long lashes framing what he saw moments before, scared, beautiful, golden-brown, eyes. He told himself to be gentle.

She murmured.

"Can you wrap your arms around my neck?" asked Brody as he leaned over the bed.

"Yes. I-I think so." Her groggy voice came out barely above a whisper, but she reached up and did as he asked.

He slid his arms under her. "Now hold on tight." He lifted her and cradled her against his chest. She felt light as a feather. Slowly, with great care, he carried her out of the room, away from her nightmare.

Jesse was ready with a gurney in the hall. Gently, Brody laid Darby down.

"Thank you," she whispered. "Thank you."

Brody watched her sink into the gurney. She lay so still, he wondered if she'd passed out, or fallen asleep, but then she stirred.

"Bri...Brianna?"

Brody saw her cheek muscles tighten when she cleared her throat and swallowed. "My daughter, Brianna." Her voice was stronger now. "He threatened her. Is she safe? Do you know?"

"Yes. She's fine. With a friend of yours and her nanny." He took the cup of water Tina handed him and gently lifted Darby's head. "Here, take a sip of water."

Darby clutched his wrist. "Stay with me, please."

Brody looked at Tina, who was putting her military medic training to use, checking Darby's vitals.

"She's good to go. The ambulance took Caleb and Eli to the hospital already, so we'll use one of the SUVs to transport her. Let's move."

Together they pushed the gurney to the front door where Jesse had already moved his SUV into place. Brody lifted her into his arms again, and slid into the back seat.

"You're safe now." He stroked her back soothingly, wanting to calm her tremors.

"I know." Her hand slid down from around his neck. It was on his chest, next to his heart. Her eyes were open, looking at him. "Who are you?" Her smile conveyed her appreciation.

"A friend helping a friend." His heart pinched in a strange new way.

"Thank you, friend."

"Brody. My name's Brody."

"First or last?"

He chuckled. He rarely spoke his full name, never felt like it fit him.

"Llewelyn Brody."

"Llewelyn Brody. Nice."

Ever so gently, he pushed strands of her chestnut hair off her face. She closed her eyes and snuggled against him. She was closer to him now than a woman had been in a very long time. And he realized he liked it, liked protecting her.

She was crying now, soft sobs flowing freely now that the danger had passed. Rocking her gently, he muttered, "It's okay. It's over. We'll get you checked by a doctor, and then get you home."

"How can I ever repay you?"

"Get well. Be happy. Live your life fully. It's all the payment we ask."

Brody felt his chest tighten as she lay in his arms. His heart picked up its pace. How long had it been since a woman had said his name? Two words shot to mind. Too long. And the lilt in her voice gave it a warm, melodic sound, like she was singing it. Or was he imagining all he was feeling? It had been two long, sleep-deprived days preparing for the operation. Maybe his body was playing tricks with his mind, with his heart.

TJ grabbed Hayden by the collar of his shirt and yanked

him to his feet, then pushed him into a seated position on the gurney vacated by Darby. Then he and Kyle left the room to make sure things were locked down elsewhere.

Moss stared at him, his hands clenching into fists, then releasing.

"Go for it." Hayden goaded. "Come on. I know you're itching to hit me again."

"In time, Hayden, in time."

"No time like the present."

"You aren't going anywhere," he said, adding flex cuffs around Hayden's ankles. "You sit tight. I'll be right back."

When Moss walked into the hall he saw TJ at the end of the hall, deep in a conversation with Detective Knight and Daniel.

"I see you decided to join the party after all." Moss gave Knight a light jab in the upper arm. "I've got Hayden hog-tied in the room back there. What do you want to do with him?"

"I'll bring him in for questioning," said Knight. "You know you're bleeding? Better get Tina to take a look at that."

"She's busy with Darby. It's just a flesh wound. A bullet caught skin, nothing more. I'll live."

"What happens now?" TJ asked Knight.

"Now we see what we can piece together. I've got a ton of questions, and I'm hoping for answers."

"What questions? Hayden's behind Darby's kidnapping and almost getting her cut up and one of her kidneys taken." Moss jerked his thumb to the room where he left Hayden. "That's got to be a federal crime."

"It is. And charges will be brought," said Daniel in a calming tone. "We just need to do it by the book so some fast-talking shit lawyer can't get him off on a technicality."

"I'll go get him," said Moss. He left the group talking, stopped at one of the supply carts, picked up a self-adhesive gauze bandage and taped it to his arm.

"What about the other two men we found? Eli and Caleb?" asked TJ.

"I don't think Hayden had anything to do with them," said Knight. "That's an entirely different operation. I'm guessing the man we photographed leaving on the medical flight got Caleb's kidney."

"Has Vivian been any help?" asked Kyle when he joined the group.

"She hasn't said anything yet. Neither have the two guys you and your friends put out of commission outside. It's unclear who they are working for."

"And finding out who is behind the larger operation here is critical. Ideas, gentlemen?" Daniel ran his fingers through his hair, and did a slow three-sixty turn, surveying the scene. "This is one hell of an operation. Florence Nightingale by day and Dr. Jekyll's friend Mr. Hyde at night. It doesn't get much creepier than this."

"And according to the map Morgan made, other Elan clinics may operate the same way," asked Kyle.

"Doesn't surprise me," said Knight. "I heard from detectives in Newport News and Virginia Beach. Elan has opened a clinic in each city within the last year. They all had similar accounts of homeless people missing for a few days, and then showing up with a scar they couldn't remember how they got."

"At least they showed up again."

"Well, not all of them." Knight shuffled his foot. "The beat cops get to know some of the homeless pretty well. Some are still missing. At first they figured they'd left the area, but my inquiry added a missing puzzle piece that's got them canvassing back alleys, marshy areas and out-of-the-way places more carefully. But if they're in a baggie in a landfill, we'll never find them."

"What the f—"

The words boomed down the hallway and brought TJ, Kyle, Knight and Daniel running to the room.

"He's gone. He's fucking gone."

"How? You said you tied him up."

"Don't know. But he had help." Moss held up the flex cuffs he'd used on Hayden's hands and feet which clearly showed they were cut. "Someone sneaked in here and cut him loose."

"How'd they get in and out without us seeing them?" asked Kyle. "This is the only door, and we were in the hall. We would have seen someone coming and two guys going. No one is that quiet."

"It's not really the only door," said Knight, pointing to the door between the two surgical theaters.

"But they'd still have to exit into the hall where we were standing to get away."

"Maybe. Maybe not." Knight surveyed the room. "The whole place is like a friggin' erector set."

Kyle picked up on Knight's point and went into the other operating room while Knight went over to the side wall. He pushed here. He pushed there. Daniel copied his actions on the back wall while TJ took the remaining wall.

"Here," yelled Knight. "He got out here." He hit pay dirt in the far corner. When he pushed it, the wall fell out of its track, revealing a narrow opening, just wide enough for a person to slide through.

TJ didn't have to look at Moss to feel his anger.

"Don't worry. We'll get him."

"I'm not worried. And I *will* get him. Trust me."

"Good thing you happened along." Hayden followed

302

Colton through the narrow space between the room wall and the outside wall of the trailer.

"I like keeping a close eye on things. Your comment about unexpected visitors last night was true. I was concerned about a repeat, so I personally monitored activities here tonight on my private video feed. Saw some shenanigans that piqued my interest, and I came to take a look. After all, guests, such as yourself are important to me. Have to protect my investment."

"And our new partnership."

"That still remains to be discussed. For now, let's get you out of here."

They exited the trailer through the loading dock. A black-clad, burly, barrel-chested man with a thick neck and muscular arms met them.

"Stay down and follow me," he barked. "We're heading over to the parking lot next door. Not too much open space between here and there, so we shouldn't be out in the open for long."

"Is this skulking around really necessary?" asked Hayden. "I think I've had more than enough of it for one night."

Colton stared at him. *What an ass.* "The area is crawling with cops. Escape or jail. Your choice." He didn't appreciate Hayden's arrogance. Or was it just plain stupidity? "I didn't take you for stupid. They'll know you're gone in a matter of minutes. Decide fast."

"Live to fight another day. Escape."

"Wise choice," the man in black barked. He led them across the parking lot, through a box-hedge row, and out into the adjacent lot. A black Hummer was waiting for them, its lights off, its motor running.

"Ms. Stamos," said Hayden, when he saw who was sitting behind the wheel, "What a pleasant surprise. I didn't expect to see you here."

She said nothing, giving him an acerbic stare. If looks

could kill, hers would have taken care of him in a New York minute.

When the man assigned to watch Hayden and monitor his activities called her to say he'd left in a taxi, she was apoplectic. She told him to follow Hayden and call her every fifteen minutes with an update. When she learned he'd gone to the clinic, she called Colton.

While they were piling into the back seat, Tiffany maneuvered herself to the passenger seat, and let the man who had led them from the clinic get behind the wheel. He pressed the gas pedal ever so gently, and slowly turned the Hummer toward the exit. But instead of going out the driveway, he continued on to the far side of the lot, where he gunned the engine to get over the curb, and raced into the woods.

"Too many police on the access road. This will get us out of the area faster. Might get a little bumpy, so hold on."

Bumpy was an accurate description. Colton thought his teeth were going to shatter while the Hummer jolted over rough terrain. His only thoughts were to get Hayden back to the Wellington Manor, and then get himself out of town, preferably out of the country.

The harrowing night exploded into another beautiful fall day. Bright sunshine and cool temperatures greeted Colton as he checked out of his room at the Williamsburg Inn and got into his rental car. He had errands to run before his ten o'clock takeoff.

The voyeur in him couldn't resist a last look at the clinic. What a sad end to an amazing venture. He pulled into the Holiday Inn parking lot, pulled out a pair of binoculars and trained them on the clinic.

A steady stream of patients with appointments for services was showing up. One by one, they were turned away. He wondered what the police were telling them. It didn't matter. The game was over.

He was surprised to see Tiffany Stamos arrive, pretty in a periwinkle blue dress, her blond hair tossed by the breeze. Appearances were important, so he told her to report to work the next day and act like nothing happened the previous night. He didn't think she'd listen, but there she was. Totally stupid. Truly amazing.

He watched her try to enter the building, and end up in a brief conversation with one of the police officers. He saw her hand cover her mouth, the feigned look of horror cross her face. Good acting, he thought. Then the man whipped her around, cuffed her, and escorted her to a waiting police car. He guided her into the back seat and closed the door.

She'll sing like a canary. Time to leave.

He'd made billions these last few years, and now had only one more stop to make before his plane whisked him away to Dubai, a rich country, and one without an extradition treaty with the United States.

Tying up loose ends by whatever means necessary was not Colton's cup of tea. Mr. Kent was better equipped for that. But this loose end he decided to handle himself. And, while murder was the option of last resort, dead men—and women—tell no tales. He had to bring closure to his dinner conversation with Hayden before all hell broke loose. And Hayden was one man whose life he would enjoy ending, even if he wouldn't be there to watch.

He pulled into the parking lot of the post office at nine thirty. He parked, pulled on a pair of black nitrile gloves, and, reaching behind him, picked up the package wrapped in plain brown paper off the back seat. Then he put on a red

Washington Nationals baseball cap, and large, dark sun glasses and went into the building.

He stood in line at the post office, calmly humming to himself, keeping his eyes downcast, staring at the nondescript linoleum floor the entire time. When it was his turn, he kept his eyes averted while the clerk took his package. He asked for Express Mail, pocketed the receipt and left.

CHAPTER 30

Private Island, Florida Keys

Three days had passed since the events at the Elan Clinic in Williamsburg. Hayden made it back to his private Florida island without being followed. Penny, the brew witch, had shown up twice for his scheduled dialysis treatments. She'd asked about Moss's whereabouts, but received only silence for an answer.

Without warning, Moss strode onto the lanai of Hayden's home. He nodded to Penny, who quickly finished unhooking Hayden from the machine, picked up her knitting, said her good-byes, and left.

"So, you've come crawling back."

"No. Only came to collect my things."

Hayden glowered at him. "You're leaving? Really? Like someone else will hire you? Give you what I've given you?"

"You've given me shit."

"Your BMW and that Rolex on your wrist ain't shit. You going to call the police?"

"In time, Hayden, in time."

"What's got you so fired-up pissed anyway?"

"You and everything about you. What you almost did to an innocent woman. If we hadn't gotten there in time, stopped you…" Moss's hands fisted, then released.

"Bullshit. Nothing would have happened, except Darby would be minus a kidney, and I'd be off this fucking machine. You still don't get it, do you?"

"Get what?"

"What I do. Who I am. I give people—men—what they want, and they in turn, have made me a very wealthy man, which allows me to continue giving them what they want. I don't give a shit what you think of me. I am who I am. Filthy rich, answerable to no one. Free."

"Arrogant. Selfish. Narcissistic."

"You think those words offend me? Asshole. I consider them fine qualities." He got up, walked across the room and took a bottle of water out of the refrigerator. "What you think of me is irrelevant. I couldn't care less about what anyone thinks. There's me, and then there's everyone else. I'm not like other people. And you can all go to hell."

Hayden gulped down some water. One truth prevailed. There would be no transplant for him. That ship had sailed. He was dying. It was only a matter of time. And of place. Right now the place was still of his choosing. Unless Moss had alerted the police and they were on their way.

Moss swallowed the bile rising from his gut. Hayden repulsed him. It took all his energy not to leap and grab Hayden by the throat, rip out his Adam's apple, and watch while he bled out. But he chose not to take that course.

Hayden needed to pay, but he, Moss, was indisputably one of the good guys, the protectors. He also knew he couldn't leave it up to some pussy-ass judge who'd feel pity for Hayden. He knew how the system worked, in theory and in practice. Justice had to be served, one way or another.

Moss needed to spend some time and some space away from Hayden to figure out how to be the arbiter of that justice.

He watched Hayden slump back in his chair. Dialysis was hard on the body, and Moss knew the last few hours, the last few days, had tested Hayden's strength. He was exhausted.

Moss also knew controlling his anger, staying calm, would unnerve Hayden.

"So what do we do now? You going to kill me?"

"Murder is illegal. I don't do illegal."

"You don't do illegal." Hayden mocked Moss. "How noble of you."

"You think mocking me will help?"

"No. You mock yourself. You've been turning a blind eye to what we do for years and living well in the process. How do you square that with your precious code of honor?"

"Can't. My time will come, and I'll answer for what I've done, what I've been part of, what I've allowed to happen."

"Then how will we end?"

A good question, thought Moss. One he had no answer for. Yet. He could see beads of perspiration forming at Hayden's hairline. His bodily functions were becoming harder to control. Taunting him provided some release, like poking a fly caught in a spider's web. But it wasn't enough. And it wasn't justice for Dawn.

The emotional roller coaster he was riding went from screaming anger to regret to guilt and back. Regret rode the ascent, slowing to give him time to think about what he shoulda, woulda, coulda done to better protect Dawn. Anger emerged as the car crested the apex and slammed down the track. And guilt—that he didn't fulfill his promise to Dawn about protecting Darby. Though tragedy was averted, she would now be forced to live with a horrifying memory.

He'd practiced what he was going to say so many times, the words, the tone, the inflection. It had to be just right, so

Hayden knew his time had come, it was time to pay for his crimes against others. But now, in the heat of the moment, he had no words.

"I'm done. I've had enough. Find yourself another boy. I quit." He flung a package at Hayden. "This came for you. It was on the doorstep. Have a nice life. What's left of it."

Hayden watched Moss leave. He was alone. Going to die alone. All his money couldn't buy him a different outcome. And he had no one to blame but himself.

"Fuck 'em all," he mumbled.

He hobbled over and picked up the package. He could see it was mailed from Williamsburg, the Wellington Manor's return address prominent. He slit open the brown wrapping to find a box of his favorite Cuban cigars. There was no note, but someone clearly knew what he liked to smoke.

Moss, he thought, it had to be him. Who else would know? He couldn't say good-bye without one last parting gift. He took a cigar from the box and ran it under his nose, breathing in its heady aroma.

No, not Moss, he thought. He was too pissed to give him a gift he knew would bring him such pleasure. But who then?

No matter. Someone would fess up to the gift eventually. Right now, he only wanted to light up and enjoy a good smoke. He took his cutter and matches, walked out to the hot tub, and turned on the jacuzzi jets. Slipping out of his terry robe, he sank into the warm water.

He clipped the tip of the cigar and warmed the end with a wooden match, spinning it around to get an even burn. Within a few moments, the tip glowed orange. He held the cigar to his mouth and drew in the smoke. Pursing his lips, he blew out one of his classic smoke rings.

There was a moment, one stunned moment…

...before he sank under the bubbling water to the bottom of the hot tub.

Williamsburg, Virginia

Morgan took a deep breath and stared at her reflection in the bathroom mirror, her emotions raw. She was thrilled that Darby was rescued and now home with her daughter. Being in the van with Brett and Carolyn, monitoring the action, had been a total rush.

Jesse and she had talked all night about their partnership on the homeless story, and its twist into the world of organ trafficking. It was jelling into a strong piece of journalism that could very well blow the lid off both homelessness and the sale of black market organs in the US. A bit more tweaking and it would be Pulitzer-worthy.

And somehow, during those discussions, he'd convinced her she was ready. It was time for her to strike out on her own, and he'd be right beside her. They had a plan, and she was eager to take the plunge into the world of freelance.

She pulled at her top, ran her fingers through her hair to spike up the tips. Her stomach was dancing a mambo, and nothing she ate was staying down. Cupping her hand under the faucet she scooped up some water and rinsed out her mouth. She looked at her reflection as she refreshed her lipstick. *This too shall pass.*

To her surprise, an editor from the *Washington World Herald* called her yesterday. He said Nadine had pitched an interesting story to him in an email a few weeks ago, telling him Morgan was the lead writer. He hadn't heard anything, and knew Nadine had passed away. He asked about the story, wanted to know if it was finished and, more important, he wanted to see it before she offered it to any other news outlet.

Tears tickled her eyes. Nadine had been a one-of-a-kind friend.

She blew out a breath and flung open the bathroom door with such force it smashed into the wall. The thumping sound startled her, and made her smile. She marched down the hall and tapped lightly on the doorjamb of Bob's office.

"Got a moment?"

"Sure. What's up?" He answered her keeping his eyes glued to his computer screen.

"I've got my week's assignments done. They're in the queue for you to review."

"Great."

She waited silently for him to look at her.

"Is there something else?" he said when he realized she was still standing in front of his desk.

"Yes." She opened her fist. The office key had left an impression in her palm, she'd been squeezing it so hard. She dropped it on his desk. It clanged against a glass ashtray holding multi-colored paper clips, which finally got his eyes off his computer screen.

He looked up at her, a quizzical expression on his face.

She met his eyes.

"I'm giving you my notice. I'm leaving."

"To do what?" His chair squeaked as he leaned back in it.

"Write the kind of stories I want to write, not the puff pieces you dole out to me."

"Ha. You think you're the next Nadine Steiner-Greene? You think you're the next hot-shot investigative reporter out to capture the big story. Give me a break." His snide laugh set her teeth on edge. "Nadine filled your head with dreams of grandeur. She was good, I'll give her that. You're no Nadine. You're lucky I even give you puff pieces to write."

312

He shook his head at her and laughed. Then he picked up the key and held it out to her. The two engaged in a mini staring contest, neither one saying anything, their eyes doing the talking. He flipped the key in her direction and she caught it against her chest.

"Tell you what I'm going to do, because I'm such a nice guy. I'll hold your job and give you twenty-four hours to think it over."

"Not necessary. I'm better than the stories you deign to give me. And I'm ready to put my money where my mouth is, take my chances, and live or die by my own skills and instincts."

Morgan took in a deep breath, her exhale mixing with her words.

She placed the key back on his desk, and with her index finger, slid it across to him. "Put this where the sun don't shine. I quit." Then she turned and headed for the door. "Have a nice day."

"Seems like we've sat around this table before," said Jesse, pouring himself another cup of coffee. Everyone was in the same seat as last time. "I'm guessing the open seat is for Detective Knight?"

"Yes," said Daniel. "He's on his way. Hopefully, the next time we gather here it will be for something more pleasant than an after-action report. But right now we're closing out our business so our Florida guests can be on their way back to the sunshine state."

"While we wait for Knight, I've got an update from the hospital," said Tina. "I went to visit Caleb this morning, and his doctor was kind enough to grant me some professional courtesy, since he knew I had a hand in rescuing him."

"What's his prognosis?" asked Morgan.

"It's good." Tina put a bunch of grapes on her plate from Rachel's breakfast buffet and sat down. "Considering what he's been through, the doctors plan to keep him for a few more days, and they've arranged a room for him at a rehab facility until he is fully back on his feet. But he's going to have to learn how take better care of himself now that he only has one kidney. He'll need a lot of support. Would be great to get him into a group home of some sort. Do they have those here?"

"Yes, but no one talks out loud about them," said Morgan. "I'll pick up Eli and go visit him later. Maybe some people at the church can help."

"How's Eli doing?" asked Kyle.

"He's good. After what happened to Caleb, he feels lucky, really lucky, that he's still got all his body parts. The hospital checked him over, and they put him in touch with a local community group that specifically helps our vets. I don't know how long it will last, but for now he's excited about meeting with his contact person and getting some help for his PTSD."

"I can talk to him before we leave, if you want," said Kyle. "Sometimes talking to another vet helps. You know, someone who's been there, done that."

"That would be great, Kyle," said Morgan. "Since Rachel's hospitality is extending through a barbecue dinner tonight, maybe I can bring him along…if that's okay, Rachel?"

"Of course. There'll be plenty of food, and the more the merrier. It will give Kyle an opportunity to talk to him without it seeming forced."

Detective Knight made his entrance carrying a tray of coffee cakes.

"These are homemade," he said. "When my mom heard about what we've been doing, she wanted to contribute, so she spent last night baking like crazy."

Rachel took the goodies out of his hands. "Sit. Let me get you coffee."

"We're just getting started, so you haven't missed much," said Daniel. "Tina was filling us in on Caleb. I'm guessing you have to get back to work, so do you want to go next?"

"Sure. The Elan Clinic has been shut down and the local staff arrested. They're pleading ignorance, saying they didn't know anything about after-hours organ transplants."

"I'm guessing if you push Vivian, she'll talk," said Jesse. "She was frightened the night of our visit. I'm pretty sure you can use her fears to your advantage."

"We're working on it, and the FBI has taken over the case. Both cases."

"Two?" asked Tina.

"Yep." Knight beamed with pride. "Pollard and the Elan Clinic case, and a separate kidnapping case starring Hayden, who was also the Grand Poobah of an extensive international sex trafficking ring. That one's yours, right Daniel?"

"Yep. It ties up all the loose ends from the Sand Isle Inn raid last spring. Brett, you and Carolyn were instrumental in both instances. We can't thank you enough for your efforts."

"Talk about when worlds collide," said Jesse.

"The Feds detained Colton Pollard at the airport just before he boarded his plane. He's being questioned as we speak about several missing persons cases in cities where Elan had clinics. He lawyered up immediately, but a smart judge recognized he was a flight risk, didn't grant bail, and ordered his passport confiscated."

"Good. He has the means to go anywhere," said Morgan. "Now he's going nowhere, except to prison for a very long time."

"What about that other guy?" asked Rachel. "The one your friend Moss worked for? Did he get away?"

"Moss sends his regrets for not saying good-bye," said

TJ. "He has unfinished business with Hayden he needs to handle. And he needed to get some records he's been keeping for the Feds about Hayden's activities. Guess Hayden killed the wrong mole. It wasn't Desiree he should have been worried about. Talk about chutzpah."

"You're saying it wrong," said Jesse. "You need to roll the ch sound, like you're a cat barfing up a hairball."

"Ch-chuzpah. That better?"

"A little. Work on it."

"Anyway," laughed TJ, "Moss wanted me to thank all of you. He knows he couldn't have done it without you…without us."

"I do have something on that front," said Knight. "I was at Pollard's arraignment hearing yesterday. I overheard a sheriff's deputy that I didn't recognize tell Pollard the whale drowned. Brought a big smile to Pollard's face."

"The whale drowned? What the hell does that mean?" asked Rachel.

"Not sure, but I know they call big Vegas gamblers whales, and I got an interesting email from a friend down in the Keys who I contacted for information about Hayden. He said a home health care worker found James Hayden dead in his hot tub."

"Let me guess. He drowned," said Morgan.

"Cause of death is still pending toxicology. But here's the interesting twist. My friend tells me one of the CSIs was talking out of school, saying they found a box of very expensive Cuban cigars with one missing, which they found in the hot tub. And when he opened the cigar box lid he thought he caught the scent of almonds."

"Almonds?" asked Rachel.

"Arsenic smells like almonds," said Daniel. "Are you saying your friend thinks Hayden was poisoned?"

"That's the going theory," said Knight, "until the ME

gets the full tox report. How's that for karma biting someone on his well-deserved ass?"

Brody needed to see Darby one more time before he left. He'd felt something when he rescued her, but what that something was he wasn't ready to define, at least not until he saw her again. When the team was packing up to head back to Florida, he asked TJ if he could take a few days of R&R. TJ had no trouble figuring out why. The kid had been moping around Daniel's house, sad-eyed as a lost puppy. He told him to take all the time he needed.

He spent the better part of the morning deciding what to wear. Even made a last-minute trip to Eddie Bauer for a new shirt. He'd never given his clothes more than a second's thought, but today was different. He felt different. Nervous. Vulnerable to emotions he'd spent years locking away.

The morning sun warmed him as he parked in the driveway. Her home reminded him of his grandpa's old farmhouse in Wyoming. An inviting wraparound front porch, hanging chair swing, and window boxes filled with flowers, all said welcome home.

He blew out a deep breath as he climbed the three steps to the front porch. He did a last-minute tug at the sleeves of his new shirt and a fly check before knocking. His stomach fluttered like it used to do in speech class.

An unexpected outburst of barking announced his presence. Darby answered quickly. Too quickly. He wasn't ready. She wore a bright red T-shirt tucked into khaki crop pants. The color brightened her cheeks.

"Wow. You look good." Realizing how lame he sounded, he quickly added, "What I mean is, compared to the last time I saw you. You were kind of blue around the edges."

"Hello to you, too. Blue's my favorite color. Better than pale gray, or chalky white—which I might have been if you hadn't barged through the door when you did. All piss and muscle." She turned away from him. "Hush, puppies. He's a friendly." The barking ceased instantly.

"How'd you do that?"

"They know who rules the roost around here. Or at least who controls the food bowls. The yellow lab is Tucker, the Cairn is Sammy Jo, and this little one," she bent down and lifted a tiny Westie puppy into her arms, snuggling him to her face, "is Casper." She put the puppy down and was back, her face bright and smiling.

"Thought I'd come by before I go home, just, you know, to see how you're doing. Are you sleeping any?"

"Not really. When I close my eyes, my mind goes wild. I see the room, the huge lights above the gurney where they strapped me down. I hear all the monitors beeping and humming. Then the what-ifs start. You know, what if you guys hadn't gotten there when you did? What if someone had actually cut out my kidney? What if I died? What would happen to Brianna?"

"It's going to take some time to get over what happened to you. Labeling it traumatic seems too technical. Downright gut-wrenching fits better. Probably talking to someone would be a good idea."

"Every time I think about the man behind it—that he's my father—my biological father. How could he do this? Kidnap me. Take my kidney without even trying to ask me? Who does something like that?"

"A very nasty man. Someone you don't want to know. Someone who will get his, one way or another."

"What's that supposed to mean?"

"Call it karma." It wasn't his place to tell her Hayden had

already been found dead. "Fate has a way of catching up to guys who do things like this guy was planning. And when fate gets involved, the outcome usually isn't pretty. You know what they say, payback's a bitch."

Darby smiled. "Look at me. Totally forgetting my manners." She pushed open the screen door. "Come on in. Hope you like dogs. I've got a full house here. Can't seem to say no to any stray that wanders by. Want some coffee? It's a fresh pot."

"Sounds good."

He followed her down the hall into a bright red, white, and blue kitchen.

"Very patriotic."

"My dad—my real dad—the man who raised me and loved me—was military all the way." She stopped pouring the coffee for a nanosecond. "He died a few years ago, and then my mom last year." She handed him a mug of steaming coffee and put a container of half and half in front of him on the counter. "Sugar's on the table."

"This is an amazing kitchen. The colors look good in this room. Lots of natural light." He sipped his coffee and nodded his pleasure. "Love the island. I could do some mighty fine cooking in a kitchen like this."

"You cook?"

"A man's gotta eat. And eating out all the time sucks. So, yes, I'm a damn good cook, if I do say so myself."

"You'll have to cook for me sometime. What do you like to make?"

"Let's say I can follow any recipe. But lately my focus has been on chicken. It's cheap, and better for you than red meat."

"So they say."

"Right. My goal is fifty ways to make chicken interesting. Kind of like fifty ways to leave your lover."

"I kind of like lemon chicken."

"Too easy. But it will be my pleasure to prepare it for you one day."

"Great. There's chicken in the freezer. Take out what you'll need."

"What? Like you want me to make it now?"

"Not now, silly. Tonight, after it defrosts. Tell me what else you'll need, and if I don't have it here, I'll stop at the store on my way home."

Darby took a good look at the man who had carried her to safety and now stood in her kitchen. His dark brown eyes, the color of melting chocolate, had an interesting twinkle, and laugh lines graced their outer corners. A patrician nose gave him regal bearing, and his mouth curved up at each corner, giving him an alluring, sexy smile. She imagined broad shoulders under his pale blue-on-blue button-down shirt. His sharply pressed jeans covered what she knew were long, strong, muscled legs. She pegged him for six three. He'd carried her effortlessly to safety, barely breaking a sweat. She remembered her hand resting on his chest, feeling him breathe under the black T-shirt and Kevlar vest he wore that night.

Yes, she thought, Llewelyn Brody is one handsome man. In her younger days, she would have labeled him a hunk. And he'd come to see her. A warm stirring tickled her insides at the thought. It had been a long time since someone who looked like Brody had come knocking at her door.

He smiled at her boldness. "You're on. But I'll do my own shopping and have dinner on the table at six. Will that work for you?"

"Yep. My daughter, Brianna, is at a sleepover tonight, so Ashley, the nanny, is off. It will just be the two of us." She dug into a drawer and pulled out a set of keys. Tossing them his way she said, "so you can let yourself in. I've got a busy day at the clinic, and an afternoon surgery. Poor dog pulled his meniscus. I'll be back in plenty of time. And hungry. Very hungry."

She pulled her soft brown curls back and secured them in a ponytail with a bright red scrunchie to match her shirt. Then she grabbed her purse and her medical bag, and gave him a peck on the cheek as she brushed past him on her way out the door.

He leaned his back against the sink staring at the back door, the scent of Darby lingering in her kitchen. This is not how he imagined his visit would go. She'd accepted his invitation to cook for her, and upped it to more of a challenge. It was time to put his money where his mouth was, put his bragging about being a good cook to the test.

The candles flickered low as Darby devoured the last remnants of dinner.

"I apologize for doubting your cooking prowess. This was incredible." She broke off a crust of bread and ran it through the lemon butter sauce. After popping it in her mouth, she licked her fingers.

Brody smiled proudly. "I never lie. When I say I can do something, I can do it."

"So...other than rescuing damsels in distress and cooking, what do you do for a living?"

"I work security at a private estate on one of the barrier islands off the east coast of Florida."

"Sounds idyllic. How'd you get such a great job?"

"Knew a guy who knew a guy. Military special ops are a tight family, regardless of branch. We help each other out. My boss, TJ, is a former SEAL."

"You like the work?"

"Mostly routine, but it does have its moments."

"Like saving me? You did a great job getting me out of harm's way."

"Yes," he grinned. "TJ and Moss served together. When Moss needed help, he made a phone call."

"That simple." Her eyes were wide.

"These guys are like family. Can't let family down."

"And that Moss guy. Even after you rescued me, he didn't say much to me directly. More the strong, silent type."

"I'm sorry I can't fill in any blanks for you. I just met him."

"I guess he made a promise to my birth mother. I used to get envelopes full of cash in the mail on my birthday and for Christmas. Never knew who they were from." She took a sip of wine. "They must have been close for him to call out the cavalry just to save me."

"Moss had your back. He made a promise, and he kept his word."

"I understand that. Air Force brat. She pointed to her chest. "We moved around a lot." She picked up her glass and finished her wine. "When Dad died, the outpouring of love and support from people I'd never met was overwhelming."

"We take care of our own." He pushed away from the table, picked up her plate along with his own, and headed out to the kitchen.

Darby sat for a moment, unsure of what was to come next. She blushed at the tempting thoughts invading her mind, her increased pulse, the uptick she felt in her beating heart.

Brody returned to the dining room for more dirty plates. He hadn't thought through how the evening would end. Seeing Darby sitting at the table created an itch in his groin that he would love to scratch.

Was it too soon for her? And he wasn't the love-'em-and-leave-'em type. His life was in Florida. Hers was here, on Virginia's Eastern Shore. In his book, long distance relationships didn't work.

"Let me do the cleanup. After all, you did the hard part." Darby blew out the candles and took the remaining dishes into the kitchen. There were no leftovers to wrap up. She rinsed off the dishes and filled the dishwasher.

"You are one very neat cook. Where are the pots and pans?"

"If you clean as you go, there's no big mess at the end. And you can do other things."

"Such as?"

Brody caught himself before answering. Unless his instincts were way off base, she was flirting with him. Unsure of how to proceed, he stalled for time. He saw Darby bite her lower lip and lean against the sink, looking at him with such intensity, he hardened with anticipation.

This is a bad idea.

Darby had gotten under his skin, and he hadn't done anything more than look at her. But this wasn't his first rodeo. He knew better. Ignoring the growing throbbing in his groin, he took a deep breath and readied himself to leave.

What was going on inside her surprised the heck out of her. A long-forgotten heat pulsed through her. She barely knew this man, who'd prepared a fabulous meal, not to mention saved her from possible death, and she was flirting with him unabashedly, wanting him to wrap his powerful arms around her now, where she stood, on her own two feet.

What must he be thinking? I don't know this guy, but I'm acting like a dog in heat, throwing myself at him.

What would mom say? God, I'm glad she's not alive to see this. What the hell, she's probably watching me from heaven. I can hear her screaming at me through the clouds to stop acting like a slut. She always said, again and again, men...good men...keepers, don't like easy women.

But his eyes...like pools of dark chocolate. The way he

makes me twitch...electric shock therapy that feels so good. And his smile. I can't stop myself.

Her cheeks flushed.

"I've got to get going. I've got an eight o'clock flight out of Norfolk in the morning, and with all the crap the TSA puts you through at the airport, I like to get there in plenty of time."

He leaned down to kiss her forehead. Lifting to her toes, she slid her arms around his neck as she tilted her head back. His mouth found hers. What he planned, a simple, closed-mouth good-night kiss, turned into something more, a soft, moist kiss. She willingly opened her mouth and his response was immediate. He pushed on in and escalated their encounter.

"Hmmm, sweet."

"Thank you. Dessert without the calories or guilt."

A bent index finger brushed under her chin, gently lifting it until her eyes met his. In those warm brown pools she found comfort. His kiss was intimate, evoking dormant sensations, now ignited and bursting forth. Her throbbing lips longed for his, and she inched up on her tiptoes.

One kiss melted into the next, and the next. Her perfume was intoxicating. His lips roamed all over her face, and returned with a vengeance to her soft, eager mouth. He was rock-hard, and beginning to think walking would be a major problem.

She felt her toes curl, her stomach tighten, her heartbeat quicken. It had been a long time since a guy had made her toes curl.

He ran a finger along her jawline, stopping under her chin and gently pushing up until her eyes met his. "I'm thinking we need to stop now before we can't stop, before I can't stop. What can I say? I'm a guy."

"You certainly are."

She could feel his manhood growing, found herself wanting to feel him inside her. She skimmed her hands up his back, feeling taut muscles ripple under his shirt. Her fingers reached for his shirt buttons. She undid the first one.

He put his hand over hers and gave it a gentle squeeze, stopping her.

"I want you to know that I don't make a habit of undressing men who save my life." She tried to continue, but he kept firm pressure on her hands.

She flashed him a seductive, let's-keep-going smile, all the while knowing, deep in her soul, he was right, of course. Their timing was off. She felt a tug at her heart. Other guys, most guys, would have taken advantage of her situation, her vulnerability. But not Brody. He was different. *She* was different. Could two differents equal a same?

Brody grinned. "Good to know. I wouldn't want to think you were using me like you've used so many others before me."

He pulled her close, held her tightly against him.

"You need to get some rest. We're heading in a direction that has enormous promise and pitfalls. You've been through a traumatic event, and it's only normal to want to do something life-affirming, like where we're heading. I don't want you to do anything in the heat of the moment you may regret later."

His fingertips caressed her cheek.

"When I make love to you, and I *will* make love to you, I want us both to be clear-eyed and ready to please each other, not fall into intimacy because we're desperately trying to make sense of something…or forget…or lose ourselves for a few moments of pleasure."

Tears welled in her eyes. "At least one of us is thinking straight."

He brushed a stray hair away from her eyes. "Probably not, but I want more than a one-night stand with you. I want the full Monty, the whole enchilada. And I'm willing to wait."

"Guess I have something to look forward to. Men friends, or should I say acquaintances, tell me I'm too picky—too serious—that I need to lighten up, go with the flow, roll with the punches."

"Picky is good. Too many losers out there expect things they shouldn't be expecting."

Darby stretched up onto her toes again, positioning herself for another kiss. He stopped her.

"I'm going to say good night. Maybe I could meander on up here for a visit in a couple of months…"

Something was happening between them. On the one hand, she was glad he was leaving so she could process her feelings. But she wanted him to come back soon. Real soon.

"Make your visit sooner rather than later so you can cook for me again."

"Sure." His boyish charm captivated her. "I've got some vacation time coming. Never had a reason to use it before."

"Then consider this an open invitation."

"One I plan to accept." He kissed her lightly, and held her hand, as she walked him to the door. The hinges squeaked when she pushed open the screen door.

"I've been meaning to get my handyman to fix that."

"I'll take care of it when I come back." He bent down for a last sweet kiss, and walked out into the night.

It was a sobering moment, realizing she met a man who gave her goose bumps, a man who saved her life, and now wanted to be part of it. A man now walking out of her life. Should she shout stop—wait—no, don't go?

From your lips to God's ear, she whispered while

standing on her front porch, watching him get into his rental car and drive away. She pressed her forehead against the door and fought back tears. The sound of his footsteps leaving her porch still echoed in her ears.

Relationships weren't her strong suit. There had been too many failures in her past, haunting any that might hold promise for her future. Her dad had been transferred so many times. The tearful good-byes, the promises to stay in touch, lost in the harsh realities of daily living. Her husband's untimely death. Heartache, one and all.

Animals were easier. You outlived them. You were their everything for their time on earth.

Darby walked into her bedroom, looked at the unmade bed and three sleeping dogs. She crawled under the covers, propped her back against the headboard, picked up Casper, and clutched him to her chest, burying her face in his neck.

"What do you think, Casper?"

He licked her nose.

There was definitely chemistry between them. She didn't know if it was the kind that set rockets exploding to a fast burnout, or the type that simmered and soothed for a long, long time. For Brianna's sake, she needed to know before she put her little girl's heart, and her own, in harm's way.

"Come back soon, Llewelyn Brody."

THANK YOU...

I am so appreciative to everyone who has journeyed with me during the writing of *Complicity*

Thank you Carolyn Koppe. Your muse gifts challenge my plot twists and turns. Our walks and talks helped me flesh out my characters and plot lines. I truly appreciate your time and energy and your belief in the story that I wanted to tell.

My editor, Faith Freewoman, at Demon for Details, totally rocks! What a pleasure and honor it has been to work with you on this story. Your generosity of spirit gently guided my writing efforts, helped me smooth out plot lines and add depth to my characters.

My heartfelt thanks goes to my beta readers Lucy Oakleaf, and Mish Kara. Your insights and suggestions were so helpful. Thank you Dar Dixon for a fantastic cover. You are a talented graphic designer and a joy to partner with. Thank you to Amy Atwell and your team at Author E.M.S. Your formatting skills are priceless.

John, your love and support is what every woman wants from her husband and what I consider myself so lucky to have. You are a blessing in my life.

Meet Jane

Writing mysteries with a touch of romance for such a kind group of readers is so rewarding. Reading your emails, telling me how much you like my stories, inspires me every day. Thank you for taking the time to write me.

My characters are definitely keeping me hopping. As Complicity comes to a close, a new story is taking shape in my mind. Not sure of a title yet, but Darby and Brody are the central characters. You'll also find some of your old favorite people involved in their new adventure, and meet some interesting new folks along the way.

I've also started a cozy mystery series set in Virginia Beach. Three BFF's—Molly, Allyson and Judi—reunite, each one opening a new business venture in an old Victorian house. Can't wait to see what challenges confront these ladies that lead to mayhem and mystery.

Come visit me at www.janeflagello.com and sign up for my newsletter so you'll know when my next stories are ready for your reading pleasure.

Made in the USA
Middletown, DE
18 April 2017